"Relatable, believable, fantastical, aspirational, and completely addictive." —SARA SHEPARD, #1 *New York Times* bestselling author of *Pretty Little Liars* and *The Perfectionists*

"With elegance, saucy secrets, and forbidden love, *American Royals* is fast-paced and utterly charming. Katharine McGee's prose sparkles, capturing the glamour and pressures of an American monarchy." —KENDARE BLAKE, #1 *New York Times* bestselling author of the Three Dark Crowns series

"Imagine a world where Meghan Markle is the queen of the United States of America. . . . *American Royals* is the next closest thing." —*Teen Vogue*

"*Crazy Rich Asians* meets *Gossip Girl*. It's easy reading, but the quality of writing from Katharine McGee is sublime. . . . [An] addictive new modern fairytale." —Yahoo Lifestyle

"More than two centuries later, the House of Washington still rules . . . with forbidden love and *Gossip Girl*–esque drama included." —*theSkimm*

"This juicy revisionist look at US history explores the dramatic inner workings of the House of Washington, which includes two princesses and a handsome prince, all of whom find themselves chafing at the restrictive rules that control their lives." —*PopSugar*

"This book is . . . just So. Much. Fun. A must-read." —Grace Atwood, *Bad on Paper Podcast*

AMERICAN ROYALS

AMERICAN ROYALS

KATHARINE McGEE

EMBER

Text copyright © 2019 by Katharine McGee and Alloy Entertainment
Cover art copyright © 2019 by Carolina Melis

All rights reserved. Published in the United States by Ember, an imprint of Random House Children's Books, a division of Penguin Random House LLC, New York. Originally published in hardcover in the United States by Random House Children's Books, a division of Penguin Random House LLC, New York, in 2019.

Ember and the E colophon are registered trademarks of Penguin Random House LLC.

Visit us on the Web! GetUnderlined.com

Educators and librarians, for a variety of teaching tools,
visit us at RHTeachersLibrarians.com

Produced by Alloy Entertainment
alloyentertainment.com

The Library of Congress has cataloged the hardcover edition of this work as follows:
Names: McGee, Katharine, author.
Title: American royals / Katharine McGee.
Description: First edition. | New York: Random House, [2019]
Summary: In an alternate America, princesses Beatrice and Samantha Washington and the two girls wooing their brother, Prince Jefferson, become embroiled in high drama in the most glorious court in the world.
Identifiers: LCCN 2018060242 | ISBN 978-1-9848-3017-3 (hardcover) | ISBN 978-1-9848-3019-7 (hardcover library binding) | ISBN 978-1-9848-3018-0 (ebook)
Subjects: | CYAC: Princesses—Fiction. | Princes—Fiction. | Courts and courtiers—Fiction.
Classification: LCC PZ7.1.M43513 Ame 2019 | DDC [Fic]—dc23

ISBN 978-0-593-70361-8 (trade paperback)

Printed in the United States of America
1st Printing
2023 Ember Edition

FOR ALEX

PROLOGUE

You already know the story of the American Revolution, and the birth of the American monarchy.

You might know it from the picture books you read as a child. From your elementary school performances— when you longed to play the role of King George I or Queen Martha, and instead were cast as a cherry tree. You know it from songs and movies and history textbooks, from that summer you visited the capital and went on the official Washington Palace tour.

You've heard the story so many times that you could tell it yourself: how, after the Battle of Yorktown, Colonel Lewis Nicola fell to his knees before General George Washington, and begged him on behalf of the entire nation to become America's first king.

Of course, the general said yes.

Historians love to debate whether, in another world, things might have gone differently. What if General Washington had refused to be king, and asked to be an elected representative instead? A prime minister—or perhaps he would have made up an entirely new name for that office, like *president*. Maybe, inspired by America's example, other nations— France and Russia and Prussia, Austria-Hungary and China and Greece—would eventually abolish their own monarchies, giving rise to a new democratic age.

But we all know that never happened. And you didn't come here for a made-up story. You came here for the story of what happens next. What America looks like two hundred and fifty years later, when the descendants of George I are still on the throne.

It is a story of soaring ballrooms and backstairs corridors. Of secrets and scandal, of love and heartbreak. It is the story of the most famous family in the world, who play out their family dramas on the greatest stage of all.

This is the story of the American royals.

1

BEATRICE

Present Day

Beatrice could trace her ancestry back to the tenth century.

It was really only through Queen Martha's side, though most people refrained from mentioning that. After all, King George I had been nothing but an upstart planter from Virginia until he married well and then fought even better. He fought so well that he helped win America's independence, and was rewarded by its people with a crown.

But through Martha, at least, Beatrice could trace her lineage for more than forty generations. Among her forebears were kings and queens and archdukes, scholars and soldiers, even a canonized saint. *We have much to learn by looking back,* her father always reminded her. *Never forget where you come from.*

It was hard to forget your ancestors when you carried their names with you as Beatrice did: Beatrice Georgina Fredericka Louise of the House of Washington, Princess Royal of America.

Beatrice's father, His Majesty King George IV, shot her a glance. She reflexively sat up straighter, to listen as the High Constable reviewed the plans for tomorrow's Queen's Ball. Her hands were clasped over her demure pencil skirt, her legs crossed at the ankle. Because as her etiquette teacher had drilled into her—by hitting her wrist with a ruler each time she slipped up—a lady never crossed her legs at the thigh.

And the rules were especially stringent for Beatrice, because she was not only a princess: she was also the first woman who would ever inherit the American throne. The first woman who would be queen in her own right: not a queen consort, married to a king, but a true queen regnant.

If she'd been born twenty years earlier, the succession would have jumped over her and skipped to Jeff. But her grandfather had famously abolished that centuries-old law, dictating that in all subsequent generations, the throne would pass to the oldest child, not the oldest boy.

Beatrice let her gaze drift over the conference table before her. It was littered with papers and scattered cups of coffee that had long since gone cold. Today's was the last Cabinet session until January, which meant it had been filled with year-end reports and long spreadsheets of analysis.

The Cabinet meetings always took place here in the Star Chamber, named for the gilded stars painted on its blue walls, and the famous star-shaped oculus overhead. Winter sunlight poured through it to dapple invitingly over the table. Not that Beatrice would get to enjoy it. She rarely had time to go outside, except on the days she rose before dawn to join her father on his run through the capital, flanked by their security officers.

For a brief and uncharacteristic moment, she wondered what her siblings were doing right now, if they were back yet from their whirlwind trip through East Asia. Samantha and Jeff—twins, and three years younger than Beatrice—were a dangerous pair. They were lively and spontaneous, full of bad ideas, and, unlike most teenagers, had the power to actually *carry out* those ideas, much to their parents' regret. Now, six months after they'd finished high school, it was clear that neither of them knew what to do with themselves—except celebrate the fact that they were eighteen and could legally drink.

No one ever expected anything of the twins. All the

expectation—in the family and, really, in the *world*—was focused like a white-hot spotlight on Beatrice.

At last the High Constable finished his report. The king gave a gracious nod and stood. "Thank you, Jacob. If there is no further business, that concludes today's meeting."

Everyone rose to their feet and began to shuffle out of the room, chatting about tomorrow's ball or their holiday plans. They seemed to have temporarily set aside their political rivalries—the king kept his Cabinet evenly divided between the Federalists and the Democratic-Republicans—though Beatrice felt certain those rivalries would be back in full force come the new year.

Her personal security detail, Connor, glanced up from where he stood outside the door, next to the king's protection officer. Both men were members of the Revere Guard, the elite corps of officers who devoted their lives to the service of the Crown.

"Beatrice, could you stay for a minute?" her dad asked.

Beatrice paused in the doorway. "Of course."

The king sat back down, and she followed suit. "Thank you again for helping with the nominations," he told her. They both glanced at the paper before him, where a list of names was printed in alphabetical order.

Beatrice smiled. "I'm glad you accepted them."

Tomorrow was the palace's annual holiday party, the Queen's Ball, so named because at the very first Christmas ball, Queen Martha had urged George I to ennoble dozens of Americans who'd aided the Revolution. The tradition had persisted ever since. Each year at the ball, the king knighted Americans for their service to the country, thereby making them lords or ladies. And for the first time, he had let Beatrice suggest the candidates for knighthood.

Before she could ask what he wanted, a tap sounded at

the door. The king gave an audible sigh of relief as Beatrice's mom swept into the room.

Queen Adelaide came from nobility on both sides of her family. Before her marriage to the king, she'd been set to inherit the Duchy of Canaveral *and* the Duchy of Savannah. The Double Duchess, people had called her.

Adelaide had grown up in Atlanta, and had never lost her ethereal Southern charm. Even now her gestures were touched with elegance: the tilt of her head as she smiled at her daughter, the turn of her wrist as she settled into the walnut chair to Beatrice's right. Caramel highlights gleamed in her rich brown hair, which she curled each morning with hot rollers and wore encircled by a headband.

The way they were sitting—a parent to either side of Beatrice, boxing her in—gave her the distinct sense that she was being ambushed.

"Hey, Mom," she said in a slightly puzzled tone. The queen wasn't usually part of their political discussions.

"Beatrice, your mother and I were hoping to discuss your future," the king began.

The princess blinked, disconcerted. She was always thinking about the future.

"On a more personal level," her mom clarified. "We were wondering if there was anyone . . . special in your life right now."

Beatrice startled. She'd expected this talk sooner or later, had done her best to mentally prepare herself for it. She just hadn't assumed it would be quite so *soon*.

"No, there isn't," she assured them. Her parents nodded distractedly; they both knew she wasn't dating anyone. The entire *country* knew it.

The king cleared his throat. "Your mother and I were hoping that you might start searching for a partner. For that person you'll spend your life with."

His words seemed to echo, amplified, around the Star Chamber.

Beatrice had almost no romantic experience to speak of—not that the various foreign princes near her age hadn't tried. The only one to make it to a second date had been Prince Nikolaos of Greece. His parents had urged him to do an exchange program at Harvard one semester, clearly hoping that he and the American princess would fall madly in love. Beatrice went out with him for a while to please their families, but nothing had come of it—even though, as a younger son of a royal family, Nikolaos was one of the few men actually *eligible* to go out with Beatrice. The future monarch could only marry someone of noble or aristocratic blood.

Beatrice had always known that she couldn't date the wrong person—couldn't even kiss the wrong person, the way everyone else at college seemed to. After all, no one wanted to see their future monarch walk-of-shaming home from a college party.

No, it was much safer if the heir to the throne had no sexual past for the press to rake through: no baggage from past boyfriends, no exes who might sell intimate secrets in a tell-all memoir. There could be no ups and downs in Beatrice's relationships. Once she publicly dated someone, that was it: they would have to be happy, and stable, and committed.

It had been enough to make her steer clear of dating almost entirely.

For years the press had applauded Beatrice for being careful with her reputation. But ever since she'd turned twenty-one, she'd noticed a shift in the way they discussed her love life. Instead of dedicated and virtuous, the reporters had begun to call her lonely and pitiable—or worse, frigid. If she never dated anyone, they complained, how was she supposed to get married, and start the all-important business of providing the *next* heir to the throne?

"Don't you think I'm a little young to worry about this?" Beatrice asked, relieved at how calm she sounded. But then, she had long ago been trained to keep her emotions hidden from public display.

"I was your age when your father and I got married. And I was pregnant with you the following year," the queen reminded her. A truly terrifying thought.

"That was twenty years ago!" Beatrice protested. "No one expects me to—I mean—things are different now."

"We're not saying you should run to the altar tomorrow. All we're asking is that you start to think about it. This won't be an easy decision, and we want to help."

"Help?"

"There are several young men whom we'd love for you to meet. We've invited them all to the ball tomorrow night." The queen unclasped her pebbled-leather handbag and pulled out a folder, colored plastic tabs peeking from its edge. She handed it to her daughter.

Each tab was labeled with a name. Lord José Ramirez, future Duke of Texas. Lord Marshall Davis, future Duke of Orange. Lord Theodore Eaton, future Duke of Boston.

"You're trying to *set me up?*"

"We're just giving you some options. Introducing you to young men who might be a good fit."

Beatrice flipped numbly through the pages. They were filled with information: family trees, photos, high school transcripts, even the guys' heights and weights.

"Did you use your security clearance to get all this?"

"What? No." The king looked shocked at the suggestion that he would abuse his privileges with the NSA. "The young men and their families all volunteered this information. They know what they're signing on for."

"So you've already talked to them," Beatrice said woodenly.

"And tomorrow night at the Queen's Ball you want me to interview these . . . potential *husbands?*"

Her mother's brows shot up in protest. "*Interview* makes it sound so impersonal! All we're asking is that you have a conversation with them, get to know them a little. Who knows? One of them might surprise you."

"Maybe it *is* like an interview," the king admitted. "Beatrice, when you do choose someone, he won't just be your husband. He will also be America's first king consort. And being married to the reigning monarch is a full-time job."

"A job that never stops," the queen chimed in.

Through the window, down in the Marble Courtyard, Beatrice heard a burst of laughter and gossip, and a single voice struggling valiantly to rise above the din. Probably a high school tour going past, on the last day before holiday break. These teenagers weren't that much younger than she was, yet Beatrice felt irrevocably distant from them.

She used her thumb to pull back the pages of the folder and let them fan back down. Only a dozen young men were included.

"This folder is pretty thin," she said softly.

Of course, Beatrice had always known that she would be fishing from a tiny pond, that her romantic options were incredibly narrow. It wasn't as bad as it had been a hundred years ago, when the marriage of the king was a matter of public policy rather than a matter of the heart. At least she wouldn't have to get married to seal a political treaty.

But it still seemed a lot to hope, that she might fall in love with someone on this very short list.

"Your father and I were very thorough. We combed through all the sons and grandsons of the nobility before we compiled these names," her mother said gently.

The king nodded. "There are some good options here,

Beatrice. Everyone in this folder is smart, and thoughtful, and from a good family—the type of men who will support you, without letting their egos get in the way."

From a good family. Beatrice knew precisely what that meant. They were the sons and grandsons of high-ranking American noblemen, if only because the foreign princes around her age—Nikolaos, or Charles of Schleswig-Holstein, or the Grand Duke Pieter—had all already struck out.

Beatrice glanced back and forth between her parents. "What if my future husband isn't on this list? What if I don't want to marry *any* of them?"

"You haven't even met them yet," her father cut in. "Besides, your mother and I were set up by our parents, and look how that turned out." He met the queen's eyes with a fond smile.

Beatrice nodded, a bit reassured. She knew that her dad had picked her mom just like this, from a short list of pre-approved options. They had met only a dozen times before their wedding day. And their arranged marriage had ended up blossoming into a genuine love match.

She tried to consider the possibility that her parents were right: that she could fall in love with one of the young men listed in this terrifyingly slim folder.

It didn't seem likely.

She hadn't yet met these noblemen, but she could already guess what they were like: the same type of spoiled, self-absorbed young men who'd been circling her for years. The type of guys she'd been carefully turning down at Harvard, each time they asked her to a final club party or fraternity date night. The type of guys who looked at her and saw not a person, but a crown.

Sometimes, Beatrice thought traitorously, that was how her parents saw her too.

The king braced his palms on the conference table. Against

the tanned skin of his hands glinted a pair of rings: the simple gold of his wedding band and, next to it, the heavy signet ring marked with the Great Seal of America. His two marriages, to the queen and to his country.

"Our hope for you has always been that you might find someone you love, who can also handle the requirements that come with this life," he told her. "Someone who is the right fit for you *and* America."

Beatrice heard the unspoken subtext: that if she couldn't find someone who checked both boxes, then America needed to come first. It was more important that she marry someone who could do this job, and do it well, than that she follow her heart.

And truthfully, Beatrice had given up on her heart a long time ago. Her life didn't belong to her, her choices were never fully her own—she had known this since she was a child.

Her grandfather King Edward III had said as much to her on his deathbed. The memory would be forever etched in her mind: the sterile smell of the hospital, the yellow fluorescent lighting, the peremptory way her grandfather had dismissed everyone else from the room. "I need to say a few things to Beatrice," he'd declared, in that frightening growl he used just for her.

The dying king had taken Beatrice's small hands in his frail ones. "Long ago, monarchies existed so that the people could serve the monarch. Now the monarch must serve the people. Remember that it is an honor and a privilege to be a Washington and devote your life to this nation."

Beatrice gave a solemn nod. She knew it was her duty to put the people first; everyone had been telling her that since she was born. The words *In service to God and country* had literally been painted on the walls of her nursery.

"From this point onward you are two people at once: Beatrice the girl, and Beatrice, heir to the Crown. When they want different things," her grandfather said gravely, "the Crown must win. Always. Swear it to me." His fingers closed around hers with a surprising amount of strength.

"I swear," Beatrice had whispered. She didn't remember consciously choosing to say those words; it was as if some greater force, perhaps the spirit of America itself, had taken temporary hold of her and snatched them from her chest.

Beatrice lived by that sacred oath. She had always known that this decision was looming in her future. But the suddenness of it all—the fact that her parents expected her to start picking a *husband* tomorrow, and from such an abbreviated list—made her breath catch.

"You know that this life isn't an easy one," the king said gently. "That it often looks so different from the outside than it really is on the inside. Beatrice, it's crucial that you find the right partner to share it with. Someone to help you through the challenges and share in the successes. Your mother and I are a team. I couldn't have done any of it without her."

Beatrice swallowed against a tightness in her throat. Well, if she needed to get married for the country's sake, she might as well *try* to pick one of her parents' choices.

"Should we look through the candidates before I meet them tomorrow?" she said at last, and opened the folder to its first page.

NINA

Nina Gonzalez clattered up the stairs at the back of the lecture hall, headed toward her usual seat in the mezzanine. Below her stretched hundreds of red auditorium chairs, each affixed with a wooden desk. Almost every seat was occupied. This was Intro to World History, a required class for all freshmen at King's College: King Edward I had decreed as much when he founded the university back in 1828.

She rolled up the sleeves of her flannel shirt, and a tattoo flashed on her wrist, its angular lines inscribed on her burnished sienna skin. It was the Chinese character for *friendship*. Samantha had insisted that they get the tattoo together, to commemorate their eighteenth birthdays. Of course, Sam couldn't very well be seen with a tattoo, so hers was somewhere decidedly more private.

"You're coming tonight, right?" Nina's friend Rachel Greenbaum leaned over from the next chair.

"Tonight?" Nina reached up to tuck her dark hair behind one ear. A cute boy at the end of the row was glancing her way, but she ignored him. He looked too much like the one she was still trying to get over.

"We're meeting in the common room to watch the coverage of the Queen's Ball. I made cherry tarts using the official recipe, the one from the Washington cookbook. I even bought cherries from the palace gift shop, to make it authentic," Rachel said eagerly.

"That sounds delicious." Those cherry tarts were famous worldwide: the palace had served them at every garden party or reception for generations. Nina wondered what Rachel would say if she found out how much the Washingtons secretly hated those tarts.

Honestly, it would have been more authentic if she'd cooked barbecue instead. Or breakfast tacos. Both of which the royal family ate with shocking frequency.

"So you're coming, right?" Rachel pressed.

Nina did her best to look regretful. "I can't. I actually have a shift tonight." She worked at the university library shelving books, as part of the work-study program that funded her scholarship. But even if she hadn't been busy, Nina had no desire to watch the coverage of the Queen's Ball. She'd attended that ball several years in a row, and it was pretty much the same every time.

"I didn't know the library was *open* on Friday nights."

"Maybe you should come with me. Some of the seniors still have finals; you might meet an older guy," Nina teased.

"Only you would daydream about a library meet-cute." Rachel shook her head, then let out a wistful sigh. "I wonder what Princess Beatrice will wear tonight. Do you remember the gown she wore last year, with the illusion neckline? It was *so* elegant."

Nina didn't want to talk about the royal family, especially not with Rachel, who was a little too obsessed with them. She'd once told Nina that she'd named her pet goldfish Jefferson—all ten of them in succession. But a deep-seated loyalty to Samantha made Nina speak up. "What about Samantha? She always looks beautiful too."

Rachel made a vague noise of disagreement, ignoring the question. It was an all-too-typical reaction. The nation adored

Beatrice, their future sovereign—or at least most people adored her, except the sexist, reactionary groups that still protested the Act of Succession to the Crown. Those people hated Beatrice, simply for having the temerity to be a woman who would inherit a throne that had always belonged to men. They were a minority, but they were still vicious and vocal, always trolling online photos of Beatrice, booing her at political rallies.

But if most of the nation loved Beatrice, they positively swooned over Jefferson, with what sometimes felt like a single collective sigh. He was the only boy, and the world seemed willing to forgive him anything, even if Nina wasn't.

As for Samantha . . . at best people were entertained by her. At worst, which was relatively often, they actively disapproved of her. The problem was that they didn't *know* Sam. Not the way Nina did.

She was saved from answering by Professor Urquhart, who started up to the podium with ponderous steps. There was a flurry of activity as all seven hundred students broke off their murmured conversations and arranged their laptops before them. Nina—who was probably the last person still taking notes by hand, in a spiral notebook—poised her pencil on a fresh page and glanced up expectantly. Dust motes hung suspended in the bars of sunlight that sliced through the windows.

"As we've covered all semester, political alliances through the turn of the century were typically bilateral and easily broken—which is why so many of them were sealed through marriage," Professor Urquhart began. "Things changed with the formation of the League of Kings: a treaty among multiple nations, meant to assure collective security and peace. The League was founded in 1895 at the Concord of Paris, hosted by—"

Louis, Nina silently finished. That was the easiest part of

French history: their kings were consistently named Louis, all the way up to the current Louis XXIII. Honestly, the French were even worse about *Louis* than the Washingtons were about *George*.

She copied the professor's words into her spiral notebook, wishing that she could stop thinking about the Washingtons. College was supposed to be her fresh start, a chance to figure out who she really was, free from the influence of the royal family.

Nina had been Princess Samantha's best friend since they were children. They had met twelve years ago, when Nina's mother, Isabella, interviewed at the palace. The former king—Edward III, Samantha's grandfather—had just passed away, and the new king needed a chamberlain. Isabella had been working in the Chamber of Commerce, and somehow, miraculously, her boss recommended her to His Majesty. For there was no "applying" to jobs in the palace. The palace made a list of candidates, and if you were one of the lucky few, *they* reached out to *you*.

The afternoon of the interview, Nina's mom Julie was out of town and Nina's usual babysitter canceled at the last minute, leaving Nina's mamá Isabella no choice but to bring Nina with her. "Stay right here," she admonished, leading her daughter to a bench in the downstairs corridor.

Nina had found it surprising that her mamá was interviewing in the actual *palace*, but as she would later learn, Washington Palace wasn't just the royal family's home in the capital. It was also the administrative center of the Crown. By far the majority of the palace's six hundred rooms were offices or public spaces. The private apartments on the second floor were all marked by oval door handles, rather than the round ones downstairs.

Nina tucked her feet beneath her and quietly opened the book she'd brought.

"What are you reading?"

A face topped by a mountain of chestnut hair peered around the corner. Nina instantly recognized Princess Samantha—though she didn't look much like a princess in her zebra-print leggings and sequined dress. Her fingernails were painted in a rainbow, each one a different primary color.

"Um . . ." Nina hid the cover in her lap. The book was about a princess, albeit a fantasy one, but it still felt strange to confess that to a *real* princess.

"My little brother and I are reading a dragon series right now," Samantha declared, and tipped her head to one side. "Have you seen him? I can't find him."

Nina shook her head. "I thought you were twins," she couldn't resist saying.

"Yes, but I'm four minutes older, which makes Jeff my little brother," Samantha replied with irrefutable logic. "Want to help me look for him?"

The princess was a storm of kinetic energy, skipping down the halls, constantly opening doors or peering behind furniture in search of her twin. The entire time she kept up a steady stream of chatter, her own greatest-hits tour of the palace.

"This room is haunted by the ghost of Queen Thérèse. I know it's her because the ghost speaks French," she declared ominously, pointing at the shuttered downstairs parlor. Or "I used to roller-skate down these halls, till my dad caught me and said I can't. Beatrice did it too, but it never matters what Beatrice does." Samantha didn't sound resentful, just pensive. "She's going to be queen someday."

"And what are you going to be?" Nina asked, curious.

Samantha grinned. "Everything else."

She led Nina from one unbelievable place to another, through storerooms of pressed linen napkins and kitchens that soared larger than ballrooms, where the chef gave them sugar cookies out of a painted blue jar. The princess bit into her cookie, but Nina tucked hers into her pocket. It was too pretty to eat.

As they looped back toward the bench, Nina was startled to see her mamá walking down the hallway, chatting easily with the king. Their eyes lit on Nina, and she instinctively froze.

The king smiled, a genial, boyish smile that made his eyes twinkle. "And who have we here?"

Nina had never met a king before, yet some unbidden instinct—perhaps all the times she'd seen him on television—prompted her to bob into a curtsy.

"This is my daughter, Nina," Isabella murmured.

Samantha trotted over to her father and tugged at his hand. "Dad, can Nina come over again soon?" she pleaded.

The king turned his warm eyes on Nina's mamá. "Samantha is right. I hope you'll bring Nina here in the afternoons. After all, it's not like we have a short workday."

Isabella blinked. "Your Majesty?"

"The girls clearly get along, and I know your wife has a busy schedule, too. Why should Nina stay home with a babysitter when she could be here?"

Nina was too young to understand Isabella's hesitation. "Please, mamá?" she'd chimed in, brimming with eagerness. Isabella had relented with a sigh.

And just like that, Nina was interwoven into the lives of the royal twins.

They became an instant threesome: the prince, the princess, and the chamberlain's daughter. Back then Nina hadn't even known to feel self-conscious about the differences between her life and Samantha's. For even though they were twins, and *royalty*, Jeff and Sam never made Nina feel like an outsider. If anything, they were all equally excluded from the glamorous and inaccessible world of the adults—even from

Beatrice, who at age ten was already enrolled in private tutoring on top of her middle school courses.

Sam and Jeff were always the instigators of their plans, with Nina trying and failing to keep them in line. They would escape the twins' nanny and set out on some escapade: to swim in the heated indoor pool, or to find the rumored safe rooms and bomb shelters that were supposedly hidden throughout the palace. One time Samantha convinced them to hide beneath a tablecloth and eavesdrop on a private meeting between the king and the Austrian ambassador. They were caught after just two minutes, when Jeff tugged on the tablecloth and knocked over a pitcher of water, but by then Samantha had already squirted honey into the ambassador's shoe. "If you don't want honey in your shoes, don't kick them off under the table," she'd said later, her eyes gleaming with mischief.

The fact that Samantha and Nina's friendship had survived all these years was a testament to the princess's determination. She refused to let them drift apart, even though they went to different schools, even after Nina's mamá left her role as chamberlain and was named Minister of the Treasury. Samantha just kept on inviting Nina to the palace for sleepovers, or to the Washingtons' vacation homes for holiday weekends, or to attend state events as her plus-one.

Nina's parents had mixed feelings about their daughter's friendship with the princess.

Isabella and Julie had met years ago in grad school. By now they were one of Washington's power couples: Isabella working as Minister of the Treasury, Julie the founder of a successful e-commerce business. They didn't argue very often, but Nina's complicated relationship with the Washingtons was something they never managed to agree on.

"We can't let Nina go on that trip," Isabella had protested, after Samantha invited Nina to the royal family's beach house.

"I don't want her spending too much time with them, especially when we aren't around."

Nina's ears perked up at the sound of their voices, which echoed through the building's old-fashioned heating pipes. She was in her bedroom on the third floor, beneath the attic. She hadn't meant to eavesdrop . . . but she'd also never confessed how easily she could hear them when they spoke in the sitting room directly below.

"Why not?" Julie had replied, her voice oddly distorted by the old metal pipes.

"Because I worry about her! The world that the Washingtons inhabit, with all its private planes and court galas and protocol—that isn't reality. And no matter how often they invite her or how much Princess Samantha likes her, Nina will never really be one of them." Nina's mamá sighed. "I don't want her feeling like a poor relation from some Jane Austen novel."

Nina shifted closer on her mattress to catch the response.

"The princess has been a good friend to Nina," her mom protested. "And you should have a little more faith in the way we've raised our daughter. If anything, I think Nina will be a positive influence on Samantha, by reminding her what exists outside those palace gates. The princess probably *needs* a normal friend."

Eventually Nina's parents had agreed to let her go, with the stipulation that she stay out of the public eye and never be quoted or photographed in press coverage of the royal family. The palace had been happy to agree. They didn't particularly want the media focusing on Princess Samantha, either.

By the time they were in high school, Nina was used to her best friend's quirky plans and contagious excitement. *Let's take Albert out!* Sam would text, naming the lemon-yellow Jeep she'd begged her parents to give her on her sixteenth birthday. She had the car, but she kept failing the parallel-parking part of her driver's test and still didn't have a license. Which meant that Nina ended up driving that obnoxiously yellow Jeep all through the capital, with Samantha sitting cross-legged in the passenger seat, begging her to swing through McDonald's. After a while Nina didn't even worry about the protection officer glowering at them from the back.

Sam made it far too easy for Nina to forget the myriad differences between them. And Nina loved her, without strings or conditions, the way she would have loved a sister if she'd had one. It was just that her sister happened to be the Princess of America.

But their relationship had subtly shifted over the past six months. Nina had never told Sam what happened the night of the graduation party—and the longer she kept it a secret, the greater the distance it seemed to wedge between them. Then Sam and Jeff went off on their whirlwind post-graduation trip, and Nina was starting her first year of college, and maybe it was all for the best anyway. This was Nina's chance to settle into a more normal life, one without the private planes and court galas and protocol that had so worried Isabella. She could go back to being her ordinary, real-world self.

Nina hadn't told anyone at King's College that Samantha was her best friend. They would probably assume she was a liar—or if they did believe her, they might try to use her for her connections. Nina didn't know which outcome would be worse.

Professor Urquhart clicked off the microphone, marking the conclusion of the lecture. Everyone stood in a shuffle of closing laptops and suppressed gossip. Nina scribbled a few final notes in her spiral before tossing it into her shoulder bag, then followed Rachel down the stairs and out into the courtyard.

A few other girls from their hallway joined them, talking in excited tones about the Queen's Ball viewing party. They started toward the student center, where everyone usually grabbed lunch after class, but Nina's steps slowed.

A movement near the street had grabbed her attention. A black town car was idling at the curb, purring softly. Propped in the car window was a piece of white computer paper with Nina's name scrawled on it.

She would recognize that handwriting anywhere.

"Nina? Are you coming?" Rachel called out.

"Sorry, I have a meeting with my advisor," Nina fibbed. She waited a few more moments before racing across the lawn toward the car.

In the backseat was Princess Samantha, wearing velour sweatpants and a white T-shirt through which Nina could see her pink bra. Nina hurried to join her, pulling the door shut before anyone could see.

"*Nina!* I missed you!" Sam threw her arms around her friend in one of her typically effusive hugs.

"I missed you, too," Nina murmured into her friend's shoulder. A million questions burned on her lips.

Finally Samantha broke away, leaning forward to address the driver. "You can just circle campus for a while," she told him. Typical Sam, wanting to be in constant motion even if she wasn't going anywhere.

"Sam—what are you doing here? Shouldn't you be getting ready for tonight?"

Sam lowered her voice conspiratorially. "I'm kidnapping you and dragging you to the Queen's Ball as my plus-one!"

Nina shook her head. "Sorry, I have to work tonight."

"But your parents will be there—I'm sure they'd love to see you!" Sam let out a breath. "Please, Nina? I could really use some backup right now, with my mom and dad."

"Didn't you just get home?" What could they already be angry about?

22

"The last morning in Thailand, Jeff and I ran away from our protection officers," Sam admitted, looking out the window. They were driving up College Street toward the soaring Gothic architecture of Dandridge Library.

"You ditched your bodyguards? How?"

"We ran away from them," Samantha repeated, unable to suppress her smile. "Literally. Jeff and I turned and sprinted into oncoming traffic, weaving between the cars, then hitched a ride to an ATV rental place. We rode four-wheelers through the jungle. It was incredible."

"That seems risky," Nina pointed out, and Sam laughed.

"You sound *just* like my parents! See, this is why I need you. I was hoping that if you came with me tonight . . ."

"I could keep you in line?" Nina finished for her. As if she'd ever been able to control the princess. No power on earth could keep Samantha from doing something once she'd set her mind to it.

"You know you're the good one!"

"I'm only 'the good one' in comparison to you," Nina countered. "That isn't saying much."

"You should be grateful I set the bar so low," Sam teased. "Look, we can leave the reception early—grab some homemade cookie dough from the kitchens, stay up late watching bad reality TV. It's been ages since we had a slumber party! Please," she said again. "I've really missed you."

It was hard to ignore that kind of plea from your best friend. "I guess . . . I could probably get Jodi to trade shifts with me," Nina conceded, after a beat of hesitation so slight that Samantha probably hadn't even noticed it.

"Thank you!" Sam gave an excited squeal and leaned forward to inform the driver of their new destination. Then she turned to Nina, pulling her slouchy leather bag onto her lap. "By the way, I brought you something from Bangkok." She dug

23

through her bag, eventually emerging with a packet of pretzel M&M's. The bright blue bag was covered in the gorgeous loops and curlicues of Thai script.

"You remembered." M&M's were Nina's favorite candy. Sam always brought a bag of them home from her foreign trips—she'd read somewhere that the formula was tweaked in each country, and decided that she and Nina would have to taste-test all of them.

"So? How are they?" Sam asked as Nina popped one of the chocolate candies into her mouth.

"Delicious." It was actually a little stale, but that wasn't surprising given how many miles it had traveled, smashed into the side pocket of Samantha's purse.

They turned a corner and the palace swam into view—far too soon for Nina's liking, but after all, King's College was only a couple of miles away. Virginia pines stretched tall and arrogant on either side of the street, which was lined with bureaucratic offices and thronged with people. The palace glowed a blazing white against the blue enamel of the sky. Its reflection danced in the waters of the Potomac, so that there seemed to be two palaces: one substantial, one watery and dreamlike.

Tourists clung to the palace's iron gates, where a row of guards stood at attention, their hands raised in a salute. Above the circle drive Nina saw the fluttering edge of the Royal Standard, the flag indicating that the monarch was officially in residence.

She took a breath, steeling herself. She hadn't wanted to come back to the palace and risk seeing *him*. She still hated him for what happened the night of the graduation party.

But more than that, Nina hated the small part of herself that secretly longed to see him, even after everything he had done.

3

DAPHNE

Daphne Deighton turned the key in her front door and paused. Out of habit she looked back over her shoulder with a smile, though it had been months since the paparazzi gathered on her lawn, the way they used to when she was dating Jefferson.

Across the river she could just see a corner of Washington Palace. The center of the world—or at least the center of hers.

It was beautiful from this angle, afternoon sunlight streaming over its white sandstone bricks and high arched windows. But as Daphne knew, the palace wasn't nearly as orderly as it appeared. Constructed on the original site of Mount Vernon, the home of King George I, it had been renovated time and again as various monarchs attempted to leave their mark on it. Now it was a confusing nest of galleries and stairways and hallways, constantly thronged with people.

Daphne lived with her parents on the edge of Herald Oaks, the neighborhood of stately aristocratic houses east of the palace. Unlike their neighbors' estates, which had been handed down these past two and a half centuries, the Deightons' home was quite new. Just like their nobility.

At least her family had a title, thank *god*, even if it fell a bit low in the hierarchy for Daphne's taste. Her father, Peter, was the second Baronet Margrave. The baronetcy had been awarded to Daphne's grandfather by King Edward III, for a "personal diplomatic service" to Empress Anna of Russia. No one in the family had ever explained the exact nature of this unspecified service. Naturally, Daphne had drawn her own conclusions.

She closed the door behind her, slinging her leather book bag off one shoulder, and heard her mom's voice from the dining room. "Daphne? Can you come in here?"

"Of course." Daphne forced herself to smooth the impatience from her tone.

She'd expected her parents to call a family conclave today, just as they had so many times before: when Jefferson had first asked Daphne out, or when he invited her on vacation with his family, or on the unthinkable day when he broke up with her. Every milestone in her relationship with the prince had been marked by one of these discussions. It was just the way her family operated.

Not that her parents had contributed all that much. Everything Daphne had accomplished with Jefferson, she'd done squarely on her own.

She slid into the dining chair across from her parents and reached nonchalantly for the pitcher of iced tea, to pour herself a glass. She already knew her mother's next words.

"He got back last night."

There was no need to clarify which *he* her mother had meant. Prince Jefferson George Alexander Augustus—the youngest of the three royal Washington siblings, and the only boy.

"I'm aware." As if Daphne hadn't set a dozen internet alerts for the prince's name, didn't constantly check social media for every last shred of information about his status. As if she didn't know the prince better than anyone else did, probably even his own mother.

"You didn't go to meet his plane."

"Next to all the shrieking fangirls? I think not. I'll see Jefferson tonight at the Queen's Ball." Daphne pointedly refused to call the prince *Jeff*, the way everyone else did. It sounded so decidedly *unroyal*.

"It's been six months," her father reminded her. "Are you sure you're ready?"

"I guess I'll have to be," Daphne replied in a clipped tone. Of course she was ready.

Her mother hastened to intercede. "We're just trying to help, Daphne. Tonight is an important night. After all we've done . . ."

A psychologist might assume that Daphne had inherited her ambitions from her parents, but it would be more accurate to say that her parents' ambitions were magnified and concentrated in her, the way a curved glass lens can focus scattered beams of heat.

Rebecca Deighton's social climbing had begun long before Daphne was born. Becky, as she'd called herself then, left her small town in Nebraska at age nineteen, armed with nothing but stunning good looks and a razor-sharp wit. She signed with a top modeling agency in a matter of weeks. Her face was soon plastered on magazines and billboards, lingerie ads and car commercials. America became infatuated with her.

Eventually, Becky restyled herself as Rebecca and set her sights on a title. After she met Daphne's father, it was only a matter of time before she became Lady Margrave.

And if things went according to plan and Daphne married Jefferson, her parents would surely be elevated above a lowly baronetcy. They might become an earl and countess . . . perhaps even a marquess and marchioness.

"We only want what's best for you," Rebecca added, her eyes on her daughter's.

You mean what's best for you, Daphne was tempted to reply. "I'll be fine," she said instead.

Daphne had known for years that she would marry the

prince. That was the only word for it: *known*. Not *hoped* to marry, or *dreamed* of marrying, or even *felt destined* to marry. Those words involved an element of chance, of uncertainty.

When she was little, Daphne had pitied the girls at her school who were obsessed with the royal family: the ones who copied everything the princesses wore, or had Prince Jefferson's picture plastered on their lockers. What were they doing when they swooned over his poster, pretending that the prince was their boyfriend? Pretending was a game for babies and fools, and Daphne was neither.

Then, in eighth grade, Daphne's class took a field trip to the palace, and she realized why her parents clung so obsessively to their aristocratic status. Because that status was their window into *this*.

As she gazed at the palace in all its inaccessible grandeur— as she heard her classmates whispering how wonderful it must be, to be a princess—Daphne came to the startling realization that they were right. It *was* wonderful to be a princess. Which was why Daphne, unlike the rest of them, would actually become one.

After that field trip, Daphne had resolved that she would date the prince, and like all goals she set for herself, she achieved it. She applied to St. Ursula's, the private all-girls school that the daughters of the royal family had attended since time immemorial. Jefferson's sisters went there. It didn't hurt that Jefferson's school, the all-boys Forsythe Academy, was right next door.

Sure enough, by the end of the year the prince had asked her out, when she was a freshman and he was a sophomore.

It wasn't always easy, managing someone as spontaneous and heedless as Jefferson. But Daphne was everything a princess should be: gracious and accomplished and, of course, beautiful. She charmed the American people and the press.

She even won the approval of the Queen Mother, and Jefferson's grandmother was notoriously impossible to please.

Until the night of Jefferson's high school graduation party, when everything went so horribly wrong. When Himari got hurt, and Daphne went looking for Jefferson—only to find him in bed with another girl.

It was definitely the prince; the light glinted unmistakably on the deep brown of his hair. Daphne tried to breathe. Her vision dissolved into spots. After everything that had happened, after the lengths she'd gone to—

She'd stumbled back, fleeing the room before either of them could see her.

Jefferson called the next morning. Daphne felt a momentary stab of panic that he somehow knew everything—knew the terrible, unthinkable thing she had done. Instead he stammered through a breakup speech that might as well have been written by his PR people. He kept saying how young they both were: how Daphne still wasn't finished with high school, and he didn't know what he was doing next year. That it might be better for both of them if they spent some time apart, but he hoped they could still be friends. Daphne's voice was eerily calm as she told him that she understood.

The moment Jefferson hung up, Daphne called Natasha at the *Daily News* and planted the breakup story herself. She'd learned long ago that the first story was always the most important, because it set the tone for all the others. So she made certain that Natasha reported the breakup as mutual, that Daphne and Jefferson had agreed it was for the best.

At least, the article ever-so-subtly implied, for the time being.

In the six months since the breakup, Jefferson had been out of town, on a royal tour and then on a rambling post-graduation trip with his twin sister. It had given Daphne ample opportunity to think about their relationship—about what they both had done, and what it had cost her.

Even after everything that had happened, even knowing what she knew, she still wanted to be a princess. And she intended to win Jefferson back.

"We're just trying to look out for you, Daphne," Rebecca went on, as gravely as if she'd been discussing a life-threatening medical diagnosis. "Especially now . . ."

Daphne knew what her mother meant. Now that she and Jefferson were broken up and it was open season again, flocks of girls had started trailing after him. *Prince poachers*, the newspapers called them. Privately Daphne liked to think of them as Jeffersluts. No matter the city, they were always the same: wearing short skirts and sky-high heels, waiting for hours at bars or in hotel lobbies just hoping for a glimpse of him. Jefferson—oblivious, as always—flitted happily from place to place like a butterfly, while those girls stalked him with nets at the ready.

The prince poachers weren't really her competition; none of them were even in the same league as her. Still, each time she saw a photo of Jefferson surrounded by a flock of those girls, Daphne couldn't help feeling worried. There were just so *many* of them.

Not to mention that girl in Jefferson's bed, whoever she was. Some masochistic part of Daphne wanted, desperately, to know. After that night, she'd kept expecting the girl to come forward with a sordid tell-all article, but she never did.

Daphne glanced up at the mirror above the sideboard to calm herself.

There was no denying that Daphne was beautiful—beautiful in that rare, dazzling way that seems to justify all successes and excuse a good many failures. She'd inherited Rebecca's vivid features, her alabaster complexion, and most of all her eyes:

those snapping green eyes with a glint of gold, which seemed to hint at untold secrets. But her hair came from Peter. It was a glorious riot of color, everything from copper to red currant to honeysuckle, and fell in a sumptuous tumble almost to her waist.

She gave a faint smile, reassured as always by the promise of her own reflection.

"Daphne." Her father cut into her thoughts. "Whatever happens, know that we are on your side. Always."

Whatever happens. Daphne shot him a look. Did he know what she had done that night?

"I'll be fine," she said again, and left it at that.

She knew what was expected of her. If a plan didn't work, she had to make another; if she slipped and fell, she must always fall forward. It could only ever be onward and upward for her.

Her parents had no idea what Daphne was capable of—no idea what she had already done, in pursuit of this crown.

4

SAMANTHA

That evening, Samantha headed toward a nondescript door that was tucked into the downstairs hallway like an architect's afterthought. It might not look impressive, but this was the Door of Sighs, the royal family's private entrance to the grand ballroom: so named because generations of princesses had lingered there when they were too young to attend, and sighed romantically as they watched the dancing.

"There's going to be hell to pay from your parents," Nina pointed out, walking next to her.

"Maybe." Though Sam doubted that her parents had even noticed her lateness. They never noticed anything she did, unless she acted out so much that she forced them to.

Sam's protection officer trotted alongside them, his mouth set into a thin line. Sam could tell that Caleb was still angry with her for pulling that stunt in Thailand. Well, Sam hadn't *wanted* to run into oncoming traffic; Caleb had simply given her no choice. Nothing else had worked on him—not persuasion or pleading, not even Sam's last-ditch trick, which usually involved a complaint about cramps or tampons. When she'd tried it on him, the bodyguard had just handed her two Midol tablets and a bottle of water.

"Incoming with the Sparrow," Caleb muttered into his walkie-talkie. Sam swallowed back a flare of irritation at her security code name. All members of the royal family were designated as birds: the Eagle for the king, the Swan for the queen, the Falcon for Beatrice, the Bluebird for Jeff. It was only a couple of years ago that Sam had learned why security always called the second child Sparrow.

It was Sparrow as in *spare*. As in *not the heir*. Sam was the extra child, an insurance policy: a living, breathing backup battery.

The herald, who stood at attention at the Door of Sighs, didn't dare remark upon Sam's tardiness. He waited as she reached into her beaded clutch to reapply her lip gloss, a custom peony shade. She'd been offered a multimillion-dollar licensing deal for it—the company wanted to call it American Rose and put Sam's face on the tube—but she'd turned it down. She liked the idea of the lip-gloss color being entirely her own.

When she nodded at him, the herald stepped into the ballroom and thumped his enormous golden staff on the floor. The sound rebounded over the noises of the party: the clink of wineglasses, the scuffle of leather soles, the low hum of gossip.

"Her Highness Samantha Martha Georgina Amphyllis of the House of Washington!"

Samantha shot Nina one last glance and stepped into the ballroom.

Hundreds of eyes darted toward Samantha, gleaming with calculation. They were all wondering how much weight she'd gained abroad or how much her gown cost or how envious she was of her older sister. Sam tried not to flinch. She'd forgotten just how big a full court function really was, with every last noble and politician in attendance, even the life peers, even their spouses.

White-gloved waiters brushed past with flutes of champagne, and a string quartet played jazz music in the background. Swaths of holiday greenery were draped throughout

33

the room, decorated with poinsettias and enormous red velvet bows. In one corner stood the palace's official Christmas tree, its branches laden with old-fashioned garlands of popcorn and cherries, the way the royal family had decorated trees for a hundred years.

Sam caught sight of Jeff outside. The French doors had been thrown open, courtiers spilling out on the colonnaded terrace to cluster beneath spidery heat lamps. Several of the twins' friends were already out there. Jeff met her gaze, his eyes flashing with unmistakable warning, just as an arm closed around Samantha's elbow like a vise.

"Samantha. We need to talk." Queen Adelaide looked coolly elegant in a strapless black dress, her glossy hair pinned back with antique diamond clips—the ones that George II had famously won from the French King Louis XVI in a game of cards. The Louisiana Gamble, people called that bet, since it had resulted in France ceding the Louisiana Territory to America.

"Hi, Mom," Sam said cheerfully, though she knew it was useless.

"That isn't the gown I laid out for you." Adelaide had the unique ability to scowl and smile at once, which Sam had always found terrifying, and also a little impressive.

"I know." Sam had ignored the dress her mom had selected, choosing instead a one-shouldered gown covered in silver sequins: far too edgy and inappropriate for an event this formal, but Sam didn't care. Her riotous dark hair was loose and messy, as if she'd just tumbled out of bed. She'd also borrowed her grandmother's choker from the Crown Jewels collection, made of enormous cabochon rubies interspersed with diamonds—but instead of fastening it around her throat, she'd wound it around her wrist in a chunky tangle, making the elegant stones into something almost sexy.

Sam had long ago resolved that if she couldn't be beautiful, she should at the very least be interesting. And she wasn't beautiful, not in the traditional sense—her forehead was too wide and sloping, her brows too heavy, her features too starkly hewn, like those of her distant Hanoverian cousins.

But people tended to forget all that the moment Samantha began talking. There was a nebulous, infectious energy to her, as if she were somehow more *alive* than everyone else. As if all her nerves were sparking at once, just below the surface.

The queen steered her daughter firmly to one side of the ballroom, far from any eavesdropping ears.

"Your father and I are disappointed in you," Adelaide began.

What else is new. "I'm sorry," Sam said wearily. She knew the script, knew it was easier to just tell her mom what she wanted to hear. She'd managed to avoid her parents when she landed late last night, and they had been too busy with preparations for the ball to confront her today. But she'd known she couldn't put them off forever.

"*Sorry?*" the queen hissed. "That's all you have to say for yourself after running away from your security officers? Samantha, that kind of behavior is inexcusable! Those officers put their lives at risk for you every day. Their job is, literally, to step between you and a bullet. The least you could do is show them some respect!"

"Did you already give this speech to Jeff?" Sam asked, as if she didn't know the answer. Jeff always emerged from trouble completely unscathed.

It wasn't fair. Despite how progressive America claimed to be, there was still a sexist double standard quietly underpinning everything. She and Jeff were proof of it, like in those scientific studies where they treated twin babies the same except for one key variable, then tracked how it affected them.

The variable here was that Jeff was a boy and Sam was a

girl, and even when they did the *exact same thing*, people reacted to them differently.

If the paparazzi caught Jeff on an expensive shopping spree, he was splurging for a special occasion, while Samantha was spoiled.

If pictures surfaced of Jeff visibly drunk and stumbling out of a bar, he was blowing off some much-needed steam. Samantha was a wild party girl.

If Jeff talked back to the paparazzi, he was simply being firm, protecting his privacy. Samantha was a ruthless bitch.

She would have loved to see how the press might react to *Beatrice* doing any of those things, but of course Beatrice never stepped a toe out of line.

Sam knew that none of it was Jeff's fault. Still . . . it was enough to make her wish she could change things. Not that she had any power to do so.

"I don't see why it's such a big deal," she protested weakly. "We didn't hurt anyone. Why can't you just let me enjoy my life for once?"

"Samantha, no one has ever accused you of failing to enjoy your life," Adelaide snapped.

Sam tried not to reveal how much that stung.

Her mom heaved a sigh. "Please, can you at least *try* to be on your best behavior? This is a big night for your sister."

Something in her tone gave Samantha pause. "What do you mean?"

The queen just pursed her lips. Whatever was going on, she didn't trust Sam with it. Per usual.

Sam half wished that she could go back to that moment in Thailand when she'd turned to Jeff, an eyebrow raised in challenge, and dared him to make a run for it. Or earlier, even, to the days before her mom looked at her with such evident disappointment. She remembered the way her mom used to smile at her when Sam came home with stories of her day at school. Adelaide would hold her daughter in her lap and French-braid her hair, her hands very gentle as they brushed the sections and pulled them over one another.

But Sam knew it wasn't any use. No one cared what she really thought; they just wanted her to shut up and stop stealing media attention from picture-perfect Beatrice. To stand in the background. To be seen and never heard.

There was a stubborn tilt to her head as she stalked across the ballroom. Well, now everyone could gossip about her gown, which was as blindingly bright as a lit-up disco ball. Her eyes gleamed willful and turbulent beneath their lashes.

Sam was almost to the far doors when she saw her older sister, wearing a prim high-necked cocktail dress, probably her first outfit of the evening: she usually had multiple costume changes for state functions. She was talking to a sharp-featured woman with graying hair. It took Sam a moment to realize that they weren't speaking English.

She hastened past Beatrice and went to station herself at the bar, edging toward the side so that no one would see her.

Where had Nina gone? Sam pulled out her phone and tapped a quick text: *Grabbing drinks, come find me.* Then she leaned forward to make eye contact with the bartender. "Can I have a beer?"

He looked at her askance. They both knew that the palace had never served beer at events like this. It was considered too lowbrow, whatever that meant.

"Please," Sam added, with as sweet a smile as she knew how to give. "Don't you have at least *one* bottle back there?"

The bartender hesitated, as if weighing the risks, then ducked below the bar, emerging a moment later with a pair of frosted beer bottles. "You didn't get this from me." He winked and turned away, distancing himself from the incriminating evidence.

"Oh, good, I've been looking for one of these," exclaimed

a voice to her left, just as one of the bottles was plucked away.

"Hey, that's mine!" Sam whirled around on her strappy heel.

The boy standing next to her leaned his elbows back onto the bar, a light glinting in his shockingly blue eyes. He looked a couple of years older, around Beatrice's age, with unruly blond hair and chiseled features. If it hadn't been for his pair of matching dimples, his handsomeness would have been almost intimidating.

She wondered who he was. Unlike most nobles, who in Sam's experience were squishy and soft, he had an athlete's muscular body.

"Easy there, killer. No need to be double-fisting this early in the night."

"Did you just call me *killer?*" Sam demanded, unsure whether to be insulted or intrigued.

"Would you prefer Your Highness?" He gave an abbreviated bow in Sam's direction. "I'm Theodore Eaton, by the way. My friends call me Teddy."

So he *was* noble. Very noble, in fact. Though Samantha rather liked that he introduced himself with only his name, when, as the heir to a dukedom, he was technically *Lord* Theodore Eaton.

The Eatons had been one of the preeminent families in New England since the Mayflower. Some would say that they were more American even than the Washingtons, who, after all, had intermarried with foreign royalty for most of the last two centuries. Teddy's father was the current Duke of Boston: one of the thirteen original dukedoms, the ones awarded by George I at the very first Queen's Ball. The Old Guard, those families were sometimes called, because there were no more dukedoms to be had. Congress had put a ban on the creation of new ones back in 1870.

"We just met and already we're friends? You're very presumptuous, *Teddy*," Sam teased. "Where did *Teddy* come from, anyway? Is it Teddy like a teddy bear?"

"Exactly that. My younger sister called me that, and the name stuck." Teddy held out his arms in a helpless, amused gesture. "Don't I look like the teddy bear you had as a kid?"

"I didn't have a teddy bear. Just a baby blanket that I very creatively named Blankie," Sam told him. "Well, I *used* to have Blankie. Now I only have half of Blankie."

"Where's the other half?"

"Jeff has it." What had possessed her to tell this story anyway? She blamed Teddy, and that disarming smile of his. "Blankie was a gift from our grandfather before he died. He gave it to both of us."

"One blanket for two people?"

Sam idly spun her beer bottle on the bar's marble surface. "I think he wanted us to learn to share. It didn't work, of course. When my dad caught us fighting over Blankie, he took a pair of scissors and cut it clean down the middle. Now we each have half."

Teddy looked at her—*really* looked at her, those blue-blue eyes meeting hers for a beat longer than was socially acceptable. Sam found herself desperate to know what he was thinking. What he thought of her.

"Being a twin sounds rough. Makes me glad my siblings are all younger," he concluded.

Sam lifted one golden-brown shoulder in a shrug. At least she hadn't been fighting with Beatrice; the king would have just given Blankie to her without a second thought.

"And I'm pretty glad my sister had a teddy bear instead of a blanket," he went on, with another flash of those damned dimples. "Otherwise what would people call me?"

"Oh, I don't know. Blankie Eaton has quite the ring to it. At the very least it's memorable." Sam tried to fight back a smile, but the smile seemed to be winning. "So, Teddy-like-a-teddy-bear, are you dreading tonight's ceremony as much as I am?"

"Should I be?"

"You've clearly never attended the Queen's Ball. My dad and Beatrice have to knight each of the candidates for nobility, individually, *in alphabetical order*. It's like the world's worst high school graduation, except each graduate gets a patent of nobility instead of a diploma."

"Sounds like I was wrong about it being too early in the night for double-fisting."

"I'll drink to that." Sam clinked her bottle to his, not caring that it was bad luck to cheers with beer—or was that only in France?—and took a sip. It felt like the rest of the room had retreated behind a hazy curved glass, like there was no one at this party but the two of them.

"I have to ask." Teddy's voice was warm, and a little husky. "Why are you hiding here at the bar, instead of working the room like the rest of your family?"

"Trust me, the rest of my family is doing just fine on their own. Right now my sister is talking with the German ambassador, *in German*," Sam told him, and rolled her eyes.

"Wow," Teddy said slowly. "That's so . . ."

"Obnoxious?"

"I was going to say impressive," he replied, and Sam flushed at being caught out. But it often felt as if Beatrice went out of her way to make everyone else look like slackers.

When she was little—it felt very long ago, now—Sam used to think of herself as smart. She loved to read, spent hours listening to stories about the former kings and queens, and had a sharp memory for details. But then she started at St. Ursula's, and that innate cheerful confidence was systematically whittled away from her.

She didn't have her older sister's patience, or her head for numbers, or her desire to chair clubs and committees. On more than one occasion Sam overheard the teachers talking about her in low voices: *She's no Beatrice,* they would say, with evident frustration. Gradually Sam was galvanized into believing it. Beatrice was the smart, beautiful future queen, while Sam was just the Other Washington Sister.

She glanced over at Teddy, who was shifting his weight as if he might walk away. But Sam didn't want him to go, not yet.

"We can head over to the throne room if you want. The ceremony is starting soon," she offered.

Teddy held out his arm in a show of careless chivalry. "Lead the way, Your Highness."

"My friends call me Sam." She looped her arm through his, still holding the half-empty beer in the other hand.

The sounds of the party chased after them, laughter and music echoing through the old, high-ceilinged rooms. A constant flow of traffic—footmen dressed in tails, PR people and camera crews—buzzed back and forth along the hall.

Teddy paused in the doorway to the throne room, to stare up at the domed ceiling that soared above them. It was painted with the famous mural of King George I crossing the sky in a flying chariot.

"Charles Wilson Peale did that one," Sam murmured, ignoring the confused glances from the support staff who were stationed inside. Caleb was already in there—Sam tried not to make eye contact with him—standing next to Beatrice's security detail, a tall, fierce-looking young man in the uniform of the Revere Guard.

"As in the Peale family from Pennsylvania?" Teddy asked.

Sam shrugged. She much preferred Charles Wilson to his modern descendants. She was pretty sure the Peale girls had started that rumor that she was sent to rehab in tenth grade—and that was just because she'd danced with one of their ex-boyfriends at a party.

"He was a lieutenant in the Revolutionary War. He painted the pillars, too." Sam nodded at the corners of the room, where four columns soared upward. "They're supposed to represent the four pillars of American virtue: truth, justice, honor, and family. The weird one with all the bales of hay and piglets is family, in case you didn't get it."

Teddy's eyes twinkled. "How do you know so much history?"

"I used to sneak away from my nanny and hide in the middle of palace tours," Sam confessed. "Sometimes people didn't even see me there. Or if they did, I would whisper that I was playing hide-and-seek against my brother, and could they please help me hide? They usually did. My nanny searched all over the palace, but she never thought to look for me in the middle of a crowd."

Teddy shook his head wonderingly. "I think you're too clever for your own good."

Trumpets sounded from the other end of the hall, indicating that the ceremony would begin in fifteen minutes. The noise was followed by an answering thunder of footsteps as hundreds of people began the slow procession toward the throne room.

Sam's heart skipped. Etiquette, as well as common sense, dictated that she should lead Teddy to his seat—but she didn't want to. She wasn't done with him. She wanted his warm golden energy to be focused on *her* for just a moment longer.

She grabbed Teddy's hand and dragged him down the hall, then threw open a nondescript door and pulled it closed behind them.

The cloakroom smelled of fur and cedarwood and Samantha's Vol de Nuit perfume. A thin light crept in through the doorframe.

Sam was still clutching her beer bottle. She lifted it to her lips, well aware of the juxtaposition she posed: wearing a couture gown and priceless Crown Jewels, chugging a beer. Teddy raised one eyebrow, evidently amused, but he didn't try to leave.

She set the empty bottle on the floor and turned to face him, the sequined fabric of her dress contorting around her.

"You might be aware that I outrank you," she whispered, teasing.

"It's been mentioned once or twice."

She reached her hands up to his shoulders to pull at the stray end of his bow tie, which fell uselessly to the floor. "I outrank you," Sam repeated, "and as your princess, I command that you kiss me."

Teddy hesitated, and for a moment Sam worried that she had misread him. But then his face relaxed into a smile.

"I don't think monarchs get to make autocratic demands like that anymore," he said softly.

"I'm not a monarch," she reminded him. "So, do you refuse?"

"In this instance, I'm happy to oblige. But don't assume this means I'm going to obey all your commands."

"Fine with me." Sam grabbed a fistful of his shirt and yanked him forward.

Teddy's mouth was warm on hers. He kissed her back eagerly, almost hungrily. Samantha closed her eyes and leaned back into the darkness, falling onto someone's mink. Her blood bubbled, as light and fizzy as champagne.

On the other side of the door, she heard the bleating pack of courtiers marching toward the throne room. As if by unspoken agreement, she and Teddy held themselves absolutely still, falling ever deeper into the kiss.

It didn't matter whether Samantha showed up to the ceremony. No one would notice if she wasn't there. She was only the Sparrow, after all.

5

BEATRICE

Beatrice kept her eyes shut, reminding herself to breathe.

Once, during the fitting for the flower-girl dress she'd worn at her uncle's wedding, she had fidgeted so much that her mom had snapped at her not to move a single muscle. So she hadn't—not even her lungs. Seven-year-old Beatrice had held her breath with such determination that she actually passed out.

"Would you look up, Your Royal Highness?" the makeup artist murmured. Beatrice reluctantly lifted her gaze, trying to ignore the eyeliner pencil prodding at her lower lid. It had been easier to keep her anxiety at bay when her eyes were closed.

She stood at the center of the Brides' Room, a downstairs sitting room across the hall from the ballroom, named for the generations of royal brides who had used it to change into their wedding gowns. Beatrice had gotten ready here on countless occasions; she often needed to do this sort of quick costume change in the middle of an event. But the room's name had never before caused her such disquiet.

If everything went according to her parents' plan, she would be getting ready here again all too soon.

The Brides' Room was the epitome of girliness, its peach wallpaper hand-painted with delicate white flowers. There was very little furniture: just a small love seat and a side table with a bowl of potpourri made from old bridal bouquets. The space was purposefully empty, to leave room for gowns with thirty-foot ceremonial trains.

A massive trifold mirror stood before her, though Beatrice was doing her best not to look. She remembered how she and Samantha used to sneak in here when they were little, mesmerized by the sight of themselves reflected into infinity. "Look, there are a thousand Beatrices," Sam would whisper, and Beatrice always wondered with a touch of longing what it might be like—to walk right through the glass and into one of their lives, these other Beatrices in their strange mirror worlds.

There were times when Beatrice wished she were more like her sister. She'd seen the way Sam flounced into the ballroom earlier, patently unconcerned that she was forty minutes late. But then, Sam had always been one for dramatic entrances and even more dramatic exits. Whereas Beatrice lived in fear of what her mother called *causing a scene.*

She stood now on a temporary seamstress's platform, surrounded by attendants who had helped her out of her first dress of the night and into her new one, a deep blue gown with off-the-shoulder sleeves. They were rapidly transitioning her from cocktail attire into her more formal head-of-state look. Beatrice felt oddly absent from the scene, as if she were Royal Barbie, about to be covered in accessories.

She remained still as the makeup artist pressed a blotting paper to her nose before dusting it with powder, then re-applied her lipstick. "Finished," she murmured. Still Beatrice didn't look at the mirror.

One of the other attendants looped the sash of the Edwardian Order, America's highest chivalric honor, over Beatrice's gown. Then she draped the ermine-trimmed robe of state over the princess's shoulders. Its weight seemed to press down on Beatrice, heavy and insistent, almost as if it wanted to choke her. Her hands clenched and unclenched at her sides.

The attendant reached for a gold brooch. But before she could fasten the cloak around Beatrice's throat, the princess jerked violently back. The attendant's eyes widened in surprise.

"I'm sorry, I just . . . I need a moment alone." Beatrice felt a bit flustered; she'd never done anything like that before.

But then, the ceremonial trappings of her position had never before felt so stifling.

The various attendants and stylists bobbed quick curtsies before filing out. When they were gone, Beatrice forced herself to look up at her reflection.

The ivory sash was a crisp line against the blue of her gown, catching the cool undertones of her smooth, tanned skin. Various medals and awards glittered in the light, along with her massive pear-shaped earrings and tiered diamond necklace. Her dark hair had been swept into a twist so tight that bobby pins dug angrily into her head. She looked very regal, and slightly older than her twenty-one years.

Well, she probably needed to look mature at tonight's reception, since she was presumably meeting the man she was going to marry. Whoever he was.

I am Beatrice Georgina Fredericka Louise of the House of Washington, future Queen of America, and I have a duty to uphold. It was the same thing Beatrice always recited to herself, every time she started to feel this sense of panic—as if her life were slipping through her fingers like sand, and no matter how hard she tried to clutch at it, she couldn't regain control.

A knock sounded on the door to the Brides' Room. "Ten minutes. You almost ready?"

Relief bloomed in Beatrice's chest. Here was one person she *did* want to see. "You can come in, Connor," she called out.

It would have been inadequate to think of Connor as Beatrice's bodyguard. *Bodyguard* failed to encapsulate the

46

honor it was to be a member of the Revere Guard: the years of discipline and brutal training it required, the incredible self-sacrifice. The Guard was far more elite than any group of the armed forces. There were thousands of Marines, and hundreds of Navy SEALs, but the Revere Guard comprised only a few dozen men.

Founded after the assassination of King George II during the War of 1812, the Revere Guard—named for the Revolutionary War hero Paul Revere—answered directly to the Crown. Its men often served the monarch on covert missions abroad, protecting American allies, or rescuing Americans who had been captured. But members of the Guard always rotated home eventually, to serve their original purpose: ensuring the safety of the royal family. It was such a demanding and high-stakes job, with so much travel and uncertainty, that many members of the Revere Guard didn't settle down or get married until they retired.

"You look nice, Bee," Connor said, forgoing formality since they were alone. He'd been using that nickname ever since she admitted that it was what Samantha used to call her.

Of course, it had been a long time since Beatrice and her sister were on nickname terms.

She smiled, warmed by his compliment. "You don't look bad yourself."

He was wearing the Guards' dress uniform, a double-breasted navy blazer. It was devoid of any braid or insignia save the traditional gold lantern pin: in memory of the two lanterns of Paul Revere, the warning signal against the British invasion. At Connor's waist hung a gold ceremonial sword. It might have looked ridiculous and outdated if Beatrice didn't suspect that he knew precisely how to use it.

Connor had been assigned to her last autumn, at the start of her final year at Harvard. Beatrice would never forget that morning: when Ari, her protection officer for the previous two years, showed up to walk Beatrice to her lecture, accompanied by a tall stranger in a charcoal-colored hoodie. He looked a year or two older than Beatrice.

"Your Royal Highness, this is Connor Markham. He'll be taking over your security upon my departure tomorrow," Ari had explained.

Beatrice nodded. She tried not to stare at the young man, but he was hard to look away from, with arresting blue-gray eyes and fair skin. His light brown hair was cut short, emphasizing the strong, clean lines of his face.

Connor inclined his head in a bow so shallow that it bordered on impertinence. The neck of his sweatshirt dipped lower, revealing a line of black ink. A tattoo.

Beatrice found herself wondering about that tattoo, how far it snaked over Connor's chest, his broad shoulders, his torso. Her face grew hot, and she looked up. Connor met her gaze—and didn't look away.

His expression was blank, yet Beatrice couldn't help thinking that Connor had suspected the wayward direction of her thoughts.

She and her new Guard said little to each other, those first couple of months. Not that Beatrice was in the habit of constantly chatting with her security detail. But Connor was especially taciturn, almost . . . brooding. He never volunteered any information about himself, never made small talk. He was just a tall, silent figure at Beatrice's side, accompanying her to lectures or to the dining hall, wearing a backpack and a crimson sweater. Unlike most of her security officers, who'd been in their thirties at least, Connor could have passed for a student. Except that by now, everyone on campus was aware of Beatrice's "incognito" Guards.

Beatrice knew from the beginning that Connor was frustrated with his assignment. Maybe he'd assumed he would be on her father's detail, in the palace and at the center of the action, instead of babysitting her on a college campus. He was too much of a professional to say anything, but sometimes—when Beatrice was in a study group or grabbing a late-night pizza with friends—she saw the bored amusement tugging at his features. He clearly felt that Guarding her was beneath his capabilities. Well, Beatrice reminded herself, this wasn't her fault. She certainly hadn't *requested* that Connor be here.

One night in November, Beatrice headed to the Boston Museum of Fine Arts, accompanied, as always, by Connor. She was taking an art history class, a requirement for her American Studies major, and the professor had assigned an essay on one of the paintings in this collection. The other students had all come this afternoon, but Beatrice hadn't wanted to join them. It would have caused such a scene—all those people gawking at her, snapping covert pictures on their phones, whispering and elbowing each other. She felt much more comfortable asking the curator if she could stop by after hours.

Her steps echoed through the empty museum as she searched for the painting. She'd been certain all the Whistler portraits were downstairs, but she didn't see it. She kept re-checking the room numbers, wishing she hadn't been in too much of a hurry to pick up a map.

"We need to go upstairs. This hallway only holds art through 1875, and the portrait you're looking for was done in 1882."

Beatrice blinked. "You remember that?"

"I was in all the same lectures as you, Princess," Connor said laconically. That was another annoying habit of his: to call her *Princess* instead of *Your Royal Highness*. Beatrice would have corrected him, except that she suspected he wasn't doing it out of confusion. He was perfectly aware of the protocol, and was trying, subtly, to goad her.

"I thought . . ." She cut herself off before saying she'd

assumed he hadn't been listening to any of those lectures. But she had been taking notes, and she *still* didn't remember the year of that painting off the top of her head.

Connor began to lead her up the stairs. "Eidetic memory is something we worked on in training," he offered by way of explanation.

Sure enough, he led her straight to the painting she needed: Sir James Whistler's portrait of Lady Charlotte Eaton, Duchess of Boston.

Beatrice perched on the bench and pulled out her laptop. She jotted down a quick series of thoughts about the painting, biting her lower lip in concentration. The room felt very quiet and still.

Finally she shut her laptop with a satisfied click and glanced up. Connor said nothing, just nodded in the direction of the exit.

Beatrice picked up her pace when they reached the room full of Picasso and other postmodernists. "I never really liked these. Especially the ones with two eyes on the same side of the face," she said, if only to break the silence. "They always make me feel a little drunk."

"That's the point," Connor said drily. "Well, really it's to make you feel like you're high on acid. But drunk is close enough."

Beatrice was startled into laughing. Connor glanced over at her with something akin to surprise.

Perhaps it was because of that laugh that he slowed his steps and paused to examine a series of graphic art prints: the ones from the fifties that looked like pages ripped straight from a comic book.

Beatrice came to stand next to him. "You're a comics guy?"

She saw Connor debate how much of himself to reveal. "My mom is," he said at last. "When I was growing up, she worked as a graphic artist. She did sketches for some of the major superhero comics: Poison Rose, the Ranger, Captain Storm."

"I bet you loved getting free comics," Beatrice ventured.

He glanced back at one of the prints, lined in electric-blue ink. "She used to sketch me a comic strip of my own whenever she had the time. *The Adventures of Connor.* I had a different superpower each week—flying, invisibility, high-tech battle suits. She's the reason I wanted to apply for the Guard. I thought it was as close as I could get to being a real-life superhero. Not just the physical stuff, but also the sense of . . . honor, I guess." He shrugged, as if unsure why he'd admitted all of that.

"That makes sense," Beatrice said quietly. Even if she hadn't seen all the comic-book movies, she knew that super-heroes operated according to a code of morality that felt almost archaic in the modern world. They protected the weak, served something much greater than themselves. No wonder Connor had felt called to the Revere Guard.

"Your mom sounds really special," she went on.

Connor nodded. "She would like you." It was a casual enough statement, but there was something else folded into it: a promise, or at least a possibility.

Things between them shifted after that—slowly, but they shifted all the same. Connor began sitting next to Beatrice during her lectures, instead of in the row behind her, then debated the course material with her on the walk back to her dorm. They traded books. He had a wicked sense of humor, and did impressions of her professors or classmates that made her laugh so hard she cried. Sometimes, in un-guarded moments—when they were running along the Charles River and he challenged her to a race, or when Beatrice in-sisted that they go to the frozen-yogurt shop and he dared her to try every flavor—he seemed almost *playful.*

And when he accompanied her to royal functions, Connor

no longer stood stone-faced to one side. Now he caught Beatrice's eye whenever someone made a bad joke or an outlandish remark, forcing her to look away lest she burst out laughing. They even developed a silent system, using her purse as a signaling device. If she slid it back and forth from one forearm to another, it meant she wanted to leave, at which point Connor would walk over with a fabricated excuse and help her escape.

As time went on, Beatrice slowly pieced together Connor's story. He'd grown up in West Texas, in a town called El Real—"How typically Texan to call a town *real*, as if the rest of the world is just made up," Connor had joked. His dad worked as a post office clerk, and his younger sister, Kaela, had just started college.

The more she learned about Connor, the more Beatrice revealed about herself: her opinions of people, her frustrations. She attempted *jokes*. As strange and unexpected as it might be, she'd begun to think of Connor as her friend.

And Beatrice had never had a close friend, not the way that Sam had Nina or Jefferson had Ethan. Even in elementary school, she'd struggled to form connections with her classmates. Half the time she had no idea what they were talking about—their references to TV shows or Disneyland were completely lost on her, as if they were speaking a bewildering foreign language. The other girls were unerringly polite, but always held themselves at a distance. It was as though they could *smell* her inherent otherness, like wild cats.

Eventually Beatrice had given up on trying to make friends. It was just easier to keep to herself, to seek the approbation of adults rather than that of her peers.

Until Connor, she hadn't realized what a relief it was, having someone who knew her so well. Someone she could simply *talk* to, without having to weigh every last word before she spoke.

It had been jarring when she graduated, and they left the informality of Harvard to come back to court, with all its etiquette and expectations. Beatrice had secretly feared that things between her and Connor might change. But while he did start calling her *Your Royal Highness* in public, in private they slipped right back into their easy camaraderie.

"You're so quiet," Connor said now, interrupting the princess's thoughts. His eyes met hers in the mirror. "What's going on, Bee?"

"My parents want me to interview potential husbands tonight."

The words rattled out violently into the room, like the discharge of musketry during the annual Presentation of the Troops.

Beatrice wasn't sure what had possessed her to say it so bluntly. She hadn't wanted to talk about this with Connor at all. Which was foolish, really, given that he knew practically everything else about her: that she hated bananas, and called her grandmother every Sunday, and had dreams of her teeth falling out whenever she got stressed.

Why did it feel so strange, then, to tell Connor that her parents wanted her to start thinking about marriage?

Maybe her subconscious had made her say it, hoping to gauge his reaction—to elicit a flare of jealousy.

Connor stared at her with a curious expression, tinged with something that might have been disbelief. "Let me get this straight," he said slowly. "You're going to meet some guys that your parents have picked out and then *marry* one of them?"

"That sums it up pretty accurately." Beatrice had seen a couple of the young men across the room during the cocktail hour. She'd managed to avoid them thus far, but she knew she would have to face them after the ceremony.

"How many . . . potential suitors are there?" Connor went on, clearly uncertain what to call them.

"Why do you care?" Beatrice meant it to sound flippant, but it came out slightly defensive.

"Just trying to do my job."

Of course. It didn't matter whether they were friends. At the end of the day, Beatrice was still his *job*.

When she didn't answer, Connor shrugged. "They need you back outside. Are you almost ready?"

Beatrice reached for a flat velvet box on the side table and unhooked its clasp. Nestled inside was the Winslow Tiara, made over a century ago and worn ever since by the Princess Royal, the oldest daughter of the reigning monarch. It was breathtaking, the whorls of its lacelike pattern covered in several hundred small diamonds.

She placed it on the hairsprayed nest of her hair and began to pin it into place. But her hands fumbled, the pins slipping from her fingers. The priceless tiara began to slide off her head.

Beatrice barely caught it before it could shatter against the floor.

"Here, let me try," Connor offered, taking a swift step forward.

Beatrice bent her knees into an almost curtsy, though Connor was so tall he probably didn't need her to. She felt oddly out of body, like she was swimming through the watery depths of a dream, as she watched him lift the tiara. Neither of them spoke as he used a series of bobby pins to fasten it in place.

The rise and fall of Beatrice's chest was shallow beneath the silk faille of her gown. He barely touched her, yet every motion, every brush of a fingertip against the back of her neck, felt scalding.

When she stood up again, Beatrice blinked at her own crowned and glittering reflection. Her eyes were still locked on Connor's in the mirror.

He reached for Beatrice's cloak, as if to imperceptibly adjust it, though it was already perfectly placed. Was it Beatrice's imagination, or did he hold his fingers on her back for a moment longer than was strictly necessary?

A flourish of trumpets rebounded down the hallway. Connor stepped back, breaking the moment—or whatever it had been.

Beatrice squared her shoulders and started toward the door. As she turned, the dense blue velvet of her cloak swept majestically behind her. It had to weigh at least fifteen pounds. Her tiara glittered, sending a spray of shadows and lights over the wall.

When they reached the door, Connor instinctively fell back a step, so that he would walk out of the room behind the princess, as befitted both their ranks. It had happened so many times before, yet Beatrice's heart still fell a little as Connor lingered. She much preferred having him *next* to her, being able to see his face.

But this was the way things were. Connor was simply doing his job—and so should she.

6

DAPHNE

You had to hand it to the Washingtons, Daphne thought, from where she sat in the audience of the knighthood ceremony. They really knew how to do pomp and circumstance.

As far as royal dynasties were concerned, they were hardly the oldest. The Bourbons, the Hapsburgs, the Hanoverians, the Romanovs: those families could trace their sovereignty back a great many centuries, or in some cases—the Yamatos had been rulers of Japan since 660 BC—*millennia*. The Washingtons were such *nouveaux arrivés* by comparison that they were practically the Deightons of royal families.

But what they lacked in age, the Washingtons more than made up in style.

Hundreds of courtiers sat on wooden benches, facing a dais with three massive thrones. The central and largest was that of King George IV himself, upholstered in red velvet with his interlocking initials, GR for Georgius Rex, stitched in gold thread. Queen Adelaide was seated in the neighboring throne, while the king and Princess Beatrice stood before her, conducting the knighthood ceremony.

Beatrice held out a scroll of parchment—one of the patents of nobility, tied with a red silk ribbon. The robe of state swept behind her, shimmering with embroidery and trimmed in fur.

"Ms. Monica Sanchez." Beatrice spoke into the microphone pinned to her sash.

One of the figures in the first few pews, presumably Monica Sanchez, jumped to her feet. Her movements were stiff with nervousness, as if she were a marionette whose strings had been cut. Honestly. People got so worked up about meeting the royal family. They seemed to forget that the Washingtons were humans too—who breathed and had nightmares and vomited just like everyone else. But then, Daphne had seen all that firsthand.

Monica trailed up the steps and knelt before the king.

"For the services you have rendered this nation and the world at large, I thank you. From this day forward, I grant you the honors and dignities of a Knight Defender of the Realm." The king was holding a ceremonial sword, its hilt engraved with the American eagle: not the sword that had belonged to King George I, because that had been lost long ago, but a replica based off an old portrait.

The king tapped the blade of the sword flat against one of Monica's shoulders, then lifted it over her head to tap the other. Daphne was quite certain that she saw Monica flinch. Probably she'd heard what happened last year, when Jefferson had drunkenly decided to knight people using one of the antique swords on the wall. He'd ended up nicking their friend Rohan's ear. Rohan laughed about the whole thing, but you could still see the scar.

"Arise, Lady Monica Sanchez," the king concluded, holding out a hand to help her to her feet. There was a polite smattering of applause, noticeably softer than it had been at the beginning of the alphabet. At least they were finally on S.

"Jeff looks *amazing*," a girl in the next row whispered.

Daphne felt her mouth curl in a proprietary smile. Jefferson did look fantastic, standing there on the side of the dais, a glaring space next to him where Samantha should have been. On a normal man, the royal dress uniform might have looked ludicrous, all that ribbon and decorative braid and those shiny gold epaulets. Yet Jefferson somehow made it seem distinguished, even sexy.

"Mr. Ryan Sinclair," Beatrice went on, and Daphne quickly checked herself before anyone could catch her staring at the prince. There were so many cameras, clustered on both sides of the room like a thicket of eyes, and she never knew which of them might be trained on her. She clasped her hands in her lap and looked forward, arranging herself like a mannequin on display.

The ceremony concluded at last. Slowly, like a great lumbering elephant, the herd of elegantly dressed people shuffled back down the hallway and into the ballroom. Toward the entrance, a few journalists spoke rapidly into their microphones, completing their coverage of the evening. Daphne didn't bother searching for her parents as she began to circumnavigate the room.

She knew where Jefferson was at all times. She could *feel* him, as if he were holding the opposite end of a rubber band, and its constant tugging let her know in which direction to look. But she didn't look. She would wait until the time was right.

She'd forgotten how good it felt, being at court. Her blood thrummed at something in the air—as thick as the scent of rain, but more raw and primal and heady like smoke. It made Daphne feel brutally awake, all the way to her fingertips. It was the scent of power, she thought, and if you were smart, you knew what it meant.

She couldn't go a few a feet without someone stopping to greet her. Here was Countess Madeleine of Hartford and her wife, the Countess Mexia. Daphne noted with a spark of envy that both women were wearing gowns straight off the runway. Next the Minister of the Treasury, Isabella Gonzalez: her mousy, poorly dressed daughter was a close friend of Samantha's. And now fast-food heiress Stephanie Warner was rustling over to pose with Daphne for the photographers, making certain to stand on Daphne's right, so that her name would appear first in the photo captions.

"How's your friend Himari?" Stephanie asked when the bulbs had stopped flashing. The question caught Daphne off guard.

"Himari is still in the hospital," she replied, with perhaps the first genuine emotion she'd shown that day.

Stephanie pursed her lips into a moue of sympathy. She was wearing a dark shade of lipstick that wasn't right for her pale complexion. It made her look garish, like some kind of vampire bride from the crypt. "She's been in there a while, hasn't she."

"Since June." Daphne said a quick goodbye and moved along the room. She couldn't let herself think about Himari, and what had happened to her the night of Jefferson's graduation. Once she did, the memory would grab hold of her mind and refuse to let go.

This was the greatest game in the world, the only game that truly mattered: the game of influence at court. So Daphne glanced around at her smiling enemies and smiled right back at them.

Looking slender and shadowy in her dusky silk gown, she started at last toward the prince. Her heels made emphatic little clicks on the hardwood surface of the ballroom. She'd worn her hair down tonight, its fiery layers framing the perfect oval of her face. She'd even managed to borrow a pair of emerald droplets that brought out the vicious green of her eyes.

When she reached him, Jefferson made a show of looking up as if startled, though he'd probably been watching her from across the ballroom. After all these years, he was just as attuned to her presence as she was to his.

Daphne dropped into a curtsy: straight down like a bucket,

like a ballerina at the barre. The fabric of her skirts pooled architecturally around her. She kept her head lifted the whole time, her eyes on his. They both knew there was no reason for her to greet him like this, except to give him a good view down the front of her dress. A bit desperate, but then, so was she.

After a moment, Jefferson reached to pull her out of the curtsy. She looked up at him wistfully, as if to say, *Here we are again, after all,* and was relieved by Jefferson's answering grin.

"Hey there, Jefferson." The familiar syllables of his name rolled in her mouth like candy.

"Hey, Daph."

"Dance with me?" She flashed her most beguiling smile, the one Jefferson had never been able to resist. Sure enough, he nodded.

As they stepped onto the dance floor, he twined a hand in hers, resting the other on her waist, the way he had so many times before. God, he was so gorgeous, so achingly familiar. All the old tenderness and warmth was bubbling back up, and the hurt, too, as she remembered what he'd done to her— what she'd done to *him*—

"Did you have fun in Asia?" she asked, to cover her momentary confusion.

"It was incredible. There's nothing like sitting at the top of Angkor Wat and watching the sun rise to really put things in perspective." Jefferson gave a lazy smile. "How's senior year treating you? I heard you got prefect, by the way. Congratulations."

She wondered how he knew that—whether someone had told him or whether he'd read it himself, in the news blurb she'd pressured Natasha to publish. Either way, it was nice to know that Jefferson was still keeping tabs on her.

"The real benefit of being prefect is that Sister Agatha no longer chases me down for hallway passes when I'm out of class."

"As if you ever cut class." Jefferson spun her in an expert twirl, causing the folds of her gown to flutter and settle around her with a pleasant whisper.

"I cut class that time we went to the World Series."

"Was that when Nicholas got so drunk that he bartered away his shoes for a hot dog?"

"His shoes *and* his phone."

They both laughed at the memory, the kind of easy, intimate laugh that they hadn't shared in a long time, and when it was over, Daphne knew she had scored her first point.

Not to mention that people had noticed them together. She felt herself glowing ever more vividly, with the spark that collective attention had always struck from her.

"Daphne," the prince said hesitantly, and she leaned forward, expectant. "I owe you an apology. I'm sorry for the way I ended things."

"It's okay." She didn't need an *apology* from Jefferson. She needed him to want her back.

"I just feel like you deserved better," he added.

Daphne knew he was thinking about that girl in his bed, and for a moment she almost despised him, for being too cowardly to tell her the truth about their breakup. For apologizing without actually telling her what he was apologizing *for*.

"It's all in the past," she said quietly, hiding her emotions behind the courtier's mask of her face. "Jefferson . . . I've missed you."

She waited for him to say it back. And for an instant, it seemed like he might.

But then he was stepping away, lowering his hands to his sides. "I have to—sorry, but I have to go."

"Of course." Daphne forced herself to smile as if nothing were amiss, even though Jefferson was leaving her alone midsong. Turning her into a source of gossip.

Tomorrow various versions of this story would make

their way through drawing rooms and dinner parties. *Jefferson abandoned her on the dance floor,* people would say; *there's no chance of them getting back together now.*

"May I cut in?" Ethan Beckett, Jefferson's best friend, appeared at her side so quickly that one could only assume he'd been watching their whole interaction.

Daphne opened her mouth to make some incisive comment, then caught herself. If she danced with Ethan, just for one song, it would distract people from the prince's abrupt departure. Which might have been precisely what Ethan was counting on.

"All right." She tried to rest her hands lightly on his shoulders, so lightly that they almost weren't touching, but through the fabric Daphne felt the warmth of his skin.

Ethan had been Jefferson's best friend since elementary school. He was good-looking, with laughing dark eyes and a smattering of freckles. He wasn't noble: his mom worked as a public school teacher, raising Ethan on her own. Daphne had always assumed he attended Forsythe on scholarship, because there was surely no way his family could afford the tuition. Now Ethan was a freshman at King's College—where Jefferson would likely go, as soon as his gap year ended.

Daphne had always liked that about Jefferson, that he had someone like Ethan as his best friend. Someone who came from a background so drastically different from his own.

Then again, it was easy to ignore things like money and status when you had near-infinite amounts of both.

They danced in silence for a few moments. Without quite realizing it, Daphne had overstepped Ethan to take the lead, her steps growing faster and faster until they outpaced the tempo of the music.

When she almost tripped over Ethan's feet in her agitation, his grip on her hand tightened. "It's a dance. You can enjoy it, not attack it."

She didn't apologize, but she did back down. Slightly.

"I take it things didn't go so well with Jeff," he went on, in a conversational tone.

Daphne fought back a swell of indignation. She didn't owe an explanation to anyone, least of all Ethan. Yet he'd always had a particular talent for getting under her skin.

"I have no idea what you're talking about."

"Come on, Daphne, you guys are over. Is it really worth throwing yourself at him like this, just so you can get a tiara someday?"

Daphne stiffened. Only Ethan had ever accused her of dating Jefferson for the wrong reasons. "I wouldn't expect you to understand. Relationships never make sense from the outside; the only people qualified to weigh in on them are the people in them."

"Except that you and Jeff aren't *in* a relationship anymore," Ethan pointed out ruthlessly.

"For now."

They were both speaking softly, their eyes locked on each other. Daphne had almost forgotten that they were in the ballroom at all.

"You're wasting your time. You won't snap your fingers and get him back, just like that," he countered.

"Not *just like that*." It wouldn't be easy, and she might have to wait a while. So what if Jefferson hung out with some of those skanky, stalkerish girls from the prince posse? Those girls didn't mean anything to him. He would come back to her, because in the end they belonged together, and he knew it as well as Daphne did.

And yet . . . something in Ethan's words gave her pause. "Where did Jefferson run off to?" she asked, wishing it didn't sound so much like she was begging.

"Wouldn't you like to know?"

"I'm asking as a friend." The words were knives in her

throat, but she delivered them with as much grace as she could muster.

"Oh, are we friends now? I thought, after—"

"*Don't* mention that."

"Careful, Daphne," Ethan said meaningfully. "We wouldn't want this to look like a lovers' quarrel."

He was right. The way their heads were tilted close together, the quick play and ripple of their conversation—it looked suspect. Daphne put some distance between them, her face glazing with a smile, though it came out as hard and brittle as the crystal flutes lined up on the bar.

"You can't say those things," she whispered.

"You mean, I can't talk about us?"

"There is no *us!*" Daphne shook her head so violently that her earrings whipped around to smack the sides of her face. "What happened that night was an awful, terrible mistake."

"Was it? Or is going after Jeff the mistake?"

"Don't mention that night. Please," Daphne entreated, scared into politeness. Normally she and Ethan didn't bother with the niceties.

The prince could never, ever find out what she and Ethan had done. If he did, all her plans would crumble to dust.

"You seriously think you'll get Jeff back, don't you," Ethan replied, with evident disbelief.

But Daphne knew that she could make it happen. She could make anything happen for herself.

"I know I will," she told him.

7

NINA

"Nina! There you are!" Princess Samantha tugged her friend to one side of the ballroom, moving in the same impatient, long-legged way that she had since she was a child, no matter how hard the etiquette masters had tried to train it out of her.

"More like there *you* are. You're the one who went completely MIA." Nina shook her head in amusement. "Where were you during the knighthood ceremony?"

Sam's hair was escaping its pins, her face glowing with a telltale flush. Despite her glittering gown and the diamonds flashing at her wrists and throat, she resembled nothing so much as a creature half-tamed, as if she might run wild at any moment.

Sam lowered her voice to a near whisper. "I was in the cloakroom with Teddy Eaton."

"Who?"

The princess tipped her head toward a guy on the dance floor, blond and aristocratic-looking. Nina would have said that he didn't seem like Samantha's type, except that Sam had never really *had* a type. The only consistent thing about her flings was the shock value they elicited. "He's cute," she said noncommittally.

"I know." Samantha couldn't hide her smile. "Sorry I disappeared on you. How's your night going? Are you miserable yet?"

Nina shrugged. "These things just aren't my scene."

She had already talked to everyone she actually liked at this party, which wasn't that many people to begin with, except for her parents. Most of the guests seemed to look straight through Nina as if she were invisible. But that was just the way of things at court: until you were someone, you were no one at all.

"Well, thank you again for coming," Sam said earnestly. "Next time I promise we can go to one of your college parties instead. I'm dying to meet all your new friends."

Nina smiled at the thought of Samantha meeting Rachel. Her two closest friends, both with such headstrong personalities, both accustomed to getting their own way. They would either adore each other or despise each other.

Before Nina could answer, a man came to stand behind Samantha. Lord Robert Standish, who had taken over as chamberlain after Nina's mamá left.

"Your Highness. His Majesty requests that you dance with the Grand Duke Pieter." Robert kept his eyes on Samantha, ignoring Nina even though he knew perfectly well who she was.

Samantha cast Nina a glance of apology tinged with irritation. "Sorry, but it seems I've been *summoned*," she said, and headed off in search of the Grand Duke—the Russian tsar's younger son, who was currently in America as a guest of the court.

Nina stayed to the side of the ballroom, gazing at the dance floor with the dispassionate eye of an outsider. So many people had crowded onto it, all of them wearing their titles or wealth or connections ostentatiously on their sleeves. Seeing them walk around in that stiff Washington Palace sort of way, Nina gave a quiet sigh of resignation.

Nothing had changed. It was the same stale gossip, the same sparkling wine poured into the same crystal flutes, the same people bickering over the same small dramas. It even *smelled* the same, the scents of greed and government mixed with rose sachets and musty old furniture.

It reminded Nina of the soap operas that Julie used to love, where you could miss weeks at a time and then seamlessly pick the story back up. Because despite the whirl of action that seemed to affect the characters, nothing much had actually happened.

She watched Samantha approach Pieter; he bowed stiffly and held out a hand to lead her forward. Courtiers crowded around them, gentlemen-at-arms and yeomen of the guard whose names blurred together in Nina's mind. She was part of Samantha's private life, not this public, royal sphere, and no matter how many of these events she'd attended, Nina had no idea who most of these people were.

Though she did recognize Daphne Deighton, dancing with Prince Jefferson.

Daphne's arm was curled over his shoulder, her mouth red and smiling. Everything about her—the blaze of her earrings, the glitter of her gown—seemed rare and expensive and impossibly elegant. Maybe the rumors were true, and she and Jeff were going to get back together after all.

Nina felt suddenly desperate for fresh air. But too many of Jeff's friends were out on the terrace, and the last thing she wanted was to run into the prince.

Then she remembered where else she could go.

She started forward, her reflection in the ballroom's antique mirrors moving with her. She never would get used to the sight of herself in formal attire. Her gown, a gauzy violet one of Sam's with a halter neckline, billowed around her heels as she walked.

Nina headed out the ballroom's main doors and down a side hallway lit only by antique sconces every few yards. She moved quickly, past ghostlike statues on marble plinths and landscapes in heavy frames. The only security guard she saw was stationed at the top of the stairs; he gave her a disinterested nod before turning back to his phone.

Most of Washington Palace had been renovated many times over. All that remained of the original Mount Vernon house was a small set of rooms along the southeast corner. They were low-ceilinged and outdated, never used for official court functions. But Nina had always loved it here, especially at night, when the building's age was softened beneath a cloak of shadows.

Kicking off her silver shoes, she stepped out onto a balcony. The flagstones were deliciously cold beneath her bare feet.

Below her stretched the gardens, a patchwork quilt of light and dark. Nina leaned her elbows on the iron balusters and gazed past the cherry orchards—the most popular stop on the palace tour, because of that old story about King George I and the cherry tree—to the city beyond.

Washington, the nation's capital. The city of dreamers and hustlers, of nobility and commoners alike, of finance and fashion and politics and art—the greatest city in the world, its residents always said, where anyone could come make a name for themselves. It was a glorious clutter of stone roofs and new high-rises, loud with neon billboards. The twin domes of Columbia House, the meeting place of both bodies of Congress, rose above the skyline in gilded splendor.

A door creaked open behind her. "Nina?"

Her breath snagged in her lungs. She should have known this might happen.

"I've barely seen you all night," said Jeff. Or rather, Prince Jefferson George Alexander Augustus, third in line for the throne of America.

"I wanted to be alone," Nina said curtly. Her tone failed to send him away.

"Smart, coming out here right before the fireworks start. You'll have the best seat in the house." He flashed his usual cocky smile, though it didn't make Nina go weak at the knees the way it once did. *Seriously?* The last time she'd seen the prince, he'd been *in bed* with her, and now he was acting as if nothing between them had changed. As if they were still the same easygoing friends as always.

"I was just leaving."

Nina started to turn away, but Jeff's hand closed around her wrist. The feel of his skin on hers shot erratically up her nerves. She glared at him, and he let go, chastened.

"I'm sorry. I just wanted to say, about the night of graduation . . ."

Nina crossed her arms over her chest. She wasn't wearing a bra with this dress, which made her feel suddenly self-conscious, though what did it really matter? Jeff had already seen it all. "Don't worry. I never told anyone, if that's what you're asking."

"What? No," he said quickly. "I wanted to tell you that I'm sorry."

"Sorry that it happened, or sorry you never bothered to text me afterward?" Nina didn't usually talk like this, but these words had been rattling around her mind for months, and now that she was with the prince again, they seemed to be spilling out independently of her.

"I didn't know. . . ."

"You didn't know that you're supposed to *acknowledge* a girl the next morning?"

Jeff winced. "You're right. I should have said something. That was just such a weird night, after what happened to Himari. I guess I didn't think."

Nina had readied herself for an excuse—that he'd forgotten, or lost his phone, or that she was overreacting, since after all they hadn't even slept together. But this caught her off guard.

"Was that the girl who fell?" She'd heard about Himari Mariko, how she tumbled down the palace's back staircase the night of the graduation party. It was a miracle her parents hadn't sued the royal family.

Perhaps aristocrats considered it poor form to accuse their monarchs in a court of law. Nina wouldn't really know.

"After it happened, security came banging on my door. I decided to let you sleep through all that," Jeff added, glancing at her awkwardly. "And then the next morning we left so early for the royal tour, and I didn't really know . . . I mean . . . I'm sorry," he said again, helpless.

His apology knocked some of the air from Nina's chest. The wave of her anger seemed to break, leaving her with a strange sense of uncertainty.

As if on cue, a low, rumbling boom sounded from the lawn, and the sky erupted in a pinwheel of spinning flame. The annual Queen's Ball fireworks.

Nina remembered how she and the twins used to love watching these, back when they were all too young to attend the party. Sam would insist that Nina come sleep over, and they would sneak onto this very terrace before the fireworks began, all three of them wrapped in a heavy wool blanket.

"I'll stay for a minute," she heard herself say. "Just until the fireworks are over." For old times' sake.

Jeff gestured toward the flagstones as if offering Nina the most elegant chair in the world. She ignored his hand and lowered herself to the stone floor of the balcony, pushing up the skirts of Sam's gown to slip her legs through the railings. Her bare feet with their unpolished toes dangled over the expanse of air.

"Do you see that?" Jeff pointed back toward the palace, where an empty birds' nest was tucked precariously in one of the beams. A hook seemed to tug and pull at Nina's heart. She'd forgotten that she and the twins used to prowl around the palace looking for birds' nests. Usually they would leave crumbs out, hoping the birds would eat them.

"Next time we need to bring some leftover scones to crumble," Jeff mused.

Next time? Nina shot him a questioning glance, but Jeff was looking away.

There was something inherently regal about his profile, his square jaw and high cheekbones and aquiline nose. It was the sort of face that the Romans would have stamped onto a coin.

They sat there for a while in companionable silence. The fireworks kept erupting overhead, shades of American red, blue, and gold unfurling in vibrant showers of sparks. They were so fast that each firework lit up the whisper of smoke left over from the one before.

Sitting like this, watching the fireworks the way they always used to, Nina could almost pretend that they were friends again. But she knew there would be no rewinding the clock, no going back to being "just friends." Not for her.

Nina couldn't pinpoint when, exactly, she'd fallen in love with Jeff. She'd been friends with him for years, had grown up with him right alongside Sam. All she knew was that one day she woke up and her love for him was simply *there*, like newly fallen snow. Maybe it had been there all along.

When he'd started dating Daphne, Nina had almost doubled over from the pain of it. Suddenly Daphne was invited to all the same events and vacations that Nina came to with Sam, and Nina had to watch, powerless, as their relationship unfolded before her.

She hated Daphne. Hated her perfect smile, her shining hair that never seemed to fall out of place, the sweet yet proprietary way she rested a hand on Jefferson's arm. Most of all she hated Daphne for being so utterly *eligible*—for being the type of girl everyone expected Jeff to go out with. Nina could never compete with a girl like that.

Until the night of the twins' graduation party, when everything changed.

The twins were leaving early the next morning, for one of the royal family's annual tours of the country. Even so, the king and queen had agreed to let them throw a graduation party at the palace. Nina laughed, dancing with Samantha and a couple of Sam's private-school friends. They'd all had a lot to drink; the party's signature cocktail was some fruity mixed thing that Sam had invented, playing bartender in the palace kitchens.

Eventually the party felt too hot and crowded for Nina. She stepped into the hallway—only to collide with the prince.

Jeff put his hands on her shoulders to steady her, because she tottered a little in her wedges. "You okay?"

Nina was curiously unsurprised to find Jeff here, alone. Of course he was here: in her drunk, happy mind, it seemed that fate had led him here, just for her.

"I can't believe you're leaving tomorrow. It won't be the same without you," Nina blurted out, then immediately wished she could take it back. "I mean, without you and Sam . . ."

"Nina Gonzalez." Jeff grinned. "Are you saying that you'll miss me?"

Nina couldn't tell whether he meant it seriously or not. She didn't know how to answer.

He leaned forward. Magic lay thick and heavy in the air. And somehow—Nina had replayed that moment in her head a million times, and even now she couldn't say for certain which of them had started it—somehow they were kissing.

It felt to Nina like she'd spun out of this universe altogether, and into some new place where anything might happen.

"Do you want to go upstairs?" Jeff murmured. Nina knew she should say no, of course not.

"Yes," she whispered instead.

They stumbled through his sitting room and into his bedroom. Nina fell back onto the bed, pulling Jeff down next to her. The air seemed thinner, or warmer, or maybe all the oxygen had simply drained from her blood, because the entire world had turned on end. She was here, with Prince Jefferson.

His hand slipped under the strap of her dress, and it forced Nina brutally to her senses.

She'd made out with a few boys from her class at school, and that one guy at the bar in Cabrillo, on a trip with Sam, but none of it had gone past kissing. It was crazy and foolish and Nina had refused to even admit it to herself, but she knew that some part of her had been waiting, hoping, for this. That she would eventually be here, with the only boy she'd ever loved.

She couldn't let herself go any further right now, because if she did, she wasn't sure she could bring herself to stop.

Reading her hesitation, Jeff carefully replaced the strap of her dress. "No pressure," he said quietly.

Nina kissed him again, because she didn't know how else to explain what she felt—that it wasn't that she didn't like Jeff; it was that she liked him *too* much.

For a split second Nina thought she heard a noise from the door. She glanced over, panic spiking through her system, but no one was there. And then all thoughts were driven from her mind as Jeff pulled her close and kissed her again.

When she woke the next morning, he was gone.

She lay there for a while in sleepy confusion, blinking into the early-morning light. He was leaving for his royal tour this morning, but surely he wouldn't go without saying goodbye? Maybe he'd just left to check on something.

Eventually Nina slid out of bed and began hunting for her things. She tiptoed into the hallway wearing last night's dress.

"Miss?" One of the palace security guards stood outside

Jeff's door, his expression carefully bland and professional. "We have a car waiting to drive you home."

"Oh" was all Nina could say, her entire body hot with mortification. The pleasant glow of last night rapidly melted away. She knew she and Jeff hadn't made each other any promises; it wasn't as though she was expecting a handwritten love note, but she'd thought she would at least *hear* from him in the morning.

Maybe he was annoyed with her for putting on the brakes. Maybe he'd only invited her upstairs because he'd assumed she would sleep with him, and once she told him no, he'd rushed off the first chance he got, leaving his security to shuffle her away like a dirty little secret. Well then, thank god she hadn't slept with him after all.

Nina angrily clicked onto her phone, determined not to think about Jeff—only to find that the internet was flooded with a single news story. JEFFERSON'S GREAT MISTAKE, one headline proclaimed; another ROYAL SPLIT: BUT IS IT FOR GOOD?

Apparently, after almost three years of dating, Jeff and Daphne had mutually agreed to break up.

In article after article, the columnists seemed to share the same opinion: that Jeff would regret his decision. *Daphne Deighton was the best thing to happen to the monarchy since Queen Adelaide. She is relatable, intelligent, and kind, and she brought out the best in the prince,* proclaimed a staff writer at the *Daily News. In losing Daphne, the Crown has lost one of its most forceful and vibrant assets. Whoever Jefferson decides to date next, she simply won't measure up.*

Nina felt sick to her stomach. Of course she wasn't Daphne. Daphne was the type of girl who could walk for hours in heels without complaint, who knew which fork to use at a formal dinner, who could tell a joke that was funny without being crass—probably in four languages.

Daphne was the girl Jeff would marry, and Nina was the girl he'd snuck upstairs at a party, then sent home in a hired car before anyone found out. The knowledge made her feel cheap and tawdry, and oddly hollow.

She had been so elated when they kissed, but it had only been the product of good, or rather bad, timing. All last night meant was that Nina had happened to run into him before anyone else did: that she was *there*, and apparently stupid enough to hook up with him. Like every other stupid girl in America.

Now the light of the last firework dissolved into the velvety darkness of the sky.

It was getting colder; the wind lifted the hair on the nape of her neck. "I should go," she murmured, wrapping her arms around herself.

Jeff wordlessly slid out of his jacket to drape it over her shoulders. It was heavy, jangling with various medals and pins.

Against her better judgment, Nina slipped her arms through the sleeves. The jacket smelled like him, warm and a little bit sweet.

When Jeff leaned forward to brush his lips against hers, she didn't pull back.

She felt a sizzle of shock as the kiss ricocheted through her body. *This* was what she'd been chasing, when she'd kissed those boys at school whose faces receded into a blur. This was how a kiss should feel—electric and pulsing and smoky all at once, like you had discovered a new source of fuel that could warm you from within.

Then her senses snapped abruptly back into focus, and she remembered everything Jeff had done.

Nina put her palms on his chest and pushed him violently away.

Silence fell like a curtain between them. Nina stumbled to

her feet. Jeff blinked up at her, his face twisted in shock, as if he couldn't believe what had just happened. Neither could she. Oh god, wasn't it *treason* to strike royalty?

"I'm sorry. I misread the situation," Jeff said hesitantly. He stood up, his features still etched with confusion.

No one ever tells him no, Nina realized. Not anymore. That was the curse of royalty.

Well, there was a first time for everything.

"You shouldn't have done that," she snapped, though she knew it wasn't entirely fair. She *had* been sitting close to him, out here in the cold in a thin gown. Wearing his jacket.

Jeff's hair fell forward; he reached up to push it back with an impatient gesture. "I know I didn't handle things well last time—"

"Didn't *handle things well?* Do you have any idea how it felt, waking up in your bed after that?" Her voice broke with suppressed emotion. "And then I never heard from you, not once in the past six months!"

"I'm sorry," he said again, as if to remind her that he'd said it already.

"*Sorry* isn't a magic eraser that undoes whatever wrong thing you did! You can't just say sorry and expect everything to be the way it was, not when people have been hurt!"

Tears gathered at the corners of her eyes, and she stuffed her hands into Jeff's pockets. He had a stray button in one of them. She kept toying nervously with it.

"I never meant to hurt you," the prince said slowly. "But I felt embarrassed about the way I handled things. I wasn't broken up with Daphne when you and I . . . I mean, I didn't actually break up with Daphne until the next morning."

"The press made it sound like the breakup was mutual." Nina felt an instant bolt of shame, that she'd admitted to reading those articles.

"You of all people know the tabloids make that stuff up.

I called Daphne the morning after the graduation party to break up with her. But I never told her about us," Jeff added. "It just seemed unnecessarily cruel. I don't know, maybe that was wrong of me. Or cowardly."

Nina wasn't sure how to respond. She had gone up those stairs too, had muddled the line between right and wrong.

"I wanted to talk to you at the reception earlier, Nina, but you ran off before I could find you. I took a chance that you might be out here."

"You came looking for me?" She'd thought Jeff's appearance on the balcony was a coincidence.

"Yeah," he said hoarsely. "Nina . . . do you think there's any chance that you and I could start over? Try again?"

"I don't know." It was as much of a truce as she was willing to give.

A corner of Jeff's mouth lifted, as if he wanted to smile but wasn't sure whether he was allowed to. "Well, *I don't know* is much better than a flat-out *no*. I'll take it for now."

His words were both a question and a promise. All Nina could do was nod. She shrugged out of his jacket and handed it to him before heading back inside.

8

BEATRICE

Beatrice had been going on royal tours her entire life.

She'd only been six months old on her first tour, of the American South and Southwest. She didn't remember it, of course, but she'd seen the photos so many times—of her parents stepping out of *Eagle V*, holding her in their arms—that she felt like she remembered it. Her parents had apparently carried her everywhere on that trip, even when she was asleep. At the sight of the infant who would be the first-ever Queen of America, the crowds had roared with a frenzy that bordered on hysteria.

Beatrice had grown used to the tours, the way she had to smile and make eye contact with every person she met, thanking them for their time, greeting them by name. She knew just how important these moments were for the image of the royal family. As her grandfather had put it, *A monarch must be seen by his people, all his people, in order to truly be believed.*

Even so, Beatrice occasionally caught herself rolling into autopilot mode, saying *Thank you* and *It's a pleasure to meet you* so many times that she forgot what the words even meant.

She felt that way now, at the Queen's Ball. Like she wasn't inhabiting her own life but had turned into an actress, reciting a script that someone else had written.

It didn't help that she was struggling valiantly, and with little success, to avoid being stepped on by her dance partner.

". . . and that's why the harvest went so much more smoothly this year," explained Lord Marshall Davis, grandson of the Duke of Orange. He was very handsome, especially when he smiled, white teeth flashing against his smooth ebony skin.

They were box-stepping around the ballroom in a languid waltz. It was rare for Beatrice to dance so much at an event like this; usually she and her parents refrained from dancing. *When you're dancing, you can only talk to one person*, her father always said. *It's a more effective use of your time to stand to the side, and circulate through the crowds.*

Tonight was an exception, of course, because tonight Beatrice needed to get to know the various candidates. She still refused to think of them as potential husbands.

She was grateful, at least, that the young men already knew what was going on, because that saved her from having to explain why she was introducing herself. And they each seemed to know who the others were; that much was clear from the way they kept staring at one another across the ballroom.

So far she'd met most of the young men. There was Lord Andrew Russell, future Earl of Huron, whose father was currently serving as the ambassador to Brazil. Lord Chaska Waneta, future Duke of the Sioux, and Lord Koda Onega, future Duke of the Iroquois, were the two heirs to Native American duchies who were closest to Beatrice in age. There was even a pair of brothers, Lord James Percy and Lord Brandon Percy, heirs to the Duchy of Tidewater, the narrow strip of land that encircled most of the Gulf of Mexico.

The one thing they all had in common was their eagerness to brag about their own accomplishments. Marshall, for instance, was currently boasting about a vineyard his family owned in Napa.

Beatrice forced a smile on her face. She rarely even *drank* wine. "I'm glad the harvest was successful. Agriculture is such an important part of the American economy, especially in Orange." She was tired, grasping at straws, but clearly she'd said the wrong thing.

"Creating wine is not *agriculture*. It's an art," Marshall informed her.

"Of course it is," she hastened to say. He nodded stiffly before leading her into a careful promenade turn.

As she spun, Beatrice caught sight of a blond head across the ballroom. That was Theodore Eaton, the only young man on her parents' list who hadn't yet sought her out. She recognized him from the photos in her manila folder.

"Excuse me, but I need to step away," she murmured. No matter how Beatrice felt, her manners never seemed to abandon her. "It's been a pleasure."

"Oh—okay." Marshall retreated, letting Beatrice cross the dance floor toward Theodore. In her full-skirted gown, weighted down with her sash and medals and the Winslow tiara, she felt a bit like a ship at full sail, making slow but stately progress across choppy seas.

"Theodore Eaton. It's nice to finally meet you," she declared. It was a bit more direct than Beatrice might usually have been, but she was feeling frayed and scattered.

"Your Royal Highness." He held out a hand expectantly, his feet already pointed toward the dance floor. "And please, call me Teddy."

"Actually . . ." Beatrice swallowed. "Would you mind if we just sat down for a minute instead?"

He nodded and followed her through the double doors into a sitting room, which was mercifully empty. Beatrice settled onto one of the couches with a sigh of relief.

"So, where were you all night? Hiding from me?" She meant it to come out teasing, but clearly she'd made yet another mistake, because Teddy reddened slightly.

All the years of etiquette training she'd received, and still she had no clue how to talk to boys.

"I figured that I should wait my turn," Teddy said tactfully.

A shadow materialized in the doorway. Beatrice knew even before she looked up that it would be Connor.

He took in the scene with a single glance. Beatrice met his gaze, giving him the slightest of nods, and because after a year together they could communicate without words, Connor understood. His brow furrowed into a frown, but he made a stiff bow and retreated.

Beatrice braced herself for the inevitable half hour of bragging she was about to endure. Yet before she could ask Teddy to tell her about himself, he interrupted her thoughts.

"How are you holding up?"

She blinked. "I beg your pardon?"

"This must be awkward and incredibly stressful for you, meeting a bunch of guys that your parents are trying to set you up with. How are you feeling?" he asked, then shook his head. "Sorry, I'm sure everyone has been asking you that all night."

"Actually, you're the first person to ask." Beatrice felt oddly touched by his concern. "The truth is, yeah. It's kind of weird."

"Totally weird. Like that reality speed-dating show," Teddy agreed, which made her want to smile. She knew the show he was talking about; Samantha and Nina used to watch it.

Teddy wasn't all that tall, certainly nowhere near as tall as Connor, but as he leaned back against the pillows, he seemed . . . imposing. Not in a bad way, Beatrice decided: in a solid, steady way. But something off-kilter about his appearance kept nagging at her.

"Your bow tie isn't on right." To her immense surprise, she found herself leaning forward. "Here, I can redo it."

Teddy gave an apologetic smile, though she caught another

flicker of self-consciousness. Oh god. Did he think she was flirting with him? But then, wasn't that precisely what she was supposed to be doing?

"Are you always such a perfectionist?" he demanded.

"It's part of the job description." She focused on her hands to keep from feeling flustered: twisting the bow tie over itself, looping it, and then pulling it through.

"How did you learn to do this?" Teddy asked as she leaned back. The bow tie was perfectly symmetrical, with crisp edges. Beatrice never attempted any task that she couldn't complete perfectly.

"My etiquette master taught me."

He started to chuckle, then caught himself. "Oh my god," he said. "You're not joking. You really had an etiquette master?"

"Of course I did." Beatrice squirmed beneath his scrutiny.

"And what did this etiquette master teach you?"

"Table manners, how to curtsy, how to get in and out of a car safely—"

"I'm sorry, why is *that* part of etiquette lessons?"

Beatrice tried not to feel even more embarrassed. "I have to swing both legs out at once, my knees locked together, to keep the paparazzi from . . ." She couldn't bear to say *getting a crotch shot*, but she didn't have to, because Teddy's eyes widened in understanding.

"I'm really glad I don't wear skirts," he joked. It made Beatrice want to burst out laughing. She settled for pursing her lips against a smile.

The sounds of the ballroom emanated toward them, growing softer as the night wore on. Teddy looked over at her, thoughtful. "I saw you around Boston a few times, you know, when I was home on break."

"Really? Where?"

"At Darwin's. I used to go there to study," he said sheepishly. "I always knew when you were coming, because one of your protection officers would do a sweep of the place. Ten minutes later you'd pull up on your bike, hiding your face under a baseball cap, to pick up bagels and cold brew. I thought it was cool of you," he added softly. "That you went to get bagels yourself, when you clearly could have sent someone."

Beatrice flushed. She was aware that the baseball cap hadn't fooled anyone, but the nice thing about college was how much people respected her privacy. Even when they recognized her, they generally didn't bother her. "I loved biking to Darwin's. It was a lot of work to get me there, but I never wanted to give it up."

"What do you mean, it was a lot of work to get you there?"

"One of my protection officers would follow in a car with darkened windows, while the other—the one who'd done the sweep—would be waiting at Darwin's to greet me," Beatrice said sheepishly. "It was a lot of intricate choreography, just for a bagel."

"In your defense, those bagels taste best fresh out of the oven. They would never have lasted if you'd had them delivered to the library, or wherever you were studying," Teddy assured her.

"Police station." Beatrice corrected him before she could catch herself.

"What?"

"I couldn't ever get work done at the library. It was so crowded, and I don't really like being in small, enclosed spaces, not when they're full of people. . . ." Beatrice swallowed. "I used to bike to the Cambridge police station with my bagels and hang out on the top floor doing my homework. No one ever bothered me there."

She felt a little silly confessing this, but Teddy nodded in understanding. "What was your go-to bagel order?" he asked, deftly changing the subject.

"Blueberry, with extra cream cheese. Unless I got a butterscotch brownie," she confessed. "I used to eat those once a day during exams. They were my personal anti-stress routine." She tilted her head to look at Teddy. "What was your Darwin's order?"

"The Brawny Breakfast Sandwich, the one with chorizo and jalapeños. I'm addicted to that spicy kick," he confessed, and laughed. "I worry that I'm being judged by my bagel choice."

"I don't have much else to judge you on. The other guys spent most of the time talking about themselves." Beatrice had given him the opening, but Teddy refused to take the bait.

"Maybe I have less to talk about."

"You aren't going to brag about Yale?" she said lightly.

"I didn't want to rub it in that I went to such a better school than Harvard," he replied, with another smile. "Though I used to wonder why you chose not to go to King's College." Where America's future kings have always gone, he didn't need to add.

"I'm trying to set a new precedent," Beatrice told him, skating around the question. People usually assumed that she'd attended Harvard for its academic rigor, when the truth was, she'd simply wanted to get away from the capital for four years. As far as she could go.

She would have preferred one of the colleges out west, except that her parents would never have allowed her to go all the way to Orange.

"Remind me, weren't you on the crew team?" Beatrice asked, attempting to change the subject.

"Only my first year. And now I have proof that you've seen my résumé." Teddy propped an elbow on one knee. "Do you have color-coded files on all of us, sorted in alphabetical order?"

"It's sorted by precedence of title, actually," she countered, attempting a joke. "How did you know?"

"Because it's what my parents would have done."

She wasn't sure how to answer that, but Teddy went on. "My parents are very . . . opinionated," he said tactfully. "As I imagine yours are. Right now, they're upset that I'm not going straight to law school. All my family are lawyers," he added, as if that explained everything.

"And you want to be a lawyer too?"

"I don't know if wanting has anything to do with it," he said softly.

Beatrice felt a pang of empathy. She was no stranger to that kind of situation.

"I think I saw a portrait of one of your ancestors at the Boston Museum of Fine Arts. Lady Charlotte Eaton," Beatrice recalled. A wistful smile stole over her features at the memory of that night.

"The Whistler portrait," Teddy said knowingly. "She was my great-grandmother."

Beatrice nodded. "There must be a lot of your personal art on display at that museum. It was nice of your family to lend it."

Most of the Washington family's art was on permanent loan at the National Portrait Gallery. Except when Beatrice was younger, and one picture a week had been rotated in from the collection, to hang in her lesson room. Some of the bloodier historical paintings used to give her nightmares.

"We sold that portrait, actually," Teddy told her—and immediately stiffened, as if he regretted his words. Beatrice felt like she'd invaded some personal territory.

"Well, I had to write a paper on that painting, and it was one of the worst grades I received in my entire college career," she went on. "So let's hope for both our sakes that you aren't as confusing as your great-grandmother. Because if so, I'll never understand you."

Teddy seemed to be studying her with thoughtful curiosity.

"You know," he said at last, "I was a little surprised when my parents told me why I was meeting you tonight. I mean . . . you could have literally anyone you want."

Not anyone. Beatrice thought again of how slim her folder of options was.

"It's not quite that simple" was all she said.

Moonlight danced through the enormous windows on one wall, catching the startling sapphire of Teddy's eyes. He nodded in understanding. "I can only imagine."

The other boys had been so predictable, so one-note. None of them had really paid attention to Beatrice. They'd just postured and preened, dancing over the surface of their conversations without truly listening to her.

She might not feel butterflies with Teddy, but there was something genuine about him that struck her as a mark in his favor.

Beatrice tried to hide her nervousness. She'd never actually done this before, except in dialogue with her etiquette master—yes, Lord Shrewsborough had made her practice asking guys on dates, since most men would be too intimidated to ask *her.*

"Teddy . . ." She broke off, swallowed, and rallied her words. "Next weekend my family will be at the opening night of *Midnight Crown*, the new show in the East End. Do you want to come with me?"

He hesitated, causing Beatrice to wonder if she'd made a misstep, asking Teddy to see a *musical*, and with her entire family, no less. But then he relaxed into a smile.

"I'd love to," he assured her.

Connor was conspicuously quiet as he walked Beatrice back to her suite at the end of the night.

She reached up to rub her temples, still sore from the tiara. If only she could kick off her shoes and skip through the halls barefoot like Samantha did, but even now, some deep-rooted sense of propriety refused to let her.

She glanced over at Connor. He was looking away, his jaw set firmly. It wasn't like them to be this silent. Usually at the end of an event they were both brimming with stories, comparing notes about the people Beatrice had talked to, sharing a complicit laugh at someone's expense. Tonight, though, he seemed determined to ignore her.

Finally Beatrice couldn't stand it. "What's going on?"

They were alone in the upstairs hallway, their footfalls muffled by the heavy scrolled carpet. Still Connor refused to look her way.

"Come on," she insisted. "You're the only person who's really honest with me. What's bothering you?"

"Honestly?" He finally turned that gaze on her, as clear and sharp as a hawk's. "I can't believe you agreed to go along with this. What's your plan, exactly? To eliminate these guys one by one, and whoever's left at the end gets the final rose?"

"I'm sorry, do you have a better idea?"

He made an angry, disbelieving sound. "I just don't think you can summon a bunch of noblemen to meet you and expect to find happily ever after with one of them."

"It doesn't necessarily need to be happily ever after. At least not according to my parents," Beatrice heard herself answer, with an uncharacteristic touch of bitterness. "Just *happy enough* ever after."

They had reached her suite. Her sitting room was beautiful, if rather impersonal: full of antique furniture and enameled lamps, the pale blue walls hung with demure watercolors. Near the door to her bedroom, a serpentine desk was littered with invitations and official documents.

Connor followed her inside, closing the door and leaning against it with crossed arms. "Why are you doing this, Bee?" He sounded upset. Which wasn't fair, given that this really had nothing to do with him.

She let out an angry breath. "What other choice do I have? You know how strange my life is. I can't just *go on dates* like a normal girl."

"And you think choosing some guy from an aristocratic lineup is your best bet?"

"Please, just . . . don't," she said helplessly. "I'm anxious enough as it is."

"You said you wanted me to be honest." Connor stuffed his hands into his pockets, his posture stiff and closed off. He was still leaning against the door, a few yards' distance separating him from the princess. "And why are *you* feeling anxious? These guys are all here for your sake. You're the one holding all the cards."

"I'm terrified because I have no idea what I'm *doing*, okay? This is all new to me! I've never had a real boyfriend, never even—"

She stopped herself before she could finish that sentence, but Connor probably knew it anyway. These days, the entire country seemed to have an opinion on Beatrice's virginity.

"I've never been in love," she said at last. "Given the circumstances, I never really had a chance to."

Then, for some reason she couldn't explain, she let her eyes lift to Connor's. "Have you?"

It was as personal a question as she had ever dared ask. Connor kept his gaze on hers. "I have."

Beatrice was surprised at the resentment that twisted through her at his words. "Well then," she said coldly, "I'm happy for you."

"You shouldn't be."

She recoiled a step. Whatever he was talking about, whatever past love affair of his had gone wrong, she didn't want to hear about it. "This is really none of your business. You may go."

Never in all their time together had Beatrice *dismissed* him like that. She saw him flinch at her words, and opened her mouth to take them back—

A roar sounded through the palace. An explosion, maybe, or a blast.

Connor leapt forward, fast as a liquid shadow, before Beatrice had even fully registered the sound.

He pulled her back toward the wall, then whirled around, keeping her safely behind him. In the same fluid motion he slid a gun from its holster.

His eyes darted from the door, to the hallway, back toward the windows, assessing the likelihood of a threat from any direction. He had run to her with impossible speed, and now he stood before her with preternatural stillness, the sort of bone-deep stillness that clearly resulted from years of training.

Beatrice's heart raced. She was hyperaware of every place their bodies touched, from her legs up to her chest, which was pressed against Connor's back. His uniform was scratchy against her cheek. She could feel the rapid rise and fall of his breath, smell the spiciness of his soap. The warmth of his body seemed to burn through her dress, to scorch her very skin.

The oath of the Revere Guard echoed in her mind. *I am the lantern of honor and truth, the light against the darkness. In life and limb, to live or die, I swear to guard this realm and its Crown.*

To live or die. Connor had literally sworn to protect her with his very breath. Beatrice had known this, but it was another thing entirely to *see* him fling his body in front of hers as a living shield. To know that he would fight for her, if it came to it. She felt oddly humbled.

It felt like an eternity passed before a voice crackled over the palace's intercom system. "False alarm, everyone! One of the fireworks accidentally went off on the South Portico!"

Connor turned, placing his hands on Beatrice's bare shoulders to steady her. They were the hard palms of a man used to physical exertion, a man who lifted weights and held a rifle and was no stranger to the boxing ring. His face was alight with something—alertness, and concern, and something else that radiated from him like heat.

"Bee, are you okay?"

Her throat felt very dry. She managed a nod.

Seemingly satisfied, Connor stepped away, holstering his weapon. In all the excitement, the collar of his suit had shifted, and there it was again: the edge of that tattoo. It hinted at the real Connor, the private body that he kept hidden beneath weapons and uniforms.

The palace was probably full of voices and running footsteps—it should have been, after a security scare like that. Beatrice heard none of it. The rest of the world seemed to have receded to nothing.

She stepped forward and lifted her mouth to his.

Her good sense must have momentarily fled her body, because she acted entirely without thinking; but all her senses came rushing back as their lips touched. The utter *rightness* of that kiss struck her, deep in her core.

Connor broke away and stumbled back. Something, maybe his lantern pin, had snagged on her ivory sash, ripping it from her shoulder as he stepped away. It fluttered to the floor like a white flag of surrender.

Oh *god*. What had she done?

Connor's breath was as shallow and uneven as hers. Neither of them spoke. She imagined them frozen in time like cartoon people in a comic strip, little speech bubbles floating out of their mouths, but empty of any text.

A knock sounded at the entrance to her suite. "Beatrice!"

Just like he always did, her father pushed open the door before she could even say *come in*.

Nothing about their position was compromising; they were standing in her sitting room, Beatrice still dressed in her full ball gown and heels. She just hoped that her expression didn't give them away.

"Are you all right?" the king exclaimed. "Sorry about the firework. I'm not quite sure how that happened."

"I'm all right," Beatrice said steadily.

Next to her, she felt Connor bob into a stiff bow. "Your Majesty," he murmured, and hurried from the room.

"I just wanted to check in. How do you feel about the young men you met tonight?" the king asked, as the door shut behind Connor.

Beatrice's ears were still ringing from what had happened. She had kissed her *Guard*. The knowledge of it echoed like the sound of the firework that had exploded several minutes ago.

Had it really been only a couple of minutes? It felt more like a lifetime.

"Can we talk tomorrow? I'm exhausted," she asked her dad, with a wan smile.

"Of course. I understand."

When her dad had left, Beatrice crossed her sitting room and bedroom and retreated into her final refuge—her closet. There was a deep bay window along one of the walls, with an old window seat piled high with cushions.

Climbing onto it, she kicked off her shoes and drew her knees up so that her skirt flowed over the cushions. She closed her eyes and rested her forehead on the cool silk of her gown, willing her pulse to slow down.

What did Connor think of what had happened? Was he still standing there at attention outside her front door?

Beatrice couldn't bear the thought of losing him.

She was afraid that she'd messed things up with him forever, but even more afraid of herself—and the thrilling, terrifying new feelings that coursed through her.

Feelings for a person who would never end up in a manila folder of approved, appropriate options. A person who could never be hers.

9

SAMANTHA

Samantha pulled the coverlet over her head and squeezed her eyes shut, but it was no use. She'd forgotten to close her drapes, and the gray predawn light seeped into her room, highlighting the delicate pillows that she'd kicked unceremoniously onto the carpet.

Her ears felt pinched. She reached up, realizing that she'd accidentally slept in the diamond earrings from the Crown Jewels collection. Oops. She unscrewed them and tossed them onto her bedside table, then lunged for her phone, suddenly desperate to know whether Teddy had texted.

He hadn't. But then, had she even given him her number? She swiped over to her various social media handles to find his profile, but it was frustratingly unhelpful. Just a few infrequent photos: a lobster roll, a Nantucket sunset, pictures he'd taken last year at a friend's birthday. She clicked through them all, burning with curiosity for any last shred of information about him.

Finally Sam flung back the covers and headed into her closet, changing into a pair of electric-pink workout pants and a matching top. She debated going down the hall to bang on Jeff's door, but he was always so grouchy in the mornings. Instead she sent him a text: *Movie later?* If she put in a request now, they might actually get clearance to go to a real movie theater, with actual *people* in it, which was always more fun than watching something in the screening room here—even if they did get advance copies of all the films before their official release. She just needed a pair of security officers to sweep the theater about a half hour before their arrival.

Sam was unusually quiet as she headed toward the protection officers' control room downstairs. The palace on the day after a party always felt curiously evocative, the empty rooms echoing with the aftereffects of the night before. Already maids were wiping down tables and unrolling carpets, retrieving misplaced champagne flutes from wherever drunk guests had forgotten them: on a shelf in the library, inside a potted orchid, or in Sam's case, on the floor of the coatroom. She chuckled at the broken plaster and scorch marks out on the South Portico, where the firework had gone off. At least this accident, for once, *hadn't* been her fault.

"Beatrice?"

Her dad was seated on the tufted bench at the foot of the stairs, leaning over to lace his running shoes. "Oh—Sam. I thought you were your sister," he explained when he glanced up. "Have you seen her?"

"Not yet."

"She must have decided to sleep in." The king braced his hands on his knees and stood up with a sigh. His eyes lit again on Sam, in her all-pink workout outfit, and he cleared his throat. "What about you, up for a jog?"

Of course. Samantha wasn't her dad's first pick for a running partner, just the second-string option when Beatrice didn't show.

"Um. Sure," she muttered, and followed her dad out into the brisk winter morning.

A pair of security officers fell into step alongside them, wearing matching all-black performance gear, their guns holstered to their waists. They had long ago resigned themselves to the king's running habit: he went out almost every day, on a preapproved loop through the center of town. Often he asked someone to come with him: a foreign ambassador, or a politician who wanted to lobby him on a particular issue, or most often, Beatrice. Invitations to run with His Majesty were more highly prized than an audience in his office.

That was the thing about Sam's dad—he never stopped working. There was no clear division for him between office and home. His mind was never still. Even when they were on vacation, Sam would catch him at work, in the early mornings or late at night: composing speeches, reading reports, emailing his staff or his press secretary or the people who ran his charities about a new idea he'd had.

They headed out the palace's discreet side exit, and the city unfurled before them, from Aviary Walk to the broad green strokes of John Jay Park. Past the blur of apartments and office buildings, the iridescent spire of the Admiralty Needle rose into the horizon, which was tinged with the saffron light of dawn.

A few other joggers passed their way, but aside from some curious glances and the occasional *Good morning, Your Majesty*, they left the king in peace.

Sam glanced over at her dad, but his gaze was fixed resolutely forward. He didn't seem as fast as usual—normally he clocked four eight-minute miles—but maybe Sam was just running at top speed, hyped up on adrenaline. Daydreams of Teddy kept spinning through her brain. The very air felt heavy with possibility, as thick and tangible as the mist curling in off the river.

And even though she knew she was just the backup option, Sam felt oddly glad that her dad had asked her to join him this morning. She couldn't remember when she'd last gotten any time alone with him.

Things had been different before Sam's grandfather died, before her father ascended to the throne and was forced to become the world's greatest multitasker. He used to spend hours with his children, playing games that he'd invented. One of Sam's favorites was Egg Day, when their dad gave them an egg in the morning and told them that they had to carry it with them at all times. If the egg was still safe at the end of the day, they won a prize. The palace staff ended up cleaning egg yolk out of everything from place mats to curtains.

The king was also a history enthusiast, and an endless source of stories about America's former rulers. Sam had loved to walk into a room and ask him who'd lived here, then listen as her dad recounted the adventures of their ancestors. He could spin a story out of anything.

She knew she could be a handful, but back then her antics had made her father laugh rather than shake his head in disappointment. She remembered one time when she wrote her name in permanent marker on the wall between the elevator shaft and the third-floor staff hallway. She wasn't sure what mischief had prompted her to do it, but her dad hadn't been angry at all; he'd just roared with laughter. "You've made your mark on history," he had teased, pulling the red marker from Samantha's hands.

That was probably the only mark she ever *would* make on history. No one ever remembered the younger sisters of kings or queens, except as a footnote to their older siblings' biographies.

The sun had risen higher in the sky. Its watery light illuminated her father's features, underscoring the lines of weariness etched across his brow. Sam realized, suddenly, how old he looked. When had his hair gone entirely gray?

"Samantha," he said at last, as they turned around the great reflecting pool, "what happened last night? First you showed up late to the Queen's Ball; then you completely missed the knighthood ceremony."

"I'm sorry." Sam wanted to get this over with as fast as possible, but her father shook his head.

"I don't want you to blurt out a token apology," he admonished. "I want to *talk* to you."

The protection officers sped up a little to give them space, though they probably heard everything anyway.

"Your sister has been thinking about her future," the king went on, in a strange tone. Sam wondered what he meant by that. Was Beatrice starting a new government initiative? "I was hoping that you would too. I haven't seen much direction from you."

"I just graduated high school!"

"Samantha, you graduated in June. It's December," her father pointed out. "When I agreed to let you and Jeff take a gap year before college, I hoped that you might use this time constructively: for reflection, or to learn something new. But all you did was jet from one place to the other."

"You approved the itinerary," she said defensively. She had a feeling that Jeff wasn't about to hear what a disappointment *he* had been.

Sam wished she could explain how she'd felt throughout that trip—that she was searching for an indefinable something, and no matter where she went, she never managed to find it. Maybe she never would. But then, how could she be expected to find it if she didn't even know what she was looking for?

Her father nodded, conceding the point. "I did approve it. But now that you're back, it's time for us to discuss what comes next. You can't spend the rest of your life ditching your bodyguards, sneaking off to ride ATVs. You haven't even decided where you're going to school next year."

Sam had halfheartedly sent in a bunch of college applications last spring. To no one's shock, all the schools had accepted her. She knew that everyone expected her to go to college, but for what? It wasn't as if she could ever get a *normal people* job, even if she'd wanted one.

Perhaps she and Jeff would just be professional wastrels, a drain on the economy for the rest of their lives. The modern incarnations of a pair of medieval court jesters. At least, that was what they always told each other: that they had a constitutional responsibility to stir up trouble, if only to make up for how excruciatingly *good* Beatrice was.

"I get it," she told her dad. "I'll accept one of the college offers."

The king let out a frustrated breath. "Sam, this isn't just about college. It's about your behavior. I know it's not easy, being unable to do so many things that other teenagers take for granted. I was your age too, once. I understand what you're going through."

"I don't know if you do," Sam insisted. Her father couldn't possibly understand what it was like to be the spare. He had been the heir, the one who could do no wrong, the one everyone fussed and exclaimed over. The one whose face was printed on money, and stamps, and coffee mugs.

"You're right. It's harder for your generation, with all those gossip sites and social media things," her father replied, misunderstanding. "This life—being a Washington—is a life of privilege and opportunity, but also a life of unusual constraints. My hope for you has always been that you'll focus on the open doors, instead of the ones that are closed to you."

His breath was coming more heavily; he slowed to a walk. Sweat beaded his brow.

"I know it isn't easy," he went on. "You're young, you're bound to make mistakes, and it isn't fair that you have to make them in front of the entire world. But, Sam, please try to give this some thought."

She still didn't understand. "Give what some thought?"

"What you want to do until you start college next fall. You could get an internship somewhere—a design firm, perhaps, or with an event planner? Or you could volunteer, find a charity to focus on."

"Can't I keep traveling?"

"You could go on a royal tour, just you and Jeff."

Samantha snorted. She hated getting dragged on the royal tours—parading down the streets of various small towns while the crowds shouted, "Look this way, Beatrice!" and "I love you, Jeff!"

They turned on to the last mile back toward the palace. The city was stirring to life, people lining up at the coffee cart on the corner. Sam's shadow danced long and distorted on the gravel trail before her.

"You're so fiercely stubborn," her father went on, though the way he said it made it sound curiously like a compliment. "Whatever you do, I know it will be great. You just have to channel all that tremendous energy into something positive. You remind me of your aunt Margaret," he added, smiling. "You act like her too. You're all Washington, you know."

Aunt Margaret, the king's older sister, had been the wildest and most controversial member of the royal family. At least until Samantha came along.

Sam adored her aunt Margaret. They had always been two of a kind, because unlike Sam's father, Margaret knew precisely what it felt like to be the unimportant Washington. And it must have been even more painful for her, because she was older than Sam's dad, and had to watch her younger brother pass her in the order of succession.

That was how it had always been for the princesses of America: the closest they ever got to the throne was at the moment of their birth. Because eventually, no matter how long it took, a boy would follow—and the boys had always taken precedence. Those princesses had stood by, silently watching as their place in the hierarchy slipped ever further, as they were demoted in importance with the birth of each successive male. Until Beatrice.

If the law had changed in Aunt Margaret's time, instead of a generation later, she would have been the first queen regnant instead of Beatrice.

Sam suspected that the law changed *because* of Aunt Margaret. Because Sam's grandfather knew how smart Margaret was, how much potential she had—and watched as she grew bitter and hard-edged, falling in with a reckless, bohemian set, deliberately distancing herself from the royal family. Maybe King Edward III had regretted what happened with his oldest child, and wanted to ensure that history didn't repeat its mistakes on Beatrice.

The security guards melted away as Sam and her father reached the palace. Its white stones soared above them, a glorious second-floor balustrade spanning the air above the Marble Courtyard. Arriving via the front drive, one had a deceptive impression that the palace was symmetrical, but from the back entrance its unevenness was glaring.

Sam reached up to retie her hair. She wondered what Teddy was doing right now. Was he dwelling on their kiss the way she was?

"Dad, what do you know about the Eatons?"

"Why do you ask?"

The king's eyes lit on hers, and for a moment Sam felt certain that he knew *Teddy* was the reason she'd missed the knighthood ceremony.

"I met Teddy last night, and was curious," she offered, striving to sound casual.

"You've met Teddy before, actually. You don't remember?" Her dad didn't seem surprised when Sam shook her head. "Well, you were both quite young. Teddy served as a pageboy at my coronation."

"Oh," Sam breathed. She shouldn't have been surprised. Royal pages—the children who served as attendants at ceremonial events like coronations and weddings—were always drawn from the aristocracy.

"We've known the Eatons a long time," her father explained. It was clear that *a long time* meant *for several centuries*. "The Dowager Duchess—Teddy's grandmother Ruth—was once a lady-in-waiting to your grandmother. And of course the current duke used to serve as one of my equerries, before his father passed away."

"You were friends with Teddy's dad?"

The king smiled wistfully at some memory. "We used to get into so much trouble, breaking into the wine cellar and hosting parties at Walthorpe. The Eatons' ducal mansion," he added, in answer to Sam's questioning look. "It's probably hosted more royal visits than any other private home in America."

"I wonder why he doesn't come to court," Sam mused aloud. She would definitely have noticed a guy like Teddy if she'd seen him before last night. Most aristocratic families made a point of spending at least part of the year in the capital. No matter how vast or luxurious their estates at home, they all possessed some kind of pied-à-terre in Washington, for the occasions when they needed to be at court.

"Well, last night he came to meet Beatrice."

Before Samantha could ask her dad what he meant, they had crossed into the warmth of the back hallway. A few doors down was the security control room; farther, the glow of the kitchens. Already the great beehive of the palace was buzzing to life around them.

Beatrice stood just inside the entrance, seeming flustered. She was dressed for running in a long-sleeved top and black athletic pants, her hair pulled into a sleek high ponytail. "Sorry, Dad, I didn't mean to—oh," she breathed, seeing

Samantha, and registering their sweaty appearance. "*You're up early.*"

"Jet lag." Sam didn't bother being offended by the implication, that Beatrice assumed Sam was too lazy to be awake at this hour.

"It's okay, Beatrice. It was an eventful evening; you deserved to sleep in," the king assured her.

Sam saw her sister visibly blanch at his words. "Eventful? Not really."

Now it was the king's turn to look puzzled. "You didn't like anyone you met?"

"Oh. Right." There were spots of color high on Beatrice's cheeks. Samantha glanced back and forth from her sister to their father, wondering what on earth they were talking about. The newly minted knights?

"No, I mean yes, I did like some of them." Beatrice swallowed. "Actually, I invited Theodore Eaton to the theater with us."

"That's wonderful," the king exclaimed, just as Samantha blurted out, "You asked Teddy on a *date*?"

"How do *you* know Teddy?" Beatrice asked slowly.

The king beamed at Beatrice, oblivious. "Samantha was just telling me how she chatted with Teddy last night. That was smart of you, enlisting your sister's help. It's always good to get a second opinion from someone you trust." With that, he started toward the staircase. "Don't forget that we're meeting later, Beatrice, to prepare for next week's private audiences."

Sam turned to her sister. "What's he talking about?"

There was something unsettled about Beatrice this morning. Her eyes kept flicking down the hall as if she were looking for someone. "Private audiences are meetings we do twice a week, usually for twenty minutes each," she said impatiently. "High commissioners, military personnel, judges, visiting dignitaries—"

"No, the part about you and Teddy."

Beatrice seemed surprised by the question. But then, she and Sam hadn't exactly talked about personal stuff for a long time now.

Sam wasn't sure when the distance between her and Beatrice had begun. It had just . . . *grown*, each of them drawing back one slight inch at a time. Now it was so vast that Sam couldn't begin to fathom how she might bridge it.

"I asked Teddy Eaton on a date, and he said yes," Beatrice repeated.

"But . . ."

But I'm the one he kissed, Sam wanted to cry out. Teddy had missed the knighthood ceremony to linger in the cloakroom with *her*, and now he was going out with her older sister?

"But you never date."

"Well, I decided that now is a good time to start," Beatrice said wearily.

"Why Teddy?" There had been so many young men swarming around the ball last night. Why couldn't Beatrice have gone for any of them, instead of the one boy Samantha liked?

"He comes from a good family. And he's very handsome," Beatrice replied. Even here in private, her words sounded stilted and rehearsed, as if she were standing on a podium and delivering a speech.

"That's it? You picked him out of a crowd for his face and his *title*?"

"Why do you care anyway? No one is asking *you* to find a husband!"

"What?" Sam blinked in confusion. "Who said anything about *marriage*?"

There was a momentary flash of something, vulnerability or confusion or maybe even hurt, behind the immutable expression on Beatrice's face. It was enough to make Samantha take a single step forward.

103

But then that mask slid over her sister's features again. "I wouldn't expect you to understand. This is a Matter of State." The way Beatrice pronounced it, Sam could practically hear the capitalization.

"Right," Sam said evenly. "There's no way I could comprehend the intricate socioeconomic and political implications of the boys you go on *dates* with."

She tried not to reveal how much it stung, that Teddy had apparently chosen Beatrice over her. Though she shouldn't have been surprised; this was what had happened their entire lives, with everything else—their parents' attention, the throne, the entire *country*.

Samantha never could keep hold of anything once Beatrice had decided that it should be hers.

10

DAPHNE

Daphne hated hospitals.

She hated how cold and antiseptic they felt, with that tangy metallic smell underlying everything. She hated the waiting rooms, with their depressing vending machines and outdated magazines, some so old that they dated from the previous king's reign. Most of all, Daphne hated hospitals for how quiet they were, the silence broken only by those machines beeping their soulless refrains.

But Daphne was no fool; she knew that certain charity hours were worth more than others. She couldn't just be a docent at the art museum and sponsor the ballet. If she wanted the American people to truly love her, she needed them to feel like they'd had a real, meaningful interaction with her.

Which was why Daphne had embarked upon a tireless self-directed PR campaign. She tutored underprivileged students in math and physics. She volunteered at a local homeless shelter. And every Sunday she came here to the children's wing at St. Stephen's Hospital, because Daphne knew that volunteering just once would get her nowhere. It had to be a habit to really count.

And count it she did. Last year Daphne had logged over four hundred hours of volunteer work, carefully recorded and time-stamped. Princess Samantha, meanwhile, had done fourteen. All year. Daphne didn't hesitate to slip those numbers to Natasha, who gleefully ran them in the *Daily News*. The comments of support had, predictably, poured in for Daphne. Though she wasn't sure anyone at the palace had even bothered to reprimand the princess.

Besides, what did it matter that she beat out Samantha, when saintly Princess Beatrice had completed even more hours than Daphne, all while she was a full-time student at Harvard?

For years, Daphne had tried to model her behavior on that of the older princess. Beatrice clearly managed her reputation with the same meticulous caution that Daphne did. As the first female heir to the throne, she had to. Far too many people were silently willing the princess to slip up.

There was no room for error in either of their lives.

If only they could commiserate about it, Daphne sometimes thought. How hard it was to be a woman in this world of monarchies, whose structures and traditions had all been built by men.

Maybe things would improve when Beatrice someday took the throne—when, after two hundred and fifty years, America would finally be ruled by a woman. Or maybe it would have been better if America had never been a monarchy at all, and had some other form of government.

Daphne doubted it.

"Daphne! It's good to see you." The aide at the front desk gave a shy smile, though he'd known her for years now. He was an acne-prone guy in his mid-twenties who always seemed on the verge of asking for her autograph.

"Thanks, Chris. How's the new kitten doing? Daisy, right?" Daphne prided herself on remembering the small details. It was what made her a professional.

Chris brightened under her interest and pulled out his

phone. Daphne made little "aww" noises as he scrolled through photos of his cat.

She heard footsteps on the linoleum floor and turned around to see Natasha. Right on schedule. "Chris," Daphne said sweetly, "would it be all right if Natasha accompanied me today? Just to snap a few pictures, get some quotes."

"We're doing a special piece to prompt holiday donations, a spotlight on philanthropic young people. We were hoping to include Daphne," Natasha chimed in.

"It would be a crime not to include Daphne. She's here every week," Chris proclaimed, and rocked forward on his toes. "Just make sure you get permission from the parents before you publish any photos of kids."

Daphne had never understood why the royal family was so allergic to the press. In her experience, if you helped them out a time or two, they were perfectly willing to do the same for you. With Natasha, Daphne had long ago reached a silent understanding: she would pass along stories—some of them about her, some about other figures at court—and in exchange Natasha ensured that her coverage portrayed Daphne in the most dazzlingly favorable light.

Today, Daphne had reluctantly called Natasha to ask a favor. This whole article was her idea; the other charitable young people, if any, would scarcely be mentioned alongside the extensive coverage of Daphne. She hated resorting to this—planting deliberate, self-promotional stories—but she wasn't sure what else to do. She still couldn't get over the way Jefferson had left her at the ball or the fact that she hadn't heard from him since.

Of course, Daphne didn't expect the prince to really care that she was volunteering. But he would care that *America* cared, because he liked being liked. Jefferson had always avoided discord or tears or harsh words of any kind, probably because, as the spoiled youngest child, he had so rarely encountered them.

If Daphne could convince America that she should be their princess, eventually Jefferson would end up agreeing with them.

She and Natasha walked down the hallway toward one of the younger wards. Past a sliding glass doorway was a long row of treatment rooms. Crayon sketches of fairies and snowflakes were tacked to the walls, alongside several red and green felt stockings. A gold tinsel tree squatted cheerfully in one corner.

Several parents glanced up at her arrival, and their eyes widened. Daphne smiled at them: the disarming, winning sunbeam of a smile that she'd practiced so many times in the mirror.

One of the little girls tumbled out of bed and ran toward Daphne, who crouched down to make her face level with the girl's. "Hello there," she said. Behind her, she could hear the steady series of clicks that meant Natasha was documenting all of this. "What's your name?"

"Molly." The girl reached up to pick her nose. Daphne wondered if she still had to shake her hand.

"It's nice to meet you, Molly. I'm Daphne."

"Are you a princess?" the girl asked, with a child's tactlessness.

Daphne forced herself to keep on smiling. *Someday*, she thought. *And when I am, you'll have to curtsy to me.* She held on to the girl's hand until her mother came to collect her, assuring the woman that it was no problem at all.

"I knew it," Daphne heard the mother say as she rejoined the rest of her family. "I knew she was even prettier in person. And so *sweet*."

This was why Daphne deserved to be princess someday—

because she could play the part. If only Jefferson could see it as clearly as she did.

Natasha unobtrusively approached Molly's mother with an electronic release form for the photos she had just snapped. The woman, still basking in the glow of having met the famous Daphne Deighton, didn't hesitate to sign.

As she progressed down the hallway, Daphne made a point of pausing at each bedside: to pour a cup of water and lift it to a boy's lips, to play with a little girl's doll, to read a favorite story from a picture book with sticky pages. She never tired, never let her smile slip even a fraction of an inch, as all the while Natasha's camera kept clicking away.

"Lovely evening," Natasha said crisply as they stepped out into the parking lot. The light was slowly leaching from the sky, a few scattered stars beginning to dust the horizon. The air felt heavy and cold; Daphne shrugged deeper into her parka.

"I got some great shots," Natasha went on, yanking open the door of her car to wedge her camera bag inside. Her angular dark hair swung forward with the movement. "Want me to send them to you for review before I run the article?"

"Please."

The reporter paused, her car keys jingling in one hand. "Are you waiting for someone? I can give you a ride home."

Daphne shook her head. "Actually, I'm heading back inside. I have one more visit to make. A personal one," she added, in answer to Natasha's questioning look.

"Your friend in the coma. I remember," Natasha purred.

Of course she remembered, because Daphne had handed her that scoop, had practically composed the article herself. Underage drinking inside Washington Palace, and a girl who ended up in the ER? It was one of the most successful stories Natasha had ever run.

"Yes. Her condition hasn't changed."

"I'm sorry to hear that," Natasha replied, in the unconvincing way of someone claiming an emotion she didn't feel. Her eyes drifted toward the camera in her backseat. "Want me to come with?"

The analytical part of Daphne knew that Natasha had a point. The future princess grieving at the bedside of her friend: it would make a great sidebar photo to complement all the coverage of her philanthropy.

But this grief was too real for Daphne to share with anyone.

"Thank you, but I think I'll visit her alone."

This time when Daphne walked into the hospital, she moved quickly, keeping her head down to deflect attention. She didn't really want to advertise why she was here.

In the long-term care ward, Daphne headed down a series of hallways, then turned toward a familiar door. She reached her hand up to trace the nameplate—HIMARI MARIKO, it said, on a square of laminated paper. At the beginning, back when everyone kept expecting Himari to wake up at any minute, her name had been written in dry-erase marker on a square of whiteboard.

Daphne had known it was serious when they hung the laminated name card.

There was a chair pulled up next to the bed; Daphne sat in it and tucked her feet to one side, kicking off her ballet flats so that her toes in their black tights curled over the cushions.

Himari lay there before her, under a silver-and-blue quilt that her mom had brought from home. Tubes and wires connected her to various IVs and machines. Her face was hollow, deep purple shadows inscribed beneath her eyes. Her breathing was so slight that Daphne could hardly hear it.

"Hey. It's me," Daphne said quietly.

When Himari had first fallen into a coma, back when it seemed like a temporary condition, Daphne had filled her visits with chatter. She would tell Himari everything she was missing: the cute new spin instructor who was teaching at their favorite studio; the eighties-themed gala at the science museum; the fact that Olivia Langley was organizing a weekend at her family's lake house and hadn't included Daphne. But now it felt strange to pour all those meaningless words into the silence. It wasn't as though Himari was listening anyway.

She reached out to take her friend's hand, surprised as always at how limp it felt in her own. Himari's nails had grown grotesquely long, and so uneven that they were starting to snag on the blanket. Of course the nurses had more important things to worry about than Himari's cuticles, but still.

Biting back a sigh, Daphne reached into her purse for the nail file she kept with her at all times. She began to meticulously shape her friend's nails, rounding them at the edges.

"Sorry I don't have any polish with me. Though I wouldn't have the right one for you anyway." Daphne only ever wore pale, almost translucent pinks—she feared that shades of red might remind people of claws, or grasping talons. But Himari had no such hesitations. She'd always gravitated toward the loud, fiery colors, just like her mom did.

You can tell a true lady by her red nail polish and red lipstick, Himari's mom used to tell them as she swished along to some event in a chic black dress and towering heels. Himari's parents were the Earl and Countess of Hana, a title that had been in their family for almost a century, ever since Himari's great-grandparents came from Kyoto as ambassadors from the Japanese Imperial Court.

Daphne used to love going to the Marikos' house. They lived in a sprawling estate in the center of Herald Oaks, with manicured gardens and an enormous swimming pool. Himari had three brothers, and their home always felt rowdy and full of laughter, no matter the priceless watercolor screens and terra-cotta bowls that decorated each room.

"I don't approve of your friendship with that Mariko girl. She's too smart," Daphne's mom announced one day when Daphne came home from a sleepover at Himari's. "You need to surround yourself with girls who make you shine, not girls who compete with you."

"She's my *friend*," Daphne said hotly.

Rebecca looked into her daughter's eyes with eerie prescience. "A pair of girls as beautiful and clever as the two of you, it can only end in disaster."

Daphne wished her mother hadn't been right.

Throughout high school, she and Himari had shared almost everything: their hopes, their successes, their position as the two most popular girls in the class. What an entrance they had made, walking into some court function together, both of them young and stunning and aristocratic. It had seemed like no one could resist them, like nothing at all could come between them.

Until Daphne started dating the prince.

As it turned out, Himari had wanted Jefferson too. Of course she did; half of America had daydreams about him. Yet somehow Daphne, who prided herself on knowing people's intentions almost before they knew them themselves, hadn't seen it coming.

"We *were* friends, weren't we?" she said softly, knowing that Himari wouldn't answer. "You weren't just pretending the whole time?"

Those seven days, from Himari's birthday through the twins' graduation party, had caused Daphne to doubt and second-guess everything. She wanted to believe that Himari had cared about her, that once upon a time their friendship had been real.

Because, even after everything that had happened, Daphne missed her friend. Her haughty, snarky, insightful friend who always seemed to know too much for her own good.

She cast a swift, cautious glance around the room. Even now, behind a closed door, she couldn't be too careful. Then she leaned forward and pressed her forehead to the back of Himari's hand, closing her eyes as if begging for a benediction that would never come.

"I never meant for any of this to happen," Daphne whispered. "It all went so wrong. I just wish . . . I wish you had *talked* to me. You didn't leave me many options, Himari."

Daphne wasn't like the other aristocrats, the ones whose families had been titled since the Revolution, who grew up trained in the rules of elegant behavior. She had a boxer's instinct when it came to fighting, and Himari had backed her into a corner.

She wished she could shed a tear for her friend. But Daphne couldn't remember the last time she had cried. Probably before Himari's accident.

Maybe she'd lost the ability to let herself show weakness. Maybe the guilt had dried up her tear ducts, and she would never be able to cry again.

"I never meant for this to happen," Daphne repeated.

There was no reaction from Himari, not even a flicker of an eyelid, to show that Daphne's words had registered at all.

11

NINA

"What's the name of Juliet's cousin in *Romeo and Juliet?*" Rachel glanced up from her laptop to where Nina stood at the opposite table, organizing books onto wheeled metal carts.

They were in the workroom at Dandridge, the main library at King's College. Technically this space was supposed to be employees only, but no one minded when Nina brought Rachel back here. None of the other library staff were even working today.

"Tybalt," Nina answered automatically, then paused. "Why are you writing about Shakespeare for your Russian history paper?"

Rachel pulled her arms overhead in a stretch, as if she'd been in the library all day rather than a single hour. "I took a break to do an online crossword. It's important to take breaks, you know, to keep the creative well full."

"You're writing a four-page history paper, not a novel," Nina teased.

Her phone buzzed with an incoming call from Samantha. Nina declined the call, then typed a quick text. *I'm at work, can I try you later?*

Her mind whirled as she tried to figure out what exactly she would tell Sam. The princess had been checking in with her all week, urging Nina to spend New Year's at the Washingtons' house in Telluride. Nina had gone on that trip almost every year for the past decade; she'd even learned to snowboard with Sam and Jeff's private instructor.

She wanted to be there for Sam, who'd been noticeably dejected ever since the ball last weekend—when she kissed that guy from Boston, only to learn that he was going on a date with *Beatrice.*

But how could Nina face Jefferson after what happened on the balcony that night?

"How about this one: 'empire founder.' Caesar? Except it's eight letters . . ."

"Augustus," Nina supplied, trying and failing not to think of Jeff. Augustus was one of his names, as was Alexander: the only thing missing was William, or perhaps Attila, and then he would literally be named for all the great conquerors of world history. For someone who wasn't the heir, he sure had a lot of power packed into those four names.

"You know, you could use the internet for this, instead of asking me," she pointed out.

"Where's the fun in that?"

Nina shook her head, smiling. She didn't actually mind that Rachel kept peppering her with questions. It would have been different if she were reading, but sorting books was second nature to Nina by now. She knew the Dewey decimal system by heart. Honestly, she might have taken this job even if it hadn't been required by the work-study terms of her scholarship, if only for an excuse to spend extra time in the library.

Nina had been raised on a steady diet of books. The weekends that her parents used to work, when she didn't want to go to the palace, Nina would beg them to drop her at their local branch library. She happily spent the whole day there, working her way through the library's children's section, in both English and Spanish. She and her mom always played a game at the end of the day, where Nina had to describe the book she was reading in as creative a way as possible. Never cross a reptile—*Peter Pan*. Don't be fooled by a reflection—*Alice in Wonderland*. And so on.

Here at the campus library, Nina's job was to collect books from the return chute and put them back in their places on the shelves. It was actually pretty fun, seeing how diverse people's research needs were. She never knew what she would come across, from the memoirs of King Zog of Albania to a seventeenth-century cookbook that she'd actually copied a recipe from. It reminded Nina just how much knowledge there was, out in the world.

"Logan is an awful texter," Rachel complained, frowning down at her phone. A bright turquoise sweatshirt slid off one shoulder. In the months Nina had known her, she'd never seen Rachel wear an article of clothing that was either black or white; her entire wardrobe seemed positively fluorescent.

"What did he say?" Nina paused over a tattered clothbound book titled *Extinct and Dormant Peerages*. Did this go under gentry, or heraldry? She waved its bar code under the scanner to check.

"I told him that I couldn't go to the party tonight because I have to write this paper, and all he said was 'Best of luck'! What do you think that means?" Rachel pursed her lips. "Is he *trying* to blow me off?"

"You might finish in time for the party if you tried to work, instead of procrastinating," Nina reproved gently. "It's only seven."

Rachel reached up to ruffle her curly hair, making it stick up as though she'd emerged from an electrical storm. "I just wanted to hang out with you before winter break. I missed you last weekend."

Nina shifted uncomfortably. She hated lying, but no way

could she tell Rachel that she'd missed the Queen's Ball watch party so that she could actually *go* to the Queen's Ball. She especially couldn't tell her about what had happened afterward, on the balcony.

"Besides," Rachel went on, "I like working in here. It makes me feel like a VIP of the library."

"I know, it's totally glamorous," Nina deadpanned.

Rachel laughed, tipping her chair up onto its back legs, then letting it clatter down. "Remind me, you'll still be in town on New Year's Eve, right? I was thinking of organizing something."

Before Nina could answer, her phone buzzed with another incoming call. She started to decline, assuming it was Samantha again—but then Nina saw who it was, and her heart leapt into her throat. She stepped out of the small workroom and into the hallway, lowering her voice.

"Nina! Please tell me you haven't had dinner yet," Prince Jefferson said warmly.

"No—um, I'm working," she stammered.

"Does that mean you can come meet me at Matsu?"

"You mean *Matsuhara*?" It was one of the most expensive white-tablecloth restaurants in Washington.

"I'm craving sushi," Jeff said simply. "Come on, please? Don't make me eat that crispy tuna rice all by myself."

Nina swallowed against a flurry of conflicting emotions. Was he asking her on a *date*?

"I'm wearing jeans and sneakers," she said, evading the question. "Besides, I'm not sure . . ." *I'm not sure it's the best idea.*

"Oh," he said slowly. "Um—that's okay. I understand."

The words were casual, yet threaded with a distinct note of disappointment. For some strange reason that changed Nina's mind.

Why *shouldn't* she go to Matsuhara? Was she so afraid of Jeff that she couldn't handle a single sushi dinner across the table from him?

"Actually . . . okay. I'll meet you there." Her throat felt very dry.

She swore she heard his smile on the other end of the phone. "That's fantastic. Should I send a car for you?"

"*No.* It's okay." The last thing Nina needed was to be seen getting into one of the royal town cars here on campus. She'd barely gotten away with it last time.

She ducked back into the staff room, trying not to reveal how suddenly flustered she felt. "Hey, Rach, I need to go. If anyone asks, will you tell them I'll come back tomorrow morning to reshelve those?" She nodded at the books stacked on the metal wheeled cart. "And just make sure that the door locks behind you when you leave."

Rachel stared at her, not bothering to hide her curiosity. "Of course. Is everything okay?"

"Sort of. I mean, yes, it's okay, but I need to go." Nina considered saying that her mom had called, but decided it was better to be vague than to tell a flat-out lie. She'd seen enough of the royal family's PR operations to know that it was a safer policy.

Rachel nodded, her eyes scouring her friend. "Sure thing. See you soon."

Tossing her bag over one shoulder, Nina headed out the library's main doors and trotted down the steps. The iconic carved lions that stood on either side of the stairs bared their teeth at her in perpetual growls.

♛

Matsuhara was empty when she got there. Empty, that is, of everyone except the security guards stationed at the entrance, their arms folded impassively over their chests—and Jeff, who was seated alone at a central table.

"What is this?" Nina breathed, halting in her tracks. "Where is everyone?"

Jeff stood to pull out her chair. Numbly, she sat in it. "It's just us tonight," he told her, as if a complete restaurant buy-out were no big deal. "I know you don't really like the spot-light, so I thought it might be better if we kept a low profile."

"Um . . . okay." Nina glanced around the rest of the din-ing room, at the round tables with their empty banquettes of buttercup-yellow leather. Behind a sushi bar of sanded hinoki wood, a pair of chefs worked in coordinated silence.

"Why did you do all this?"

Jeff leaned his elbows onto the table. He was wearing a button-down, its creases crisply ironed. "I remember your parents used to always take you out for sushi on special occa-sions," he said. "And this felt like a special occasion. I mean, I did consider flying us to Tokyo, so we could get it directly from the source," he went on, "but my parents have both of the planes today."

"Jeff . . ."

He burst out laughing at the expression on her face. "I was kidding, Nina."

Oh. With the royal family, sometimes it was hard to tell.

She was saved from further talk by the arrival of a Japa-nese man in a white chef's coat and oversized glasses. "Your Highness, it is an honor to host you this evening. May I pre-sent the first course?"

Nina was about to tell him that they hadn't ordered, but a pair of waiters had already sailed in from the kitchen to de-posit an appetizer before each of them. "A selection of toro and caviar. Please enjoy." The chef gave a deferential nod and melted away.

She glanced down at her plate. The soy-sauce reduction

was drizzled so beautifully that it seemed almost sinful to disturb it. The carved chopsticks looked like works of art in her hands. Nina realized how out of place her tattoo was, and started to pull her sleeve farther down her wrist, then decided against it.

"What were you working on when I called?" Jeff asked, politely waiting for her before he took a bite.

"I was at my job. I work in the library, as part of my scholarship." Nina said it proudly. She had no shame about where she came from.

She forced herself to try the caviar, which she generally avoided when it was served at royal functions. As usual, all she tasted was salt. She set her chopsticks down with an inadvertent clatter.

"You don't like it?" Jeff asked, watching her.

Nina saw the sous-chefs glance over with sharp eyes. She couldn't do this, couldn't sit here in this vast room, which should have echoed with voices and laughter and the clinking of glasses, but was instead heavy with silence. It was all too stifling. Too *much*.

Jeff had probably taken Daphne Deighton on this type of date every weekend. But Nina wasn't anything like Daphne, and if she and Jeff were going to have the slightest chance of making this work—whatever this even *was*—then he needed to understand that.

"Honestly, no. I hate caviar." Nina's voice was barely audible over the ambient classical music. "Jeff, you shouldn't have done all this."

"I told you, it's a special—"

"No," she insisted. "This date is . . ." *Extravagant, glitzy, over the top.* "Thoughtful," she said, compromising. "But it isn't *me.*"

Jeff blinked at her in astonishment. Nina wondered if she'd upset him, after all the money and planning he had obviously put into the evening. Then his eyes brightened, and he laughed.

"You want to know something? I hate caviar too."

The prince stood in a single motion, tossing his napkin onto the table next to the half-eaten tower of toro and caviar. Nina hurried to follow. Seeing their movement, Matsuhara swept out of the kitchen in evident dismay.

"We're so sorry, but an emergency came up. We won't be staying for the rest of the meal. Of course, you'll still be paid in full," Jeff announced to the startled chef.

"But Your Highness—all the food . . ."

"You and the staff should eat it. I bet you never get a chance to enjoy your own cooking." Excitement blossomed on the chef's face.

Jeff waited until they had slipped out the shadowed side door before turning to Nina. "Where to? I have to admit, I'm still a little hungry."

Nina gave an appreciative laugh. "I know just the spot."

The incredulous delight on Jefferson's face was totally worth it—even if his protection officer did look like he wanted to throttle Nina in retribution.

They had walked to the Wawa from Salsa Deli, Nina's favorite taco shop, where they'd sat at a plastic-covered table and ordered carnitas tacos. In the low light, no one had cast them a second glance. Especially after Jeff borrowed the navy sweatshirt that his protection officer kept in the trunk of his car.

Eating chips and canned salsa was the opposite of the five-star dinner they'd just abandoned, but it was much more Nina's speed. Free of all that expectation and gourmet food, she and Jeff had finally been able to relax, and just talk.

When he asked where they could get dessert, Nina led him across the street to Wawa.

It was cold inside; fluorescent lights beamed down on aisle after aisle of brightly colored packaging. The store was empty except for the cashier, who barely looked their way before returning to her magazine. Nina had to bite back a laugh when she saw the cover: a WHO WORE IT BETTER? review of the gowns from the Queen's Ball. If only the cashier knew that a Prince of the Realm was in her store, his features hidden behind a navy hoodie.

But Nina knew the hoodie wasn't the only reason Jeff had gotten away with this. It was simply a matter of context. The cashier didn't *expect* to see Prince Jefferson at the Engletown Wawa, which was why she failed to notice his presence right here before her.

And now Jeff was running around the Wawa like . . . well, like a kid in a candy store. He kept pulling items from the shelves with gleeful abandon: flaming hot potato chips, a frosted Tastykake, jalapeño poppers.

He turned to her in delighted confusion, his arms brimming with packaged foods. "I don't understand this place. Is it a fast-food restaurant or a convenience store?"

"Both. Wawa is where those two worlds converge."

Jeff grinned. "I feel so cool. So hipster and bohemian."

"To a boy who wears a tiara, I guess everything looks bohemian," Nina teased, and Jeff reddened at her reference.

"It's a *circlet*, not a tiara, and I haven't worn it since I was ten!" he protested. "Just for those portraits my mom made me take as a kid!"

"It sure looked like a tiara to me." Nina ducked as Jeff tossed a bag of chips in her direction. "A rose by any other name . . ."

"Let's look up some photos of you when *you* were ten. I seem to remember that you went through a rough patch of your own."

"I think you mean my infamous bowl cut. Also known as my bad hair year." Nina laughed.

"At least your photos weren't circulated worldwide," Jeff pointed out. "Besides, you were still cute, even with that terrible haircut."

His voice had softened. They both fell still.

Nina felt a sudden need to say something, anything, to break the moment. "We came here for dessert, and all you've gotten are salty snacks," she pointed out.

"Fair enough." Jeff veered toward the freezer section and grabbed a pint of mint chocolate chip ice cream.

Nina made a face. "There are dozens of flavors to choose from and you went with mint chocolate chip?"

"What do you have against mint chocolate chip?"

"Nothing should be that shade of green. It's unnatural."

"Fine, then. More for me." Jeff smiled: a lopsided, genuine smile, which was how Nina knew that the other one—the one he showed the rest of the world—was false.

It gave her a stupid rush of confidence, knowing that she was the one who'd elicited that smile. Nina found herself desperate to see it again.

"If you insist upon that *monstrosity*"—she nodded at his ice cream carton—"then you leave me no choice but to get my own dessert. Watch and learn."

She marched to the front counter and caught the cashier's attention. "Excuse me, could I get a chocolate milkshake with double M&M's?"

"Double M&M's? That's shockingly greedy." Jeff came to stand behind her, close enough that Nina could have leaned back into him, if she dared.

"Or it's the secret to true happiness," she replied, over the sudden pounding of her heart. "All I know is that when I need to eat my feelings, my feelings taste like Wawa milkshakes with extra M&M's."

Jeff smiled. "Are you and Sam still trying to sample all the M&M varieties from around the world?"

Nina was startled that he had remembered. "We haven't gotten to all the countries yet. Turns out there's a whole lot of world out there."

Something flashed in Jeff's eyes at her words, and he nodded, thoughtful.

Nina insisted on paying for their snacks. It was the least she could do, after she'd cut off the elaborate, expensive date that Jeff had planned. As she signed the receipt, she noticed that the cashier was looking at her companion in the hoodie a little too closely. The girl opened her mouth—but before she could say anything, Nina had grabbed their shopping bag in one hand and the prince's arm in the other. "Let's get out of here."

"Should we make it a race?" Jeff asked, as playful and challenging as he'd been when they were kids and used to slide down the palace stairs on sofa cushions.

"You're on." Nina took off sprinting down the street, Jeff running alongside her.

When they reached the section of John Jay Park that stretched along the river, they both collapsed onto a bench, their breathing uneven. The darkness was broken only by pools of buttery light cast by scattered streetlamps along the footpath behind them.

Jeff pulled the sweatshirt over his head and tossed it to one side. The moonlight gleamed on his dark hair, turning it into the silver helmet of a knight. "Sorry, Matt," he told his protection officer, not sounding sorry at all. Matt just shook his head and retreated a few yards down the path, still in their line of sight.

"That place was *amazing.*" Jeff reached for his ice cream carton before passing Nina the shopping bag. "Where does the name Wawa come from, anyway?"

"I'm not sure." Probably, like everything else in this country, it traced back to Washington.

Nina pierced the lid of her milkshake with a straw. "I feel honored to have led you on your very first Wawa excursion," she went on, in a lighter tone. "Promise me that next year, when you go to the campus Wawa for late-night snacks, you'll remember that I'm the one who showed you how it's done."

"There's a Wawa at King's College?"

"Oh, yeah. It's always crowded, especially at one-fifty-five a.m., five minutes before closing time," she told him. "Once when I was at the front of the line, someone offered me thirty bucks for my milkshake."

"Did you take it?"

"Absolutely not! You can't put a price on this kind of happiness."

Jeff shifted on the bench, his leg momentarily pressing against hers. And even though there were two layers of fabric between them, his khakis and her black jeans, Nina still felt her face go hot. She took an enormous, unladylike slurp of her milkshake, hoping it would calm the clamor of her thoughts.

The prince cleared his throat. "To be honest," he said, "I don't know if I want to go to King's College next year."

The statement caught Nina off guard. "Really?"

"I know, I know, it's where my family has always gone. My parents keep pressuring me to sign on the dotted line and be done with it."

"But . . . ," Nina offered, waiting.

"But I would rather go abroad. To Spain, maybe, or Australia. Not that they'll ever let me. An American prince, studying in a country that isn't America?" Jeff shook his head. "The press would lose it. I'm not asking you to feel sorry for me," he hurried to add.

Nina shook her head, surprised. She had assumed Jeff

would automatically choose King's College—because it was predictable and easy, because he could sail through his classes and be the president of a fraternity, just like his dad and uncle and grandfather and great-grandfather.

Maybe she didn't know Jeff that well anymore, or maybe he had changed. Nina wondered if it had happened to her, too—if Jeff was having just as much trouble reconciling the current Nina with the one he used to know.

Her phone buzzed in her pocket. Nina glanced down at the screen, only to see that it was a text from Samantha: *Want to come over tomorrow?*

She quickly tucked the phone away. If this were any other boy, she would have surreptitiously tapped out a reply, then called Sam the moment the date ended to hash out every last detail. It felt strange, keeping something like this from her best friend, but there was no possible way she could tell Samantha that she was with her twin brother.

At least, not until Nina figured out what this was between her and Jeff, and whether it was even going anywhere.

Midnight arrived with a sudden chorus of bells from the capital's churches, St. Jerome's and Holy Rosary and downtown Liberty Church. The sounds chased each other through the streets and alleys of the city, ushering in a new day.

Jeff started to rise to his feet, stammering something about how late it was, but Nina tugged at his sleeve, and he sat back down.

"It's tomorrow; make a wish," she murmured.

"What?"

"It's something my parents used to say when we stayed up till midnight: that now it's tomorrow, and you get to make a wish."

"I've never heard of that." Jeff's voice was laced with an amused skepticism. "Sounds to me like they were looking for excuses to grant you wishes."

"So what if they were? The world could use more wishes."

Nina didn't tell Jeff what she'd silently wished for all those years, that most of those wishes had been centered on *him*.

The final notes of the church bells reverberated around them.

Jeff reached tentatively for Nina's face, his thumb lightly brushing against her cheek. He leaned in to kiss her.

It was a slow kiss, almost careful, as if Jefferson was afraid of rushing or getting it wrong. When they finally broke apart, Nina leaned her head against his chest. She could feel the thumping of his heart through his expensive button-down shirt. The sound was oddly comforting.

"This is a terrible idea." Her words were muffled, but the prince still threw an arm around her, pulling her closer.

"I disagree. It's a brilliant one."

"We could just—I don't know, walk away and pretend it never happened—"

"Why would we do that?"

"Because." Nina forced herself to tear away from his warmth, even as her body cried out at the sudden distance between them. "Aside from the fact that your sister is my best friend, I'm not your type."

"Sam will be the biggest fan of us, trust me," Jeff assured her. That single word, *us*, seemed to carry more weight than it should. "And since when is smart and beautiful not my type?"

"That's not what I meant," Nina insisted, flustered. "I hardly own a hairbrush, I hate wearing heels, and in case you forgot, I'm a *commoner.*"

"Hairbrushes are overrated, those sneakers are way cooler than heels, and who cares about whether your family has a title?"

"*America* does! You know what I mean, Jeff," she said impatiently. "I'm hardly the type of girl you should be taking to Matsuhara."

"I thought we established that all our future dates were going to be at Wawa." Jeff hazarded a grin. "I *like* you, Nina. I know that I messed up, before. But I really want to change your mind. At the very least, could you stop being so difficult and give me the chance to try?"

Despite her lingering misgivings, Nina smiled. "Don't take it personally; I'm always difficult."

"It hasn't scared me away so far," Jeff reminded her.

Nina shifted closer and kissed the Prince of America again.

12

BEATRICE

Beatrice didn't dare glance back at Connor as she headed up the curved staircase of His Majesty's Theater. The rest of her family, along with all their security, walked alongside her. Even Jeff was here, which should have surprised Beatrice, given that he usually went to great lengths to avoid the theater. But she was too preoccupied with her own anxiety to notice.

After the Queen's Ball—after she'd crossed an uncrossable line and *kissed* him—she'd been half afraid that Connor might hand in his resignation. Yet he had just shown up to work the next morning as usual.

They'd barely spoken all week, their usual easy conversation and good-natured teasing replaced by a heavy silence. The few times Beatrice ventured a question, Connor's answers were clipped and distant. He had clearly resolved to put the entire mess behind him and act like it had never happened.

Which was precisely what she should be doing.

"Beatrice, you sit here," the queen commanded, as they swept through the curtain that led to the royal box.

Adelaide gestured to the seat that was front and center. It was the most exposed to the other theatergoers: in the orchestra below, on the balcony above, even the other occupants of the private boxes, which wound around the mezzanine in a gilded semicircle. Beatrice recognized all the curious faces on those balconies, from the Nigerian trade envoy to the elderly

Baroness Västerbotten, who was openly staring at the royal family through her opera lorgnettes.

Beatrice took the seat her mother had indicated. She clasped one hand over the other in her lap, then reversed them. Strains of music floated from the orchestra, conversations overlapping as people found their way to their seats.

"Your Royal Highness," said a voice at her shoulder, and Beatrice glanced up into the dancing blue eyes of Teddy Eaton.

She rose to her feet in a fluid motion, only to freeze with indecision. How was she supposed to welcome Teddy? A handshake felt too impersonal, given that this was a *date*, but a hug seemed a bit familiar.

As if sensing her panic, Teddy reached for her hand and lifted it to his lips in an old-fashioned, courtly gesture. His kiss just barely brushed the surface of her skin.

Beatrice swallowed. It took every last shred of her self-control not to turn around and glance at Connor. "Thank you for coming," she declared, her words hollow and formal even to her own ears.

The moment they took their seats next to each other, a dull roar of interest swept through the theater. People craned their necks to catch a glimpse of them, held up their phones to snap a quick photo. Even the occupants of the other boxes didn't bother to hide their stares.

Beatrice ground her back teeth, wishing she hadn't suggested something so high-profile and public. *Of course* people were going to gossip about this. Beatrice never went on dates, and now she was at the season's most anticipated show with the handsome, eminently eligible Theodore Eaton?

Teddy turned to her, ignoring the flurry of excitement at his arrival. "So, are you looking forward to the show? They're saying it's completely revolutionary."

Beatrice saw her sister try to slip toward the back, but the

130

queen put her hands on Samantha's shoulders and steered her into the seat on Teddy's left. She winced at the memory of how she'd snapped at Sam the other morning. She hadn't meant to; she'd just been so on edge about what had happened the night before with Connor, and Sam's accusations had caught her off guard.

"I'm looking forward to it," she told Teddy, and glanced in her sister's direction. Maybe she could extend an olive branch by drawing her into the conversation. "Though Samantha is the one who's really into musicals."

"Really?" Teddy asked, glancing at Samantha.

"Beatrice is the official patron of the arts, not me," Sam said sullenly. She turned to her friend Nina, in the chair on her other side.

Beatrice blinked at her sister's rudeness. "That position is just a formality," she hurried to explain. "I've never had any musical ability."

Teddy's eyes flicked briefly to Samantha, and a shadow of something darted over his expression. Then he gave Beatrice a smile. "You're not a singer?"

"I'm so tragically off-key that I got cut from fourth-grade choir."

But there was more to it. The truth was, Beatrice had always lacked the patience for theater, for the same reason she rarely read novels: she couldn't relate to the characters. She remembered how frustrated she'd been as a child, when she saw a play about a princess on a quest. The whole thing had felt so deceitful to her—this story about a princess who drove the action, who got to make *choices*. Because the life of a princess was decided for her, long before she was even born.

Writers got to pick the endings of their novels, but Beatrice wasn't living a story. She was living history, and history went on forever.

She flipped open the Playbill and saw that the opening number would be performed by Melinda Lacy, in the role of Emily.

Of course, Beatrice realized: the title alone should have given it away. This was the story of Lady Emily Washington, the Pretender—or as some people persisted in calling her, Queen Emily.

The only child of King Edward I, Emily remained one of the most controversial, romantic, and tragic figures in American history. Her parents had done their best to arrange a marriage for her. But despite being pursued by half the world's kings—supposedly the kings of Greece and Spain once fought a duel over her—Emily refused to ever marry. Upon her father's death in 1855, twenty-five-year-old Emily attempted to establish her claim to the throne, as a woman, alone.

And then, after just a single day of being the so-called queen, Emily vanished from history.

Scholars still debated what had happened to her. The prevailing theory was that her uncle John had her killed so that he could become king. But rumors persisted, each wilder and more outlandish than the next—that Emily fell in love with a stable boy and ran away to live in anonymity; that she became a lady pirate and spied for the British; that she escaped to Paris, assumed the name Angelique d'Esclans, and married the French dauphin, which therefore meant that the true heirs to the American throne were actually the kings of France.

"I didn't realize this was about Emily," Beatrice said softly. "I wonder which ending the show will give her." She scanned the list of musical numbers in search of a clue.

"I like to think that she escaped to safety. Canada, maybe, or the Caribbean." Teddy leaned an elbow on the armrest between them.

"Unfortunately, *like to think* isn't the same as *believe*,"

Beatrice argued. "The evidence suggests that her uncle murdered her."

"That very same uncle is your ancestor," Teddy reminded her. He had a point. "And until you, Emily was the only woman who could ever claim to have been America's queen. Don't you want her story to have a happy ending, even in fiction?"

What use was fiction when confronted with cold hard facts? "I guess so," Beatrice said noncommittally.

She felt relieved when the houselights dimmed and the curtain lifted, shifting Teddy's attention, and that of most people in the theater, away from Beatrice at last.

An actor in a braided red jacket and paste crown stepped onstage, accompanied by an actress in a glittering rhinestone tiara: most likely the pair playing King John and doomed Queen Emily. Their eyes fixed on the royal box directly across from them, they both sank into a deep reverence.

It was a tradition dating back to the founding of this theater two hundred years ago: any actors portraying royalty must bow and curtsy to the *real* royalty before the show could begin.

The lights softened, gleaming on the reflective sheen of Emily's costume. The rest of the world dissolved into oblivion as she began to sing.

And Beatrice's self-control began to slip.

She'd never heard music this powerful and emotional and poignant. It reached deep into her core, grabbed at the feelings that were tangled there in hot angry knots and unspooled them like a skein of thread. She leaned forward, rapt, her hands clutching tightly at the program. She felt so brittle and transparent that she might snap in two.

Emily sang of nation-building, of legacy and sacrifice. She sang of love gained and lost. And as the score swept toward the end of the first act—as Emily launched into a heart-wrenching ballad about how she would need to give up the person she loved, for the good of her country—Beatrice realized that she was trembling.

She stumbled to her feet and fled, ignoring the startled glances of her family and Teddy. The hallway was mercifully empty, save the flock of her family's security stationed outside the door to their box.

She didn't let their murmured protests slow her down, didn't stop even when her heels almost tripped over the red carpet. She just charged frantically down the hallway, not sure where she was going, knowing only that she couldn't bear to be still.

"Are you all right?" Connor fell into step alongside her. "Did that duke say something to upset you? Because if so, I promise I'll—"

"It's okay. I just got emotional, watching the show." She tried to dab at her eyes without Connor seeing, but he reached into his jacket to give her a handkerchief.

"A musical made you cry," he repeated, with evident disbelief.

Beatrice gave a strangled laugh. "I know it doesn't sound like me." But then, she hadn't really been herself since the Queen's Ball.

She drew to a halt partway down the mezzanine's hallway. Snatches of music drifted through the closed doors to the boxes. The light of the ornate wall sconces fell on Connor's uniform, on his hair, on the molten steel of his eyes. Those eyes were now locked meaningfully on Beatrice's.

So many things lay unspoken between them, and Beatrice didn't know how to begin to say them.

"Connor," she whispered. His name on her lips was a plea, a prayer.

He ventured a step closer, so close that Beatrice could see

each individual freckle dusted over his nose. Her face tilted upward—

"Your Royal Highness! Are you okay?"

At the sound of Teddy's voice, Connor took a quick step back. Beatrice had to bite her lip to keep from reaching for him again.

Quieting the expression on her face, she turned around to where Teddy was striding briskly down the hall in their direction. "I'm fine," she said evenly. "I just needed a minute, after that song."

"And here I thought you weren't really into musicals," Teddy said gently. His eyes drifted to a velvet-covered settee against the wall. "Do you want to wait a minute before we head back?"

Beatrice couldn't help looking over at Connor, who gave an imperceptible shrug. "Whatever you want, Your Royal Highness."

The way he said her title was utterly cold. As if he needed to remind himself, remind *both* of them, of her rank.

Beatrice sank wordlessly onto the cushions, trying not to glance over to where he stood: a few meters away, but most likely within earshot. What was he *thinking*? Was his blood sparking and spinning with as much wild abandon as hers?

Teddy came to sit next to her. Slowly, the panic in Beatrice's veins began to subside. Neither of them rushed to speak, yet the silence didn't feel tense or awkward, just . . . simple. Companionable, even. Perhaps because, alone among all the courtiers she'd met, Teddy had made no demands of her.

Everyone else wanted something. They wanted money or a title or a position in government; they wanted their names next to hers in the papers. Except Teddy. He hadn't asked anything of her, except perhaps for honesty.

Which she wasn't entirely sure she could give.

"When I was little, my parents used to bring me and my siblings to the opening night of every show." Beatrice stared down at her lap, but she could feel Teddy's gaze on her. "Sam always begged my parents to let us leave at intermission."

"Why?"

"She hated unhappy endings. Or really, she hated *all* endings. I think Sam preferred to imagine her own ending, rather than stay and watch everything unravel into a tragedy." Beatrice glanced over at Teddy. "Now I know how she felt."

"We don't have to stay," he offered, and Beatrice knew he understood that this was about more than the musical.

"I'm sorry for running out like that, and for the way everyone was staring at us. I haven't been on a lot of dates before," she fumbled to say, "but I do know that they aren't supposed to go like this."

"Our first date was never going to be normal."

Beatrice managed an uncertain smile. "Probably not, but we still could have gone somewhere without a literal audience."

Teddy chuckled at that, then quieted.

"Beatrice. I want you to know that I . . ." He spoke slowly, as if choosing his words with care. "Respect you," he decided at last.

That didn't sound particularly romantic, but Beatrice realized that Teddy wasn't striving for romance. He was just telling her the truth.

"Thank you," she said cautiously.

"Before we met, I wasn't sure what to expect of you. I didn't realize how thoughtful, and smart, and dedicated you are. You're going to be an amazing first queen. If this was a world where people could, I don't know, *vote* for their monarch, I know that America would still pick you. *I* would pick you."

Elect the king or queen—what a funny concept. Everyone knew that elections only worked for judges and Congress. Making the executive branch pander to the people, go out begging for votes—that could only end in disaster. That structure would attract the wrong sort of people: power-hungry people with twisted agendas.

Teddy gave an uncertain smile. "I realize this is all a setup, that your parents are the ones who asked you to go out with me."

She stiffened. "Teddy . . ."

"I get it," he said smoothly. "I'm under the same kind of pressure."

"You only came here tonight because your parents asked you to?"

"No—I mean yes, they did—but I'm trying to tell you that I understand how it feels. Being the heir to a dukedom isn't that different from being the heir to a kingdom, just on a smaller scale. I know what it's like to have burdens and commitments that other people can't understand. And even if they did understand them . . ."

They would run in the other direction, and leave the tangle of responsibilities with us, Beatrice silently finished.

Teddy shifted on the seat next to her. "I didn't go into this thinking that I would *like* you, but I do. So I hope that our first date isn't also our last."

Beatrice gave a slow nod. He was right: among all the young men her parents had picked for her, Teddy was a pleasant surprise. "Me neither," she admitted.

As they returned to the shadows of the royal box, her family cast her a few curious glances, but Beatrice ignored them. She settled back into her chair, smoothing her black cocktail dress around her legs so that it wouldn't wrinkle.

She told herself that Teddy was right. They might not be *in love* with each other, in a passionate, head-over-heels, romance-novel sort of way, but at the very least they understood each other.

Maybe she was watching for him, or maybe her nerves

were just on high alert, but Beatrice noticed the moment Connor slipped into the box. He planted himself just inside the door, standing in the typical Revere Guard manner, his spine straight, his holstered weapons within reach. She wondered if he'd come here under orders, or out of curiosity—to see the musical that brought even Princess Beatrice to tears.

Some foolish instinct made her try to catch his eye, but Connor didn't look her way. His gaze was fixed on the stage, as inscrutable as ever.

13

SAMANTHA

Not even *Midnight Crown* could distract Samantha from the fact that Teddy Eaton was sitting mere inches from her, on a date with her sister.

She spent the entire second act in a low throbbing agitation, hyperaware of how close Teddy was. So close that Sam could slap him across the face, or grab his shirt with both fists and yank him forward to kiss him.

Honestly, she hadn't ruled out either possibility.

For some masochistic reason, she kept replaying their interaction in her head, examining it from every angle, like a jeweler studying the facets of a gemstone in various lighting. Maybe it was foolish of her, but she'd thought there was something *real* between her and Teddy. What had prompted him to ping-pong from her straight to Beatrice? Was he really just another of those shallow guys who went after Beatrice for the wrong reasons, who wanted nothing more than to be America's first king consort?

How had Sam's instincts about him been so off base?

She was relieved when the performance ended and they all filed into the reception hall for the afterparty. Servers passed with trays of hors d'oeuvres: deviled quail eggs, goat cheese arancini, smoked salmon arranged on tiny slices of cucumber. Most of the cast was already here, still wearing their costumes, their faces slick with makeup and sweat.

"You okay?" Nina asked meaningfully. She knew how difficult it had been for Sam, seeing Teddy with Beatrice.

Sam cast her friend a grateful look. She was so glad Nina had agreed to come with her tonight. Something about her friend's no-nonsense humor, her fierce and unwavering sense of self, made Samantha feel like she could face anything.

"I need a drink," Sam decided. "Want to come?"

Nina hesitated. Her gaze drifted behind Sam and softened imperceptibly. "That's okay. I'll wait for you here," Nina murmured. Sam glanced around, wondering who had prompted that look, but the only person standing there was Jeff.

When she reached the bar, Sam asked the bartender for two glasses of wine and a whiskey sour, just as an all-too-familiar figure stepped up next to her. "No beer tonight?" Teddy asked.

As if it hadn't been enough for him to spend the entirety of the performance tormenting her, now he had to ruin the afterparty, too.

Samantha pursed her lips and said nothing, determined to be cool and aloof. She didn't owe Teddy an answer. She didn't owe him *anything*, even if her traitorous body persisted in leaning toward him. She tried—and failed—not to remember how it had felt, being pressed up against him in the scented darkness of the coatroom.

Teddy seemed determined to try again. "What did you think of the show?"

Sam glanced up at him, her eyes snapping fire. "If you must know," she said coldly, "I thought it was utterly inspired. It reminded me of the Henriad."

She'd expected the reference to go over his head, but to her annoyance, Teddy nodded in understanding. "Of course—Shakespeare's early history plays. Because *Midnight Crown* tells America's story to America the same way that Shakespeare told England's to the English." He smiled at her, an off-kilter smile that set her stupid heart racing. "I wouldn't have pegged you for a Shakespeare enthusiast."

"Right, because Beatrice is the smart one," Sam said venomously. "I'm just the girl you made out with in a closet, until my sister finally deigned to meet with you."

Teddy recoiled at her words. "I'm sorry. That wasn't what I—"

Sam ignored him, reaching for the drinks that the bartender slid toward her. "See you, Teddy." Her peacock-blue dress fluttered around her stilettos as she stalked back across the room toward her friend.

Nina was still chatting with Jeff; the sight of them deep in conversation, their heads tipped together with surprising intimacy, caught Sam off guard. She didn't remember them getting along this well in the past.

"How'd you know I wanted a whiskey?" Jeff exclaimed in delight, reaching for the cocktail as Sam handed Nina one of the glasses of wine.

"That was for *me*, actually, but you can have it," Sam replied. "I love you just that much."

"And here I was thinking our twin telepathy had finally started working." Jeff clinked his glass lightly to hers. "Thanks."

Sam's eyes cut back to Nina. "Why does he keep trying to talk to me?"

"I think Teddy is just trying to be polite," Nina offered, realizing at once who she meant.

Jeff frowned in confusion. "Teddy Eaton? We barely know him."

"Exactly," Samantha snapped. Teddy barely knew her, yet already he had judged her, found her wanting, and upgraded to Beatrice. She swirled her wine over and over, building her own little tornado within the confines of her glass.

"What did he say to you?" Jeff asked, clearly confused.

Nina shot him a warning glance, silently urging him to drop the subject.

"It doesn't matter," Sam said heavily.

She hadn't told her brother about her and Teddy, but she knew he'd sensed that something was going on. When the twins were children, their emotions had always blurred together: whatever one of them was feeling, the other instantly amplified it. Their nanny used to joke that they were incapable of laughing alone or crying alone. Even now, it was hard for one of them to be happy if the other one wasn't.

Samantha forced herself to smile. She hated herself for wondering if Teddy was watching—if he even bothered to care how she felt.

"Let's take a pic," she suggested, holding out her phone for a selfie. Nina, predictably, stepped aside; she never posed in photographs with Sam. Jeff gave an easy grin and sidled closer as Samantha snapped the photo.

"Are you still Fiona von Trapp?" Nina asked.

Samantha swiped across the screen to add silly cartoon sunglasses atop her and Jeff's faces. "Jeff is Spike Wales. That's equally absurd," she pointed out, fighting back a smile.

The twins' social media presence was a source of endless frustration in the palace's PR department. Members of the royal family weren't supposed to have personal profiles; the only approved account was the palace's official one, @WashingtonRoyal, which had a full-time manager and photo editor. Ignoring that rule, Sam and Jeff had created private accounts of their own, using fake names, and limiting their followers to their hundred or so closest friends.

It never lasted. Inevitably, the palace discovered the accounts and shut them down. But Sam and Jeff would just decide upon even more outlandish names, pick out cartoon hedgehogs or unicorns or something equally comical for their profile pictures, and start the whole thing over again.

"I'm starving, and these appetizers are bird food," Jeff announced, draping his arms casually over Sam's and Nina's shoulders and pulling them close together. "Anyone want to go home and order pizza? Or we could stop by a Wawa," he added in a strange tone.

Nina chuckled at that, though Sam didn't really get why. "We'd better text in the order now," she said, setting her still-full wineglass on a side table. Of course, no one actually *delivered* pizza to the palace; they would have to send one of the footmen out in plainclothes to pick it up.

As they headed out of the party and toward the front drive, Samantha reminded herself that it didn't matter what Teddy thought of her. It didn't matter that the entire *world* thought she was less than Beatrice, as long as she had Nina and Jeff. These two people, at least, knew the real her.

Later that evening, Sam yawned as she shimmied into an old T-shirt and silky blue sleep shorts. They had devoured two enormous thin-crust pizzas and watched a bad action movie—the opposite end of the spectrum from *Midnight Crown*, at least as far as cultural sophistication went. She wished Nina had stayed; there was a guest bedroom next to Sam's suite that they normally used for sleepovers. But when she suggested it, Nina had gotten a weird look on her face and stammered that she should probably head to campus.

It dawned on Sam that Nina might be going back for a boy. But if she was dating one of her classmates, why hadn't she told Sam about it?

Sam's thoughts were interrupted by a hesitant knock.

"Come in," she called out, and was startled to see her sister, hovering uncertainly at the entrance to her suite.

"I guess congratulations are in order," Sam heard herself

say. "The internet practically broke itself tonight, drooling over you and Teddy."

"What?"

"You guys are trending nationwide. Hashtag #Beadore." Sam gave a derisive snort. "Personally, if I was going to smash your names together, I would have gone with Theotrice, but no one asked me."

"Oh . . . all right." Beatrice looked surprisingly young and vulnerable in a white silk robe and pajama set. Her hair, which earlier tonight had been twisted into an intricate updo, spilled in a great dark river over one shoulder. "I didn't see you at the afterparty," she went on.

"Nina and Jeff left early with me, to get pizza." Sam was surprised by the hurt that darted across Beatrice's face. Was she feeling left out? "Did you want something?" she went on, with a little less bitterness.

Beatrice sighed. "Sorry to bother you. I just . . . I keep wondering . . ."

Sam's resentment began to gutter and die out. She couldn't remember the last time Beatrice had come to her room like this. They lived just down the hall from each other, but they might as well have been on separate continents.

"What is it?" Sam gestured to her couch, an eighteenth-century love seat that she'd unearthed in palace storage and reupholstered in a bright persimmon-colored silk.

Beatrice sank wordlessly onto the cushions. She glanced around the room with something like confusion, as if she were seeing it for the first time—the mismatched bamboo tables, the multicolored pillows. Sam had the strangest sensation that her sister was trying to figure out how to ask for her advice, or maybe her *help*.

"Do you think Aunt Margaret is happy?"

Whatever Sam had expected, it wasn't that. She sat tentatively on the other side of the couch. "What do you mean?"

Beatrice played idly with the fringe of a silk pillow. "Because she was in love with that airplane pilot when she was younger, and Grandma and Grandpa made her give him up."

"They didn't *make her* do anything. Aunt Margaret could have married him if she wanted. But she would have given up her titles and income and status, and relinquished her place in the order of succession. If she'd *really* loved him, don't you think she would have chosen him anyway?" Sam had always thought of the pilot as just another of Aunt Margaret's youthful acts of rebellion. Which Sam could relate to.

"Maybe she did love him, but felt that it was impossible for them to be together, because she was a princess," Beatrice said softly.

"I don't know." Sam shrugged. "She wasn't the heir to the throne. If they'd gotten married, she wouldn't have even been exiled or anything. She could have found a way to make her life work."

Beatrice's head shot up. "Exiled?"

"A British king tried to marry a commoner and was forced to abdicate over it. He lived in Paris the rest of his life."

Her sister blanched, hugging the silk pillow tighter to her chest.

Sam shot her a confused look. "Beatrice, what is this really about?"

Before her sister could reply, steps thundered down the hallway, and another knock sounded at Sam's door. It opened to reveal the king and queen.

"Beatrice! Here you are," their dad exclaimed, his features creased in a smile.

Of course he hadn't actually come to Sam's room looking for Sam.

The queen smiled at Samantha, but then her eyes, too, rounded on Beatrice. "You and Teddy looked like you were getting along tonight. Everyone certainly loved seeing you together."

Sam wondered if her parents had seen the internet's wild surge of excitement at #Beadore.

"He's very nice," Beatrice replied. *Nice*—the most meaningless of all adjectives. A word you reserved for distant acquaintances and events you had no desire to attend.

Did Beatrice even *like* Teddy?

"Of course, it was just a first date," Beatrice added, as if to explain away her lack of gushing enthusiasm.

Their parents exchanged a glance. "We've been thinking the same thing. Which is why we invited Teddy to Telluride for New Year's," the king announced proudly.

"You invited Teddy to Telluride?" Beatrice's voice scraped wildly over the words, with something that might have been panic.

The queen tilted her head, puzzled. "We thought it would be a fantastic way to accelerate things. Help you get to know Teddy in a familiar, low-stress setting."

From the way Beatrice's nostrils flared in panic, it seemed like this was hardly low-stress. "Right," she hedged. "It's just . . . Telluride has always been our private place, where we get to be together as a family, and now you've invited someone who's practically a stranger."

"He's not a stranger. We've known the Eatons for generations," the king countered.

This was too much. Sam wasn't sure why Beatrice didn't want Teddy there, but whatever her reasons, they were in agreement for once. Sam had no desire to spend her New Year's vacation watching Teddy on an extended date with her sister.

"This is moving a little fast," she interjected. "From first date to a weekend away—what will people think? Maybe Beatrice should wait until we're back, and then if she wants to ask Teddy out a second time, she can do it then."

Beatrice shot Sam a grateful look, but the king waved away her protest. "Don't worry about the message it sends. Teddy will be staying in the guest cottage, not the main house. The way Daphne used to."

Daphne Deighton was the only significant other who'd ever gotten an invite to Telluride. It wasn't lost on Samantha that her father had just equated Jeff's three-year former relationship to the guy Beatrice had gone out with *once*.

"Besides," the queen persisted, "we're never there as a family, just us. Jeff is inviting Ethan this year, and Sam, aren't you bringing Nina?"

"Yeah," Sam admitted.

Beatrice nodded, having obviously realized that she wasn't going to win this one. "No, you're right. Bringing Teddy to Telluride is a good idea. Thank you for thinking of it." She stood up, her movements stiff and jerky, almost robotic.

"Beatrice," Sam ventured. Didn't her sister want to finish talking about . . . well, whatever it was they were talking about?

Beatrice just shook her head, her eyes hollow-looking. "Good night, Sam." She followed their parents out of the room, her white robe billowing in her wake. The door shut behind her with a resounding thud.

14

NINA

The Washingtons had gathered at the top of Bald Mountain, the breathtaking backdrop of the Rockies falling away behind them. Sunlight glittered over the pristine white snow. Watching them tease and torment one another, you might almost have thought they were any other family, posing for a quick picture before tearing down the slopes.

Except this wasn't a normal vacation photo, but an all-press photo call.

The palace's PR office had long ago struck a bargain with the various media outlets: the royal family would conduct an interview at the start of their annual trip to Telluride, in exchange for complete privacy thereafter. It was much like the deal that had protected Beatrice while she was in college, where she did an in-depth interview once a year, and otherwise was able to move around Cambridge relatively unbothered.

Nina still couldn't quite believe that she'd come on this trip after all. Just a few weeks ago she'd been certain that she would stay in the capital: go to the party that Rachel was planning, have a *normal* New Year's Eve for once. But that was before she went out with Jeff, and everything changed.

It hadn't been easy keeping this a secret. At Christmas with her family, Nina had to constantly check herself to keep from mentioning the prince. She and Jeff were texting nonstop;

Nina had even changed his name to *Alex* in her phone, just in case anyone happened to glance at her screen while she was typing. Who would ever expect the vaguely-labeled *Alex* was actually the prince?

They'd seen each other alone just a couple of times since that first date, always somewhere public where Jeff went incognito. Nina didn't dare bring him to campus, where he would definitely get recognized, and she was too scared to hang out at the palace, in case Samantha caught them together.

They kept seeking excuses to attend the same events, if only for more chances to be near each other. Jefferson had even come to the *theater* for once, simply because Nina had told him she would be there with Sam.

Hiding it from Samantha was the worst part. So many times, Nina had felt herself on the verge of telling her best friend everything, but some innate cautiousness, or perhaps fear, restrained her. It wasn't that Nina worried about Sam's reaction. If anything, Sam would get too excited at the news, and end up spilling the secret to the rest of the world.

And Nina couldn't help thinking that if she and Jeff weren't going to last, she would rather Sam never find out at all. As weird as things would be for the three of them once Sam knew that Nina and Jeff were secretly together, it would be even *weirder* if they then broke up—and Sam had to deal with her brother and her best friend as exes.

Being in Telluride as Sam's guest rather than Jeff's was equal parts bliss and torture. Sometimes, when no one was looking, he would sneak up behind her and pull her into his arms, or spin her around to drop a lingering kiss on her lips. Just last night at dinner, the prince had taken the seat next to Nina. She'd been so distracted by the feel of his leg brushing against hers that she'd almost forgotten to eat.

He was standing now with the rest of his family, their skis

and snowboards carefully posed before them, their boots crunching on the snow. Almost everyone was here: the king and queen and the twins. The king's younger brother, Richard, Duke of Manchester, and his wife, Evelyn, along with their two small children, Annabel and Percy, who were currently drawing stick figures in the snow with the points of their ski poles. The king's older sister, Samantha's wild and controversial aunt Margaret, Duchess of Louisiana, and her husband, Nate. The Hollywood Hottie, the press liked to call him, because he was a soap-opera actor, and ten years younger than Margaret—luckily for her, he also happened to be the grandson of a viscount, otherwise their marriage wouldn't have been approved. The Queen Mother had tried on numerous occasions to make Nate give up his work; she didn't want members of the royal family engaged in something so openly commercial, so *trashy*. But Nate cheerfully ignored her complaints. Nina had always liked him for that.

The only member of the Washington family noticeably absent was Princess Beatrice, who would be joining them tomorrow afternoon.

Nina had observed plenty of photo calls through the years. She was used to being shuffled to one side and asked to wait until the interview was over. Today she had stationed herself beneath the overhang of a chairlift, a few yards past the raucous bubble of photographers and reporters. Jeff's friend Ethan Beckett stood next to her, alongside Teddy Eaton.

It couldn't be easy on Sam, having Teddy here in Telluride. Nina worried that it would only get worse once Beatrice arrived at the house tomorrow, and Sam was forced to observe their flirting at close range.

"All right, everyone!" The king's chamberlain, Lord Robert Standish, shouted over the noise of the photographers. He looked a bit ridiculous in his typical navy suit, his only concession to the cold weather a patriotic striped scarf, but

Robert had always been a stickler for protocol. No matter the conditions.

"We'll take a few questions at this time," he offered, with all the self-importance of someone who delivers news about people more powerful than himself.

"Who's the surprise entertainment at this year's New Year's party?" one of the press corps called out. The clacking of cameras was like the sound of a million insects.

"If we announced that, it wouldn't be a surprise." The queen gave a good-natured smile.

The Washingtons' private New Year's Eve party, at local members-only club Smuggler's, was the event of the year. Nina had heard of noble families who rented houses in Telluride for the week, just *hoping* that they would run into the king on the slopes and snag a last-minute invite. Someone world-famous always ended up giving a private performance—a pop star or comedian, or once, a boy band Beatrice had been a little obsessed with.

"I'd say this beats being in Urquhart's lecture right now," Ethan drawled, sliding closer on his snowboard.

Nina realized, startled, that the comment had been directed at her. She kept forgetting that Ethan was also a freshman at King's College this year. "Wait—you're in the World History class?"

"Yeah." He shrugged. "I assumed you were, too. You don't seem like the type to leave mandatory credits until senior year."

Nina nodded absently, wondering why she hadn't seen Ethan around campus more. Then again, King's College *was* a big school.

She and Ethan had known each other for years. It was inevitable that their paths kept crossing, given how close they both were to the twins. But Nina would never have ventured to claim that they were friends. No matter how often he laughed or lounged around with the others, she couldn't shake the sense that Ethan was holding something back, out of self-preservation or wariness.

"What do you think of all this?" Ethan asked, edging his board a little closer.

Nina wondered why Ethan was bothering with her now, when he'd never paid her much attention before.

"It's just a press call. We've both seen our fair share of them," she said easily.

Still, Nina couldn't help glancing back over at the Washingtons, so artfully arranged against that dramatic background. The lights of the cameras flashed over their perfect white smiles and dark hair, their flawless golden-brown tans. When they stood all together like that, there was something sleek and powerful about them, something that left Nina with an unbidden foreboding.

"Jeff!" shouted one of the reporters. "We keep hearing rumors that you're seeing someone. Who is it?"

Nina's heart skipped a beat.

The *Daily News* correspondent chimed in, thrusting her microphone forward. "Is it Daphne Deighton? All of America keeps hoping you and Daphne will get back together."

"You know I don't comment on my love life," Jeff said tightly.

"So you *are* seeing someone!" one of the reporters cried out, elated.

"Who is she?"

"What's her name?"

"*Is it Daphne?*"

Nina began stomping the heel of her boot angrily into the snow, the way that ten-year-old Annabel had been doing not so long ago.

"What the prince means is *no comment*." Robert stepped

smoothly between Jeff and the reporter. "And that will be all for today. Let's give Their Majesties a chance to enjoy the snow, shall we?"

There was a final burst of flashbulbs, and then the Washingtons quickly dispersed: Aunt Margaret whooshing down the slope in pursuit of her Hollywood Hottie, Richard and Evelyn leading their children off to a private instructor. The press corps began the laborious process of packing up their cameras and gear, to load it into the snowmobiles that would cart them back down the mountain.

Jeff strapped his foot into his binding and snowboarded the few yards toward them. "Sorry about that."

"I know," Nina replied quietly, just as Ethan said, "No problem."

Oh, right. Jeff had been talking to Ethan, apologizing that he'd been forced to wait through yet another press call. Nina had thought it was for *her*, that Jeff was sorry the paparazzi had somehow found out about them.

Ethan cast her a sharp glance, as if wondering what she meant. Because of course, Nina wasn't *supposed* to be here for Jeff. She was here for Samantha, her best friend.

Sam chose that moment to join them, cutting a razor-sharp turn so that her arrival flung a spray of ice crystals into their faces.

"Hey!" Nina cried out, wiping the snow from her shoulders. Sam laughed. It was her dad's laugh, that great Washington roar of laughter that sparked an answering smile in everyone.

"Sorry, but you all looked drowsy," she said, not sounding sorry at all. "Consider this your official wake-up."

"I knew I would regret brewing you that second mug of coffee," Jeff countered, though he was smiling.

"I blame the frosted bear claw as much as the coffee." Nina

directed the comment at Sam, though she was watching Jeff's mouth for a smile.

Sam ignored them, reaching up to pull her goggles down over her eyes. "Where are you guys headed? I'm thinking if we want to do Prospect, we should go now, before it gets choppy and skied-over."

"That sounds perfect," said Teddy, who'd been quiet up to this point.

Nina hoped she was the only one who saw Sam flinch at his words. "You go ahead. I just remembered something." The princess pulled her phone from her pocket as if to send a text, though Nina saw she was really just scrolling through her social media feeds.

Jeff's eyes lit on Nina's, then darted rapidly away. "Last one to the lift is in charge of the hot-tub jets!" he called out, and dropped down into the slope, Ethan and Teddy on his heels.

Nina turned to Sam, but the princess's eyes had widened at something on her phone. "You won't *believe* who's in Telluride!" Sam answered her own question before Nina could hazard a guess. *"Daphne Deighton."*

"Really," Nina said carefully. It was an effort to keep her features bland and disinterested. Just when things seemed to be going so well, she would have to face Jeff's ex-girlfriend?

"I know, it makes her look totally desperate," Sam agreed, misunderstanding.

Sam and Daphne had never really gotten along—though they'd pretended to, for Jeff's sake. Nina wasn't sure why, but Sam didn't like Daphne. It was the biggest thing the twins had ever disagreed upon.

"We need to find someone else for Jeff to date, so that he doesn't relapse and end up back with *her*," Sam declared.

Nina made a strange noise of protest that she quickly tried to hide with a cough. "I think you might be overreacting."

Sam only smiled as she shoved her phone into her pocket and kicked off. Nina hurried to follow.

Halfway down the run, she took a narrow traverse through the trees, only to realize she'd gone the wrong way. She'd missed the turnoff for the Prospect lift.

Though she'd learned to snowboard alongside Jeff and Samantha, Nina had never gotten the hang of it the way they did. The twins loved extreme terrain, which required sharp turns and serious finesse. While most of the time, Nina secretly wished she could call Ski Patrol to come collect her, and have them take her home in what Jeff and Sam called the "toboggan of shame."

She turned her board edge-on to the mountain, slowing almost to a halt, leaning back as she scraped down the traverse inch by painstaking inch.

"I knew you'd come this way."

Nina whirled around, breathless—and saw the prince off to one side, his board slung casually over his shoulder.

"Jeff! How did you . . . ?"

"Because you always miss that turnoff. Every year." He grinned and pulled her a few feet down, into the thick cover of the trees. Nina let out a startled yelp.

"Shh." Jeff set his board to one side and stepped forward, trapping her against the broad trunk of a tree. He braced both gloved hands against the frozen bark to hold Nina in place. Not that she wanted to go anywhere.

She could see the cloud of his breath in the cold winter air, mingling with her own.

"Aren't you worried about being the last one to the lift?" she managed to say. No one ever wanted to be on hot-tub-jet duty. It meant that while everyone else was warm in the water, you had to run across the patio and hit the button that turned the jets on for another thirty-minute cycle.

"I have more important things on my mind right now."

Still pinning her there, as if he was terrified she might change her mind and snowboard away from him, Jeff reached to unsnap her helmet and pull it off her head. He began trailing a line of soft, teasing kisses along her jawline.

Nina went still, her eyes fluttering shut. Jeff's lips were freezing, but his tongue was hot. The twin sensations of ice and fire sent shivers of longing through her body, fusing deep within her into something sharp and newly forged. She kept trying to twist her head, to catch Jeff's mouth with her own, but he seemed determined to torture her.

When Nina couldn't take it anymore, she reached around his waist to grab fistfuls of his jacket, yanking him closer. Her hair brushed against the tree as she tipped her head back, arcing into the kiss with reckless abandon. In the distance, they could still hear scattered laughter and the whoosh of skiers gliding past.

"I guess we should head down," Jeff finally said, with obvious reluctance.

Nina's blood pounded with adrenaline. "You should at least give me a head start. It's the chivalrous thing to do."

She gave him one last rushed kiss before setting off downhill, unable to stop smiling.

That night, Nina stood just inside her doorway, rising on tiptoe and lowering back down again. She was waiting for silence—for all the rustling and footfalls and general ambient noises of an eighteen-bedroom house to finally fall still.

At least she was here as Sam's friend. If Jeff had invited her, Nina knew she would have been relegated to the guest cottage, the way Daphne used to be. There was a twenty-four-hour security guard stationed on the property, which would complicate things if she tried to sneak across the yard back to the main house. She wondered how Jeff and Daphne used to do it, then flinched at the thought.

There was no point in tormenting herself with questions about Jeff's ex-girlfriend. So what if Daphne was in Telluride right now? Maybe they wouldn't run into her at all.

When Nina judged that she'd lingered long enough, she held her breath and darted silently into the hallway, tiptoeing along the corridor until she reached Jeff's room.

"Finally!" He pulled the door shut behind her. "I was worried you might not be coming."

"I had to wait until the coast was clear."

Jeff's room was larger than Nina's, though decorated in the same style: suede pillows, a braided rope ottoman, cozy cashmere blankets. On one wall hung a series of framed black-and-white photographs that the former king had taken in the mountains.

Nina sank gratefully onto Jeff's bed, tugging his arm to pull him down next to her.

"Nina," Jeff began, and the way he said her name, Nina knew he'd been thinking about this for a while. "I still don't understand all the secrecy. Why can't we at least tell Sam?"

She tried to play it off in a lighthearted way. "Sam can't keep a secret. Remember how she ruined your parents' twentieth wedding anniversary?"

"She didn't mean to," Jeff reminded her. The Washington siblings had tried to plan a surprise anniversary party for their parents, but the surprise was blown when the *Post* got wind of their plans and ran a story about it the week before. Apparently Samantha had gossiped about the party at a brunch with some friends, and another table had overheard them.

"I mean it," Jeff insisted. "When that reporter asked today whether I was dating anyone, all I wanted was to shout about you to the whole world. How much longer do we need to keep it a secret?"

Nina ran a hand over the red-and-black tartan of his bed-spread. She didn't know how to explain the confusing geometry of her emotions: that she was falling for Jeff all over again, and far too fast. And whatever this was between them, it was still too uncertain, too eggshell fragile, for her to share it.

She took a shallow breath. "I'm just not ready to tell anyone. Once we do . . . it won't be just us anymore." Their relationship would be public property.

"Why is that such a bad thing? People are going to find out eventually."

"Because they won't approve! I'm different from the type of girl America wants you to be with, and it *scares* me, okay?"

To his credit, Jeff didn't automatically dismiss her objections, or tell her that none of those things mattered to him, the way he had last time. He was silent for a while.

"I can't pretend to know how everyone will react," Jeff said at last. "But I don't care about public opinion, and neither do you. For what it's worth, I like the ways that you're different. I like that you're smart, and ambitious, and that you call me out when I'm wrong. That you talk to *me*, and not to my titles, the way everyone else does."

"Wait a minute, you have titles? This changes *everything*."

She made as if to push him away, but he circled his hands around her wrists and held her close. His eyes danced appreciatively. "You're funny. I'll take two of you, please."

"As if you could handle two of me," she scoffed.

Jeff laughed, a great hearty laugh that seemed to emanate from deep within his chest. "True," he conceded. "I'm in enough trouble with just the one."

She settled against him, her head tipped onto his shoulder. His hand curled around her waist, not in a demanding way, but simply because it seemed to belong there.

"I'm sorry," Nina said at last, "but can't I just . . . keep you to myself, for a little while longer?"

Jeff smiled. "No arguments here. I quite like when you keep me to yourself."

The wind crooned as it brushed the snow against the windows. It felt like the rest of the world no longer existed: as if they had fallen under a temporary spell, and there was nothing but the two of them, and this moment.

Nina shifted. "You know, I seem to remember that we had some unfinished business from this afternoon."

"Did we now?" Jeff's voice was a low rumble.

Nina's hair fell loose around them, curtaining their faces as she leaned forward to kiss him.

Out there was the world: cold and harsh, full of contradictions and judgment. Out there, he was His Highness Jefferson George Alexander Augustus, while Nina was a commoner whose mom *worked* for his family. But here, in this cocoon of golden warmth, they were safe.

Here they were just a boy and a girl, kissing in a cabin in the mountains.

15

DAPHNE

Daphne made slow, wide turns down the last fifty meters, drawing to a halt at the entrance to the Apex lift. There was still no sign of Jefferson.

The liftie, a guy in a Raiders beanie with a scruffy beard, gave her a puzzled smile, as if he knew that he should recognize her, but couldn't remember what she was famous for. It needled Daphne a little, though she hated to admit it.

Or maybe he didn't recognize her at all, and was looking at her with such confusion because he couldn't understand why she was heading up yet again, repeating the same exact run she'd been skiing for the past hour and a half.

This was the first time in three years that Daphne hadn't been invited to join the royal family for New Year's, but she wasn't about to let a small detail like that stop her. She and her parents had come to Telluride themselves, renting a hotel room for the week, so that Daphne could find an opportunity to oh-so-conveniently run into the prince.

Which was why she was here, lapping off of Apex, alone. She'd skied with Jefferson and Ethan enough to feel certain that they would end up on this run: it was their favorite place to ski on mornings like this, when it was warm enough to soften the top layer of snow.

Except that Jefferson was nowhere to be seen. Daphne cast another glance back over her shoulder—and caught sight of a figure in a nondescript gray parka, snowboarding over from Ophir Loop. She allowed herself a slow, dangerous smile. She would recognize that particular shade of gray anywhere.

There were a few other people here with Jefferson: his uncle Richard; his aunt Margaret and her husband, Nate; a protection officer. And, of course, Ethan.

Daphne poled to one side and bent over in a pretense of tightening her boots. When she heard them coasting toward the entrance to the lift, she turned around slowly, for maximum effect. She was well aware how amazing she looked, even in ski gear. Her all-black ensemble—a thin down parka with a hood trimmed in rabbit fur, ergonomic stretchy pants that belted at the waist—was surprisingly chic. No one would know that she'd spent months monitoring the luxury sports websites, ready to buy it all the instant it went on super sale.

"Jefferson!" she exclaimed, in a show of surprise, and turned brightly to the others. "And Your Highnesses, Ethan. It's good to see you all."

The twins' uncle Richard smiled warmly at her, but Aunt Margaret, who was wearing a yellow one-piece ski suit that made her look curiously like a tall skiing banana, gave her a cool nod before deliberately turning aside. She was the only one who didn't like Daphne.

Well, aside from Samantha. No matter how intensely Daphne had amped up her charm, Jefferson's twin sister had never warmed to her. Eventually Daphne had given up trying, and treated the princess with the same pleasant cordiality that she did everyone else.

Jefferson pulled out one of his earbuds: he always listened to music while snowboarding, despite constant protests from the king and queen, who worried that it was somehow unsafe. "Hey, Daph. I didn't know you were in town this weekend."

She thrilled a little at his use of the old nickname. "My

161

parents and I decided at the last minute. Were you about to head up?" she added, her eyes cutting toward the lift.

Jefferson nodded, and her chest seized in relief. She felt the weight of everyone's gazes on them as they poled over to the loading station. Daphne was gratified by the flash of recognition on the liftie's face when he realized that the other person on the chair was Prince Jefferson. Now, at least, he finally recognized her.

With any luck he might phone in a tip to one of the national magazines, that she and the prince were spotted skiing together in Telluride.

She tucked her poles beneath one of her pant legs, resisting the urge to pull the safety bar down. Jefferson always scoffed at anyone who needed it. So she swallowed her fear and leaned back, trying not to think of how far they were above the cold hard ground, rushing on at a thousand feet per minute.

"It's good to see you, Jefferson." It felt strange, talking to him in such a stilted way, as if they barely knew each other—worse even than when they'd first started dating, all those years ago. "How's the trip going?"

"You know how it is," he said, with a laugh. *I do know,* Daphne thought furiously. "My mom and Aunt Margaret are constantly at each other's throats, and Percy and Annabel keep racing up and down the stairs early in the mornings, when we're all still trying to sleep. We're pretty much the same as always."

It stung a little, that it was so apparently easy for Jefferson to be in Telluride without her, when to Daphne this place was indelibly printed with their memories. So much of their relationship had unfolded here. All those long afternoons when Samantha would lead them off piste into the glades, and Jefferson and Daphne would laugh and follow. Stopping at the crêpe stand for a chocolate-almond crêpe, which they would eat right there, standing up, because it was piping hot and they were too impatient to wait. Lingering in the hot tub until their fingertips were pruney, talking about anything and nothing.

The ski house was where Jefferson first told Daphne that he loved her.

The slopes fell away before them as their chair climbed ever higher. To their right, behind a curtain of snow-dusted fir trees, Daphne could see the glittering curves of a run called Allais Alley. Over the steep back side of the mountain lay the Revelation Bowl, its broad white canvas crisscrossed by the lines of various skiers. Nestled between the sleeping forms of the mountains was the village of Telluride itself, the distance making it look like the miniature toy town that the royal family used to put beneath their Christmas tree.

Daphne had realized early on how important Telluride was to the Washingtons. It represented their chance to get away, to close their doors and briefly let down their guard. Two generations of Washingtons had honeymooned at this very house after their weddings. And some of the most famous photos of the royal family had been taken here, like the infamous one of the king skiing with Princess Samantha on his shoulders. He was given a lot of safety lectures after that incident.

Daphne had worried that her skiing ability might be a deal-breaker—that she might lose Jefferson's interest if she couldn't keep up with him on the slopes—and therefore had thrown herself into ski lessons with an almost violent aggression. Her decision to ski, rather than snowboard like Jefferson did, had been a no-brainer: Queen Adelaide and Princess Beatrice skied, and therefore so would Daphne.

"How was your Christmas?" Jefferson asked.

"It was great," Daphne said automatically, though she'd kept so busy that Christmas had come and gone almost without her noticing. It wasn't as if her family was the type to curl up with cookies and carols, anyway.

Daphne had spent the holiday season at a whirlwind of public events. She'd attended the opening of the National Portrait Gallery's new exhibit, a welcome reception in honor of Lady Siqi, the new ambassadress from China, and dozens of Christmas carol concerts. She had RSVP'd yes to so many cocktail parties and benefits that she sometimes stopped by five events in a single night. Daphne kept hoping that Jefferson might turn up at one of them, might see her and realize just how much he missed her. By the end, she felt like the bait at the end of a fishing hook, being tossed over and over into the water, waiting powerlessly for the prince to bite.

He didn't bite. He didn't even attend any of those events. The only member of the royal family Daphne kept seeing was Princess Beatrice, often accompanied by Theodore Eaton.

If only she'd gone to the opening-night performance of *Midnight Queen*. She could so easily have been there; she knew plenty of people who rented a box for the season, many of whom owed her a favor in some form or another. But Daphne hadn't guessed that Jefferson would attend a *musical*, not when he hadn't been to a single one in all the years they'd dated. The king and queen must have insisted on it, for Beatrice's first public outing with Teddy.

They were nearing the end of the lift; Daphne needed to say something now, or lose her chance. "To be honest, it was a weird Christmas," she told Jefferson. "It didn't feel the same without you."

"Daphne . . ." The prince edged closer on the chair, his dark eyes burning.

They'd reached the unloading point. Whatever he'd been about to tell her, he let it go, placing his back foot between his bindings and slipping down a few meters. By the time Daphne had untucked her poles and come to join him, his grin was as bright and careless as ever.

"The snow looked great over on Giant Steps," she offered.

Jefferson gave an easy nod. "I'm always game to do Steps."
Behind them, the rest of the group had disembarked from
the chairlift. Daphne was relieved to see them ski farther
down, toward one of the other, less intense runs that fed off
this lift.

Jefferson had already edged down to the entrance to Giant
Steps. It was a thin funnel that shot just below the chairlift,
and hadn't been groomed in what looked like weeks. The
snow was deep, thick banks piling up on the edges as people
turned down the steep middle.

Daphne was about to drop into the chute when Ethan
coasted over. He slid to a stop directly in her path.

"What are you doing here, Daphne?"

"I was *trying* to ski, except that you seem to be in my way."

"Are you really this desperate?" Ethan stared at her through
the curved lens of his blue-tinted goggles. "You don't seriously expect any of us to think this was a coincidence?"

"I don't really care what you think."

As if she was about to share her plans with Ethan Beckett.
Daphne played her own game and kept her own counsel, and
the last thing she needed was his interference.

Ethan didn't budge. "Daphne . . . I'm pretty sure that Jeff
is with someone else now."

She laughed. "Is this because of what Natasha said at the
photo call? Because *I'm* the one who planted that question."
Anything to get Jefferson thinking about her again, to remind
him how much America adored the idea of the two of them
together.

"No," Ethan persisted. "There's something going on between him and Nina."

"Nina?" Daphne scoured her memory of St. Ursula's, of
all the various daughters and granddaughters of the aristocracy, but couldn't think of a single one named Nina.

"Samantha's friend, Nina Gonzalez."

"The Minister of the Treasury's daughter?"

Ethan snorted. "I should have known that's how you would think of her. In terms of her proximity to power."

Daphne ignored him. She could have laughed from sheer relief. Of course she knew Nina—that girl with split ends and atrocious fashion sense, who was always trailing along after Samantha, probably hoping to get invited on another five-star vacation.

"You're wrong," Daphne said dismissively.

"I don't think so."

"Did you *see* them together?" She hated herself for the way her voice rose with the question.

"They've been staring at each other all weekend. And at the press call yesterday—"

"Jealousy isn't a good look on you," Daphne cut in. She pushed past Ethan, and this time, he didn't stop her.

The run was narrower than Daphne remembered, forcing her up onto her edges for each rapid turn. Far below she saw Jefferson's gray form, carving loosely down the center of the run.

She knew that Ethan's instincts about these things were usually right. But even if Nina and Jefferson were hooking up—which Daphne tried her best not to think about too closely—there was no way that Jefferson could be *serious* about a girl like that.

A bank of ominous clouds gathered in the distance. It would snow soon; Daphne could feel the landscape holding its breath in anticipation. Pines rose on either side of the path, their heavy branches dusted with white. A bird burst from the trees in a flurry of falling snow.

Daphne loved skiing—the pulse of blurred colors around her, the powerful, tensed sensation of carving turns into the side of the mountain. She loved the profound, hallowed silence, the only sound the hiss of the crisp powder as she sliced through it. When she was skiing, Daphne felt like she had control over everything in her life, over the entire *world*, even over gravity itself.

She was gaining on Jefferson. He had more mass than she did, but he was turning lazily, while Daphne flung herself forward like an arrow from a bow. She knew she'd long since left Ethan in her dust. Maybe he hadn't even dared try this run at all. The thought was inordinately satisfying.

"That was incredible," she exclaimed, after she had finally caught up with the prince. Her shins were sore from pressing against her boots, and her quads burned pleasantly.

"Seriously." Jefferson's smile echoed her own. He pulled off his helmet and ran a hand through his damp hair. Even now, sweaty and breathing heavily, he looked tall, dark, and handsome, like a prince from a storybook.

Jefferson waited for Ethan to make his way toward them before nodding at the chairlift. "Should we head back up?"

"Absolutely."

Grinning, Jefferson reached down to unfasten his back binding, then began to shuffle toward the entrance to the lift. Daphne curled her gloved hands around the grips of her poles and followed, still smiling her bright, perfect smile.

She would show Ethan just how wrong he was. She had already come this far; she would get Jefferson back, no matter the cost.

No matter what she had to do to poor Nina Gonzalez, to push her out of the way.

16

BEATRICE

The plane's windows were nothing but a frosted darkness. Still, Beatrice kept staring out them anyway, because she couldn't bear to glance across from her: where Connor sat, reading a hardcover book, ignoring her.

They had traveled like this, just the two of them on a small plane, so many times before. Beatrice secretly looked forward to those flights. It was one of the only opportunities she and Connor had to simply *talk*, for hours on end: about their families, or politics, or whatever bad movie they'd put on to pass the time, while they munched on bagged popcorn from the plane's onboard snack drawer. If the pilots were curious about how unusually close the princess seemed with her bodyguard, they were too professional to ever say anything.

But it had been this way between her and Connor for weeks now, their usual camaraderie and easy conversation replaced by a strange, strained silence. Beatrice had no idea what he was thinking. His face revealed nothing as he accompanied her everywhere she went, to ribbon-cuttings and meetings with ministers. And on dates with Teddy.

Things had accelerated after her dad invited him to Telluride the night of the musical. They'd gone out several times since then, to parties and charity functions and once on a school visit.

Beatrice knew that America was infatuated with their relationship. Most of the press had started calling Teddy her *boyfriend*—and to her utter surprise, Teddy had picked up the term, and started referring to Beatrice as his girlfriend.

It seemed particularly strange given that they hadn't even kissed.

Perhaps Teddy was waiting for some cue from her. That was fine with Beatrice; she had no desire to rush things. She hadn't pushed Teddy to explain any further, but she still remembered what he'd said at the theater, that he was under obligations just as pressing as hers.

She wondered whether he was enjoying Telluride. Somehow she couldn't muster up an ounce of regret that she'd stayed in town for the Maddux Center's day of service, and would be arriving a day late. Her parents had done their best to talk her out of it, reminding her in a pointed tone that Teddy was going to Telluride as *her* guest. Well, Beatrice hadn't been the one to invite him.

As she told her parents, she and her father would need to fly on separate planes anyway—the first in the line of succession could never travel with the reigning monarch, for security reasons—so what difference did it make if she stayed in the capital an extra day?

Secretly, Beatrice was relieved that she would arrive late, and save herself that extra day of forced intimacy with Teddy.

Her thoughts were interrupted by a violent swoop as the plane jolted through sudden turbulence.

"Your Royal Highness." The pilot's words emanated from the speakers. "Unfortunately, due to the weather, we won't be able to land at Telluride Airport as planned. Air traffic control insists that we divert to Montrose Regional. I'm sorry—I told them who the passenger was," he added apologetically. "But they were very firm."

"I understand. Thank you." Beatrice's mind felt oddly

numb. Montrose? It was at least two hours' drive from Telluride.

The pilots must have been landing by instruments alone, because there was no visibility; their plane descended through a cloud of opaque white. Beatrice said a prayer of gratitude when they touched down smoothly on the runway.

A dark SUV had already pulled up alongside the private jet, its driver rushing out to collect their luggage from the plane's cargo hold. The snow fell more heavily now, fast and thick as rain, obscuring Beatrice's vision. It dissolved in icy sparks on her skin.

She bundled herself into the backseat of the waiting car. Connor slid in alongside her, bringing a cold rush of air in with him.

"Your Royal Highness," the driver said hesitantly, as he backed out of the parking lot, "I have more bad news. They just closed both highways due to unsafe road conditions. There's no way you'll make it to Telluride tonight."

♛

Barely an hour later, she and Connor were standing in a tiny cottage on the outskirts of Montrose. It wasn't exactly what Beatrice was used to, but her options had been fairly limited, given that it was late at night and in blizzard conditions.

The woman who owned the property had been nearly apoplectic with anxiety when she realized her guest's identity. She had signed the standard NDA, of course, but she'd still insisted on trudging here through the storm to open the front door herself. There was a lot of curtsying and *Your Majesty*-ing, which Beatrice acknowledged with a smile. She didn't have the heart to tell the woman that Your Majesty was an honorific reserved exclusively for the king and queen.

When the woman finally retreated, Connor cleared his

throat. "Sorry there wasn't anything more . . . spacious. I'll sleep on the floor, of course."

Oh. Beatrice hadn't fully registered that there was only one bed.

"Don't be ridiculous. You should at least take the couch." To hide her confusion, she knelt before the fireplace and began to build a fire.

"Let me do that," Connor offered, when he saw what the princess was up to. Beatrice shook her head.

"My grandfather taught me to build a fire. He said it was a critical life skill." Methodically, she stacked larger logs atop the smaller ones, adding bunched-up newspaper as tinder beneath. "Besides, it's nice for me to get to do something useful, for once. I don't often have the chance."

"Everything you do is useful," Connor insisted.

A lock of hair fell into her eyes; Beatrice blew out a breath to toss it back. "You know what I mean."

She flicked the side of the lighter and touched it to the kindling. There was something deeply satisfying about watching the flame curl steadily upward. When she was certain that it wouldn't gutter out, Beatrice retreated to the couch, pulling her feet up beneath her to sit cross-legged. Connor hadn't moved from where he stood against one wall, his body tensed in the usual Revere Guard stance. His gaze was fixed straight ahead, as if he was scanning the room for possible threats.

"You can come sit down, instead of growling over there in the corner."

"Maybe I like growling." Shadows from the fire flickered over his features.

"Not when there's no one to growl at." It was the closest they'd come in weeks to their normal easy banter. "How could anyone possibly get here through that storm? You're officially off duty for the night," she insisted.

Cautiously, Connor came to sit on the couch, leaving a

generous space between him and Beatrice. He took one of the faded taupe pillows and put it on the seat next to him like some kind of safety barrier.

They sat there for a while, watching the fire dance tranquilly before them. Eventually Connor stood to toss on another piece of wood. The flames blazed and popped contentedly in response. Beatrice imagined she could see various shapes there, stars and pinwheels and trumpets all melting and re-forming in columns of red-gold light.

"Do you remember the time it snowed like this at school?" she asked as he returned to the couch. It might have been her imagination, but he seemed to settle a little closer than before.

"Winter Storm Nemo," Connor recalled. "We got so much snow that the entire campus shut down for days. We had to live on cereal."

Beatrice smiled at the memory. The dining hall had been closed all day long, so Harvard ended up sending someone through the snow to hand-deliver food to each of the dorms. It was nothing but a milk crate containing some prepackaged cereal. She and Connor had made a picnic of it, sitting on her floor as they ate dry Cheerios and played Trivial Pursuit.

"And then we built that awful snowman," she replied. When they woke the next morning, Beatrice and Connor, along with most of the student body, had ventured out into the quad. For once, no one was in a rush to get anywhere. People were laughing and starting snowball fights, while groups of girls in furry boots and pom-pom hats took heavily posed pictures. They were the type of girls who normally pretended to fawn over Beatrice, yet she was so bundled up in her scarf and jacket that no one noticed her. She and Connor were free to make their absurdly lopsided snowman, which kept toppling over despite their best efforts. "Remember how some of the kids in my dorm built an igloo and tried to hotbox it?"

"I think snow days make people reckless," Connor said, then paused as he seemed to realize what he'd said—because this, too, was a snow day.

Before Beatrice could answer, her stomach gave a loud, angry rumble. She flushed, trying not to feel self-conscious. "Guess I didn't eat enough popcorn on the plane."

Connor rose to his feet. His silhouette glowed like warm amber against the fire. "Why don't we do a little investigating?"

He headed into the kitchen with long, lazy strides and began to scavenge through the cupboards. Moments later he emerged with a bag of macaroni and some Alfredo sauce in a jar. "Looks like your options are pasta and . . . pasta."

Beatrice tilted her head, pretending to consider the question. "Pasta sounds delicious," she declared. "Can I help?"

"You could grab a colander." Connor filled a pot with water and turned on the stove, then pulled out another saucepan and poured in the Alfredo.

"A colander?" Beatrice stared at him. She had no idea what that was.

Connor's mouth twitched against a smile. "Never mind."

She watched as he brought the water to a boil and added the macaroni, then drained the noodles in something that must have been a colander. It struck Beatrice how utterly normal this was. Hanging out in a kitchen, cooking pasta sauce from a jar: this was something that other people could do whenever they *wanted*.

"Want to try stirring?" Connor offered.

Beatrice ventured toward the stovetop and began whisking the sauce. Connor laughed in protest. "Not so fast—you aren't trying to make whipped cream!" He nudged Beatrice out of the way and grabbed the wooden spoon, stirring the pot at a slower, more sedate pace.

"Sorry I'm so hopeless in the kitchen."

"It's okay; I don't exactly like you for your culinary skills."

Something about his words, about the way he said *like*, lingered in Beatrice's ears. But before she could think on it too closely, her Guard's face hardened. "I'm guessing it doesn't matter to Lord Boston, either."

Beatrice knew she should let the comment go—but a catch of vulnerability in Connor's tone, beneath the layers of sarcasm, gave her pause.

"You know his name is Teddy," she said quietly.

"Honestly, Beatrice, I'm happy for you, that—"

She cut in. "And if you'd been paying the *slightest* bit of attention this past month instead of glowering in the corner, you would realize that there's nothing real between us."

Connor frowned. "You seem happy when you're together. And . . . he's a nice guy." Those last words were delivered with obvious reluctance.

"Sure, he's nice." And warm, and friendly, and scrupulously *good*. She could envision her future with Teddy, straightforward and simple, stretching on and on into the distance. He would do a wonderful job as America's first king consort.

Beatrice braced her palms on the counter, fighting back a sudden feeling of dizziness. She had the sensation that her entire world was poised on a knife edge, and her next words would determine which way it fell.

"Trust me, I *wish* I could fall for Teddy," she said helplessly. "It would make everything so much easier if I could. But he isn't . . ."

"Isn't what?"

Silence stretched taut between them.

Beatrice was so very tired of running from this, of hiding it all beneath a smooth layer of denial. She needed to say it— to risk rejection, even if she had to carry that rejection with her for the rest of her life.

"He isn't *you*."

Slowly, her meaning unmistakable, she reached for

Connor's hand and laced her fingers in his. He gave a sharp intake of breath, but didn't move.

It was strange, Beatrice thought, over the deafening pounding of her pulse. She had felt Connor's touch so many times: his touch on her elbow as he helped her navigate a crowd, or the accidental knocking of knees that might happen when they sat next to each other in a car. This felt monumentally, unbelievably different. As if some magic glowed and gathered there, where their hands were intertwined.

Then Connor forcibly broke away.

"Beatrice, *no.*" The kitchen seemed to vibrate with what he'd said.

She took a step back, crossing her arms to hide their sudden shaking. "I'm sorry. Just—forget I ever said anything."

She began to sweep past him, but his next words stopped her cold.

"You think I don't want this too?" Connor's voice was ragged. "God, Bee, it's all I've thought about for the better part of a year! So many times I've marched up to my commanding officer, to tell him that I need to be reassigned, because I care about my charge *too much.* Because it's a torment, being around you when I can't be *with* you. But then, every single time, I turned away at the last minute."

He was still so close, his mouth dangerously near hers. "Apparently I would rather be around you like this, would rather chaperone your *dates* with Lord Theodore *Eaton,* than say goodbye to you forever." He gave his head a bitter shake. "Clearly I have a bit of a weak spot when it comes to you."

Beatrice's heart seized and skittered in her chest. "You think this has been any easier on me?"

"Easy enough, given that you've been going out with Teddy Eaton!"

"I told you, there are *no* real feelings between us! I'm only dating him because my parents asked me to!"

This time, Connor finally seemed to register her words. His blue-gray eyes were veiled.

"This is still impossible," he insisted, his fists clenched at his sides. "Beatrice, you are completely off-limits to someone like me. I work for your father. I'm your *Guard*. I swore a sacred, unbreakable oath that I would protect and serve the Crown to my dying breath."

"I know." She, too, was bound by a sacred oath.

"Your family would never allow it," he added. As if she needed another reminder.

It struck Beatrice that none of them were the masters of their own fates. Not Connor or Teddy and especially not her. Any decisions she had made in her life were an illusion—the choice of what gown to wear, what charity to sponsor—a selection between two equally limited options.

She had never, ever chosen for herself before. Not when it came to anything that mattered.

"Let's just put all this behind us," Connor said, very formally. "As soon as we get back to the capital, I'll request my reassignment."

"*No.*"

Beatrice was surprised by the vehemence of her own response.

"You can't leave," she said hoarsely. "Please, Connor. You have no idea how important you are to me. You're the only one in my life who makes me feel like a real person."

At his confused look, she fumbled for the words to explain. "Until I met you, I never knew what it felt like, for someone to look at me because of *who* I am, not *what* I am. I can't bear to lose you," she said baldly.

Connor swallowed. "I would never do anything to hurt you. But, Beatrice, I can't promise that you won't come to any harm. That you won't get hurt, if you get involved with me."

"I'm *already* hurt." She felt tears pricking at her eyes. "I never get to make my own choices. I have always put my family first—my *country* first—and it costs me, every single day of my life. But losing you . . . that's not a cost I'm willing to pay."

Connor brushed back a loose strand of her hair. Before he could lower his hand, Beatrice had reached up to cover it, cupping his fingers around her cheek. His skin felt rough and callused.

"We shouldn't be doing this," he said again.

"We aren't *doing* anything yet." She lifted her gaze to meet his. "If you're going to break the rules, Connor, then go ahead and break them."

He gave a familiar half smile at her words, then bent down to claim her mouth with his own.

Beatrice rose on tiptoe, her lips parted. Connor's hands slid from her face to settle gently around her waist. She tipped back against the stone island in the center of the kitchen, and Connor leaned forward in response, the warmth of him settling against her. He kissed her slowly, with a hushed sense of wonder that bordered on awe. As if he didn't fully believe this was happening either.

Kissing Connor felt terrifying and familiar all at once, like returning home after a lifetime of being lost.

At some point the stone counter was digging into her hips, and Beatrice shifted. Connor seemed to take that as a signal to pause. "We should probably . . . um . . . ," he said, in a questioning tone.

Beatrice's eyes darted instinctively toward the couch. No way was she ready to take this into the bedroom.

Seeing that look, and knowing what it meant, Connor turned off the stovetop—at least one of them was remembering not to burn this place down—and scooped Beatrice into his arms as if she weighed nothing at all. He carried her toward the couch and set her delicately back on the cushions, never breaking the kiss the entire time.

Outside, the snow tumbled ever faster toward the ground; a fringe of icicles hung along the top of the windowsill. Beatrice felt like she had stepped inside a snow globe that someone had shaken. She prayed that the little white flakes never settled, that she could stay here forever, outside time itself.

"I'm scared." Connor whispered it so softly that she thought she'd misheard.

"You? I thought you were too arrogant to be scared."

"There's the Beatrice I know." He gave a wry smile, then let out a breath. "But I *am* scared. I'm scared of losing you, of somehow hurting you. Most of all I'm afraid of failing you."

Beatrice shifted her weight so that she could look into his eyes. "I'm scared, too," she admitted. "At least we can be scared together."

The fire burned on before them, untended.

17

SAMANTHA

Samantha was at the chairlift's loading station with Teddy and Jeff, humming a disjointed melody under her breath, when Jeff's phone fell out of his pocket.

"Sorry!" he exclaimed, ducking off to one side to collect it. Before Sam could react, the chair had whirled around the central rotary toward them—leaving her no choice but to ride up with Teddy.

He turned toward her as if to say something, but Sam angled deliberately away from him. It wasn't her job to entertain him just because his *real* date hadn't yet arrived. She kept staring out at the mountain, onto which she couldn't wait to be set loose.

Sam had woken that morning to a world of drifting white: white clouds shivering into snow, white wind whipping everything around them. She'd hurried into her snow gear and headed downstairs, where a few family members were already gathered.

Jeff jumped to his feet at her arrival. "We've gone inter-lodge! Both highways are closed, 145 *and* the pass from Red Mountain."

"Which means that Beatrice is still stuck in Montrose." The queen's eyes drifted uncomfortably to Teddy, who was at the kitchen table, eating a homemade breakfast sandwich on a bagel. "If the roads aren't open again by the afternoon, she'll miss the party."

Sam wasn't particularly worried about whether Beatrice made it to the New Year's Eve celebration. Her eyes met Jeff's; they were both grinning with a complicit excitement.

Interlodge was every skier or snowboarder's dream condition: when it had snowed so much that the roads closed, but the mountain remained open. Snowfall in itself wasn't enough to shut down a ski resort, only severe winds, which made chairlifts unsafe to operate. Interlodge therefore meant unbelievable snow, *plus* having the mountain mostly to yourself—because the road closures kept anyone else from skiing, except the people already in town.

"In that case, we'd better get going." Sam headed toward the mudroom to pull on her boots and jacket, then grabbed her snowboard, which was covered in stickers and decals. "Who's coming?"

Sam's eyes were on her dad, who normally lived for days like this, but he just shook his head. "I'll let you kids have the mountain to yourselves this morning."

He said it cheerfully, but Sam couldn't help noticing how completely tired he looked. There were fine lines crinkling around his eyes, and a new slump to his shoulders.

She glanced over at Nina, who gave an apologetic smile and held up a thick fantasy novel. "I might stay home. Besides, I'll only slow you down on a day like today."

Then, to Sam's horror, Teddy jumped in. "I'd love to come, if you don't mind."

"Sure," she said, after a beat. She couldn't think of any reasonable way to get rid of him.

They'd started on the Gold Hill chutes, making their way steadily across the mountain. Sam had to grudgingly admit that Teddy was a very good skier. She couldn't shake him off her tail even if she tried—and she had been trying, all morning.

"We're heading to the Revelation Bowl, right?" Teddy attempted now.

"Jeff and I are," Sam said stiffly. "You can rip-cord out on some easier blacks before the hike. Otherwise you'll have to walk along the ridge for the last five hundred meters carrying your board. Or in your case, skis," she added pointedly. She'd always found skiers so . . . conventional.

"I can handle it." Teddy gave a bold smile. "Unlike you, I learned to ski on terrain that's *actually* difficult. The icy, unforgiving, set-an-edge-and-hope-you-don't-die runs at Stowe."

Sam winced in mock sympathy. "East Coast skiing? I'm sorry you had to suffer through that."

"Sam!" Jeff hollered from the chair behind them. "Revelation, right?"

Sam twisted around; her brother was sprawled out on the chair, one leg kicked up onto the seat while the other dangled below, still fixed to his board.

"Absolutely. Race?" she called out in reply.

"Dare?"

"You're on."

Teddy glanced back and forth between them. "Have you and Jeff always used that kind of twin-speak?"

"You think that was twin-speak?" Sam scoffed. "That's just lazy ski-lift talk. When we were kids Jeff and I communicated in complete gibberish. It drove our nanny nuts."

Teddy smiled beneath his wool neck gaiter. The tip of his nose had gone red from the cold. "Did I misunderstand, or did he just challenge you to a race?"

"Jeff and I always race down Revelation Bowl. The winner gets to make the loser complete a dare." She chuckled. "Last year after I won, I made him freeze Daphne's long underwear out in the snow overnight. She was *furious* the next day."

They were above the tree line now; the landscape raced along below them in an unbroken sheet of white.

"I've heard the ski team at King's College is surprisingly good given that they aren't in the mountains." A smile ghosted Teddy's lips. "Granted, it *is* East Coast skiing, but you could still look into it."

"Why does everyone always assume I'm going to King's College?" Sam struggled to check her irritation. "Who knows, maybe I won't go to college at all."

"You don't mean that," Teddy countered, with surprising conviction.

She gave a disinterested shrug. "What's the point, for someone like me?"

"*Someone like you*, meaning one of the most influential people on the planet? Someone who actually has the power to make the world a better place?"

"You're confusing me with my sister. Which is understandable, given that you've made out with both of us." Sam ignored Teddy's sharp inhale. "Beatrice is already part of Cabinet meetings, is helping to set the national agenda and negotiate treaties. *She* has power, not me."

The wind picked up, swaying the chair lightly back and forth. Teddy raised his voice to be heard over it. "Don't you realize that millions of people look to you for inspiration? You have such a unique position, Samantha—you can use it to drive people to action, to spotlight issues you care about—"

"You're talking about *advocacy*, not policy-making or governing," she cut in. "Which means being a glorified cheerleader. Throwing a bunch of fancy parties and asking people to donate to my cause of the week? I don't think so." That was the type of thing *Daphne* wanted to do with her life. Not Samantha.

"It's more than glorified cheerleading if it causes real change," Teddy countered. "Or what would you rather do?"

Sam started to deliver some flippant, incisive comment, to

mock Teddy for his starry-eyed idealism—but the truth came out instead. "I don't know what I want to do. I don't even know what I would be *good* at."

"Maybe if you went to college, you would figure it out."

Suddenly they were lifting the safety bar and sliding out onto the windswept peak. Sam snapped out of her board and lifted it onto her shoulder, not waiting for Teddy, who had pulled a nylon strap from his jacket pocket, to loop his skis behind him like a backpack.

She wordlessly started along the ridge, following the icy footprints etched into the snow by previous skiers and snowboarders. To her left, every several yards, wooden stakes were anchored in the snow with red DANGER tape looped between them—not that the tape would do anything to help, if someone slipped. Past the tape, the mountain fell off in a sheer vertical drop.

At last they reached the top of the Revelation Bowl: a wide expanse of snow that funneled off the side of the mountain. Sam reached to unzip her jacket, feeling warm from exertion. The sun had finally dispersed the clouds. She tilted her face upward, letting its rays kiss her brow.

"You ready to lose?" Jeff asked, still breathing heavily. He flashed her his usual cheeky grin.

"Bring it on." Ignoring Teddy's quiet presence behind her, Sam strapped back into her snowboard. Then she edged over the lip of the slope and dropped in.

The air whipped at her, tore mercilessly at her clothes. Knee-deep powder flung itself to each side of her board in a spray of white. Sam felt like she'd been stagnant every minute that she wasn't on her snowboard—that only now when she was falling off the side of a mountain was she alive again.

Jeff had shot ahead, and she felt Teddy nipping at her heels, the whoosh of his skis a softer sound than the boards' loud carving. Sam curled her ankles and threw her weight forward with more blind force than usual, as if spurred on by what Teddy had said. What right did he think he had, to pass judgment on her?

Her board slipped out from beneath her.

Once, at five years old, Sam had tried to escape her private instructor and barreled straight down the mountain. She ran out of snow, skidding across twenty meters of mud before she crashed into a bush. When Ski Patrol finally dug her out, she'd lost two teeth and was grinning ear to ear.

Sam felt that way now. She was careening ever faster down the slope, trying desperately to slam her back foot onto her edge—

She flew forward, hitting the snow with a thud and tumbling head over heels downhill. The world was reduced to a spinning whirl of white.

She curled her body in on itself, waiting until everything finally fell still.

"*Sam!*"

To her surprise, the voice wasn't Jeff's, but Teddy's.

He grabbed her elbow to pull her upright. "Are you hurt?"

"I'm fine." Sam fumbled for her board in the drifts and fastened herself back in, one foot at a time. She felt suddenly embarrassed—not for falling, but for the reason it happened. Because she'd been thinking about *Teddy*.

"Congratulations," she forced herself to say, looking down the mountain at Jeff. "It would appear that I owe you a dare."

Wrapped in a fluffy white towel, Sam padded toward the indoor hot tub, which was built into the side of the house, bordered by floor-to-ceiling windows that looked out over the mountains. There was an outdoor hot tub too, of course, but

Sam's every muscle felt sore, and she didn't want to keep running out into the cold to reset the jets.

She turned the corner, only to realize that she wasn't alone.

"Oh—sorry. Never mind," she said hesitantly.

Teddy stood, shaking his head. "Please, don't let me scare you off. There's plenty of room."

It was true; this hot tub had been designed to accommodate fifteen people. But wasn't it a little weird for her to be out here alone, with the guy her sister was dating?

Then again, Sam realized, she hadn't heard Teddy mention Beatrice's name all weekend.

She reluctantly dropped her towel and lowered herself into the water. She was wearing a bright fuchsia one-piece, which technically might not qualify as a one-piece at all given how many cutouts had been strategically sliced into it. It was the kind of thing she couldn't wear in the summer, because the tan lines it left were too weird.

"Besides, you probably need the hot tub more than I do, after that wipeout," Teddy went on, and ventured a smile. "Has Jeff decided on your dare yet?"

"Not yet. He'll have to come up with something really great, because this opportunity won't come along again. I don't usually lose to him," she boasted.

Teddy chuckled. "As long as you guys don't freeze my long underwear."

"I can't make any promises."

Sam drifted so that her back was over one of the jets. She forced herself to look out the window, because otherwise she would be staring at Teddy—at his muscled arms, the fine line of stubble along his jawline. Steam curled around his hair, making it a little darker than usual, the color of fine-spun gold.

"Samantha." Teddy cleared his throat. "I'm sorry for what I said earlier. I was out of line."

"No, you were right."

Sam was as shocked by her answer as Teddy seemed to be. She glanced down at the surface of the water, biting her lip. "Unlike Beatrice, Jeff and I have no defined role or purpose, no job we're being trained for. We just . . . exist."

Teddy shook his head. "Sorry to break it to you, but you aren't boring or lazy enough to *just exist*."

Sam felt curiously grateful for his words. And perhaps it was the sympathetic glow of his eyes, or the delicious warmth of the hot tub, but she felt lulled into admitting the truth. "That isn't the only reason I'm dragging my feet about college," she said slowly.

"What do you mean?" A bead of sweat slid down the curve of Teddy's neck to settle distractingly at the hollow of his throat. His lashes were spiky and damp.

Sam tore her eyes forcibly away from him. "Beatrice hated Harvard. Not the academics, but the social aspect. She always felt like she was isolated, like she wasn't really *part* of it." She gave a half smile. "I know I put on a good show, but I don't actually have many friends."

"Really? Not even the girls who went to your school?"

For some reason Sam thought of elementary school, when some of the girls used to steal things that belonged to her or Beatrice and sell them online. Their old name tags went for a hundred dollars; anything with a signature on it, like homework or tests, even more. When the palace found out, Beatrice had just grown even more quiet and reserved, while Sam responded by ignoring her female classmates altogether, and hanging out with Jeff and his friends.

Come to think of it, that was probably the beginning of her reputation as a flirt.

"Those girls aren't really my friends."

"Why do you say that?" There was no challenge in Teddy's tone, just curiosity.

"Because a real friend forgives your faults, and those girls store them up, to spread around as gossip items." She rippled her fingers over the surface of the water, letting out a breath. "I only have one true friend, and that's Nina."

"You're lucky to have a friend like her."

Sam nodded in agreement. "Still, I have this fear that going to college will only highlight how lonely I already am. And I'll spend four years being just as miserable as Beatrice was. Except probably worse, because I'm not the academic star that she is."

"You could try talking about this *with* Beatrice, you know."

"Beatrice doesn't have time for me these days."

Teddy gave a gentle shake of his head. "I think you'd be surprised."

Sam thought back to the night of the musical—when Beatrice had knocked on her door, wide-eyed and lost, and Sam had greeted her with nothing but disdain. She colored at the memory.

"What about you? Did you make any good friends at Yale?" she decided to ask.

"Yeah, but I'm more like you. I've had the same best friend since childhood," Teddy admitted. "It's just easier with people who've known you for most of your life, rather than people who judge you after the first glance."

She twisted a lime-green hair tie up and down her wrist. "I know what you mean. People never have a good first impression of me."

Teddy's blue eyes deepened. "Or sometimes the first impression is fine, and it's the second impression that goes all wrong."

Sam wondered if he was talking about them—about her first impression of Teddy, and how drastically it had changed after he went out with her sister.

Her confusion was broken by the buzzing of her phone,

where it lay perched on a nearby ledge. Sam lurched out of the hot tub to grab it. Her eyes widened when she saw the text she'd received.

"Beatrice is on her way back. She should be here in a couple of hours," she said slowly. She hadn't realized just how much she'd hoped Beatrice would remain stranded in Montrose.

"I'm glad she's okay," Teddy replied, though some strange emotion darted over his face at the news.

"Teddy . . . what's really going on, with you and my sister?"

For a moment Teddy tried to shrug off her words. "I'm not good enough for Beatrice," he said, with a self-deprecating smile. "She'll end up with someone far more important than I am—the Duke of Cambridge, maybe, or the tsarevitch."

Sam rolled her eyes. "She can't be with another heir; that's a political impossibility."

"Is it?"

"Of course! The last time heirs to their respective thrones married each other was Philip of Spain and Queen Mary, and we all know how *that* turned out."

"We do?"

"Not well," Sam said curtly.

"Too bad, then." Teddy let out a sigh. "The truth is, I've enjoyed getting to know your sister. I really admire her."

"That's the least romantic endorsement I've ever heard." Sam hadn't quite meant to blurt it out like that, but to her relief, Teddy didn't seem bothered by her words.

"She's the future queen. I don't think I'm *supposed* to feel romantic about her," he said abruptly. "She exists on a higher plane than the rest of us, at the level of . . . I don't know. Symbols and ideals."

The way Teddy said it, he made it sound pretty impossible to feel romantic about Beatrice.

"I'm grateful, of course, that your parents thought I was worthy of being considered—"

"My *parents* set you guys up?"

"Beatrice didn't tell you?" At her stunned look, Teddy let out a breath. "Your parents made a list of guys they wanted her to meet at the Queen's Ball. And I made the cut. Of course," he added, "my parents didn't tell me the real reason we were attending the ball that night until after I'd already met you." His eyes pleaded with her, a silent request for forgiveness. "I would never have gone into that coatroom with you if I'd known I was on Beatrice's short list."

Short list. Oh god.

Sam remembered what Beatrice had said the morning after that ball: *No one is asking you to get married.*

She'd gotten it all wrong. She had assumed Beatrice was pursuing Teddy just because she could, when in fact their parents apparently wanted a royal wedding. Maybe they'd seen all those op-ed articles complaining about Beatrice's lack of a boyfriend, or maybe they were simply anxious for some grandchildren, to secure the all-important succession for another generation.

"I didn't realize," she said quietly.

"Look, Beatrice and I get along," Teddy said. "We understand each other. But if it was up to me . . ." He didn't finish that sentence.

She could only manage a single word. "Why?"

Teddy looked down, avoiding her gaze. "There are certain expectations of me, because of who I am. Especially since my family lost our fortune."

Sam startled. "What?"

"Like so many old New England families, we made our money generations ago, and have been managing it ever since. Until the last recession hit, and it turned out that my grandfather had placed a lot of it in some volatile investments. He died later that year.

"My family is about to lose everything. All our houses, our positions, our way of life. We've already had to lay off hundreds of people, sell off our businesses—did you know my family was the single biggest employer in the Boston area?" Teddy's voice was rough with anguish. "When you're in that kind of position and the heir to the throne asks you out . . . it's not a question that you say no to. You just *don't*."

Sam glanced out the window, her mind spinning with everything he'd said. One of the Old Guard families about to lose everything, the future of an entire community on their shoulders . . . it was a lot of weight for one person to carry.

Teddy's transformation was slight, but Sam noticed it: the way his back went ramrod straight, the new distance in his eyes. It was eerily similar to the transformation she'd seen Beatrice make a thousand times—the way she would snap into her formal, remote self, as if putting on the Washington mask.

"I shouldn't have told you any of that," he said, his voice heavy. "No one knows. Not even your sister. Please, can we keep it between us?"

"Of course. What happens in the hot tub stays in the hot tub." Sam was striving for lightheartedness, but she suddenly heard another meaning to her words.

She saw from the glow of Teddy's eyes that he did too.

Sam waded toward him, holding out her hands beneath the bubbling surface of the water. Teddy hesitated, then laced his fingers in hers.

"This is a lot for you to take on," she murmured.

"I've always known what's expected of me, as I'm sure your sister does. It's why we understand each other." Teddy gave a lopsided smile. "Though things would have been easier for me and Beatrice if I hadn't met *you* first."

"Teddy . . ."

"I don't regret it," he hurried to say. "No matter what happens, I'm glad that I got to kiss you. Even if it was just once, in a coatroom."

No matter what happens.

That sentence was a loud, grating record scratch, like nails on chalkboard, because Sam knew the words that Teddy had left out. No matter where things went with him and Beatrice.

No matter if they ended up getting *married.*

But her sister wasn't here right now, and Sam refused to cede her this moment. Beatrice might get Teddy for the rest of his life, but she didn't get him now. This parcel of time existed unto itself, removed from the rest of the world, from consequences or regrets or what-ifs. It didn't belong to Beatrice at all, but to Teddy and Sam.

Their hands were still clasped under the surface of the water. Sam felt almost light-headed, from the altitude or the heat or the sudden nearness of Teddy's face.

Their lips touched.

The kiss was gentle and soft, nothing like their fevered kisses in the cloakroom that night. It was the kiss they might have shared if they'd met under other circumstances. If they'd had the chance to go on real dates, if Beatrice had never gotten between them.

Sam lifted her hands to splay them over the planes of Teddy's chest, then draped them over his shoulders. She held tight to him, as if she were still tumbling down the mountain and he was the only solid thing left in the world. Everything seemed to go luscious, and slow, and still.

Finally, after an impossible stretch of time, Teddy leaned his forehead against hers. "I'm sorry," he said, breathing hard. "I shouldn't have—"

"Don't ever apologize for kissing me."

There was that smile, the one that Sam found herself desperate to see again. "Noted" was all he said.

"It's getting late." Reluctantly, Sam reached for her pony-tail and wrung it out over one shoulder like a wet rag. She stepped out of the hot tub and shrugged into one of the robes in the heated cedar closet.

Before she headed back inside, she cast one last glance back out at the mountains, still covered in the glittering carpet of last night's snowfall. There was something evocative about the sight, something bright and glittering and full of promise.

18

DAPHNE

Daphne shivered; the night air felt slippery and cool on her arms, like a silken court gown. She was wearing a cocktail dress of black tulle with gold detail, a cropped fur jacket thrown over her shoulders. But then, she hadn't dressed for the weather. She had dressed for battle. To remind Jefferson of everything he'd given up.

Her stiletto heels clicked pleasantly on the sidewalk as she headed toward Smuggler's. There was no sign out front, no indication that you were in the right place except for a single word, MEMBERS, in polished brass letters on the door.

Some said that the owners of the ski-and-be-seen private club were the Washingtons themselves, though no one knew for certain. The identity of the proprietors was as closely guarded as the secrets of what happened behind that famous wooden door.

Smuggler's required that all guests check their phones at the entrance, particularly when the royal family was in residence. No unauthorized photos ever emerged of what went on inside. Of course, that only fueled the rumors: that the newlywed Dukes of Roanoke once got into a lovers' quarrel there, so terrible that one of them threw a fork at the other (no one would ever say which); that the king's sister Margaret hosted her bachelorette party there, and used the land line to drunkenly prank call all her ex-boyfriends, including the Duc d'Orléans and the maharaja of Jaipur. Most famous of all was tonight's event, the Washingtons' annual New Year's Eve party.

Despite the royal family's efforts to keep this party low-profile, the entire town clearly knew about it. A massive crowd surrounded the entrance to Smuggler's, everyone jostling eagerly for position, as if the security team might miraculously change their minds and suddenly let them inside. Toward the front of the crowd Daphne saw a few of the "it girls" who were busy on the capital's social scene, wearing too-short dresses and too-large diamonds. They glanced her way, but Daphne pointedly refused to make eye contact. She marched to the front of the line as if she belonged here—because she did.

"Hey, Kenny." She nodded at the guard as she sauntered past, hoping that he wouldn't—

"Daphne?" Kenny startled to attention, giving her an uncomfortable smile. He had a space between his two front teeth. "I didn't see you on this year's list."

As a rule, Daphne loved barriers, but only when she was on the correct side of them.

"Jefferson invited me," she said innocently, and held out her phone. Sure enough, there was a series of texts from Jefferson. She clenched her hands at her sides, willing Kenny not to click on the contact icon, because then he would realize that the texts actually came from her mom's phone. Daphne had composed them herself, while she was getting ready.

"You guys are back together?" Kenny asked, then shook his head, handing her phone back. "I'm sorry, but I can't. Not today."

Daphne's stomach plummeted in panic. She could *not* afford for all these people to witness her humiliation. "You know I'm not a safety hazard," she insisted, and made a show of opening her gleaming black purse, to show him the hair-brush and lip gloss tucked innocuously inside.

Before Kenny could refuse her again, the front door of Smuggler's swung open, and Ethan stepped out. He took in the entire situation with a single glance. Daphne unwillingly lifted her eyes to his.

"I'm so sorry, Daphne." She heard Ethan struggling to mask his amusement. "This is my fault. Jeff asked me to add you to the list, but I completely forgot. Can't she come in?" This last was directed at Kenny.

Daphne kept on smiling her sweet, ingenuous smile, but inwardly she was seething.

Kenny seemed to think it over, then visibly relented. "Okay, just this once."

Daphne handed in her phone at the mandatory check-point, collecting a plastic claim ticket in its place. She started down the staircase, but Ethan pointedly held out an arm. She had no choice but to take it.

Dim light gleamed from the chandelier overhead, which was made entirely of antlers. The lounge's dark green walls were lined with Western-style paintings, the knotted pine floors covered in throw rugs and leather furniture. Women in sequined dresses and men in bow ties spilled into the next room, which held a bar and, farther, a dance floor.

Daphne's swift glance confirmed that it was the usual crowd: earls and countesses and Supreme Court members, a few scattered businesspeople, various members of the extended royal family. The king stood with his back to the massive stone fireplace, his arm brushing the queen's as she recounted some story. Usually he was so jovial at these events—laughing, gesturing for the footmen to keep everyone's wineglasses full—yet tonight Daphne noted a new gravity to his manner.

"You can go now," Daphne murmured, unhooking her arm from where it was looped through Ethan's.

"Your gratitude, as always, is overwhelming."

"You've made your point, Ethan. There's no need to gloat."

"But I'm so good at it." His eyes glittered like dark stars.

"I'm not in the mood, okay?"

He gave a lazy, sensuous grin. "Come on, Daphne. I know we've had our moments—"

"*That's* an understatement—"

"—but you should be glad I'm here. Otherwise you'd still be standing on the doorstep, waving around your fake text messages."

She pursed her lips against an incisive retort. "Thank you for helping me get in," she forced herself to say.

Ethan chuckled at her discomposure. "No worries, you can owe me one."

Daphne didn't deign to reply. She had zero intention of owing Ethan anything.

He grabbed two flutes of champagne from a passing tray and tried to hand one to her, but she shook her head. She never drank in public: no matter that she was turning eighteen in a few months, and that underage drinking was tacitly permitted, or at least politely ignored, at private events like this. She had worked far too hard to risk her image over a *cocktail*.

"It's New Year's Eve; no one cares," Ethan countered, but Daphne ignored him.

Her eyes had locked on a girl who stood to one side of the room, wearing a strapless black dress and cropped booties— *booties*, to a formal New Year's Eve party.

It was the look in Nina's deep brown eyes that gave Daphne pause. Because she was staring at the patio, to where Prince Jefferson stood.

It killed Daphne that they were both watching him. She hated that they had that in common, that they had *anything* in common.

Daphne walked briskly toward her. "Nina! It's been a while . . . since this summer, at least?" She said it hesitantly, implying that the other girl wasn't memorable enough for her to be certain.

Nina shrugged. "I was at the Queen's Ball a few weeks ago. Maybe you were there?"

Daphne's smile froze on her face. Was *Nina* the reason that Jefferson had run off in the middle of their dance? "You look fantastic, by the way. I love those earrings."

It was an old tactic of hers: to use compliments to get the measure of her opponents, set them at ease.

Nina reached a hand up to one ear, as if to verify which earrings she was, in fact, wearing. A tattoo flashed on the inside of her wrist. "Oh—these are Samantha's."

Of course they were. "Well, they look lovely," Daphne declared, and slightly tilted her head. "You know, I had no idea that you were in town. I guess I haven't seen you post anything?"

"I don't really do social media," Nina said dismissively. "Come to think of it, I didn't realize *you* were in town this weekend either. Are you here with your parents?"

The nerve of her. "I am. Actually, I ran into Jefferson the other day off the Apex lift. If I'd realized you were here, I would have suggested you come meet us," she added, in a politely puzzled tone.

Nina gave a self-deprecating laugh. "That's okay. I can't keep up with Jeff on those intense runs."

You can't keep up with us anywhere. "I remember, you were always happier reading a book by the fire than out on the slopes. It's nice to know that things haven't changed."

"At least, most things," Nina countered, as if to remind Daphne of what had changed most of all—her relationship with the prince.

There was nothing more to be accomplished here; Daphne

had made her point. "If you'll excuse me . . . ," she said vaguely, and headed off in a flutter of spangled tulle skirts.

Jefferson was out on the back patio, surrounded by a cluster of people, most of them young women. They cast him sidelong glances, fidgeting with their clothing as if their dresses had suddenly become too hot, or too loosely fastened.

Daphne didn't let it faze her. Girls were always throwing themselves at Jefferson. Things had been like this even when she and the prince were dating—and wouldn't stop, she knew, until they were engaged. Maybe not even until they got married.

When she met Jefferson's gaze, he relaxed into an easy smile and followed her past an outdoor fire pit. Fairy lights had been strung throughout the space, echoing the sparkle of the stars overhead.

"Can you believe the snow we've gotten this year?" the prince exclaimed. "I'm thinking of heading back to Apex tomorrow, if you want to meet up with us."

Daphne tried not to flinch at the fact that his *us* no longer included her. "I'd love that." She took an unobtrusive step forward, letting her dress slip ever so slightly lower. Jefferson's eyes drifted predictably downward, to the shadowed curve of her cleavage. For a moment, the look in them—a look Daphne knew well—struck her as one that she could play to her advantage.

"I had so much fun, spending time with you the other day. More fun than I've had in months." She gathered her breath and took the plunge. "I really miss you, Jefferson."

He blinked at her uncertainly.

"I know we ended things . . . messily," she murmured, her voice rippling with seduction. "But I'm here now, and I want to try again. This time we don't have to wait. For *anything.*"

There was no mistaking her meaning.

Ever since the breakup, Daphne had wondered whether

her mistake was that she'd never slept with Jefferson. It had just seemed like the right thing to do—these might be modern times, but she was aiming for the highest of goals, and therefore held herself to the highest of standards. Certainly to the standard set by Princess Beatrice.

She'd told Jefferson that they were too young, that she wanted to wait until they were both a little more mature. And to be fair, they *were* young; she was barely fifteen when they started dating.

Well, she was older now, and much surer of herself—of what she wanted.

Daphne didn't usually make such spectacular errors in judgment. But she knew at once that she had said the wrong thing. Jefferson took a step back, rapidly doubling the distance between them. Her smile slipped from her face.

"I'm sorry if I gave you the wrong impression," the prince said hastily. "When we were snowboarding, I thought you knew that it was just as friends. I'm with someone else now."

Daphne's lungs constricted. She took a great, gasping breath, fighting to stay upright. There was nowhere near enough oxygen at this elevation.

"Oh." Her voice seemed to emanate from a great distance, as cool and elegant as always. "I'll see you later, then."

She had been so certain that Jefferson still cared, that she could persuade him to come back to her. Especially now that she was finally, after all these years, willing to put sex on the table.

She tried not to think of the implications of that—of what must be going on at that ski house between him and Nina. But no matter how hard she tried to shut them out, a barrage of images flooded Daphne's mind, each more excruciating than the next. Jefferson introducing Nina to his grandmother. Texting her a string of cartoon hearts in the middle of the day. Lifting her hair to drop a kiss on the back of her neck.

All the things he had done with Daphne, at least at the beginning, he would be doing with *her*.

Daphne had given up everything for Jefferson, had designed her entire *life* around him. Now her future seemed to flatten out before her, shadowing and blurring at the edges until it led nowhere at all.

The sounds of the party receded to a dull roar beneath the thudding of her heart. She pushed blindly back inside.

"Daphne?"

Princess Samantha stood near the bar, clutching a tumbler of clear liquid that certainly wasn't water. She leaned forward, a little too close to Daphne; but that had always been Samantha's way. She simply refused to inhabit the normal space between people.

"Are you having fun?" Samantha asked, a touch of challenge to the question.

"This party is amazing, as always."

Daphne thought she'd sounded convincing, but Samantha gave a huff of amused disbelief. "Really? Because you seem as miserable as I am."

Daphne was so startled by the comment that she didn't bother denying it. "My night didn't quite go as I'd hoped," she heard herself say. And then, shocking herself even further—"Why are *you* miserable?"

"Does it matter?" the princess asked, with a touch of bitterness. She kept darting glances at someone across the room.

Daphne followed her gaze, to where Princess Beatrice stood next to Theodore Eaton. They were both smiling, both talking to the same group of guests; yet the longer Daphne watched them, the more it seemed that their movements were coordinated but disparate, as if they were trains operating on parallel tracks. Beatrice never seemed to look *at* Theodore, but *around* him.

"I see that your sister made it back in time."

"Yeah," Samantha said dismissively. She held up her now-empty glass and gave it a shake, a provocative gleam in her eyes. "Care to join me?"

Daphne's eyes flicked toward the dance floor, where hordes of people were gathered, awaiting the countdown to midnight. Several of the party planner's interns had begun to circulate glowing necklaces and noisemakers.

Why *shouldn't* she have a drink, for once?

♛

For the first time in her life, Daphne was drunk in public.

After she and Samantha took that first round of shots, Daphne had insisted on switching to champagne, which at least *looked* classy. But she was on her third—or was it fourth?—glass, and at that altitude, on an empty stomach, it was really going to her head.

She and Samantha were on the dance floor now, jumping and giggling as if they'd always been the best of friends. If Daphne hadn't been so drunk she might have smiled at the irony of it. For years she'd driven herself to distraction, brainstorming ways to make Jefferson's twin sister like her—when the entire time, all she'd needed to do was be Samantha's drinking buddy.

Daphne twirled in a circle, her stack of glowing necklaces bouncing as she moved. Near the DJ booth she saw Sir Sanjay Murthy with his two teenage sons, who'd attended Forsythe Academy with Jefferson. They both winked at her encouragingly. Daphne blew them a breezy kiss in reply.

She'd never known how utterly liberating it was, to drink until the edges of reality felt liquid and blurred. To do something delightfully illicit, just to prove that none of it mattered. Was this how Samantha felt all the time? If so, small wonder she'd turned out the way she had.

A pair of hands closed around her waist, and Daphne didn't even swat them away, just leaned back provocatively.

"Come on, Daphne. You're better than this," Ethan whispered into her ear. His breath was somehow warm and cool at once, sending uncanny shivers down her spine.

"I'm doing just fine, thank you," she informed him.

When Ethan tried to spin her around to face him, Daphne's heel slipped, and she lost her balance.

A few people glanced over, but Ethan managed to catch her before she crashed to the dance floor. He expertly folded her into a spin, making it seem like the whole thing had just been an overeager dance move. The onlookers turned away, rapidly losing interest.

"Five minutes till midnight!" proclaimed the DJ, who proceeded to amp up the volume even higher.

Ethan's arms were still closed tight around her elbows. "I think it's time we got you home."

For once, Daphne let her eyes drag unabashedly and appreciatively over Ethan: the gleaming intelligence of his eyes, the soft curve of his mouth. He was wearing a tailored blazer that emphasized the broad lines of his shoulders. Daphne looped her arms easily around them, trying to find her balance.

"I have to at least stay until midnight," she informed him, and lowered her voice to a whisper. "You can kiss me at the countdown, if you want." Maybe it would break through the wall of Jefferson's indifference, make him jealous.

Or maybe part of her wanted to kiss Ethan again.

For the second time that night she'd said the wrong thing. Ethan recoiled at her words, anger—or perhaps hurt—flashing over his features. "You're being unfair, Daphne," he said quietly. "You know this isn't how I want you. Not like this."

Before she could argue, he'd grabbed her wrist and carved a path through the crowded dance floor. Daphne cast a glance back at Samantha, who hardly seemed to have noticed her departure, before stumbling after him. They turned a corner, past a bar where more flutes of champagne were lined up. She was acutely aware of how narrow the hallway was, how close she was to the heat of Ethan's body.

"Where are you taking me?"

"You don't want to leave through the front door. There are way too many people out there with phones, trust me."

"I don't trust anyone," Daphne was drunk enough to admit. It was true. The only people she'd ever trusted were her parents, and even them she only trusted halfway.

"I know," Ethan said quietly.

Her protests died off as she passed a mirror that hung on one wall. Where her reflection should have been, a stranger's face floated before her: a hollow face with shadowed eyes and heavy, smudged makeup. Her hair had lost all its curl, to fall damp and listless around her shoulders.

"I can't go out there," she said softly, almost to herself. If she did, this image would be all over the tabloids tomorrow morning.

"It's okay; I have a taxi for you out back."

"A taxi?" Taxi drivers weren't always trustworthy, especially picking people up from a party like this one.

"You're paying in cash, don't worry." Ethan handed her a plastic Mardi Gras–style mask, lined with writing that said HAPPY NEW YEAR! "You can wear this, if you're feeling extra paranoid."

Daphne pulled the mask over her face, then turned to Ethan. "I don't know why you're being so nice, but thank you," she said, summoning as much dignity as she could.

"Maybe I know how it feels, living through a broken heart," he said gruffly.

Daphne's breath caught. She couldn't understand Ethan's expression. He was looking at her as if she had no secrets from him, as if he could see through the gold plastic of her mask to the second mask beneath—her perfect face—and then even farther, beneath her skin and her muscles to the sticky dark ambition beneath. None of it bothered him.

Ethan nodded once before heading back toward the party.

As he walked away, Daphne's eyes lingered on the back of his neck, between his hairline and the collar of his shirt. She knew she shouldn't be looking at Ethan like that. But it didn't matter anymore, now that she and Jefferson were over.

Except . . . did it have to be over? Was she really ready to admit defeat?

Daphne closed her eyes, leaning back against the wall as her mind raced through her various options. She smiled in a sudden flash of inspiration.

This game between her and Nina wasn't finished, not while Daphne still had one last move to play.

19

BEATRICE

The following week, Beatrice woke to Connor stirring alongside her. Early-morning light bled through the curtains of her bedroom, casting a pearly glow over the ivory wallpaper, pale blue carpet, frothy lace pillows. When she'd first moved here from the nursery, Beatrice used to imagine that she was falling asleep inside a cloud.

"Don't go," she pleaded, and instinctively tugged him back down so that she lay curled against him. She burrowed deeper into her sheets, which were stitched in the corner with the royal crest.

"Five more minutes," Connor breathed into her hair. He didn't bother reminding her how dangerous this was. They both knew the risks.

They had been sneaking around ever since that night at the cabin in Montrose. Beatrice wished that snowstorm had raged on for weeks, wished that she and Connor were still there now, tucked away from the rest of the world. But the roads had reopened the next afternoon, leaving her no choice but to head on to Telluride, to her family's annual New Year's party—and to Teddy.

As she'd walked into that party, Beatrice had brushed her fingers against Connor's: a swift, subtle reminder that she was his. Connor's only response was a slight tightening of his jaw when Teddy appeared. And the territorial glances he kept sending her all night from the edge of the room.

Beatrice's life now felt cleaved into two parts. There was her public self, who went to events with Teddy, who mechanically carried out her duties as heir to the throne.

And then there were her stolen moments with Connor.

He snuck into her room each night, when security switched to the late shift, and left again at dawn. They weren't doing *everything*, but still, Beatrice had barely slept all week. She offered, once, to come by his room instead, but Connor's refusal was adamant. If someone caught Connor outside her rooms at odd hours, they could at least give a plausible explanation. There was no reason for the Princess Royal to be up on the third-floor staff hallway.

Each morning Connor lingered a minute or two longer, both of them stretching out the night as if they couldn't bear for it to end.

They talked for hours, about everything in the world except this—the sheer madness of what they were doing. It was as if they both thought that they could keep getting away with it, as long as they never spoke of it aloud.

Beatrice knew that they *should* talk about it. If she were braver, she would turn to Connor and ask him that very question: "What are we doing?" But then, she already knew the answer.

They were being reckless and foolish; they were tempting fate; they were breaking the rules; they were falling in love.

Or they had fallen in love a long time ago, and only now had the chance to act on it.

Lately, Beatrice had started to let another thought in, one so radical that she hadn't even voiced it aloud.

What if there was a way that they *could* be together?

Sure, no commoner had ever married into the royal family. But no woman had ever sat on the throne before, either.

Times were changing. Maybe a future with Connor wasn't as utterly impossible as she thought.

Beatrice propped herself on one elbow, to gaze down at Connor's outstretched form. She traced her fingers lightly along his jaw, rough with stubble, relishing the shiver that her touch evoked.

She let her hand skim still lower; over his sculpted shoulders, along the corded strength of his forearms. Connor swallowed. She felt his pulse jumping over his skin, as erratic and feverish as her own.

Finally her fingertips came to rest over his heart, above the sweeping lines of his tattoo. She loved that she could see it at last.

"Will you tell me the story behind this?"

It was an eagle, drawn over the broad planes of Connor's chest in stark black ink. Its massive wings were unfurled, stretching from the top of his ribs up to the base of his throat. There was a boldness to the lines that evoked movement and a firm eternal strength.

"It's the original symbol of the Revere Guard, from back when the Guard was just a few men guarding King Edward I. Well, not the *real* symbol," Connor amended. "None of the drawings of that one have survived. This is just a modern sketch, based on descriptions from old journals. I got it after our first tour of service—after I lost one of my fellow Guards," he added, his eyes shadowed.

Beatrice held her palm against the steady beating of Connor's heart. "Who drew it for you?"

"I did it."

He looked away, self-conscious, but Beatrice kept her eyes on his. "It's magnificent. I had no idea you were an artist."

"I'm not. My mom is the artist," Connor argued. "I'm just a guy with a pen and ink."

"Hmm," Beatrice murmured. "As much as I'd like to

debate your artistic talent, I can think of better ways to spend our time. If I only get a few more minutes, I'm going to make them count." She leaned forward to steal a quick kiss.

When she pulled back, she was startled by her Guard's expression. "I'm sorry, Bee. I wish it didn't have to be this way. I'm sure no other boy ever made you skulk around like this."

"First of all, I can't believe you said *skulk*," Beatrice declared, which elicited a ghost of a smile. "And secondly, none of those guys mattered. Prince Nikolaos and I had the most miserable dates of all time."

She was purposefully avoiding the mention of Teddy, but pushed her guilt aside.

"What about you? Who have you . . ." She trailed off before she could finish the sentence.

"No one, really," Connor replied. "The Revere Guard doesn't leave time for much else. Like you, I haven't had the opportunity."

"But the night of the Queen's Ball, you told me you'd been in love before." *I'm happy for you*, she had said coldly, to which he'd replied, *You shouldn't be.*

It seemed to take Connor a moment to remember the conversation. When he did, his blue-gray eyes glowed from within. "Bee. I was talking about you."

The world slowed, then stopped.

Before Connor could react, Beatrice had flipped herself up so that she was sitting on top of him, straddling his torso. "I love you, too," she told him, laughing a little at her dizzying, delirious joy. "I love you, I love you, I love you."

It felt to Beatrice that she was the first person in history to say those words—that they had just been empty syllables before, had never meant anything until she spoke them now, to Connor.

She said it again and again, kissing him each time: on his nose, his temple, the corner of his mouth. A kiss for all the nights they had spent apart before they discovered each other. A kiss for everything Connor had suffered, for the lines of ink that swooped over his skin. A kiss for the future that Beatrice hardly dared hope for.

She felt Connor smile, even as a low growl echoed in his chest. He reached to pull her closer, running a hand down her back, the other tangled in her hair—

The intercom on Beatrice's bedside table emitted an angry buzz.

She heaved a sigh and slid off the bed, pressing the intercom's bright green button. "Yes?"

"Your Royal Highness, your father has requested to see you in his study." It was Robert.

"Now?" Beatrice glanced over her bare shoulder at Connor, but he was already out of bed, fastening the buttons down the front of his shirt. "Are we going for a run?"

"No," Robert replied. "Just come as soon as you're ready."

"I'll be there in ten," Beatrice conceded. She heard the whisper of the front door sliding shut, and realized that Connor had already slipped out.

When she emerged from her sitting room wearing jeans and a deep aubergine sweater, he was standing at attention in the hallway, as if he'd just arrived for the morning. "Oh— Connor," she made a show of saying. "Walk me to my dad's office?"

He nodded and fell into step alongside her. "I seem to recognize that uniform," Beatrice added nonchalantly. "Any chance it's the one you had on yesterday?"

"I'm going to make you pay for that," Connor said. His gaze was still fixed straight ahead, but his mouth curled in a smile.

"I look forward to it," Beatrice replied, and was gratified by the way Connor almost stumbled.

When they reached the entrance to His Majesty's study,

Connor stepped aside to stand opposite her dad's Guard. Beatrice knocked at the double doors, waiting for her father's muffled *come in* before she pushed them open.

This had always been her favorite room in the palace, all warmth and dark wood. A pair of massive bookcases held her dad's private library, mostly leather-bound volumes of history and law, though tucked away here and there was a paperback thriller. On the wall gleamed a biosecurity-enabled alarm panel.

Before the window sat the king's desk, made of heavy oak and topped with leather. It was scattered with papers and official requests. A ceremonial gold-plated fountain pen— with which the king signed all official laws, treaties, and correspondence—sat propped on its stand.

Her dad was on the leather couch near the fireplace, an old photo album in his lap. Beatrice sat down next to him, uncharacteristically stilled by something in his manner.

"Sorry for asking you here so early. I couldn't sleep," the king confessed. "I need to talk to you about something, and it can't wait any longer."

"Okay," Beatrice said hesitantly.

He passed her the photo album. "This was the happiest day of my life, you know. Except for the day I married your mother."

He had paused on the photos from St. Stephen's Hospital, taken the day she was born: close-ups of Beatrice wrapped in a white wool blanket, her tiny fists closed, and then the posed family photos on the steps outside.

"These are great pictures." It never failed to amaze Beatrice how gorgeous her mom had looked right after giving birth. She'd made a point of wearing her old pre-pregnancy jeans home from the hospital, just because she could.

"Your mother and I were utterly infatuated," the king

went on, his gaze softening. "You were this perfect creature who belonged to us, and yet it was clear that you belonged to everyone else as well. There were such scenes outside the hospital that day, Beatrice. Even then, America adored you."

Beatrice loved it when he smiled like this. When he stopped being the king, and went back to being her dad.

She continued to flip through the pages, past school pictures and photos from the garden, to a state dinner where Beatrice had fallen asleep in her mother's lap. "What made you decide to look through these?"

"Just . . . reminiscing," her dad said vaguely. "By the way, I have something for you."

He shuffled over to the desk, returning with a tattered clothbound book. The pages were crinkly and yellow, with that distinct smell of aged paper. She opened it to the first page, curious.

The American Constitution, it read, in bold block letters. *Article I: The Crown.*

Someone had underlined the opening paragraph: *The King is the Head of State, the symbol of its Unity, Glory, and Permanence. Upon ascending the throne of this Realm, the King is charged by God to administer this Nation's government according to its laws, and to protect the rights of its People. The King assumes the highest representation of the American State in International Relations. . . .*

The King, the King, it said over and over. The Founding Fathers had never imagined that a *woman* might run their nation.

Beatrice made a mental note to revise the Constitution so that it said *the Sovereign* instead.

"This was your grandfather's old copy, and then mine. You'll find some of our annotations in the margins. I hope you'll seek guidance from it," her dad told her in a strange tone. "Being the monarch is a solitary job, Beatrice. When you have a question someday, after I'm gone, promise me that you'll look in here for the answer."

He wasn't usually this morbid. But then, that was always the weirdest part of being heir to the throne: the fact that she spent her entire life training for a job she would only assume once her father died.

"Luckily that won't be for a long time," Beatrice said firmly.

The king stared down at the rings on his clasped hands. "I'm not sure that's the case."

Her heart skipped a beat. "What do you mean?"

When her father looked up at her, every line of his face was etched with sorrow. "Beatrice, I've been diagnosed with stage-four lung cancer."

The air seemed to abruptly vacuum from the room. Everything was silent, as if the grandfather clock in the corner had halted in time, as if even the wind outside had stilled at her father's words.

No. It couldn't be possible, no, no, no—

"No!" Beatrice didn't remember standing, but somehow she was on her feet. "Who's your doctor? I want to come with you, review your treatment plan," she said frantically, thinking aloud. "You can beat this, Dad, I'm certain you can; you're the strongest person I know."

"Beatrice." Her father's voice broke. "This is stage four. There is no treatment plan."

It took a moment for the implication of his words to sink in.

Pain exploded in her head. And there was a roaring in her ears, the sound of different pieces of reality fragmenting and shattering all around her.

"Dad . . . ," Beatrice whispered, her eyes burning, and she saw that tears were trailing down his face, too, as he nodded.

"I know," he said heavily. "I know."

She collapsed back onto the couch and threw her arms

around his shoulders. Her dad just hugged her and let her cry, great forlorn sobs that split her chest open from within. He ran a hand lightly over her back, the way he used to comfort her when she was a child. It made Beatrice wish she could melt back down to little-girl size: back when everything was so simple, when a kiss and a Band-Aid could solve almost any problem.

She couldn't bear the thought of losing him. Her dad, who used to throw her into the swimming pool and pretend that he was rocket-launching her into space; who read stories to her stuffed otter when she was too proud to ask for them for herself; who had always been her greatest advocate and fiercest champion. Her dad—and also her king.

"I love you, Dad," she whispered through the rawness in her throat.

"I love you so much, Beatrice," he told her, over and over. His voice was steady, but she could tell that he was still weeping, because her hair was damp with his tears.

He didn't have to say it for Beatrice to know what he was thinking. She needed to do all her crying now, in private, because she wouldn't get another moment like this. From now on, she would need to be tough, for her father's sake. For her family's. And most of all, for her country's.

Beatrice's resolve quavered a little at the thought of what was coming—the fact that she would have to rule, so much sooner than she had ever imagined—but she would deal with that later. That fear was nothing compared to the grief coursing through her.

Eventually she sat back, her sobs subsiding. The early-morning light filtered through the window to dance over the scrolling carpet beneath their feet.

"Who else knows?" she asked, still sniffling. "Have you told Mom?"

"Not yet." The king's voice sounded ragged. "And if I

could have kept from telling you, I would have. I wish there was a way for me to tell Beatrice, my successor, without telling Beatrice, my daughter. This is a matter of state, a matter between monarchs," her father said.

"I understand." Beatrice willed herself to be strong for her dad, to be Beatrice the successor. But Beatrice the daughter couldn't stop the silent tears that kept sliding down her cheeks.

"I promise that I'll tell your mom soon—and Sam and Jeff," her dad hastened to add. "But right now I want to enjoy this time, however long it is, without the shadow of my illness hanging over us. And over the country."

As if to prove just how little time he had left, he subsided into a fit of coughing: heavy, racking coughs that seemed to shake his entire frame. Finally he looked up at her, his mouth set into a grim line.

"How long?" she asked.

"Hopefully a year," her father said softly. "More likely, months."

Beatrice bit her lip until it felt like she might draw blood.

"You will be a great queen." Her father spoke slowly, as if choosing his words with care. "But as I've said before, this isn't an easy job. It's so much more than the charity work, or the politics—the Cabinet meetings, the ambassador appointments, being the commander in chief of the armed forces. More than any of that, the most important role of the monarch is still a symbolic one.

"When you are queen, the people will look to you as the ultimate symbol of stability in a confusing and ever-changing world. The Crown is the magic link that holds this country together, that keeps all the different states and political parties and types of people peacefully interwoven."

Beatrice had heard all of this before. But hearing it now,

knowing her time would come far too fast, she felt the sentiment take on a whole new meaning.

"I'm just—" She braced her hands on the fabric of her jeans to steady herself. "I'm not ready for this."

"Good. If you thought you were ready, it would have been certain proof that you're not," the king said gruffly, yet with unmistakable warmth. "No one is ever ready for this, Beatrice. I certainly wasn't."

Her heart careened wildly from sorrow to panic. "I'm terrified I'll mess up."

Instead of assuaging her fears, her dad only nodded. "You will. Countless times."

"But . . ."

"You think your predecessors never made mistakes?" he asked, then swiftly answered his own question. "Of *course* they did. Our nation's history is woven from their errors in judgment, their wrong decisions, as much as it is from their achievements."

Beatrice followed her father's gaze to the portrait of King George I that hung above the fireplace. She knew precisely what her dad was talking about, because it was something they had discussed before—the horror of slavery.

George I had *known* that slavery was wrong; he had freed all his own slaves upon his death. Perhaps if he'd listened to his conscience instead of to the Southern congressmen, he would have abolished the institution altogether. Instead that hadn't happened for another two generations.

"I wish I could tell you that becoming the monarch will give you infallible judgment. If it did, maybe America would have a history I felt unequivocally proud to represent." Her father gave a disappointed breath. "But unfortunately, this is the history we've got."

Beatrice had never quite thought of that part of the job.

That as the living symbol of America, she would be the in-heritor of the nation's legacy, the bad as well as the good.

"I wish we could erase all those—those atrocities," she stammered, and was surprised by her father's reply.

"*Never* say that," he insisted. "Say you want to make things right, to build a better future. But erasing the past—or worse, trying to rewrite it—is the tool of despots. Only by engaging with the past can we avoid repeating it."

Beatrice remembered something her history tutor used to say: a good queen learns from her mistakes, but a great one learns from the mistakes of others.

She reached for the photo album, which had slid off her lap onto the carpet. It had fallen open to a photo from an old balcony appearance. Beatrice's eyes quickly moved past her waving parents to focus instead on the roiling sea of people beneath. The sight of them, the sheer *number* of them, suddenly felt overwhelming.

"How do you do it?" she whispered. "How do you represent tens of millions of people who all want such different things? Especially when . . ."

She didn't finish the sentence, but her dad had always been able to guess the direction of her thoughts. "Especially when some of them would rather have Jefferson than you?"

"Yes, exactly!"

"You do it with grace," he said gently. "You listen to those people with respect, and try to address their concerns, even when they refuse to grant you the same courtesy. Because you *will* be their queen. Whether they like it or not."

Beatrice flipped to another page in the photo album. She knew her dad was right. But sometimes—when newspapers accused her of "getting emotional," whatever that meant, or when the media spent more time critiquing her outfits than her policies—she wished she could act with a little less grace and a little more aggression. That she could be a little more like Samantha.

She blinked, surprised by that last thought.

"Beatrice," her father went on, sounding hesitant, "there is one thing I was hoping to ask you."

"Of course," she said automatically.

"You are the future queen, and the people have known you, have *loved* you, since you were born. But as you pointed out, there are still so many Americans who aren't ready to have a woman in charge." He sighed. "I hate to say it, but not everyone will like the idea of you ascending the throne as a young woman, alone. The transition would be so much easier on you if you had a king consort by your side."

No. Surely he wasn't asking this of her.

"I—I don't understand," she stammered. "You just told me that our duty is to learn from our forefathers' mistakes. To be *better* than they were."

Her dad inclined his head in agreement. "It is."

"But suggesting I get married . . . You're saying I can't do the job on my own."

"*No one* can do this job on their own," the king clarified, and attempted a smile. "Beatrice, this is the hardest role in the world, and it never lets up or slows down or offers you any kind of reprieve. I love you far too much to let you take on this burden without someone to share it."

Beatrice opened her mouth in protest, but no words came out. Her dad didn't seem to notice.

"I wouldn't suggest it if I didn't think you were ready, but I watched you and Teddy at the New Year's Eve party. You seemed so at ease with each other, so well matched. And more than that, you couldn't stop smiling to yourself. You looked so happy." Her dad's voice was urgent and earnest.

Beatrice blanched. If she'd looked like that on New Year's,

it was because of the secret glances she'd been exchanging with Connor. It had nothing at all to do with Teddy.

"I just—I haven't known Teddy very long," she stammered. "It's barely been a month."

"Your mother and I had only been on eleven dates before we got married, and look how it turned out for us." Her dad's expression softened, the way it always did at the mention of her mom. "I know that other people sometimes wait years before they commit to decisions like this, but we aren't like other people. And your instincts about Teddy are sound. I got to spend some more time with him in Telluride, and I liked what I saw. He has strength, integrity, and humility, and most of all, a warm heart."

Beatrice twisted her hands in her lap. "I'm not ready to be engaged."

"I know this seems fast. But let me tell you from experience, you would be miserable as sovereign without a partner to help you face it. It's such a lonely, isolating job." Her father's eyes glimmered. "Teddy will take good care of you."

Beatrice wrapped her arms around her chest, trying not to think of Connor. "It all feels so . . ." Overwhelming, impossible, *unfair*. "It feels like a lot," she finished.

Her father nodded. "I understand if this is too fast for you. But I've always dreamed of walking you down the aisle. I would love to do that, before I die," he finished.

Those three words, *before I die*, seemed to echo plaintively around the room.

Those words were like the ruler Beatrice's etiquette master used to snap across her knuckles, yanking her sharply back to reality. All the things she'd been dreaming this morning felt like just that: dreams. Foolish, impossible, hopeless dreams.

From now on, you are two people at once: Beatrice the girl, and Beatrice, heir to the Crown. When they want different things, the Crown must win. Always.

She thought of the task that lay ahead: of all the things she would have to embody and build and improve and unite. Of all the millions of people whose voices she was charged with representing. The colossal weight of that duty settled over her shoulders like a cloak sewn with stones, pressing her downward.

Beatrice's spine instinctively stiffened, her shoulders squaring, bracing themselves beneath that weight. This might be a near-impossible burden, but it was *her* burden. The one she had been training for her entire life.

She could never be with Connor. She knew it, and so did he. Hadn't they both said it that night in Montrose, before they flung themselves at each other?

"I love you, Beatrice," her father told her. "Whatever you decide. And I'm so proud of you."

Beatrice rubbed at her eyes, reached up to run her fingers through her hair, took another breath. Somehow she found the self-control to stand up.

"I love you too, Dad," she told him. Enfolded in that sentence was her promise, her solemn vow—part of the same vow that she had made long ago, that had been sworn on her behalf the moment she was born. She saw that her dad understood, because his features visibly relaxed with relief.

She knew, now, what she had to do.

20

NINA

"I'm thinking of dropping Film Studies," Rachel announced, reaching across the table to swipe one of Nina's French fries.

They were in the freshman dining hall at King's College. It was one of the older buildings on campus; the arched wooden ceiling rose high above them, and massive pendant lights hung over each table.

"Same," agreed Logan, the guy who Rachel was on-again, off-again seeing. They must be on-again right now, from the way they'd been deliberately bumping elbows throughout the meal.

"Wait, why?" Nina asked. When Rachel tried to steal another fry, she slid the plate across the table in amusement.

The three of them had agreed to take Film Studies together: Rachel and Logan needed a fine arts credit, and as for Nina, she'd just thought it sounded interesting. Plus, it counted toward her departmental GPA. Perks of being an English major.

Logan shrugged. "Too much work. Who wants to attend film screenings every Thursday night?"

"You can still go out Fridays and Saturdays," Nina reminded him.

"And Tuesdays and Wednesdays and Sundays," Rachel added, only somewhat kidding. Nina had known her to go to parties on pretty much every day of the week. Honestly, she appreciated it; anytime she felt like doing something, she could count on Rachel to know what was going on.

Nina leaned back in her chair, stifling a yawn. She'd gone over to the palace last night to curl up in one of the media rooms and watch a movie with Jeff. After they'd gotten away with it in Telluride, it felt silly telling him that she couldn't come over—though Nina still felt weird about sneaking around, trying to avoid Sam.

When the movie ended, Jeff had insisted on driving back in the car with her: "A normal boyfriend would take you home."

"A normal boyfriend would walk me to my door," Nina had countered.

Perhaps because it was so late, the campus quiet and deserted, Jeff had taken her words to heart. Ignoring his protection officer's angry grunt of disapproval, he'd followed Nina out of the car and walked her to her dorm's entrance, watching as she scanned her campus ID over the key-card reader.

"Let it never be said that I can't act like a normal boyfriend. At least a fraction of the time," he'd teased, and dropped a quick kiss on her mouth.

Nina smiled at the memory of his thoughtfulness, then started to push back her dining hall chair. "Either of you want froyo? I saw that the machine has salted caramel today."

"Could you bring me some?" Rachel had her phone out and was scrolling idly through her newsfeed. "You still owe me, since you missed my New Year's Eve party."

"I was sick." It was a flimsy lie, but Nina hadn't come up with anything better.

She was getting tired of all the secrets that kept crowding into her life, multiplying and building on each other.

"Fine, fine, I'll come with you," Rachel started to stay— and froze. She was staring at something on her phone, her mouth open in shock.

"Everything okay?"

Logan leaned toward Rachel to read over her shoulder. His eyes widened, and he lifted them incredulously to Nina.

"Are you dating the *prince?*"

Nina's stomach plummeted. "How . . ."

Rachel wordlessly slid her phone across the table.

Nina was stunned to see her own face sprawled on the home page of the *Daily News.* THE PRINCE'S SECRET NEW GIRL! ran the headline, which had been posted just fifteen minutes ago—along with photos of her and Jeff, from last night's goodbye kiss.

"I *recognize* that archway! *Nina!*" Rachel squealed, incredulous. "You've been making out with Prince Jefferson outside our dorm and never *told* me?" A few students at nearby tables turned in their direction, curious.

"Oh my god," Nina whispered, her mind racing.

Someone must have known about them. She hadn't seen anyone nearby last night, and from the high resolution on the photo, she could tell it hadn't been taken on a phone. This wasn't an accidental royalty spotting.

Someone had been lying in wait for them, stationed across the courtyard with a long-lens camera, just hoping for the chance to snag a picture like this. But who had possibly known? Had Jeff told someone?

Nina zoomed in to look at the photos in closer detail, then winced in immediate regret. She looked disheveled and sloppy. Her coat wasn't fastened, and beneath it her shirt was riding up, revealing a line of bare midriff. Somehow the angle made it look as though *she* was the one draped over Jeff, as if she was coming on to him rather aggressively.

The article contained just enough truth to make it dangerously credible. It stated that Nina was the daughter of the Minister of the Treasury, who also happened to be the king's former chamberlain, and that she now attended college just a few miles from the palace—which she had apparently chosen because she wanted to stay near Jeff. She was clearly a fame whore, a social climber—"though the prince is so far above her, *social mountaineer* is a better term," the article pointed out.

People Nina hardly knew had come out of the woodwork to denounce her: *She wasn't even pretty or nice enough to make homecoming court,* sniffed a girl from Nina's high school class, who spoke on the condition of anonymity. *She's been friends with Princess Samantha for years, and the whole time she's been using the princess to get access to Jeff,* someone else chimed in. The article had even tracked down an unflattering picture from one of the football games in the fall—with Nina in the background, taking an enormous bite of a hot dog as mustard spilled down her shirt.

The adjacent picture was of Daphne Deighton, reading to kids in the children's wing of the hospital. When you stacked them next to each other, it made Nina look . . . trashy.

"The picture really isn't all that bad," Rachel said, watching Nina's face. "At least you have a healthy appetite? *And* school spirit!"

"Daphne Deighton would never allow that kind of photo to be taken," Nina said quietly. Because that was the problem, wasn't it? She wasn't Daphne.

People didn't hesitate to say as much in the comments. Nina was taken aback at how vicious they were. Everyone seemed to have their own reason for despising her—because she had two moms, or because she was Latina, or simply because she was a commoner. They attacked her tattoo and her pierced cartilage and her hipster wardrobe. #TeamDaphne, cried out one commenter after another.

Seriously, Jeff, get rid of that skanky commoner
I don't know who she is but I hate her
The beginning of the end for the royal family

Or, strangest of all: *Don't worry, the queen will just have her killed.*

The blood drained from Nina's face. She had *known* this would happen, had *told* Jeff that America would never approve of her as a match for their beloved prince. And events had played out exactly as she'd feared. In the span of a single half hour, she'd gone from blissful anonymity to being the most hated girl in America.

Someone must have started circulating the article around campus email chains, because it suddenly felt like the dining hall, normally a low rumble of conversation, had erupted into agitated gossip. Nina sank farther down on the bench.

"I'll find out who took that football photo and *incinerate* them," Rachel said under her breath.

If only it were as simple as a single photo, Nina thought sadly. Though she was still grateful for Rachel's vehement and unquestioning support.

She glanced down at her phone and saw, belatedly, that she'd received dozens of text messages in the past ten minutes. Most were from Jeff, variations on *Are you okay?* and *I'm so sorry* and *Please call me.* A good number of the rest were from Samantha, alternating between versions of *I can't believe you didn't tell me!!* and *I'm getting worried—please call?*

Her parents had only sent a single message: *We're here if you want to come home and talk.*

Nina forced herself to stand, ignoring the hungry, curious eyes around the room. "I'm sorry, I—I have to—I can't—" she stammered. Rachel nodded in understanding.

Somehow Nina made it outside. She started toward the bus stop on the corner, wrapping her arms around her torso. She was wearing a thin fleece, but she couldn't bring herself to go back to her dorm room for a real jacket; she couldn't wait another instant before getting out of here. She stared down at her chunky brown boots.

"Look, it's *her*," someone whispered. Nina glanced up and saw two women staring at their phones, then at Nina, and back again. They began snapping hurried photos of her.

"Jeff could have had any woman in America, and *this* is who he chose?"

"Is she seriously about to take the *bus* with us?"

They were no longer even pretending to keep their voices quiet.

Nina brushed past them with her head held high, stepping out onto the curb to hail a taxi. She couldn't remember ever being so grateful to slide into a backseat. She told the driver her home address and closed her eyes.

Her phone kept buzzing. Nina fished through her purse for it and saw that Samantha was calling, again. She started to accept—but her finger paused over the bright green icon. Did she really want to talk to Sam right now? Part of her longed to, if only to unload some of this onto her best friend. But she knew she would also have to explain why she'd kept a secret this big. She didn't have the energy for that conversation right now.

"Miss? Are you sure this is the right house?" the taxi driver asked hesitantly. Nina looked up, and cursed aloud when she saw her street.

It was flooded with paparazzi.

Their townhome lacked any sort of gate or fence, so the photographers had flocked all the way onto the front lawn, in a cluster that was at least six people deep. The moment they realized she was pulling up, they swarmed toward the car, their bulbs flashing in a steady eruption of light.

"This is the right house," Nina said hoarsely. She thrust a wad of cash toward the driver, then threw open the car door and tried to run toward her porch.

The paparazzi shuffled alongside her, thrusting their cameras into her face, bombarding her with questions. *Nina, baby, are you in love? Nina, what's the prince like in bed?*

She ducked her head and tried to move faster, but several of them had darted ahead to get in front of her, circling her tighter and tighter, like a noose. A few of them actually grabbed at her with rough hands in an attempt to slow her down.

Nina pushed through to her front door, fumbling with her keys, which she dropped in her confusion. She knelt down to scramble on the front step for them, and just as she picked them up, Julie opened the door and pulled her swiftly inside.

The door slammed shut behind her, and the entire world went from roaring chaos to blissful silence.

"Mom," Nina said, broken. She started to step forward, but her mom's expression stopped her.

"Nina. You have a visitor." She nodded to the man poised on a wingback chair, one leg crossed over the opposite knee. It was the king's chamberlain, Lord Robert Standish. His graying hair was close-cropped, his mouth drawn into a harsh line.

Isabella sat across from Robert, the two of them staring at each other—two sets of warring brown eyes, one fierce and protective, one cool and disdainful.

"Miss Gonzalez," Robert began, which was oddly formal; on the rare occasions he'd addressed Nina in the past, it was always by her first name. "Please, have a seat," he offered, as if this weren't the Gonzalezes' house.

Well, technically this house did belong to the Crown. It was a grace-and-favor house: a property owned by the royal family, and leased rent-free to those who worked in their service. Nina and her parents had lived here for twelve years, ever since her mamá took the job as chamberlain.

Nina remained standing. "Can't you get *rid* of them?" She jerked her head toward the front door, to indicate the raucous hordes of paparazzi outside.

Robert held out his hands in a helpless gesture. "If you

were a minor, you would be protected by the privacy laws of the Press Compliance Commission, but now that you're eighteen, there's very little I can do."

Nina sank onto the deep blue couch across from him, next to Isabella. Her mom took the spot on her other side. It was reassuring, Nina thought, having a parent on either side of her. Defending her flanks from the attack that was surely coming.

"I'm here to discuss your relationship with His Highness Prince Jefferson," Robert began. "But before we get started, let me say that I am here in an *un*official capacity. The palace can't officially be seen encouraging this sort of behavior."

"What sort of behavior? Nina has done nothing wrong!" Isabella challenged him. Julie wordlessly reached for Nina's hand and squeezed it.

"We can't condone premarital *relations*," Robert said carefully. "Which you should know, Isabella. You've been in my position before."

Nina squirmed. "We haven't—I mean—" She couldn't believe she was saying this, but she felt the need to clarify. There had been absolutely zero premarital relations between her and Jeff.

Not that she hadn't been considering it.

"Miss Gonzalez, that part of your relationship is none of my business," Robert hurried to say. "I'm simply here to discuss *appearances*. As long as you and His Highness are together, we'll need to strictly regulate any trips that you attend with the Washington family, make sure you stay in a separate building. If I had known," he added forcibly, "I would have housed you in the guest cottage at Telluride, along with Lord Eaton. But you were *supposedly* there as a guest of Her Highness Princess Samantha."

It was irritatingly pompous, the way Robert couldn't talk about anyone without using their full titles.

But if she wasn't allowed to stay over at the palace . . .
"Does that mean that Jeff can come see me in the dorms?"

Robert winced. "That would be far too public."

Nina pursed her lips. She couldn't help wondering how this conversation had gone when the palace had attempted it with Daphne Deighton. Or maybe they never had. Maybe Daphne was so perfect and proper that no one had ever needed to reprimand her for anything.

"I get it. No royal sleepovers," she said stiffly.

"And we'll need to discuss your security as well, now that you're a figure of public interest."

"My . . . security?"

"Unfortunately, unless you are engaged or married to a member of the royal family, we cannot provide private security using taxpayer dollars. I encourage you to reach out to your local police chief—or the campus security when you're at school—if you ever feel unsafe. Especially if any of the reporters and photographers attempt to gain illegal entry to your home."

"*What?*" Nina's mom cried out, her face a dark thundercloud.

"They'll start going through your trash, so either shred it or drive it all the way to the processing center yourself," Robert said in a maddeningly matter-of-fact tone. "Especially sensitive items, like receipts or prescriptions—they will sort through the bins for that kind of thing. I sincerely hope you don't keep a diary."

"Not since I was in third grade."

He nodded. "As for your wardrobe. Unfortunately, unless you are engaged or married to a member of the royal family"— he had this speech down pat, Nina thought, unamused—"the palace cannot be seen funding your wardrobe. However, we were hoping you might invest in some new pieces if you plan on attending any upcoming events with His Highness. I know that you and Her Highness Princess Samantha are friends, but you can't be seen constantly rewearing dresses of hers. The fashion bloggers track her clothing choices; they're bound to take notice."

Her mom let out a low hiss. Nina held the chamberlain's gaze. "I didn't realize my outfits were such a problem," she said levelly. Didn't he have better things to do than worry about her *clothes?*

The palace had definitely never had *this* part of the conversation with Daphne, because Daphne never looked less than absolutely perfect.

Robert visibly struggled to find an answer. "The palace does prefer that hemlines be kept to right above the knee. And it might be better if you refrained from being photographed in sweatpants in public."

"She's a *college student,*" Nina's mom cut in. "She's perfectly entitled to wear sweatpants!"

But Robert had already moved on. He held out a manila folder containing a heavy stapled packet. Nina glanced at the opening line: THE UNDERSIGNED, NINA PEREZ GONZALEZ, HEREBY AGREES TO ENTER INTO THIS CONFIDENTIALITY AGREEMENT.

It was a nondisclosure contract.

Nina had seen these before: they were distributed to Samantha's and Jefferson's friends, to anyone they invited over to the palace or who attended one of their parties. But never in all her years of friendship with the princess had anyone requested one from her.

Her mamá Isabella stood, gesturing toward the front door. "I think we're done here. Please feel free to tell the gathered press that they can leave as well."

But something else had occurred to Nina. "Even if you can't touch the press, can you do something about the online commenters? What they're saying about me . . . doesn't it count as abuse?" she asked quietly.

Robert's features relaxed into something approaching

sympathy. "Unfortunately," he began—Nina waited for him to say *unless you are engaged or married to a member of the royal family*, but instead he went on—"freedom of speech is a constitutional right in America. I sincerely wish I could have those comments removed, and have the commenters banned from the internet. But it's completely legal to be ugly, and petty, and mean-spirited. I truly am sorry, Nina," the chamberlain added, sounding human for the first time that day.

Isabella shut the door behind Robert, then turned to lean against it. "Oh, sweetie. Are you okay?"

Nina struggled to hold back the onslaught of tears. "Honestly, mamá, I've been better," she managed, with a broken attempt at a laugh.

Nina's mom still held tight to her hand. Isabella moved swiftly to her other side and began rubbing her back with soft, soothing gestures. "I wish you'd told us."

"I'm sorry." Nina felt awful that they'd had to find out like this: from the media, instead of from her. "I wanted to wait until I figured out whether there was anything real between me and Jeff."

"And is there?"

She glanced around their open-air first floor, with its warped wood dining table, ferns and succulents cascading off various surfaces. Along one wall, an old library ladder had been repurposed as a bookshelf.

"I thought there was," Nina admitted. "Except . . ."

"It's a very big *except*." Her mamá heaved a sigh. "Trust me—I know firsthand how it feels, being pulled into the orbit of the royal family. It's a lot to sign on for. We would understand if you wanted to walk away from it all."

"Is that what you think I should do?" Nina asked slowly.

"Yes," Isabella declared, just as Julie said, "Not necessarily."

Her parents glared at each other over Nina's head. Clearly,

they hadn't had time to get their official verdict ready before her arrival.

"This is *exactly* what I always worried would happen," her mamá went on, reaching to gently tuck back a strand of Nina's hair. "From that very first day I interviewed at the palace and found you running around with Samantha, I worried about you. Living this royal life when you aren't actually royal . . . it messes with your sense of reality. And now you've been forced into the spotlight, where all those awful people can judge you. It's too *public*."

"Your job is public," Nina reminded her. "People write hateful things about you all the time."

"I'm a *grown woman*, and I took on this job knowing exactly what it entailed!" Isabella burst out. "You are eighteen years old! It isn't right that people are saying all these disgusting, heinous things about you. It's vile, it's perverted, it's—"

Julie cast her wife a warning glance, then turned back to Nina. "Sweetie, you know all we want is for you to be happy. But . . ." She paused, hesitant. "*Are* you happy?"

If her mom had posed this question a week ago, Nina would have said yes without hesitation. But even then, she'd been leading a double life.

"I don't know," she admitted. How could she still be with Jeff, knowing what America thought of them? "The things those people wrote . . ."

Her mom placed her hands firmly on Nina's shoulders. "Don't you *dare* worry about what those people think. They are small-minded and jealous, and frankly, I feel sorry for them. The people who love you know you for who you are. The rest is all just noise."

At least she would always have this, Nina thought gratefully. No matter how utterly messed up the rest of the world became, at least her family would always be on her side. "Thank you," Nina whispered.

They leaned forward, and all of them held each other tight in the same three-person hug they'd been doing since Nina was a toddler.

Her phone kept buzzing, but Nina ignored it. She had no idea when she would be ready to talk to Jeff. Maybe she never would.

21

BEATRICE

What did one wear to one's own proposal? Beatrice thought, with an oddly clinical sense of detachment. Something white? She settled on a long-sleeved creamy lace dress and matching heels.

"You look beautiful," Connor told her when she stepped into the hallway, and started across the palace toward the East Wing. "What's the occasion?"

She felt color rising to her cheeks. "No reason."

Beatrice had been in a silent, screaming turmoil since the conversation with her father a few days ago. Every morning she would wake up next to Connor with a bolt of happiness—and then the knowledge of her dad's sickness would hit her all over again, flooding her body with excruciating waves of grief. Yesterday's news about Jeff dating Sam's friend Nina hadn't even been enough to snap her out of it.

She and Connor had just reached the Oak Room when a figure appeared at the opposite end of the hallway. Right on time, of course.

"You didn't tell me that this meeting was with Theodore Eaton."

"Connor . . . ," she said helplessly.

"I'm kidding, Bee." He turned to her with a smile so genuine, so intimately trusting, it knocked the air smack out of her chest. "I promise I won't be a jealous idiot anymore. I know what's real and what's just for show."

He leaned forward, lowering his mouth toward hers—momentarily forgetting that Teddy was right *there*, halfway down the hall and closer every second, because Beatrice knew from the look in his eyes that he was going to kiss her.

She made a strangled sound deep in her throat. Connor startled to awareness. He managed to turn the movement into an abbreviated bow, as if he were responding to some command of hers. His face impassive, he went to stand near the door.

Beatrice forced herself to smile at Teddy. "Thank you for coming."

"Of course I came. You don't exactly ignore a summons from the future queen." He said it lightly, but the words twisted like a knife in her gut.

Her posture as rigid as a ballerina's, Beatrice stepped into the Oak Room, and Teddy followed.

She'd chosen the Oak Room for its privacy. She could have invited Teddy to her sitting room, but that felt too intimate—which was ridiculous, really, given the conversation they were about to have. But the Oak Room was the type of place nineteenth-century courtiers might have gone to whisper treasonous secrets. It had only one window, and was lined in heavy oaken panels the color of dark honey, so thick that no sound escaped.

This conversation would be painful enough without Beatrice having to worry that Connor might overhear from the hallway.

She had broached this topic with her father the other day, once her initial wave of shock had begun to subside. Any proposal would have to come from Beatrice. Like so many queens before her—the British Queen Victoria, Empress

Maria Theresa of Austria, supposedly even Mary, Queen of Scots—she would have to ask the question herself. That was just part of being next in line to the throne. She was so stratospherically high in the hierarchy that no one could presume to ask her for her hand in marriage.

"Teddy," Beatrice began, sounding formal and tense even to her own ears. "There's something I wanted to ask you."

"Okay," he said hesitantly.

How different he felt from Connor, who had looked at her just this morning with such clear, vibrant love. Compared to that, Teddy was a stranger. Yet she was about to ask him to spend the rest of his life with her.

She dug her fingernails into her palms, trying to remember the words she'd memorized. *Think of it as a speech,* she reminded herself, *like you're addressing Congress.*

"Teddy, in the time we've spent together, I feel like I've gotten to know you. Or at least, I know the important things. Your love for your family, your warmth, your thoughtfulness."

He was looking at her so intently that Beatrice had to close her eyes. She couldn't say what she needed to, not beneath the scrutiny of that gaze.

"I know all the important things," she repeated, her voice wobbling only a little, "which is why I'm ready to ask you this. I know it might seem . . . fast, or rushed. But trust me when I say that I have reasons for asking you now.

"Being with me wouldn't be the easiest decision of your life. Or the simplest," she said earnestly. "So I want you to really think this over. You don't have to answer right away. Teddy—"

She had practiced this part before a mirror, struggling to meet her own gaze. But no matter how many times she said it, the sentence failed to make sense. It just didn't sound like it had anything to do with her.

"Will you marry me?"

Teddy stared at her with visible incredulity. "Are you sure?" he said at last.

"Would you believe me more if I got down on one knee?"

She was curiously glad when Teddy laughed at that. "Sorry," he said swiftly, "I just didn't think . . ."

I didn't either, Beatrice silently agreed. *Not this soon—really, not ever.*

She held his gaze. "I believe that you and I could accomplish great things together. That we could be a fantastic team. But I understand that it is a sacrifice to be wedded to the Crown." *To be wedded to me, when we both know that we don't love each other.*

She didn't insult Teddy by reminding him of the implications of his decision. He knew them just as well as she did. If he said yes, if they went through with this, it would be for life. As her grandmother always said, divorce was something only the *European* royals did.

Teddy was silent. He seemed to be reaching some decision deep within himself, various weights and tumblers falling into place in his mind. His eyes held hers, and Beatrice saw that he'd guessed what was going on: maybe not everything, because he couldn't know about her relationship with Connor, but enough.

He reached to take her hands in his. The shock of his touch was like a bite.

To her consternation, Teddy knelt before her and bowed his head. A beam of sunlight sliced through the window to touch upon his golden hair.

"You don't have to . . . ," Beatrice began, but fell silent at Teddy's next words.

"I, Lord Theodore Eaton, solemnly swear that I am your liege man. I will honor and serve you in faith and in loyalty, from this day forward, and for all the days of my life. So help me God."

Teddy had just sworn the Oath of Vassal Homage. The words that peers of the realm recited upon the accession of a new king.

He was speaking to her not as a woman he was going to marry, but as his future sovereign.

Beatrice glanced down, marveling at how strange and awkward his grip felt, as if their hands were puzzle pieces that didn't quite fit. It felt fundamentally *wrong*, but she supposed she would get used to it in time.

There was a scripted response to the oath—*I humbly and gratefully accept your service*—but it didn't feel right. Beatrice settled for gently pulling on Teddy's hands, to tug him to his feet.

His blue eyes met hers, and he nodded. Beatrice knew in that moment that they understood each other, both of them conscious of the pledge they were making—and what they were giving up.

"Thank you for entrusting me with your future happiness. I swear that I will try to be worthy of the honor you are doing me." Teddy sounded as if he was accepting a job offer, which, she supposed, he was.

Teddy might not be the love of her life, but he was so many other things—honorable and true, reliable and steady. He was the type of man a girl could lean on in an ever-shifting world.

She just hoped it was enough to build a life on.

"So I can take that as a yes?" she asked.

"Yes," he assured her.

Slowly, with a quiet reverence, Teddy kissed her.

Beatrice had sensed that this was coming, and tried not to think about it too closely—not to think anything at all. But it took every ounce of her willpower not to recoil from the feel of Teddy's lips on hers.

Just this morning she had been tangled in bed with Connor,

their kisses so electrified that they sizzled all way down each of her nerve endings, while this kiss felt as empty as a scrap of blank paper. She wondered if Teddy sensed her reluctance, if that was why he kept the kiss so swift and chaste.

Beatrice cleared her throat. "One more thing. I know we'll both share the news with our families, but would you mind if we didn't tell anyone else, just until the press announcement? I don't want to risk a media leak."

She didn't need Connor finding out any earlier than he absolutely had to. Maybe it was selfish, but she wanted as much time as possible with him before he knew.

She didn't think he would look at her the same way once he learned what she'd done.

"Press announcement?" Teddy glanced down at their hands, and his eyes widened. "Should I bring you a ring?"

"You could pick one out from the Crown Jewels collection and give it to me at the press conference," Beatrice offered, and managed a smile.

Teddy nodded. Normally when the heir to the throne proposed, he brought his fiancée a ring from the royal vault. Except that every heir to the throne up till now had been a man.

Beatrice had considered bringing Teddy a ring today, but honestly, she hadn't been able to face the thought of going down to the vault to pick one out. It would make all of this feel too sharply real.

"That sounds great. I'll call my parents now with the good news, but don't worry, I'll swear them to secrecy," Teddy replied.

Beatrice nodded her thanks. She had to force herself not to reach up to her lips, where that unfamiliar kiss still lingered, now grown cold.

♛

Beatrice paced across her room with all the caged panic of a jungle cat. It was almost midnight, and Connor still wasn't here.

She knew she wouldn't be able to fall asleep, not after what had happened today. She kept envisioning the way Teddy had knelt before her like a medieval knight, swearing to forever bind his life to hers. It was too much, far too fast, and her heart simply couldn't keep up.

Before she could second-guess herself, Beatrice had pulled an old college sweatshirt over her pajamas. She ducked out of her suite and started soundlessly across the palace: down a series of hallways, then up another flight of stairs. The marble floor pushed the cold up through the soles of her slippers.

She only had to knock at Connor's room once before the door cracked open.

His eyes widened when he saw her standing there. He reached for her arm to quickly pull her inside, then shut the door behind them.

"What are you doing here?" he whispered, looking as if he would rather shout at her for her recklessness.

"I just . . ." She swallowed. "You didn't come, and I needed to see you."

"How did you even know which room was mine?"

"I looked it up. Top security clearance." She tried to sound flippant, but she knew he heard the tremor in her voice.

"Are you okay? What happened?"

She blinked back her tears, looking around the room as she took a moment to collect herself.

It was small but very tidy, the narrow bed made with crisp military precision. On a wooden dresser stood a series of framed photographs: Connor and his family at a theme park; Connor and his sister as small children, their arms thrown around a golden retriever puppy. And then, to Beatrice's surprise, a picture of her and Connor from her Harvard graduation. She barely remembered *taking* that photo.

"We need to replace this. You're not even looking into the camera," she informed him.

"I would," Connor said carefully, "but this is the only picture of you and me."

Oh. Beatrice's mind flew to all the photos people had taken of her and Teddy—hundreds, maybe thousands of them—in magazines, all over the internet. She hated herself a little, for not taking more pictures with Connor while she had the chance.

"What's going on?" he asked again. "Do you want to talk about it?"

When she didn't answer, he put a hand on the small of her back, as if to steer her out the door. "Then you really need to leave."

Beatrice stubbornly shook her head. "You've been in my room plenty of times. Why should this be any different?"

"Because my reputation doesn't matter, and yours does."

At the rough edge to his voice, the light that burned in those eyes, some tether deep within Beatrice snapped.

Just this morning she and Teddy had agreed to get *married*. Though it had felt more to Beatrice like a political alliance than anything romantic. She remembered their kiss, so remote and chaste, and shivered.

Other girls got to marry for love. Beatrice might not be free to make that choice, but she still deserved to experience love—*real* love, in all its heat and passion—at least once before she signed her life away.

If she couldn't have a future with Connor, then she would have to live fully in what little time she did have.

"I'm not leaving." Beatrice yanked her sweatshirt over her head and took a step forward. "I came because . . . I wanted . . ." She swallowed and tried again. "If you're going to break your vow, I figured you should break it all the way."

Connor's expression faltered, his eyes raking over her pale, drawn features. He took a shuddering breath and set his hands on her shoulders. "I want you more than anything, Bee. Believe me. But this . . ." He glanced down at her with hesitation. "It doesn't feel right. You seem too upset to make this kind of decision. Are you sure you're okay?"

No. My dad is dying, and I'm going to marry Teddy Eaton, when I really just wish that it could be you instead.

Beatrice was trembling. The shaking began in her hands, spreading up her arms and down her legs so that her whole body was suddenly quivering. She pressed the heels of her palms to her eyes, her breath coming in short gasps. Her spine curled inward, her shoulders hunched—

Just as he'd done in the cabin, Connor gathered her in his arms and carried her, still shaking uncontrollably, to his bed.

Beatrice buried her face in his chest and sobbed. She couldn't bear the thought of letting him go. Not now, not ever. She clutched tighter at him, her hands digging so fiercely into his back that she was probably leaving scratch marks, as if she could forcibly anchor them both here, in this moment. Connor said nothing, his hand stroking the dark sheet of her hair.

She couldn't bring herself to share the whole truth with Connor, but maybe she could tell him part.

"My dad has lung cancer," she whispered into his shirt, now wet with her tears. "He doesn't have much time left."

Connor pulled back a few inches and gazed into her red-rimmed eyes. His face was blazing with love. But no matter how adamantly he Guarded her, some threats weren't physical. Some things he couldn't protect her from.

"Oh, Bee," he said softly. "I'm so sorry."

There were no other words, but Beatrice didn't need them.

She stayed folded in the safety of Connor's embrace, letting the tears flood through her. She thought she might shatter from how nice it was, to simply be held by someone who loved her.

Out there in the rest of her life, Beatrice had to be unwaveringly strong. But here, for just a little while, she could set down her burden, could lean on Connor's shoulders and close her eyes.

Even after her sobs subsided, she kept her arms wrapped around him, relishing his quiet strength.

"I'm sorry," she whispered.

Her face was still pressed against Connor's chest, so that she felt his answer rumble softly through her. "You have nothing to be sorry for."

She leaned back and wiped at her eyes. Her face was streaked with tears. "I came in here to seduce you," she said, with a strangled laugh, "and then I cried all over you instead."

"Let's rain-check the seduction, please," Connor replied, and then his tone grew more serious. "You know that you can cry all over me anytime. I'll always be here for you, Bee."

Beatrice nodded, though she wasn't quite certain that was true. Not once Connor found out that she and Teddy were engaged.

She looked at him for a long, searing moment, trying to fix his face in her mind, as if she were pressing her father's Great Seal into a medallion of wax. And then she leaned in to kiss him.

She focused on the feel of his mouth, the roughness of his cheek against hers, committing every last detail to memory— so that someday, when she was trapped in a political marriage, she could look back on this moment, and remember what it felt like to be truly loved.

22

SAMANTHA

Sam trailed along the downstairs hallway, lost in thought. She was debating whether to head over to King's College and try to see Nina.

Sam hadn't been able to get hold of her friend since the news about Nina and Jeff broke. She'd been calling and texting nonstop, but the only response Nina had sent to all her messages was *Thanks for checking in, but I'm not ready to see anyone.*

I'm not anyone, Sam had wanted to reply. *I'm your best friend.* Or at least she'd thought she was.

Best friends didn't keep secrets this big from each other, did they?

Sam had to admit, she'd felt an initial twinge of weirdness at the knowledge that her twin brother and her friend had been hooking up for weeks without telling her—had been sneaking around the entire trip to Telluride, right under Sam's nose. It was a little hurtful that she'd found out about their relationship from the *tabloids*, the same as the rest of America.

But that initial flush of discomfort was followed by an overwhelming wave of protectiveness. The tone of these articles, not to mention the comments, was absolutely vile. Sam wanted to publish a rebuttal, or better yet go on television and tell everyone what Nina was really like—but the palace's press secretary had put a gag order on her *and* Jeff the moment the story broke. The best Sam had been able to do was post a flurry of comments in support of Nina, under a series of aliases.

She'd tried to get some answers from Jeff, but he just had a lost-puppy look about the whole thing. Apparently Nina wasn't answering his calls, either.

The first morning after the articles came out, when she hadn't heard anything from Nina beyond that single text, Sam had asked her protection officer to drive her to the Gonzalezes' house. She'd elbowed past the scattered paparazzi to ring the doorbell. When Nina's mamá answered, she took one look at Sam and shook her head. "She went back to campus."

Sam nodded. "Thanks. I'll head over now."

"I don't know if that's the best idea," Isabella said uncertainly. "Having you there might only make things worse." She cut her eyes toward the paparazzi, who were still gathered on the front lawn like scavengers surrounding their prey.

"Oh—all right. Will you tell her I came by?" Sam had shoved her hands into the pockets of her down-filled jacket.

That was three days ago, and Sam still hadn't heard anything from Nina.

She paused now at the entrance to the Grand Gallery, a long room lined with portraits of all the American kings, in order. At this end stood the massive painting of George I after the Battle of Yorktown, smiling benevolently, one hand on the hilt of his sword. Next came his nephew George II, a bit pasty and narrow-eyed for Sam's taste, and then his son King Theodore: the one who died as a child, whom teddy bears—and probably Teddy Eaton—were named for. And so on, all the way through the official regnal portrait of Samantha's own father, George IV.

Footsteps sounded behind her. She turned around, expecting one of the footmen or bureaucrats, and was delighted to see Teddy instead. He was walking slowly, lost in thought.

She and Teddy hadn't gotten a moment alone together since their illicit kiss in the hot tub. She'd seen him a few times since their return from Telluride, always at crowded functions, when he was officially there with Beatrice. But their eyes would meet across the room, and Sam would know, with a hot glow of certainty, that he was thinking of her.

In those moments, every inch of her felt so eager and alive that she had to forcibly restrain herself from taking his arm and dragging him away with her.

"Hey. I didn't realize you were coming over today." She reached for Teddy's hand, but he neatly detangled himself from her grip and took a step back. The motion was like a bucket of cold water tossed over her head.

"I can't—not right now. I'm here to see Robert," Teddy told her.

"Standish?" Sam wrinkled her nose in a frown. "What on earth for?"

"To discuss the press announcement."

"Press announcement?" Sam asked blankly.

Teddy was silent for a moment. A series of emotions flickered over his face, too fast for her to read. "I assumed you knew. Beatrice and I had agreed to tell our families. But I guess she wanted to save the surprise."

Sam's heart struck a strange rhythm in her chest. "Tell your families what?" she asked, too quietly, because some part of her already knew and refused to face it.

"About our engagement."

The shock of it vibrated through her.

Teddy's throat bobbed as he swallowed. "Beatrice asked me to marry her, and I said yes."

Tiny white lights danced before Sam's vision. She felt short of breath, like one of her ancestors, constricted in a corset and gasping for air.

Teddy took a cautious step toward her, but Samantha stumbled back, holding up her hands to warn him off. "I can't believe you," she said viciously. "Are you seriously going to marry my *sister?*"

He winced. "I'm sorry that I kissed you in Telluride. It wasn't fair to Beatrice, or to you."

"You can't go through with this," Sam insisted, ignoring his mention of the hot tub. This was much bigger than a single kiss. "Teddy, you can't marry Beatrice just because your family expects it of you."

Steel flashed in his eyes. "I'm sorry, but you don't get to tell me what I can and can't do."

"Why not?" she pressed. "You've already lectured me about deciding what to do with *my* life! So now I'm asking you the same question. Is this really what you want—to marry Beatrice?"

"Don't make me answer that," Teddy said stiffly.

"If you don't actually want to marry her, then why did you say yes to her proposal?"

"I said yes because you can't say no to the future queen, not when she asks a question like that!"

"Yes, you can. It's easy!" Sam argued. "You open your mouth and tell her *no!*"

"I'm sorry." Teddy's voice was so hoarse, so defeated, that it seemed unrecognizable. Those piercing blue eyes were filled with remorse.

Rage shot through her like a flash of summer lightning. "Fine. If this is really how you want it to be."

"It *isn't* how I want it to be, but I told you, I don't have a choice."

"*Everyone* has a choice, Teddy. And you, apparently, choose this."

His features contorted in pain, but he didn't answer. She didn't really expect him to.

"Let me tell you something. If you think this marriage is going to give you a position of power, you're wrong." Sam spoke slowly, enunciating each syllable—even the punctuation, even the spaces between the words—with terrifying care. "You'll be forced to set aside your own desires to support Beatrice. *She* will be in the limelight and in the driver's seat, not you. Your children will have the last name of Washington." She took a dark pleasure in Teddy's anguish at her words.

"Beatrice will prioritize herself, and what she thinks is right for the country." She glanced away, her tone falling to a whisper. "I would have *always* put us first."

"Sam . . . ," he said brokenly.

She shook her head. "Like I told you when we met, only my friends call me Sam."

Teddy hesitated another moment, then seemed to think better of it. He swept her a low, formal bow before heading down the hallway.

Sam leaned her palm against the wall and took a few ragged breaths. The portraits along the gallery seemed to be staring at her, their jaws tightened in judgment, their eyes cold and disappointed. As if they were silently telegraphing their displeasure at her—the worthless spare daughter, the flighty and ridiculous Sparrow.

As if they, too, would choose Beatrice over her.

Before she'd thought it through, Sam was storming upstairs to Beatrice's suite, barging past her bewildered Revere Guard without even bothering to knock. She slammed the door behind her with a resounding thud.

Beatrice was seated at her desk, her hands poised over the keys of her laptop. She glanced up at Samantha's arrival and gave a watery smile. "Hey, Samantha."

"You proposed to Teddy." Sam was gratified to see her sister flinch.

"I guess news travels fast in this place."

"That's all you have to say for yourself? I can't believe you would do this to me!"

"Do this to you?" Beatrice gave a puzzled frown.

"I *like* Teddy! I've liked him since the Queen's Ball. And I met him first," Sam cried out, unable to stop the sudden flow of words. "Or didn't he tell you that he spent the entire ceremony making out with *me?*"

Beatrice inhaled sharply, but her expression remained unchanged. "I'm sorry that you have a crush on my fiancé—"

"It isn't a crush!" Sam cut in. "I really like him, okay?"

"You like everybody, Samantha."

She was speaking in a calm, level voice, which somehow made Sam even angrier, as if the more rational Beatrice got, the more out of control Sam wanted to spin. She was seized by an irrational desire to grab hold of something—a whorled glass paperweight, maybe—and hurl it against a wall, just to watch it shatter.

"I know that Mom and Dad asked you to date him, but why did you have to jump all the way to a *proposal?* Don't you feel like you're rushing things? Or are you that desperate to remain the center of attention?"

A darker, heavier emotion flitted behind Beatrice's deep brown eyes. "As always, you have no idea what's really going on," she said cryptically. "I hate to break it to you, Samantha, but not everything is about you."

"Trust me, I know that. It's all about *you,*" Sam shot back.

Beatrice bristled. "I don't know why you're so upset.

248

You're the one who can do anything you want, and no one even cares."

"Exactly!" Sam cried out, triumphant. *"No one cares!"*

She was shouting by now. Some rational part of her realized that the staff must have heard. That was the down-side of living in a palace—that nothing was private, certainly not her tears or displays of emotion.

At Sam's words, Beatrice seemed to fold inward, like a bal-loon that was deflating. "Sam, I would trade with you in a heartbeat." Her whisper was so quiet that Sam wasn't quite certain she'd heard.

Beatrice seemed utterly broken; the sight of her like this slammed into Samantha's anger, twisting it into something else.

Except—Beatrice had won. She had Teddy; she had the throne; she had *everything.* So why did she seem so miserable? She looked as sorrowful as Teddy had been, as if this engage-ment had somehow been forced upon them both. But they didn't get to play the victims here. Not when she was the real casualty of this engagement.

"Forget it." Sam started toward the door. "You and Teddy clearly deserve each other."

23

NINA

Nina tossed and turned listlessly. Her eyes were closed, but she knew she wouldn't fall asleep, despite the blackout shades she'd ordered online and stapled to the top molding of her window. Well, it *was* one p.m.

She'd been hiding in her dorm room ever since those horrible articles came out the other day—when the paparazzi set up camp outside her dorm. The few times Nina did leave for class, or to work at the library, she'd texted Rachel and Logan to come meet her at the door. They would stand protectively on either side of her while Nina shoved her way forward, trying her best to ignore the paparazzi's shouts.

Nina, give us a smile! they cried out. *Nina, when's Jeff coming to visit?* When she kept her head down and didn't answer, they began saying much worse things, calling her cruel, nasty names. Nina knew they were just trying to upset her, because pictures of her walking weren't any good to them. They needed a shot of her crying—or better yet, yelling—to get a real payout from the trashy blogs that bought these photos.

Even when she did make it to a lecture, Nina felt the weight of everyone's stares. She'd seen more than one student surreptitiously take out a phone and snap a picture of her looking disheveled and sad. The one time Nina had ventured to the campus convenience store, to buy shampoo and tissues, she'd seen her own face all over the magazines at the checkout counter. One of the headlines actually read, NINA TELLS JEFF: "I'M KEEPING THE BABY!"

She went back and bought an extra-large box of tampons after she saw that one.

Her parents kept calling to check on her, to ask whether Nina wanted to come home for a while, but Nina insisted she was fine. It was one thing for the press to start attacking her, but the way they'd been treating her parents was completely out of line. At least when she stayed at the dorms, she drew the paparazzi away from her family's house.

A knock sounded at her door. Nina shifted, squeezing her eyes shut. "Wrong room," she called out. The only person who ever came over was Rachel, and she was in class right now. The same history class that Nina was supposed to be in. Well, at least she knew Rachel would share her notes from the lecture.

The knock sounded again, a familiar one-two-three knock that could only come from one person. It used to be their secret knock, back when they played at being knights in a castle. "Please, Nina? I want to talk," called out Princess Samantha.

Nina's stomach twisted. She'd been avoiding Sam the past few days, for almost the same reason she was avoiding Jeff—she didn't know what to say to her. It was all so unbelievably *weird*.

She tore herself reluctantly from bed and went to unlock the door, hitting the light switch so the fluorescent bulbs flared to life.

"Nina!" Sam tilted forward a little, as if she were about to throw her arms around her friend in one of her usual hugs, then seemed to change her mind. She stood uncertainly in the doorway.

Suddenly, Nina saw her room through Samantha's eyes. It was smaller than Sam's closet, and had the worn, lived-in look that comes from decades of students. Note cards were tacked over every last inch of the wall, covered in Nina's blocky handwriting. She was always writing things down: literary quotes, reminders to herself. Alongside the note cards were collages of pictures—of Nina with her parents, or hanging out with her college friends. There wasn't a single photo of Nina and Sam.

Sam had noticed; Nina saw from the way she pursed her lips. But she didn't say anything.

"Hey, Sam. Um, you can come in." Nina gestured to the twin bed, which was starting to look a little rumpled and stale. Sam climbed obediently up onto the blue paisley bedspread, but Nina had gone to stand near the window, to peek behind the shade. The reporters were all still gathered there, their lenses gleaming hungrily in the afternoon sun, though they had taken a few respectful steps back in deference to Sam's bodyguard, who stood at the door with arms crossed.

"I kept expecting to hear from you," Sam said quietly, as Nina came to perch on the bed.

"I sent you a text." Nina glanced at the carpet, evading Sam's gaze. She knew she owed her friend more than that single message. But every time she'd pulled out her phone to call Sam, she'd thought of how the conversation would go—the apology she would have to give, for keeping this a secret—and had put it off. She had plenty to worry about without adding Sam's hurt feelings to the mix.

Sam leaned forward, her legs crisscrossed before her. "Why didn't you feel like you could tell me about you and Jeff?"

So many reasons. Nina tried to think of the simplest. "I didn't know what would happen between us," she said honestly. "I didn't want to make things weirder than they needed to be, in case it didn't work out."

Apparently it was the wrong thing to say. "So if you guys

had broken up before this happened, you would never have told me?" Sam asked, visibly hurt. "I keep thinking about all the things we did in Telluride . . . that comment I made, about how I wanted to find Jeff a girlfriend. Were the two of you laughing at me behind my back the entire time?"

Nina blinked. *We weren't thinking of* you *at all,* she wanted to reply. Didn't Sam understand that this hadn't been all fun and games for her—that it had made her miserable?

Sam sighed. "I'm just saying that I'm your best friend, and I had to find out from the tabloids, the same as the rest of the world."

"You're also Jeff's twin sister," Nina felt the need to point out. "He kept this from you just as much as I did."

"He and I have already talked about it," Sam informed her. "About twenty minutes after the article came out." She didn't need to say more; the implication was clear. She thought Nina was a bad friend for avoiding her these past few days.

Nina couldn't hold her tongue any longer. "Sorry I haven't prioritized your feelings while my life was falling to pieces around me."

Sam winced at her tone. "Right. It just . . . hasn't been the easiest week for me, either. Teddy and Beatrice got engaged. They're going to announce it at a press conference soon." She sighed and glanced down. "I really liked him, you know? I *still* like him. I get that Beatrice has to marry someone, because she's the future queen, and that her choices are limited. But couldn't she have chosen someone else?"

Nina stared at her friend. "Seriously?"

"I know, isn't it messed up?"

"I'm talking about *you,* Sam! That's really why you came by?" Nina's words came out quickly, fueled by an anger that surprised her. "I thought you wanted to talk to me about Jeff, or the fact that most of America apparently hates me. But instead of coming here to support me, you're actually here because you wanted to vent about Beatrice and Teddy!"

Sam bit her lip. "I'm sorry. I just . . . needed a friend right now."

"So do I," Nina said meaningfully.

Sam's eyes darted toward the blacked-out window. "The paparazzi will lose interest soon," she promised, clearly trying to be helpful. "They'll move on to another story and stop hanging out here. I mean, they'll still take pictures of you at official events, but you'll get used to it."

"I don't want to 'get used to it'!" Nina clawed angrily at her bedspread, her fists closing around the printed fabric. "I just want things to go back to normal!"

"*Normal* meaning a world where you've conveniently erased me from the story of your life?" Sam nodded toward the photos on the wall.

Nina had been curious how long it would take Sam to ask about those.

"It's just—no one at school knows I'm friends with you. It seemed easier not to tell everyone. Less complicated," Nina said quickly, wondering why she felt the need to explain herself to Sam, anyway.

The princess flinched at her words. "I didn't realize I was a *complication*."

"You know I didn't mean it like that," Nina insisted, though her gaze followed Sam's toward the collage.

What if this *was* an accurate depiction of Nina's life? What if her mom had never interviewed for the chamberlain job, if Nina and Sam had never become such good friends? How would Nina's life be different—or, more importantly, how would *Nina* be different?

Even as a child, Nina had instinctively known that she had to give way to Sam. Not necessarily because she was royal, though that was certainly part of it. But Sam had enough personality for two people—which always made Nina feel like she needed to back down a bit, to compensate. Sam was unpredictable and irrepressible and laughing and mischievous. She had always been the one to set their plans, come up with their schemes. And she expected Nina to follow her lead without question.

Nina thought of all the times she had quietly done whatever Sam wanted, without even stopping to consider what *she* might want. When they went shopping for new backpacks in fifth grade, Sam had demanded the bright blue one, even though she knew blue was Nina's favorite color. Last year when they got their tattoos together, Sam had chosen the design, and only then had asked Nina whether she liked it. She begged Nina to come to events where she wouldn't know many people, then ditched her to make out with some new guy in a closet.

Come to think of it, Sam was an unreliable and thoughtless friend. Selfish, even.

"Sam," she said quietly. "It hasn't always been easy, being your best friend."

"Why?" Sam demanded, instantly on the defensive.

"Because. A friendship is supposed to be equal, and absolutely nothing about our friendship has ever been equal." Nina let out a breath. "I know you never consciously tried to make me feel inferior. But traveling on all these vacations that your family pays for, driving *your* car around the capital because my parents wouldn't buy me one, going to galas in your cast-off dresses, where everyone just looks right through me like I'm not even there. The only thing worse than feeling invisible is feeling like your charity case."

She met Sam's gaze. "It's easier with the friends I've made at college. We're all taking the same classes and going to the same parties. We're just . . . equals."

Sam's face was dazed, almost incredulous, but beneath it

Nina saw an unmistakable hurt. "I didn't realize," she said, stating the obvious. "But, Nina, none of those things matter to me, not the money or the titles or the vacations."

"They only 'don't matter' to you because you *have* them," Nina replied. It came out more snappish than she'd meant it to. But really. Nina was the furthest thing in the world from a social climber, yet even she couldn't help being constantly aware of those things. Money, titles, and her lack thereof.

It was hard not to resent Sam a little bit, for being so blissfully unaware of the struggles everyone else faced.

"Well, forget what the world thinks," Sam replied, striving for an upbeat tone.

"Forget what the world thinks?" Nina asked, incredulous. "How am I supposed to do that when millions of people are currently trash-talking me? They don't think I'm good enough for your brother."

"Of course you're good enough!"

"Do you really think that?" Nina wasn't sure what instinct was urging her onward. Maybe it just felt good, pushing back at Sam for once, instead of letting the princess's desires steamroll over her own.

"I wouldn't be your friend if I didn't think so," Sam replied.

That comment sent Nina over the edge. Because in typical Sam fashion, she hadn't really answered the question—hadn't told Nina that she was smart and classy, and to ignore the internet trolls. She had just delivered her own opinion as if it were fact, and let that rest her case.

"*Are* we friends?" Nina heard herself ask, her voice terrifyingly even. "Because the way I see it, you show up here when it's convenient for *you*—barging into my dorm room, summoning me to some party or theater performance, always wanting to talk about you and *your* problems. I'm not at your beck and call, Samantha. I'm supposed to be your friend. Not an assistant, not a secretary, not someone you can take for granted. A *friend*!"

The words bubbled up out of her like acid, years of frustration and bottled-up insecurities finally boiling over. And for once, Nina felt powerless to hold it all back.

Sam flushed a bright red. "I always thought of you like a sister, Nina, but I guess I've been wrong the whole time, since apparently I've been hurting your feelings throughout our years of friendship."

"Like a sister?" Nina repeated. "That doesn't count for much, based on the way you treat your real sister."

The moment the comment left her mouth, Nina regretted it—but the damage had been done.

Her words were followed by complete and total silence.

I'm sorry, Nina wanted to say; *I didn't mean it*—except that wasn't entirely true. She *had* meant it, or at least some part of her had meant it.

Sam had pulled her lower lip into her teeth, the way she did when she was struggling not to cry. "I'll get out of here. God forbid my presence ruins your perfect college life."

"Sounds good to me." Nina didn't bother watching as Sam shut the door behind her.

She fell back onto her bed, pulling her hands up before her as she curled into the fetal position. The tattoo was mere inches from her face.

She remembered what she'd researched, when Sam had decided they would get that particular image. The Chinese character was more nuanced than the simple translation of *friendship*. It derived from an older symbol that combined the words for *two* and *hands*—meaning not just a friend, but a friend who helped you out in times of need. A friend you could lean on.

Nina tucked her tattooed wrist beneath her pillow and shut her eyes.

24

SAMANTHA

Samantha tapped frantically at her controller, willing her lime-green animated car to go faster. She *always* beat Jeff at this game. That was her favorite part of playing it: the look of shocked dismay on her brother's face when he lost.

Jeff was hunched over in the armchair next to her, his dark eyes gleaming with the reflected glow of the TV screen. Sam gritted her teeth, whipping her car around the curve of the track, only to collide with the wall in an explosion of cartoon flames.

She expected Jeff to jump to his feet, at the very least to give a low whoop of victory, but he just turned to her with an uneven shrug. "Neither of us is playing all that great," he pointed out. "Maybe we should call it a day."

Sam set aside the video-game controller and turned to her brother. "Still no word from Nina?" When he shook his head, she sighed. "She isn't really talking to me, either."

"Really? I figured you guys would have made up by now."

Slowly, her throat nearly closing over the words, Sam related what Nina had said on campus yesterday. That it hadn't been easy on her, spending so much time with the royal family through the years. How they'd inadvertently shuffled her aside, made her feel inferior. Treated her like an afterthought.

Her brother's expression hardened, and he muttered a curse. "I can't believe she felt that way and I didn't realize. . . ."

"It's my fault too. She was my best friend long before she became your secret girlfriend."

Jeff glanced over, alerted by something in her tone. "Are you angry that I didn't tell you?"

"Not angry," Sam admitted. "Just . . . hurt, I guess. I thought you trusted me with this kind of thing." Even as she said it, Sam squirmed at her own hypocrisy, because she hadn't told Jeff about her and Teddy.

Well, she definitely wouldn't tell him now, given that Teddy had just gotten engaged to their sister.

The overhead motion-detector lights flickered on as their mom strode into the media room.

"There you two are!" the queen proclaimed, her voice laced with impatience. "Samantha, I've been looking for you. I need you right now."

"What for?" Sam asked cautiously.

"Wedding prep. Come on." Adelaide turned on one heel and led her daughter along the hallway, then down multiple flights of stairs. Sam's fishtail braid swung back and forth like a pendulum with their steps.

Wedding prep. Last night, Beatrice had announced the news of the engagement to the gathered family—with Teddy at her side, of course. There had been a lot of hugging and champagne and planning of a full-court engagement party, all of which had made Sam feel slightly ill.

When they stepped into the hallway that led beneath the palace, Sam almost halted in her tracks. "We're going to the vault?"

The queen cast her a puzzled glance. "Is something wrong? Usually you can't wait for an excuse to come down here."

While the Crown Jewels technically belonged to the state, the right to borrow them was granted only at the discretion of the monarch, which meant that right now, the only people with access were the queen, the princesses, and the Queen

Mother—and, occasionally, Aunt Margaret and Aunt Evelyn. They usually scheduled a visit before each black-tie event, to coordinate which jewels each of them would wear. Sometimes the queen would bring her favorite dress designer along, so that he could make a gown specifically to showcase a particular item of jewelry.

They were probably here to pick out their jewels for Beatrice and Teddy's big party. *Another occasion to celebrate Beatrice,* Sam thought dully. What else was new.

She wondered what her mom thought about Beatrice's lightning-fast engagement. Maybe she was the one who'd pressured Beatrice into it.

"I can't believe the news about Teddy and Beatrice," Sam began, testing the waters. "Don't you think it feels a little fast?"

The queen shrugged. "When you know, you know. I knew that your father was the one by the end of our third date."

Sam lifted an eyebrow skeptically, but her mom wasn't finished. "Beatrice clearly felt certain enough in her choice that she didn't need to wait any longer. She's always been sure of what she wanted." *Unlike you* was the silent implication.

"I guess so," Sam muttered, unconvinced. It was easy to be decisive when all you did was obey your parents' orders.

They stepped into a shadowed underground hallway. The air was especially cold down here; Sam hugged herself, trying not to shiver in her thin black sweater. A pair of security guards stood to either side of a heavy metal door.

The queen pressed her palm to a biosecurity panel and the door swung inward, revealing that it was almost a meter thick. Sam followed her mom inside, feeling her spirits lift a little in spite of everything.

The room blossomed to life as display tables lit up one by one. Behind the glass panes, against a backdrop of black velvet, gleamed gold and ivory and countless jewels. Sam knew for a fact that nothing down here was insured, because how could anyone begin to assign a financial value to these items? They were all utterly priceless.

This was far and away the most lucrative part of the palace's tourism revenue: the "Crown Jewels Experience" cost an additional ten dollars per ticket, which almost everyone paid. In the crowded summer months, the entry line snaked around the hallway for hours.

Sam wandered past the first case, the one containing all the ceremonial regalia: the Great Scepter, the Orb of State, the Hand of Justice. Farther along was a collection of delicate porcelain wedding-cake boxes that, remarkably, still contained a slice of cake from every royal wedding. The fondant was solid as a brick by now.

She paused at the crowns and tiaras. There were almost a dozen of them, some heavy and masculine, others delicate and filigreed, including a few child-sized coronets for the Princes and Princesses Royal. Through the first hundred years of America's history, the kings and queens had commissioned their own crowns for each coronation, until the expense was eventually deemed too great.

Grandest of all was the Imperial State Crown, the one that had been used for every coronation since that of King George III. It glittered all over with stones—at the center was a massive hundred-carat ruby called Heart's Blood, stolen in the Spanish-American War—and a set of pearls that was said to be from Queen Martha's necklace.

Sam's memories of her father's coronation were hazy; her grandfather King Edward III had died so suddenly. No one had expected George to assume the throne for another twenty years at least.

She remembered the look on her father's face as he recited the words of the coronation oath: "I swear to you that my whole life, whether it be long or short, shall be devoted to your service, and to the service of this great nation to which we all belong."

"Who is he talking to?" she'd whispered to ten-year-old Beatrice, who'd stood next to her, looking awed and maybe a little fearful. But then, Beatrice had known that she was up next.

"Everyone. America," Beatrice answered.

Sam watched, breathless, as her father reached for the enormous gleaming crown and placed it upon his head.

In other countries, kings and queens were crowned in churches, by priests. But this was America, where the state was the state, with no involvement from any religious entity. Here the monarchs crowned themselves.

"Your Majesty. Thank you so much for making the time," she heard Teddy say as he walked through the door and into the vault. He started to bow to the queen, who brushed the motion aside and pulled him in for a hug.

"We're so thrilled for you both," Queen Adelaide murmured. Sam rolled her eyes.

Teddy stopped short when he noticed Sam. "Samantha. I didn't know—I mean, I hadn't expected you to join us."

The queen's phone buzzed, and she glanced down at her screen with a frown. "I have to take this," she said with a resigned sigh. "Why don't you two get started without me?"

Get started? Sam felt her chest seize in panic. Were they really here to pick out Beatrice's *engagement ring?*

Teddy blanched. "That's all right, we can wait—"

"Don't be ridiculous," Adelaide assured him. "You're in good hands. Samantha is the maid of honor, after all."

"I'm not the maid of honor. I mean, Beatrice hasn't asked me," Sam muttered.

The queen exchanged a loaded glance with Teddy, as if seeking sympathy for Sam's obstinacy. "She doesn't need to ask. She's your sister; it's *understood*," she said crisply. Before either of them could protest, she swept back out of the room, leaving the security guards at the door. "Go ahead; I'll just be a minute!"

Samantha briefly considered making a run for it. But that was the cowardly thing to do, and the last thing Sam wanted was for Teddy to think he had rattled her. She squared her shoulders and started toward the final row of display cases, the ones that everyone really came here for—the jewelry. One of the security guards unlocked the glass cover before retreating with a nod.

Teddy came to stand next to her. He seemed oddly wary, as if he expected Sam to whirl on him with a barrage of insults any moment now, or maybe pummel him with her fists.

She just looked over the rings, ignoring him.

"I'm hopeless at this," Teddy ventured, breaking the silence. "They all look beautiful. How am I supposed to choose?" He opened the display case to pull out one of the rings, an elegant platinum band circled with baguette-cut diamonds.

"My grandmother had that one made to celebrate her twenty-fifth wedding anniversary." She wasn't really sure why she told him that.

"In that case, maybe it has some good luck." Teddy cast a quick glance at Sam, but she still refused to meet his gaze. Instead she moved sideways along the case, studying the various showstopping jewels nestled inside.

A few of them she slipped on her own finger: a massive thirteen-carat emerald, an oval diamond on a rose-gold band. They were all unquestionably beautiful, but to Sam, their appeal was so much more than the beauty.

They were living fragments of history. Each time she put one on, Sam felt the ghosts of her ancestors whispering to her across the fabric of centuries. The rings made her feel more confident, even majestic.

Not that she would ever be a Your Majesty.

Teddy cleared his throat. "I'm sorry, but I have to ask . . . are you just angry with me, or is something else going on?"

"Oh, so you've decided that now is a good time to start caring about my feelings?"

"Please, Sam. I'm trying here."

Sam felt the anger seeping from her, just a little. After everything that had happened between them, she didn't exactly want to get into this with Teddy. But she had no one else to talk to. And he *was* a good listener.

"Nina and I got into a fight. On top of everything else . . . it just feels like a lot."

"You miss her." It wasn't a question.

"We used to talk constantly, and now all of a sudden we've gone radio silent. It feels like half my internal monologue has suddenly switched off."

"Have you apologized?"

"What makes you think I'm the one who did something wrong?" Sam said automatically, then caught her breath at the wry expression on Teddy's face. "I don't know. The things we said to each other . . . I'm not sure we'll be able to forgive and forget."

"Who said anything about forgetting? The point of forgiveness is to recognize that someone has hurt you, and to still love them in spite of it." The way Teddy said it, Sam knew he wasn't just talking about Nina anymore.

He reached for one of the rings. It looked very small, centered there on his palm. He quickly put it back. "Which would you pick?"

Her eyes darted to a cushion-cut pink diamond surrounded by a halo of smaller diamonds.

Wordlessly, Teddy took the ring in his hand. He looked at her expectantly.

A hushed spell seemed to have fallen over them. Samantha's breath caught as she placed her hand in his. Slowly, neither of them daring to speak, he slid the ring onto her finger. It fit perfectly.

Their faces were suddenly very close. Sam's heartbeat echoed in her ears. She knew what Teddy's old-fashioned gesture meant. He was silently willing her to understand that even though their love could never be, because of reasons much more powerful than either of them, he would always care about her.

She swallowed and forced herself to step back. "You aren't picking for me, though. And this ring doesn't feel like Beatrice."

Teddy let go of her hand with visible reluctance. Sam hated herself for how lonely her palm felt without him touching it.

She had never been any good at disguising her feelings. There was something too *immediate* about her face, the way all her emotions played themselves out over her features like the shadows of clouds on water. She turned away, because she knew that if she kept looking at him, he would see exactly what she was thinking.

Teddy reached for a very old ring that had once belonged to Queen Thérèse, the only French-born queen America had ever had. It looked like Beatrice, classic and elegant: a simple solitaire diamond on a white-gold band. They both gasped as a ray of light hit the multifaceted stone, throwing up a glitter of dancing pinpoints that chased themselves over the walls of the vault.

"Looks like you know Beatrice pretty well." Sam managed to sound almost normal, though she could feel her heart breaking all over again.

"Oh! That one is perfect," cried out the queen, who had just reentered the vault. She hurried to pull Teddy into another hug, beaming, exclaiming her congratulations over and over.

No one noticed as Samantha slid the pink diamond off her finger and set it quietly back against the black velvet of the display case.

25

BEATRICE

"I can't believe we're doing your engagement interview!" Dave Dunleavy exclaimed in his booming television voice. Beatrice managed a tight smile in reply.

Dave had been the media's senior royal correspondent since Beatrice was a child. He'd conducted all the major interviews in her life, from her very first one at age five—a joint interview with her father, when Dave had flashed silly cartoons on the teleprompter to make sure she smiled—to the very serious one she'd done on her eighteenth birthday. Beatrice had personally requested Dave for today's live filming. Unsurprisingly, he'd jumped at the chance to introduce the world to America's future king consort.

A small group of staff bustled around them, preparing this room—one of the smaller salons on the first floor—for the interview. A few doors down was the Media Briefing Hall, where the palace's press secretary spoke to reporters each morning from behind a podium, addressing questions of policy or budget. But for these intimate, personal conversations, the royal family preferred a sitting room.

"Teddy, how are you feeling?" Dave glanced at Teddy, who was standing utterly still as an assistant pinned a small mic to his shirt.

"Nervous," Teddy admitted. "America is going to make up their minds about me right now. Whatever they think about me after the next twenty minutes, that's what they'll think about me for the rest of their lives. So, you know, no pressure."

"First impressions are important," Dave agreed sagely, "but there's no need to worry. Your relationship will speak for itself."

Robert Standish moved to the side of the room, a Bluetooth headset tucked into his ear. He caught Beatrice's eye and nodded, all business. Next to him stood Beatrice's stand-in security, a Guard named Jake, who normally worked the palace entrance.

That was the only small blessing: Connor's absence. Beatrice felt ashamed of her own cowardice, but she'd purposefully planned this interview on a Thursday because it was Connor's day off. She didn't want to see the look on his face as he watched her and Teddy playact this relationship in front of the entire world.

She had tried, so many times, to tell Connor about her engagement. But whenever she braced herself to share the news, she would see the look on his face—and the words would die on her lips. *I'll tell him tomorrow,* she assured herself. *Just one more night where he smiles at me like this, before it all falls apart.*

This morning, Beatrice knew she couldn't wait any longer; she had to tell him, or risk him finding out from the media. But when she'd reached across her bed for Connor, he was already gone.

"All right. Are you both ready?" Dave asked, taking a seat in the armchair across from them.

Beatrice settled next to Teddy on the couch, smoothing a nonexistent wrinkle from her pleated navy dress. Someone adjusted an overhead light, and she squinted into the sudden brightness. The room felt very warm. "I'm ready."

"As ready as I'll ever be," Teddy echoed.

"Rolling," the cameraman said softly, a few feet away.

Dave nodded. "What an honor it is, to get to speak to

you both on such a joyous day. Princess Beatrice, would you like to be the one to personally share your news?"

Like the professional she was, Beatrice lifted her eyes to the camera and smiled. "I'm delighted to announce that Theodore Eaton and I are engaged. I proposed to him last week, and thankfully, he said yes."

"I know I speak for America when I say how thrilled I am for you both," Dave replied. "It's clear from the looks on your faces that you're very much in love."

In love. Right. Beatrice glanced over at Teddy with what she hoped was a dewy-eyed smile.

At that very moment, the door at the back of the room opened, and a familiar tall figure stepped inside.

Time ground to a momentary halt.

No, Beatrice thought desperately. Connor wasn't *supposed* to be here. This was all wrong.

Connor's eyes met hers, then drifted to the enormous diamond on Beatrice's finger, which suddenly felt impossibly heavy. She saw the rapid shifts of his expression, from bewilderment, to comprehension, to the devastating pain that followed.

She hated herself in that moment, for being the source of that pain.

"Tell us about your relationship, Beatrice. It seems like it's been a whirlwind," Dave went on. "How did you decide that you were ready to propose?"

Not for nothing had Beatrice lived her entire life in the spotlight. Her smile never wavered.

"As my mom always told me, when you know, you know," she replied, without missing a beat. "I knew right away that Teddy was someone I could see myself marrying." In a way, it was the truth. She *had* met Teddy for the specific purpose of finding a future husband.

Teddy reached for her hand, interlacing their fingers on the couch between them.

Connor took a sharp intake of breath at the gesture and slipped out of the room. Beatrice wished she could look over, but she didn't dare. She just kept on smiling.

Teddy must have sensed her sudden panic, because he leaned forward and lowered his voice conspiratorially. The cameras obediently swiveled toward him.

"My first impression was slightly different," he confessed to Dave. "To be honest, I thought Beatrice didn't like me, because she refused to dance with me. Not that I blamed her," he added, with that disarming smile that revealed his twin dimples. "She's so far out of my league, I assumed I didn't stand a chance."

"She wouldn't dance with you!" Dave seized eagerly on this tidbit. "Why not?"

The attention of the room veered back toward Beatrice, but by now she had regained her composure. She let her eyes meet Teddy's in a single instant of gratitude. He may not have known why she was upset, but he'd done his best to cover for her all the same.

"I know, my mistake," she said lightly. "Luckily for me, I have a lifetime of dancing with Teddy to make up for it." She saw from Dave's beaming expression that she'd said the right thing.

She could do this, Beatrice reminded herself, squeezing Teddy's hand for reassurance. She could sit before these cameras and spin her life into the fairy-tale romance America craved. She could smile until the bitter end, no matter what it cost, because she was a Washington and she had been trained to smile through anything. Even through her own heartbreak.

269

After the interview, Robert asked Beatrice and Teddy if they wouldn't mind doing a walkabout—stepping outside and greeting the waiting crowds. Apparently most of the capital had been watching their broadcast and had already flooded the streets to congratulate them.

Teddy looked to Beatrice for confirmation. "All right," she said, her throat hoarse. She kept glancing around in search of Connor, but didn't see him.

People jostled behind the palace's iron gates, waving miniature American flags, shouting Beatrice's and Teddy's names. The moment they appeared on the front steps, the decibel level soared even higher.

"You start on the left, and I'll take the right?" Teddy offered. Beatrice nodded.

She made her way methodically along the crowd, pausing to shake hands whenever she could, smiling at the phone screens that were thrust in her face. People threw flowers as she passed; Beatrice bent down to accept one of them, a handful of simple garden daisies from a little girl. "She looked at *me!*" more than one person cried out, elbowing a friend. Everyone seemed desperate to catch her gaze, to brush her coat, to feel in some way that they had claimed a piece of her. To her right, Beatrice saw Teddy graciously accepting congratulations, hugging people over the barrier. He really was a natural at this.

It wasn't until later, after Teddy had finally headed home and Beatrice started up the stairs to her room, that she looked out a window and caught sight of Connor.

He was out in the Marble Courtyard: a lonely, solitary figure holding a cigarette in one hand.

She had to force herself not to break into a run as she headed through the first-floor reception rooms and outside. Connor tensed, but didn't otherwise acknowledge her arrival.

There were a million things Beatrice wanted to say: that she was sorry and that she loved him and could he ever forgive her. All she blurted out was "I didn't realize you smoked."

"In extreme situations only," he said tersely, and turned away.

Beatrice instinctively reached for him, to pull him back—then caught herself, lowering her arm slowly to her side. "Please. Will you take a walk with me?"

She needed to talk to him in private, and had no idea where else they could go. The palace would be swarming with people right now: chamberlains and chambermaids, courtiers and tourists and ministers of state. The gardens were only open to group tours during the summer months. It was January, so everything looked drab and dead, but at least they could talk without fear of being overheard.

Connor tossed his cigarette onto the black and white marble slabs, worn down from centuries of foot traffic. He ground it beneath his heel, daring Beatrice to remark upon it, but she was silent. "Okay," he conceded.

They started down the gravel path through the center of the gardens. Gray skies arced overhead, mirroring the gray waters of the Potomac in the distance. The air had a bite to it.

"I'm sorry I didn't tell you." Beatrice's words fell sharply into the silence. "I wanted to, so many times, but . . ."

"You *proposed* to him, Beatrice. How do you think I felt, watching you do an engagement interview, and with someone like *him?*"

"Teddy is actually a nice person," she couldn't help saying, which only made things worse.

"Oh, so now you're defending him?"

The winter light filtered through the bare branches overhead, falling on the sculptures that lined the paths. The fountains were all empty, to keep them from icing over. They looked bare and lonely without their sparkling jets of water.

"This is because of your dad, isn't it?" Connor asked. "Because he's sick?"

Beatrice gave a miserable nod, unsurprised that he'd figured it out. "He wants me to get married before he dies. I think it will give him peace of mind, to know that he's leaving the country in safe hands."

"He will be leaving the country in safe hands, with *you*. There's no one smarter or more capable."

"I think he wants to ensure the succession," she clarified, her voice bleak. "Make sure things are set up for the next generation of Washingtons."

At the mention of children, Connor halted his steps. For a moment Beatrice thought he was going to storm off, turn away from her and never look back.

Instead he fell to one knee before her.

Time went momentarily still. In some dazed part of her mind Beatrice remembered Teddy, kneeling stiffly at her feet as he swore to be her liege man. This felt utterly different.

Even kneeling, Connor looked like a warrior, every line of his body radiating a tensed power and strength.

"It kills me that I don't have more to offer you," he said roughly. "I have no lands, no fortune, no title. All I can give you is my honor, and my heart. Which already belongs to you."

She would have fallen in love with him right then, if she didn't already love him so fiercely that every cell of her body burned with it.

"I love you, Bee. I've loved you for so long I've forgotten what it felt like *not* to love you."

"I love you, too." Her eyes stung with tears.

"I get that you have to marry someone before your dad dies. But you can't marry Teddy Eaton."

She watched as he fumbled in his jacket for something— had he bought a *ring*? she thought wildly—but what he pulled out instead was a black Sharpie.

Still kneeling before her, he slid the diamond engagement ring off Beatrice's finger and tucked it in the pocket of her jacket. Using the Sharpie, he traced a thin loop around the skin of Beatrice's finger, where her ring had been.

"I'm sorry it isn't a real ring, but I'm improvising here." There was a nervous catch to Connor's voice that Beatrice hadn't heard before. But when he looked up and spoke his next words, his face glowed with a fierce, fervent hope.

"Marry *me*."

In that instant, Beatrice forgot who she was—the name she had been born to, the mantle of responsibility she would soon wear. She forgot her titles and her history and the promises she had made. She thought only of the young man who knelt before her, and the fact that every last fiber of her being was screaming her answer at her—*yes yes yes*.

When it all came rushing back, it weighed a thousand times more than it had before.

"I'm sorry."

Beatrice closed her eyes so she wouldn't have to see Connor's face.

He was on his feet in a swift, fluid motion, the space between them aching.

"You're really doing this," he said heavily. "You're really choosing him?"

"No!" she cried out, shaking her head. "That's not it. Just because I'm marrying him doesn't mean I'm *choosing* him. But Connor, you know that you and me—it's impossible."

"Is it," he said dully.

Beatrice's skin prickled with the cold. "I don't want this any more than you do. But we can figure something out. We'll find a way to keep seeing each other—"

"What are you saying?" Connor cut in.

"I'm saying that I love you and don't want to lose you!"

"So you want me to . . . what? Just stay here as your Guard?

Watch from the sidelines, alone, while you marry him, eventually have *children* with him? Stealing moments together when we can get away with it, whenever your husband is out of town? No," he said bitterly. "I love you, but that doesn't mean I want to live off the scraps of time you can spare from your *real* life."

"I'm sorry," Beatrice whispered through her tears. "But Connor—you've always known the constraints on my position. You know who I am."

"I know *what* you are. But I'm not sure I know who you are at all. The Beatrice I know would never ask this of me."

Beatrice felt suddenly, terrifyingly lonely.

She reached for his hand, but he retreated a step. Panic laced down her spine. "Please," she begged. "Don't give up on us."

"You're the one who already gave up on us, Bee." He let out a ponderous breath. "If this is really your choice, then of course I can't do anything to stop you. All I can do is refuse to be part of it."

"What do you—"

"Consider this my formal resignation. When we get back to the palace, I'll let my supervisor know that I need to be reassigned."

Once, in third grade, Beatrice had fallen off her horse and broken her arm. The doctors assured her that it was no big deal, that lots of people broke their arms, and that the bones often grew back stronger in the broken places.

Standing here in the cold empty garden, she thought of that day, of how much pain she'd been in, and how exponentially worse this was. It was so much easier to break an arm than to break your heart.

Hearts didn't heal themselves. Hearts didn't remake themselves stronger than before.

"I accept your resignation. Thank you for your service," she told him, and the voice that came out of her was a voice

Beatrice had never heard herself use before—steely, calm, taut with control.

It was the voice of a queen.

Connor gave a silent nod before heading back toward the palace.

Beatrice waited until she heard his steps crunch far down the gravel path before lifting her hand to study the line of Sharpie inscribed there. She could barely see it through the blurriness of her vision.

She reached into her pocket for her diamond engagement ring and slipped it back over her finger, covering every last trace of the ink.

26

NINA

"Come to Logan's frat party with me tonight?" Rachel pleaded.

Nina shook her head automatically. All week, in the wake of her explosive fight with Samantha, she'd stayed camped out here in her dorm, emerging only to walk to her lectures or to her job at the library, a hoodie pulled low over her head. No way was she going to something as crowded and hyper-social as a fraternity party.

She curled on her side and closed her eyes, waiting for the sound of Rachel shutting the door.

Instead Rachel stormed over to the bed and yanked the blanket off Nina. "Get up," she snapped. "No more wallowing in your room."

"I can't—"

"Yes, you *can*." Rachel threw open the doors to Nina's wardrobe and began pulling out various items, tossing them one after the other onto the bed. Her vivacity was contagious. "Get dressed and let's go."

"All right." Nina was startled into agreement.

Rachel played music on her phone, singing along in a distinctly off-key voice as she waited for her friend to get ready. Nina pulled on a black crocheted top and skinny jeans, with a long multistrand gold necklace. Then she swept her hair into a high ponytail, revealing the piercings that trailed up the cartilage of her ears. *Let people stare,* she thought, with a new fierceness. Rachel was right—it was time she stopped hiding.

When they walked outside, Nina was pleasantly surprised to see that only a single paparazzo was stationed outside her dorm. He snapped a few halfhearted photos, muttering to himself, then began to pack up his gear.

Rachel gave a bright, quicksilver laugh. "Looks like Beatrice's engagement took the heat off you."

"Apparently so." Nina wasn't all that close with Sam's older sister, but still, she felt oddly grateful to her.

Rachel led Nina to an old redbrick building at the end of Somerset Drive, which students at King's College called simply "the Street," since it was lined on both sides with all the fraternity and sorority houses. On nights like this, cars didn't even attempt to drive down the Street; there were too many college kids spilling out onto the pavement, holding their phones to their ears, trailing back and forth from one house to another as they party-hopped. Despite the chilly weather, a few of the houses had kegs and music on their front lawns, so that people could bring the party outside.

The moment she stepped through the front door, Nina heard the whispers: *She's prettier than I expected; she's not all that pretty; do you think her boobs are real; look at what she's wearing.* People held up their phones to take very unsubtle photos of her, which they probably hoped to sell to some tabloid or gossip site.

"Nina! How are you?" A girl from her English class—Melissa? Marissa?—stepped forward with an eager smile. "Is Jeff here?" She glanced around Nina's side, as if Nina might be hiding the Prince of America on the fraternity's front porch.

"He isn't," Nina said tersely.

277

"Bummer! Hopefully next time," Melissa-or-Marissa replied, in the eager voice of someone who thrived on gossip. It shattered Nina's already tenuous self-control.

"Excuse me," she murmured, and brushed past the girl into the party, Rachel close on her heels.

The fraternity house's two-story living room was filled with other undergrads, many of them clutching red Solo cups. A music video played on the massive TV. In a nearby room, clusters of students gathered around a plastic table, lining up their cups of beer for a drinking game.

It might have been Nina's imagination, but she thought the noise of the party dipped a little at her arrival, as people nudged their friends and pointed her out. The moment she passed, little currents and eddies of whispers rippled out in her wake.

She came to a halt near the door to the backyard and tipped her chin up, daring people to say something. Eventually the noise level in the room recalibrated toward normal.

"Promise you'll stay at least an hour. You look too good to waste this outfit on moping around in your room," Rachel begged, as if reading her thoughts.

Nina managed a half smile. "I'm glad you dragged me out. Even if you did bring me to a frat party."

"Nothing wrong with a frat party every now and then," Rachel said evenly. "Besides, if you leave right away, the haters have won."

Some of those haters were probably here now. Nina gazed around the room, full of overt stares and glossy fake smiles. She wondered which of these students were the ones who'd sent in photos from lecture halls, poking fun at her outfit choices or so-called lack of class. How many of them had logged on to the comment boards to call her an ugly name?

She had never realized how hard it must be for the royal family, to know where to place their trust.

Rachel let out a breath. "You know they reached out to me."

"'They'?"

"Magazines, blogs. I don't know how they found me, but they figured out that we're friends. They offered me a thousand dollars in exchange for information about you, compromising pictures, anything. I told them to go to hell, obviously," Rachel said quickly. "But I thought you should know."

Nina recoiled from the shock. "Thank you. That means a lot to me."

"As if I would sell out my friend. Not to mention my hookup for my VIP library status." Rachel smiled, leaning back against the wall and crossing her arms. "Now, will you *please* tell me why you still refuse to talk to Jeff?"

A few people inclined their heads toward them, trying desperately to eavesdrop without being obvious about it. Nina deliberately turned her back on the rest of the room. "I'm just not ready for . . . whatever that conversation is going to be."

"It's been almost two weeks," Rachel said baldly. "And I know he's been calling nonstop. Or should I say, your imaginary friend *Alex* has been calling." Rachel's eyes glinted with amusement. "That was kind of obvious, Nina. Next time you're hiding a secret relationship with a prince, don't label his contact icon with one of his middle names."

This was the problem with having smart, observant friends, Nina thought wryly. She let out a breath. "I know it's not completely fair, but part of me feels angry at Jeff. This whole media firestorm is exactly why I didn't want to tell anyone, and the story still got out anyway."

Rachel tapped one chunky heel absently against the floor.

"Jeff didn't take those pictures. Doesn't he at least deserve the chance to tell you he's sorry?"

"Are you saying this because you really think he's blameless, or because he's the prince?"

"I don't see why it can't be both," Rachel said glibly, and her grin loosened some of Nina's resolve.

As if on cue, her phone buzzed with an incoming call from Jeff. She started to ignore it, but Rachel's skeptical look stopped her. "Fine, you win," she muttered, and answered.

"Um, hey. It's Jeff." He sounded nervous, as if he hadn't expected her to pick up—and now that she had, he was terrified she might hang up again. "I came to your dorm room, but you aren't answering."

"You're on campus?"

"Yeah. Where are you?"

Nina was startled into answering. "A party at one of the frats."

"Which frat?"

"Sigma something? Listen, Jeff—"

"I understand if you don't want to talk to me." There was a crackling on the other end of the phone, as if he was moving quickly and needed to say everything in a single breath. "I just want to apologize for all the madness that the press has put you through. You should have every expectation of privacy. I'm so sorry."

Nina felt her resentment slowly lessening. "I know it's not your fault."

"Is it Sigma Chi or Kappa Sig? Or SAE?"

"I don't know, the one on the corner?" It took Nina a moment to realize what he'd just said. "Wait—are you *here*?"

There was the sound of a car door slamming. "Look, at least let me deliver this Wawa chocolate shake. Especially after I waited for it and everything."

"You went to Wawa *yourself?*" Nina tried, and failed, to imagine Jeff standing in line. The entire store must have asked for selfies with him.

"I had to make sure they gave you extra M&M's. Obviously."

Before Nina could answer, a commotion rose up behind her. She felt everyone's eyes swivel abruptly toward the front door, then to Nina and back again, as if observing a tennis match. Nina knew even before she turned around what she would see.

It was Prince Jefferson George Alexander Augustus, his phone pressed to one ear, holding a Wawa milkshake in a plastic cup. "I'm here," he said unnecessarily, still speaking into the phone. Nina had the surreal sensation of hearing his voice in her ear and, at the same time, several yards away from her.

No one was even *pretending* not to stare, but Nina didn't care anymore.

She hung up and started toward the prince. He looked oddly nervous, as if he still wasn't sure how she would react to him. Neither was Nina.

"As promised, your delivery," Jeff declared, handing over the Wawa milkshake. Nina took a small sip to cover her confusion.

"Jeff!" Rachel exclaimed in her upbeat, bouncing way. She'd ignored his titles, Nina noticed in a daze, which Jeff would appreciate, and held out her hand rather than curtsying. "It's so good to meet you. I'm Rachel Greenbaum."

"I've heard a lot about you," Jeff replied. "And might I say, you have excellent taste in names for your goldfish."

"You told him!" Rachel rounded on Nina, though she didn't sound upset. "Before you judge me, you should know that every girl on our hallway has a poster of you in her dorm room, except Nina." She gave a mischievous grin. "I get it, though. Why have a poster of you when she's already got the real thing?"

"The real thing is much more work, trust me," Nina countered, only somewhat teasing.

Jeff's eyes gleamed. "But would the poster deliver you on-demand milkshakes?"

Against her better judgment, Nina ventured a step closer. Her mind was throbbing with confusion.

"Is there somewhere we can talk? In private?" Jeff asked.

"You could go upstairs to the study," Rachel suggested. "I guarantee that no one will be working right now."

"There's a study here?"

"Frat boys have homework too." Rachel shrugged, her eyes drifting to Jeff. "Actually, Jeff, they say that your uncle *and* your father both wrote their senior theses in that room."

Neither Nina nor Jeff spoke as they traipsed up the stairs and down the hallway, his security detail hovering alongside them.

The study was lined with shelves of old books, a pair of circular tables gathered beneath bank-style iron lamps. Nina held her breath as the protection officer stationed himself outside and pulled the door shut. She set the Wawa cup on the table; her stomach was too twisted with anxiety for a milkshake right now.

"Jeff, why did you come?"

"To see you," he said, as if it were self-evident.

"No, I mean—why did you come *tonight?*" *After I've been avoiding you since last week,* she didn't need to add.

"Sam told me that she came by. She also told me what you said, about how hard it's been, being involved with our family all these years. I'm so sorry for making you feel that way." His eyes were downcast. "And then last night, after Beatrice's engagement interview, when I saw all those people crowding around her and Teddy outside the palace—I should have realized that was why you wanted to keep our relationship a secret. Anyway," he said clumsily, "I really am sorry."

He sucked in his breath before his next question, as if he couldn't bear to ask but couldn't bear not to.

"Nina . . . what's going on with us? Are we going to be okay?"

Nina trailed a hand along the spines of the nearby books. She couldn't help noticing that they weren't arranged in any kind of order, not alphabetically or by the Dewey decimal system or even by *color*. A perverse part of her wanted to pull them all out, catalog them, then put them back on the shelves properly.

"I meant what I said earlier," Jeff added, rambling into the silence. "The way that the media have been treating you is completely out of line. I'm so sorry for my part in it."

"I know." Nina wasn't quite ready to say, *It's okay*.

"But I'm still curious how the paparazzi knew about us," she went on, voicing a thought she'd had multiple times this past week. "Someone must have tipped them off, for them to be ready and waiting outside my dorm with a long-lens camera."

"No one knew about us. Except for my security detail and the team at Matsuhara, and I don't think they would betray us."

"You never told anyone? Not even Ethan?" She didn't have to point out that Ethan went to this school, too. Maybe even lived in one of the dorms near Nina's.

"I told Ethan that I liked *someone*," Jeff admitted. "It was kind of hard not to, after the reporter asked that question at the photo call. But I never told him who it was. And I trust Ethan, implicitly," he added, before she could accuse Ethan of tipping off the tabloids.

Nina gave a slow nod. She believed Jeff. After all, she certainly would never do anything like that to Sam.

"Still, someone must have known," she persisted. "There's no way a photographer just happened to be on campus with that camera, happened to notice you, and *happened* to snap a photo of us in the one second that you kissed me!"

Jeff shrugged. He clearly wasn't as bothered by this as she was, but then, he was much more used to having his privacy invaded. "Maybe they were tailing the town car? I can try to get my security involved, if you want," he offered, though he didn't sound hopeful.

"It just makes me feel unsafe, thinking that there's someone who sold us out," Nina insisted. "I don't know who to trust anymore."

"You can trust *me*." Jeff took a hesitant step toward her. "Please, Nina. Tell me what I can do to make this right."

She slipped her phone from her pocket and pulled up her photo album. She had taken a picture of every page of the nondisclosure agreement Robert had asked her to sign. Nina had already read through it in its entirety, but now she watched Jeff skim through the various sections.

I will not disclose confidential information to any party . . . I shall not use or exploit my relationship to the Crown to promote my own interests . . . In the event of a dispute, I waive my right to a jury of my peers in a public court proceeding, and agree instead to a closed arbitration . . .

Jeff cursed. "I had no idea." He handed Nina's phone back to her, shaking his head in disgust. "Please don't feel like you need to sign that."

"I don't mind signing. I would never sell secrets about your family," Nina said gently. "This isn't about the contract. It's about what the contract represents. That if you and I keep dating, it won't ever be just you and me in the relationship. It's you and me and the palace—or, worse, you and me and the world. Which makes things a bit crowded."

"*If* we keep dating?" Jeff repeated.

A lock of his hair kept falling forward into his eyes; Nina resisted the urge to brush it back. "I don't know if I'm the right person to be dating you."

"Says who, someone at the *Daily News*? I couldn't care less what she thinks," Jeff shot back, but Nina shook her head.

"It isn't just her. All those thousands of comments— America used to adore you, and now they hate you, because of *me*. And what about Daphne?"

"What about her?"

"Everyone likes her better!"

"You really need to stop reading the tabloids. Those things rot your brain," Jeff said, at which Nina couldn't help but smile. "Honestly, Nina. I don't care if America 'likes her better.'" He lifted his hands into air quotes to show his skepticism. "America isn't the one trying to date you; I am. And I like *you* better."

Nina wasn't trying to validate all those articles, and yet . . . "It feels like there's still something between you, some kind of unfinished business. Don't you think that, eventually, you'll end up going back to her?"

"I'm sorry again about Daphne, and graduation," Jeff said heavily. "I know what I put you through wasn't fair. The thing is, I should have ended things with Daphne much earlier than I did."

He swallowed and looked into her eyes.

"We had just been together for so long, and my parents and all my friends and even the *media* were always telling me how good she was for me. So I kept thinking that she must be," he said helplessly.

"That's exactly my point!" Nina cried out. "You said it yourself: your parents and friends and the media were all rooting for her. I wish that didn't matter, but it does. It isn't just the two of us anymore, Jeff. And I worry that I'm not the right fit for this life. For your family."

Jeff reached for her hand, and Nina let him take it. He rubbed a thumb lightly over the back of her wrist.

"You're already part of our family," he told her. "You've been Sam's best friend for so long that you've seen behind the curtain. You know the *real* us, the bickering and the pressure. You know that my cousin Percy is a little menace and that half the time when Aunt Margaret does royal engagements, she's drunk. You of all people shouldn't worry about fitting in. You already belong with us. You belong with me."

Nina let out a heavy breath. "If only things could stay like this, when it's just the two of us. Simple, no complications."

Jeff's dark eyes seemed to possess impossible depths. "I hate that all this baggage comes with dating me. It's a lot to take on, especially for someone as independent as you. I wish I could say that things will get easier. But they never will—not for me."

He gave Nina's hand a final squeeze, then let go. "I don't have a choice, but you do. If you want to walk away from this, from all the attention and the madness and the NDAs, I won't blame you. But I will miss you."

Nina opened her mouth to say yes—that she wanted to walk away, that she wished him nothing but the best and would always be his friend. That this life and everything that came with it were just too *much*.

What came out instead was "No."

The prince looked up sharply. Nina swallowed. "No," she said again, and realized that it was true. "I'm not done with you, not yet."

Then she was flinging herself into his arms, kissing Jeff with such enthusiasm that he stumbled backward and had to lift her off her feet—literally, her boots were dangling in the air. Nina didn't even notice that the buttons on Jeff's jacket were digging into her. The impact of their kiss crashed through her like cymbals, tingling all the way to her lips and toes and the very edges of her hair.

Finally Jeff set her down. Nina reached for the table to steady herself, and her hand almost knocked over the milkshake.

She shook back her hair and took a celebratory sip, smiling around the straw. "Thanks for bringing me this," she told Jeff, and handed it over so that he could try.

He grinned. "You're right, it really does taste better with double M&M's."

27

DAPHNE

Daphne sighed with a hollow sense of discontent.

It was Saturday morning, and she was seated next to her mother in one of the luxurious pedicure chairs at Ceron's, the top salon in Washington. They were ensconced in the place of honor at the center of the room, with prime views over the rest of the salon. Daphne saw Henrietta of Hanover, one of the royal family's numerous distant cousins, with her hair wrapped in a Medusa helmet of silver foils. And wasn't that the senator from Rainier walking out of a treatment room, her face red and angry from a facial?

Daphne's mother knew Ceron from years ago, back when he did hair for magazine photo shoots and runway shows, though he moved in more rarified circles these days. His life had forever changed once he was named the official palace hairstylist. It had caused business here at the salon to triple, even if half those clients were just royalty fanatics who plopped in their chairs and declared that however Her Majesty was wearing her hair, they wanted the exact same thing.

Tiffany, the salon assistant, finished the topcoat on Rebecca's toes. "Can I get you anything else, milady?"

Rebecca couldn't help preening a little at the title. She never was happier than when she was being *milady*'d somewhere. "Not unless you have any news for me," she said meaningfully.

Ceron went to the palace several times a month, to touch

up the queen's highlights or style the princesses' hair before an event. Sometimes he brought the junior salon technicians along with him. And while Ceron was far too loyal to the Washingtons to be susceptible to bribery, not all members of his staff were. It had only taken a few carefully dropped hints and overly generous tips for Tiffany to reach an understanding with Daphne's mother. She had provided the Deightons with details about the royal family on more than one occasion. Small details, like what color gown the queen might be wearing to an upcoming event, and some that were more significant.

Tiffany leaned forward, lowering her voice to a near whisper. "He was at the palace yesterday to do a trial updo on Princess Beatrice. They're holding a black-tie ball soon, in honor of her engagement to Teddy. The invitations are about to go out."

Rebecca flashed her perfect white teeth in a smile. "Thank you, Tiffany."

Tiffany retreated, her platinum ponytail bouncing. She'd looped a thin red scarf through the belt holes of her waxed black jeans. It was the trademark of Ceron's salon: each of the stylists had to wear black and white with a small pop of red. The salon itself was decorated in the same color scheme, from the vases of vibrant red daylilies to the black-and-white photographs on the walls.

Rebecca shot her daughter a curious glance. "You need to go to that engagement party as Jefferson's date."

"I know, Mother." Though privately, Daphne was more concerned with the wedding itself. She could *not* let this play out the way the last royal wedding had—when Jefferson's aunt Margaret got married, and Daphne wasn't even invited.

Rebecca gave a vague *hmm* of concern. She looked as stunning as ever in a crisp white shirt and jeans, her light blond hair styled in seemingly effortless layers. But no matter how well she dressed the part, you could still tell that Rebecca Deighton hadn't been born to the aristocratic life. It was something hard and hungry, glinting in her catlike face.

Daphne glanced down at her nails, which gleamed with a coat of pearly sheer polish. GOOD AND PROPER, the bottle was labeled, which was so spot-on that it almost seemed ironic. The last time she'd visited the hospital, Daphne had brought a bottle of deep red Va-Va-Voom, and painted Himari's nails with it.

She didn't tell her mother about that, because she knew precisely what Rebecca would say: that visiting Himari was a waste of Daphne's time. But Daphne wasn't sure she was going for Himari's sake.

"At least you got rid of that *obstacle.*" Rebecca gestured to the magazines on her lap—*People, Us Weekly,* the *Daily News.* They were all filled with pictures of Nina Gonzalez looking tacky and second-rate next to images of Daphne. Although in the days since Beatrice announced her engagement, the coverage of Nina had decreased sharply.

"This is good work, Daphne," her mother added, a bit clumsily. She clearly wasn't used to giving praise.

The moment she'd returned from the New Year's party at Smuggler's, Daphne had sent Natasha the tip about Jefferson and Nina. She'd even figured out which dorm Nina was living in, so Natasha could stake it out; all it had taken was a bit of online sleuthing and a phone call to the school. She knew the *Daily News* couldn't run a story like that without photographic evidence.

"It wasn't that difficult," Daphne replied. "The commenters did most of the hard work for me."

Daphne knew there was no easier target than a so-called social climber, which was why she'd urged Natasha to take that angle in the article. Predictably, the internet roared in outrage that anyone would set out to ensnare their beloved prince. Some of them went so far as to claim Nina's parents had planned their daughter's entire *life* for this purpose: that Isabella had taken the chamberlain job specifically to throw her daughter in the prince's path. *That girl is like a weed,* one commenter wrote. *She's ugly to look at and has a ferocious ability to climb.*

Daphne didn't feel especially sorry about what she'd done. Nina had brought this down on herself by going after the prince, when everyone knew he belonged to Daphne.

There were plenty of other, more anonymous boys in America—millions of them, in fact. Didn't Nina understand that to date someone as high-profile as Jefferson, she would necessarily become a public figure herself?

If she couldn't take the pressure, she should have stayed out of the big leagues.

"When are you seeing Jefferson next?" Rebecca cut into her thoughts. "You should find a way to bring up this party."

Daphne pretended to blow on her nails, her mind racing, but she couldn't think of an easy way to lie. "I actually haven't heard from him," she admitted.

There it was: the reason Daphne felt this vague and caustic discontent. She had done everything in her power, had schemed and blackmailed and knocked out her competition, and still Jefferson hadn't reached out. What was he waiting for?

Rebecca's eyes drifted to her phone, where she was scrolling through several gossip blogs. Her eyes widened at something she saw.

"Perhaps *this* is why." Her mother's voice was dangerously quiet as she held out her phone. Daphne reached for it with trepidation.

It was a blurry cell-phone pic of Nina and Jefferson, taken last night at a college party.

"He went to a *frat party* with her?" Daphne forced herself

to breathe, trying not to scream. "Well—after all these articles, no *way* will the palace let him date her."

"He isn't the heir to the throne. He has more leeway than Beatrice." Her mother frowned. "Daphne, you've completely lost control of this situation."

"I—y-you were just saying I did a good job—" Daphne stammered, but Rebecca's fierce look quelled her protests.

"That was before I knew what an utter disaster it is."

Panic flooded Daphne's synapses. "I don't know what else to do! I can't just throw myself at him; I tried that at New Year's and it didn't work."

Rebecca turned toward her daughter with an impassive glare. "There are two people in that relationship. If you aren't getting anywhere with the prince, then it's time to try another approach."

When Daphne understood, she felt almost sick. She couldn't imagine seeing Nina Gonzalez again. She despised her.

"Daphne, you can't just sit around waiting for something to happen. Nothing ever gets accomplished that way," her mother hissed. As if Daphne didn't already know that.

Rebecca leaned back in her chair, running her hands along the edges of the magazines in her lap to arrange them in a perfect stack. "Haven't you learned anything from me? Never attack a rival unless you can finish them off completely. Either finish the job, or don't start it in the first place," she said quietly.

Daphne nodded, but her thoughts had drifted to Himari, lying in a coma for almost eight months now. *Either finish the job, or don't start it in the first place.*

What would happen if Himari ever woke up and told the world—told Jefferson—what Daphne had done?

28

BEATRICE

Beatrice couldn't sleep.

In the week since she and Teddy announced their engagement, their schedule had moved at a breakneck pace, crammed with dinners and speeches and charitable visits. Just this morning their entire family had gone to a homeless shelter across town. Beatrice barely had time to get her hair and makeup done afterward, for her engagement photo shoot with Teddy: to take the pictures that would be reproduced on all their wedding merchandise. Pillows and paper dolls, coffee mugs and playing cards, and of course the limited-edition royal engagement stamps: all of it would be plastered with their faces. It felt a bit ridiculous, but Beatrice knew better than to refuse any of the licensing requests, not when the latest estimates projected that her wedding would boost the economy by over three hundred million dollars.

Honestly, she was grateful for the busy schedule. She felt like one of those sharks that needed to keep swimming in order to stay alive. As long as she was in a meeting with members of Congress, or discussing the wedding, or even just *smiling* at someone, she could momentarily forget that her dad was sick—that her time as queen was coming so much sooner than anyone would have imagined.

She could forget that the Guard trailing her movements wasn't Connor, but Jake.

But the forgetting never lasted long enough. Because every-thing in the palace now reminded Beatrice of Connor: of the wicked edge to his humor, the quick, sure grace of his movements. The way his blue-gray eyes lit up every time he saw her.

Even though there were more people than ever at the pal-ace these days, even though she now had a *fiancé*, Beatrice had never felt so alone.

She got out of bed and went to open her windows, to gaze at the net of lights that glittered over the capital. The street-lamps blazed in straight, clean lines around the rectangle of darkness that marked John Jay Park.

Her stomach growled resentfully. Teddy's family had come over for dinner tonight, to discuss next week's engagement party, and Beatrice hadn't had much of an appetite. She'd forced herself to swallow a few bites of her swordfish, but it felt like shards of glass in her stomach. Luckily no one had noticed—just as no one seemed to look past her false smiles, to notice the shadow that lingered in her eyes.

With a heavy sigh, Beatrice pulled on a robe and headed downstairs to the kitchens. The stainless-steel appliances and sleek black cooktops gleamed invitingly. No one was here at this hour: the first sous-chefs and busboys wouldn't arrive until six a.m.

She opened the refrigerator, about to grab one of the con-tainers of leftovers that the cooks always kept here for just this situation, only to pause. She didn't want the cold rem-nants of tonight's dinner. For once in her life, Beatrice would cook something for herself.

After a few minutes of clattering around, she unearthed a massive saucepan. She poured water into it and set it on the stove to boil, fumbling with the knobs. What was that mesh thing Connor had used to drain the cooked pasta? And where in this vast kitchen was she supposed to *find* pasta, anyway?

That night in the cabin felt like it belonged to another lifetime, another Beatrice. How simple everything had been back then, before she knew about her father's condition. Before she'd had to give up Connor.

She braced her palms on the counter, her breath coming in short, panicked gasps. And finally—now that she didn't have to keep that fragile smile on her face, now that there was no one around to see—she let herself cry.

"Beatrice? Are you okay?"

Samantha stood in the doorway, wearing a robe identical to Beatrice's; their mom had given them as Christmas gifts this year. Her hair was pulled into a messy side ponytail that made her whole head look lopsided. Typical Samantha.

Beatrice hastily wiped away her tears. "I was trying to make pasta," she admitted. "What are you doing here?"

"Same thing as you, I guess. I didn't eat much at dinner."

"Oh." Beatrice felt suddenly tentative and uncertain around her sister. In all her own discomfort at the meal with Teddy's family, she hadn't really thought that it might be awkward for Samantha, too. But wasn't she over Teddy by now?

Sam kicked one fuzzy slipper idly against the other. "Remember the time we came in here before a state dinner and accidentally knocked over that enormous cake?"

"They had to send someone out at the last minute to buy fifty tubs of lemon sorbet," Beatrice recollected. That was back before her grandfather died, when she could get away with behavior like that. "We got in so much trouble that night."

"We were always in trouble," Sam countered, and shrugged. "At least, Jeff and I were."

The water in the pot began to boil. Beatrice made a helpless noise and turned back toward it. She still hadn't found any pasta.

"I think there's some mac and cheese in the pantry," Sam pointed out.

"Which pantry?" Beatrice knew about the crystal pantry, the silver pantry, the china pantry—

"The one with food in it." Sam sounded almost amused. "Here, I'll look for it."

Beatrice tried to hide her surprise at Samantha's offer. "That would be great, actually."

Her sister ducked into the pantry, emerging moments later with a blue-and-white box labeled MACARONI AND CHEESE: ROYAL ADVENTURE! The flat noodles were shaped like tiny tiaras and stars, as well as a girl in a ball gown that Beatrice suspected was meant to be *her*.

"Whoever's in charge of restocking has a sense of humor," she heard herself say. Sam lifted an eyebrow but didn't reply.

Neither of them spoke as Sam ripped open the box, poured the noodles into the hot water, then drained them several minutes later. She measured out butter and milk from the fridge before stirring it with the powdered cheese sauce.

"How do you know all this?"

"It's just mac and cheese; anyone can do it," Sam pointed out, then winced. "Sorry, I didn't . . ."

"It's okay. We both know I'm not anyone normal." Beatrice laughed, but there was no humor in it. She hated how helpless she was at such simple domestic tasks. She hated that this life had ruined her for a normal one.

"Most of cooking is just following the directions. It really isn't hard."

Then I should be great at it, Beatrice thought plaintively. All she ever did was follow instructions.

Sam scooped the pasta into two cereal bowls and grabbed a pair of spoons, then hiked herself up onto the counter to sit with her feet dangling over the edge. After a moment Beatrice followed suit. Well, it wasn't as if they were about to carry late-night mac and cheese into the formal dining room.

The macaroni was delicious, its warm cheesiness curiously

comforting. Beatrice wondered what Connor would say if he saw the princesses like this—sitting atop the kitchen counter, eating royal-shaped mac and cheese.

"What is that on your finger?" Sam's voice echoed around the cavernous kitchen. "Are you not wearing your ring?"

Beatrice glanced down at her left hand, so blatantly bare where the enormous diamond should have been. If you looked closely, you could see the faded Sharpie line that Connor had drawn there.

"I take the ring off at night when I wash my face, to keep the soap from getting it dirty," she lied. "I must have accidentally left it on the ring stand by my sink."

Every night Beatrice slipped off that ring the instant she was alone. It was too cold, too heavy, its enormous weight almost too much to bear. It felt like it belonged to someone else and had been given to her by mistake.

"Do you love him?"

Sam's question caught her so off guard that she almost dropped her ceramic bowl.

"I'm just trying to understand," Sam persisted. "In your room that day, after you proposed to him, you seemed so unhappy. I keep watching you and Teddy at all your engagement events, waiting for either of you to say *I love you*, but you never have."

Beatrice shifted on the counter. Samantha was far more observant than the world gave her credit for.

"I just wish it had been anyone but Teddy. At least if it was someone else . . ." Sam trailed off before she could finish, but Beatrice knew enough to fill in the blanks.

If Teddy were free of their engagement, then at least *one* of the Washington sisters might be happy.

Beatrice had assumed that Sam was flirting with Teddy out of spite, or simply because she was bored. She hadn't realized her sister's feelings ran so deep.

Beatrice twirled the spoon between her fingers. It was heavy, engraved with fruits and foliage all the way down the handle. "I'm sorry," she told her sister. "I wish things were different."

Sam's eyes blazed. "Then go *make* them different! Get un-engaged to Teddy so you can both move on with your lives!"

"I can't just get *unengaged* to him." Beatrice rolled her eyes at Sam's made-up word. "Not now. I would be letting everyone down."

"Who, the PR people and party planners? In case you forgot, they work for *you!*"

"It's not just them," Beatrice said helplessly.

"What is it, then?" Sam's face went a hot, indignant red. "If you don't love Teddy, why are you rushing to the altar?" Her temper had always been like this, cruel and lightning quick. Beatrice felt her hold on her emotions starting to fray.

"I know it might seem fast, but I've given this a lot of thought, okay? I really am trying to do the right thing for this country."

"And what reason does the *country* have for needing you to get married right now?"

Beatrice felt suddenly dizzy. "Stability," she insisted, "and continuity, and symbolism . . ."

"You're just saying a bunch of meaningless *words!*"

"Because Dad is *dying!*"

Beatrice hadn't meant to say that. She wished she could snatch the sentence from the air and swallow it back into her chest, where its razor-sharp wings had been beating furiously for weeks. But it was too late.

"What?" Sam's hands gripped the edges of the counter so tightly that her knuckles turned white.

"He has cancer," Beatrice said miserably.

"What?" Sam repeated, with an audible gasp. "What do you—how can—why didn't he tell us?" she managed at last.

A tear trailed down her face and fell into the bowl of macaroni that lay forgotten in her lap.

Then Beatrice was crying too, as the story spilled from her in a jumbled mess: their father's fatal diagnosis, the reasons he had for keeping it to himself—and what he had asked Beatrice to do.

Samantha set her mac and cheese aside with a jarring clatter and threw her arms fiercely around Beatrice.

It was the first time they had hugged like this in years. Beatrice hadn't realized, until this moment, how much she'd missed her sister.

"I can't believe you've been dealing with all of this." Sam reached up to fiddle with her ponytail. "You've held it together so well, I never would have realized that you were upset."

"Sometimes I think I hold it together *too* well," Beatrice said softly. She hated that her siblings thought she was cold or unfeeling. Just because she'd been brought up to keep her emotions hidden didn't mean that she never *experienced* those emotions.

Sam nodded. Tears still glistened on her cheeks. "I'm glad you told me. No one should have to carry this kind of burden alone."

"That's what being the heir to the throne is. Being alone," Beatrice said automatically. Walking alone, sleeping alone, sitting alone on a solitary throne.

Even once she married Teddy, Beatrice knew, she would still feel alone.

A gentle hum emanated from the refrigerators. The overhead lights fell in wide beams over Samantha's features.

"Do you ever wish that you were someone else?" Beatrice asked, after a while.

"I always used to wish I was you. Because I'm utterly

pointless, while you are literally the point of everything." Sam tilted her head to look at Beatrice in confusion. "But you shouldn't feel that way. Why on earth would *you* want to be someone else?"

Beatrice had never thought that Sam might be jealous of her—that Sam would actually prefer to be the heir.

"Because I didn't ask for this." Beatrice heaved a breath. "Trust me, I realize how lucky I am to have been born with this kind of privilege. But I'm still jealous of everyone else in the country, because they get to choose what direction their lives will take. Other kids can dream of being astronauts or firefighters or dancers or doctors," she said helplessly. "But no one in my life has ever asked me what I want to be when I grow up, because there is only one possible future for me."

"Beatrice," Sam asked, her eyes wide. "Do you even *want* to be queen?"

"Wanting has nothing to do with it," Beatrice reminded her. "I am a Washington, just like you, and becoming the queen has always been my future. My road is laid out before me, but yours doesn't have to be. You have options, you have freedom, that I never will."

They were both quiet at that.

Sam reached for her sister's hand and gave it a squeeze. "Remember when we were little, and I used to sneak into your closet to steal your clothes?"

"Your favorite was that pale pink Easter dress. The one with the matching shoes," Beatrice recalled, oddly wistful.

"I wanted so badly to be like you back then." Sam's voice was rough. "I wanted to *be* you. When I realized that was impossible—that only you were the future queen, and I could never be you, no matter how hard I tried—I set out to be everything you're not."

"You . . . what?"

"Why do you think I acted the way I did?" Sam shrugged. "You followed the rules, so I misbehaved; you were disciplined and organized, so I ran wild. I felt left out," she added softly. "You were constantly off doing important future-queen things."

Beatrice sat up a little straighter in surprise. "I felt left out, too, Sam. You and Jeff always had that unbreakable twin bond. It made me feel like an outsider."

"I'm sorry," Sam whispered. "I didn't know."

Beatrice could only nod. She wished they'd had this conversation years ago, instead of waiting until these circumstances forced it upon them.

Sam cleared her throat. "Look, I know you didn't ask for this life, but I also can't imagine anyone handling it with as much grace and dignity as you do. You are next in line for the throne, and you're going to be queen—that's just the way things are. But that doesn't mean it has to define you. You are still a person, and this is still *your* life. We can figure this out. There has to be a way to do the job you were born to do without sacrificing yourself along the way."

Beatrice was stunned by her sister's maturity and wisdom. She gave Sam's hand a grateful squeeze. "Thank you."

"I'm here for you, Bee," Sam told her, using the nickname for what must have been the first time in a decade. "After all of this . . . I just want to make sure you're okay."

Beatrice looked again at Samantha's glassy eyes, remembered the nervous way she'd walked into the kitchen earlier. "What about you?" she demanded. "Are *you* okay?"

"Not really." Sam looked down, her lashes casting shadows on her face. "Nina and I had an awful fight. I didn't feel like I could really unload it on Jeff—it's kind of weird, talking about Nina with him. Mom and Dad never listen to me anyway, and I couldn't talk to you. . . ."

"You can talk to me now," Beatrice assured her. "No more secrets, no more misunderstandings. From here on out, we have each other's backs."

Sam managed an uneven smile. "I would like that."

As Beatrice pulled Samantha in for another hug, the icy lump in her throat seemed to lessen, just a little. Whatever happened, at least now she had her sister on her side.

29

SAMANTHA

The next morning, Samantha knocked at the heavy wooden doors to her father's office. "Hey, Dad, are you busy?"

"Sam! Come on in," he called out in reply.

She didn't normally show up here uninvited, but after last night's conversation with Beatrice, Sam needed to talk to their dad herself: to look him in the eye and ask him about his cancer. Maybe there was still some way out, for all of them. Maybe the prognosis wasn't as bad as Beatrice feared.

Her father was seated behind his desk, sorting through a small leather-bound trunk filled with papers. At Sam's arrival, he glanced up with a weary smile. "I'm glad you stopped by. There's something I've been meaning to talk to you about."

Sam opened her mouth, brimming with questions—*How bad is it? Why didn't you tell us?*—but the words faltered and died on her lips. She realized with a sinking feeling that she didn't need to ask, because she already knew.

Her dad didn't look good. She wasn't sure how she'd missed the changes; they must have been gradual and subtle enough that she didn't notice them on a day-to-day basis. But now that she was looking closely, she saw how thin his skin had become, the purple shadows beneath his eyes. His movements were underscored with an alarming new fatigue.

Sam sank into the chair opposite him, trying desperately

to settle her breaths, to arrange her features into some semblance of a normal expression.

Her father didn't seem to notice her distress. "Have you seen the Box before?" he asked, still organizing papers into various stacks. Something about the way he said the word made Samantha imagine it capitalized.

"I'm not sure." The Box was the size of a briefcase, lined in embossed leather, with oiled hinges. Sam realized that her dad had unlocked it with a small golden key.

"It contains my business for the day. A lot of this is electronic now, of course." He gestured to the tablet at his elbow. "But some of it is still printed: Cabinet minutes, reports from various federal agencies, documents that require my signature. My favorite part are the letters," he added, reaching into the Box to extract an ordinary white envelope.

"Letters?"

"I receive hundreds of letters every day," her dad informed her. "Every last one of them is answered, mostly by my junior secretaries. But I've asked them to pull two letters at random each day, and those letters I answer myself. It's something your grandfather used to do, too."

"Really?"

The king nodded. "I find it useful. Like a daily snapshot of what's on Americans' minds at any given moment."

"People DM me. It's kind of similar," Sam offered.

"DM?"

"Direct message. You know, on social media."

"Ah," the king replied, evidently confused. "Well. It's important for people to feel like they have a direct line to their monarch. That we are reachable, and sympathetic, and responsive. Especially since they usually write such highly personal things."

"What kind of things do they write to you?" Samantha asked, curious.

"Everything. They want a pardon for someone imprisoned; they want to change my mind about some new policy proposal. Their local library is failing; their parent is ill; their fourth-grade classroom needs school supplies. And then, of course, there are the letters full of criticism for something I've done."

"They criticize you?" Sam burst out, leaping to her dad's defense. "Why aren't your secretaries filtering out those letters so you don't see them?" Reading that kind of letter seemed unnecessarily masochistic, like scrolling through the negative comments on social media. Sam had long ago learned to avoid those.

"Because I asked them not to," her dad replied. "Samantha, criticism is a good thing. It means you've fought for something. The only people free from censure are people who've never taken a stand."

She shifted uncomfortably in her seat. "Sure, but that doesn't mean you need to *read* strangers' attacks on you."

"On the contrary, I do," he argued. "Some of our nation's greatest moments of change were born of our family's most vocal critics. It was Red Fox James, for instance, whose efforts led to the establishment of the Native American dukedoms. Opposition is *crucial* to government, like oxygen to fire. And now those voices, those movements, are coming from your generation." The king's eyes rested warmly on Sam. "Although, historically, the people who spark change have usually done so from outside the monarchy, not from within."

"What do you mean?" she asked, confused.

"I'm talking about *you*, Sam." A corner of her dad's mouth lifted. "You've never had a problem letting your family know when we're in the wrong."

She let out an amused breath. "Are you actually *thanking* me for being a troublemaker?"

"Let's say *renegade* instead," her dad teased. "It sounds a little better."

Sam's smile faded as she glanced at the letter in his hands, still unopened. "How do you answer all the people who write to you?"

"With honesty and respect. If I can help with their request, I usually do—even if it means going around the official policy rules and making a private, personal donation. It's nice to feel like I made a difference, in some small way. Especially on the days when I feel like I've failed to resolve the bigger issues."

Her father tore open the envelope and smoothed its contents on the desk before him. His next words were softer, almost as if he were talking to himself. "I often wonder how it must feel, to blindly ask for help like that—to just write a letter to the king and await his answer. I wish I had someone *I* could turn to for guidance. But all I can do is pray."

Hadn't Sam been hoping to do exactly what he described—to lay all her troubles on her dad's shoulders? She wanted him to tell her everything would be all right, the way he used to when she was little. But she knew now that those days were over.

She glanced out the window, her vision blurring. There was a divot in the window's iron casing that her dad swore was a bullet hole from an assassination attempt on King Andrew. She tried desperately to focus on that, to keep from crying in front of him.

"Sam," her dad started to say—but before he could finish, he dissolved into a sudden fit of coughing, and reached into his pocket for a handkerchief to place over his mouth. "Sorry," he said, wheezing through a rueful smile, "got a bit of a dry throat."

Sam nodded mutely.

He leaned back at last, tucking the handkerchief into his pocket, then pressed his hands over the letter from the citizen, absently smoothing its creases. "I've been meaning to thank you. I noticed all the effort you've made with Teddy, helping him feel a part of the family. And your mother tells me that you helped pick out his engagement ring for Beatrice."

"I didn't do very much." Guilt gnawed at the inside of Sam's stomach.

"I know you've never been certain what your role should be, moving forward—that you sometimes feel out of place." Her dad's eyes lit knowingly on hers. "But Beatrice is going to rely on you when she's queen, someday."

Sam noticed that the *someday* was a little tacked on.

"Rely on me for what?" She shook her head, confused. "I'm not as smart as Beatrice."

"There are many ways to be smart, Sam. It isn't just books and memorization. It's wisdom, and patience, and understanding people, which is something you've always been able to do. Not to mention that Beatrice will be surrounded by courtiers telling her what she wants to hear—which, as we just established, isn't a problem you suffer from." He said it lightly, but Sam heard a thread of urgency beneath the words. "Beatrice will count on you for the unvarnished truth. I expect you to give her your support when she's earned it and your criticism when she deserves it. That's what siblings are for, after all."

"You're right," Sam said hoarsely. As Beatrice's sister, Sam should have been her most thoughtful critic, but also her fiercest champion. Instead she'd spent years treating Beatrice as if they were at opposite ends of a battlefield.

Well, that had ended last night.

Her dad managed a smile. "I've always felt that you and Beatrice make a great team—that the two of you embody different aspects of the monarchy. You're sort of like Edward the Black Prince and John of Gaunt."

"You're making me *John of Gaunt* in this analogy?" Sam

protested. "He married for money and manipulated his nephew, and didn't he try to steal the throne of Castile, too?"

The king threw his hands up in surrender. "The early years!" he exclaimed. "When they were teenagers, King Edward III used the Black Prince and John of Gaunt for different political purposes. They were close siblings who clearly trusted each other and were able to divide up the work in a way that made sense. There were a lot of things the Black Prince couldn't do himself, as heir to the throne, that John of Gaunt was able to take on."

"Like what, collecting taxes?" Sam teased.

Her father chuckled appreciatively. "That's not entirely off base. You will sometimes have to serve as a lightning rod: to handle all the negativity and jealousy that people don't dare show Beatrice. But you already know that."

Sam blinked. She hadn't thought of it that way—that some of the criticism she bore might actually be criticism of *Beatrice*, or of the monarchy more broadly, which funneled to her simply because there was nowhere else it could go.

Maybe that was just part of being the spare.

"As head of state," the king went on, "Beatrice won't be able to take on any charitable causes. She can't demonstrate personal preference like that. But you can. That's one of the inherent strengths of monarchy: you aren't angling for reelection like members of Congress; you aren't politically motivated, yet you have continuity. You can act on your good judgment, your empathy, in a way that would be impossible to them."

Her dad had never talked to her like this before—as if she might actually make a difference. Sam edged forward on her chair. "What do you want me to do?"

"I was hoping you might take on a more active role in the Washington Trust. I'd like to give you a board seat," her dad announced.

The trust was a charitable fund that donated millions of

dollars every year, usually by finding new and underappreciated initiatives, putting a large amount of seed money into them, and helping to boost awareness. Her great-grandfather had created the trust many years ago, when he realized that there was only so much he could accomplish through the government. The trust gave him a direct way to help Americans without having to lobby Congress for a new law.

"Thank you, Dad." Sam felt strangely humbled.

"No need to thank me," her dad said gruffly. "You've earned this. I saw you at the shelter yesterday: you were such a natural, especially with the young children. The way you made a fool of yourself, laughing and jumping around with the kids as if no one was watching. You even remembered that boy from our last visit."

When they'd visited the shelter, Sam had recognized one of the kids from last year, a boy named Pete who'd told her all about his music. She asked him if he was still playing guitar, and he'd scrambled to go get it, elated that she had remembered him. The whole thing had devolved into a fun impromptu concert.

Sam shrugged. "It wasn't that big a deal."

"It was unquestionably a big deal to that young man," her dad insisted. "That's one of your most amazing qualities, Sam—your lack of pretension, the way you can make someone feel heard. You are *relatable*, which is something the monarchy could use a little more of."

Sam thought of what she'd said to Beatrice last night, that Beatrice had to find a way to make her life feel like her own. Maybe she could, too. She might be the second-string princess, but she was still *her*. She could use her position to do something meaningful, make a real difference.

"I'm sorry if I've pushed you too hard," the king went on, staring down at his desk. "I thought I needed to give you the benefit of my experience, when all along I needed you to give me the benefit of your *inexperience*." The king smiled. "You're a force of nature, Sam. When you're being yourself, you're our family's secret weapon."

"Dad . . ." She had to swallow to keep her voice from cracking. "Thank you. It really means a lot, that you believe in me."

"I've always believed in you. Sorry if I haven't done the best job of showing it," he admitted. "Now, what did you want to ask me? Wasn't there something you came in here to talk about?"

Sam looked up at her father's calm smile, his steady brown eyes, so full of wisdom. Suddenly she couldn't bring herself to hurl accusations at him. He would tell her of his sickness whenever he was ready, and in the meantime, every moment that she got with him was precious.

"No reason, really. Just wanted to spend time with you." Her eyes drifted to the Box. "Can I help with any of that?"

"Want to answer this for me?" he offered, and slid the envelope toward Sam.

"Am I signing it as you?"

"You could," her dad said. "Or you could answer as yourself. I think the author of that letter would really love to hear from you."

She nodded, the sun glinting on her hair as she bent over the paper. "I love you, Dad."

His Majesty smiled. "Love you, too, kiddo. So much."

30

DAPHNE

Daphne swerved aggressively into another lane, resisting the urge to climb too far above the speed limit. She couldn't afford to get pulled over right now—even though she could probably talk her way out of a ticket.

She was finally going to confront Nina Gonzalez.

It had only gotten worse in the week since those pictures of Nina and Jefferson at the fraternity party surfaced. Whatever happened that night must have resolved their differences, because now they were *everywhere* together: at a local coffee shop, in courtside seats at a basketball game, walking around the campus of King's College.

Daphne knew her mom was right: she needed to talk to Nina, alone. She shouldn't have wasted time trying to go through the prince, not when Nina was clearly the weak point in their relationship.

But crafting a situation in which she could talk to Nina—without Jefferson anywhere nearby—proved more difficult than Daphne had anticipated. She'd debated trying to tail the girl from her college classes, but Daphne knew her face was far too famous; someone would see her and make the connection, and then she would look like a crazy ex-girlfriend lurking around the new girlfriend's dorm room.

Eventually she'd set internet alerts for mentions of Nina's name, and vigilantly monitored the various hashtags about

Nina and Jefferson. Twenty minutes ago, someone had finally posted something: a blurry cell-phone pic of Nina browsing the designer gowns at Halo.

Halo was a decades-old boutique in the center of Herald Oaks, widely known to have the best dress selection in the city. Daphne couldn't quite believe that Nina had shown her face here. Didn't she realize that she was in Daphne's favorite store, on *Daphne's* turf? This was tantamount to a declaration of war.

Her mind drifted to the invitation her family had received earlier this week, on gilt-edged cream paper, stamped with the Washington coat of arms.

The Lord Chamberlain is commanded by Their Majesties

to request the honour of your presence

at a reception celebrating

Her Royal Highness Beatrice Georgina Fredericka Louise

and Lord Theodore Beaufort Eaton

Friday, the seventh of February, at eight in the evening

A reply is requested addressed to the Lord Chamberlain,
Washington Palace

Daphne had every intention of going to that engagement party. And if Nina and Jefferson were there together—well, she would make sure that by the end of the night, they no longer were.

She tore into the parking lot of Halo, her nerves on edge, and charged straight through the front doors. She needed to move fast; she had no idea how long Nina would stay. That is, if she hadn't already left.

There were a lot of people inside the high-ceilinged space:

a couple gazing at the jewelry display, a pair of women giggling as they purchased identical quilted purses. Daphne had never understood women who went shopping together and bought the same exact thing. Didn't they realize the whole point of clothes was to make you stand out?

A few eyes flicked toward her with recognition, though no one greeted her. Daphne wondered which of them had posted the unflattering picture of Nina. She hoped they would think to take a photo of *her*—she looked utterly fantastic in her ivory sleeveless sweater and creamy leather pants. The monochromatic winter-white look was hard to pull off unless you had an absolutely perfect body. Which, of course, Daphne did.

"Daphne! I didn't realize you were coming. I've got some gowns on hold for you in the back, for Beatrice's party." It was her favorite sales associate, Damien: only a few years older than Daphne, with pale blue eyes and a grin that had probably charmed countless women into purchases they didn't need. As usual, he was wearing a casual button-down and skinny tie.

"It's all right; I'm here just to browse." Daphne tried to shrug away the irregularity, but she knew Damien saw right through her. Never in her life had Daphne come to Halo "just to browse." She *always* texted him ahead of time, to let him know which event in the endless rotation of court functions she was shopping for. That way, once she arrived, he would already have arranged a dressing room full of options.

In the early days, Damien had knowingly let Daphne return dresses she had worn—she would leave the tags on, tucking them behind her bra if she could, then bring the garments back to Halo the next day. Damien never said a word, just winked and gave Daphne the full refund. The moment her relationship with Prince Jefferson went public, he'd talked the manager into giving her a full promotional discount, so that she could buy items at cost. Even after she and the prince broke up, he hadn't taken the discount away.

"You're going to love the new gowns that just came in." Damien resolutely tried to steer her in the opposite direction. "There's a blush-colored one that will look *perfect* on you— Arabella Sykes tried to buy it yesterday, but I told her it was spoken for." He waved at another salesperson, who bustled off, presumably to find the dress in question.

Daphne knew what he was doing, engaging the rest of the store in a silent conspiracy to keep her away from Nina, and she adored him all the more for it. But she wasn't about to be dissuaded from her mission.

"I actually wanted to look through the formal wear myself this time," Daphne told him, and headed toward the wing of the store that housed all the gowns. This time Damien made no move to stop her.

Sure enough, there was Nina, browsing the gowns with a perplexed frown on her face. Daphne noted with pleasure that she was wearing stretchy black athleisure pants, with a baggy top that looked like it more rightfully belonged to someone's grandmother. Her combat boots kept making an undignified squeaky noise over the floors.

Didn't Nina realize that she was a public figure now, and couldn't leave her dorm room looking anything but perfect?

"Nina!" Daphne exclaimed, pleased at how truly surprised she sounded. "What a coincidence. Is Samantha here?"

"Oh, um—Daphne. Hi," the other girl stammered, evidently caught off guard. "Sam isn't here, actually. It's just me."

Daphne's ears pricked up at her tone. Something had clearly happened between the so-called best friends. Maybe Samantha didn't approve of Nina dating her twin brother. Maybe *that* was what had bothered the princess at the New Year's party—the reason she'd been standing at the bar alone, looking for someone to drink with. Because she'd just found out that her brother and her best friend were sneaking around behind her back.

Daphne put back a printed jumpsuit she'd been pretending to examine. "Honestly, I don't know who decided that jumpsuits count as formal attire," she said conversationally. "I know they make our legs look fantastic, but we can't exactly wear *pants* to Beatrice's engagement party. That's what you're shopping for, right?"

"Trying to," Nina said awkwardly.

So, she *was* going. At least now Daphne was forewarned. She could handle this. She was Daphne Deighton, and she could handle anything.

"I've actually been hoping I might run into you. How are you holding up, after those horrible articles?"

"I don't really want to talk about it." Nina pretended to examine a price tag, looking distinctly uncomfortable.

"I've been through it all, too, you know," Daphne said earnestly. "I get how totally awful it is. I just wanted to say that I'm here, if you ever need any help."

Nina seemed confused by this unprecedented gesture of friendship from her boyfriend's ex. "That's really nice, but I wouldn't want to bother you," she said warily.

Daphne shook her head. "Jefferson and I are friends," she insisted. "I know you and I have never been close, but it's clear to me that he cares about you. Trust me when I say that I understand. I'm probably the *only* person on earth who understands."

She saw Nina listening, softening, in spite of herself. "It really does suck," Nina ventured.

"Doesn't it?" Daphne asked, and their eyes met in what Nina surely thought was a look of empathy.

"This dress would look amazing on you," Daphne went on, taking the reins of the conversation firmly in hand. "Though it's too big. I wonder where Damien is?"

Unsurprisingly, he appeared right away. He'd likely been eavesdropping from the other side of the clothing rack. Not that Daphne minded. If he sold this story to the press, it could only reflect well on her.

"Can we get a fitting room, and can you please pull some things for Nina?" she asked sweetly, leading the other girl away.

"I couldn't—you don't need to—"

"Come on, the ball is in just a few days, and you clearly weren't making any progress on your own," Daphne reminded her. "Besides, this is way more fun than shopping alone."

Within minutes they were at the back of the store, twin racks of gowns rolled up alongside them. There were dozens to choose from: silk and chiffon, balloon-sleeved and sleeveless, tailored and slouchy. Though Daphne noted with a proprietary pleasure that Damien hadn't *really* brought out the best options, as if he wanted to quietly undermine her efforts to help Nina. The thought warmed her.

She smiled and began to sort through the various gowns, weeding out the rejects with brutal determination. While Nina retreated into a dressing room to try them on, one after the other, Daphne kept up a steady stream of chatter, confessing that *People* had trashed the first outfit she wore in public—"It was this awful green dress that made me look seasick; I don't know *what* I was thinking"—and that in the first few weeks, she read every one of the thousands of comments on those online articles.

Tell no one your secrets, Daphne's mom always said, *but make them think that you have. It creates the illusion of intimacy.*

"I read all the comments too! Well, for a while. Eventually I just deleted my social media handles." Nina's voice emanated through the dressing room door. "You never did that, did you?"

"I guess I thought that if I ran away from it all, the haters would win," Daphne said simply.

Nina stepped in front of the mirror, wearing a black column gown that Daphne wasn't flat-chested enough to pull off. Of course, her hair was dull and unhighlighted, and she had no makeup or nail polish on. And yet—it didn't look totally awful on her.

"How did you make everyone . . ." Nina hesitated, sounding vulnerable. "Make everyone *like* you?"

They'll never like you, because they'll always love *me.*

Aloud she said, "They'll like you eventually. And then they'll dislike you, and then they'll like you again, back and forth. That's just the way it goes." Daphne shrugged, as if she wasn't particularly bothered by it, and changed the subject.

"I'm not sure about this gown. It's kind of boring," she declared, and pulled an ivory one-shouldered trumpet gown from one of the racks. "What about this one?"

Nina gave a puzzled frown. "Isn't it weird to wear white at an engagement party? I wouldn't want anyone to think I was trying to upstage Beatrice."

Oops. Nina had grown up around the royal family; of course she couldn't be fooled by a cheap trick like that. "Right," Daphne agreed, without missing a beat. "I wasn't thinking, sorry."

"I'll try this one," Nina said, reaching for a navy gown flocked with a pattern of black velvet and pulling the dressing room curtain shut behind her. She didn't suspect Daphne of a thing. Which would explain why her purse—a woven straw hobo bag that really should only be worn in the summer—was right out here in the hallway, just begging to be explored.

In a single smooth motion, Daphne opened the bag and pulled out the cell phone tucked inside.

It was touch-ID protected. Daphne swiped up to activate

the camera function, then clicked the icon in the bottom left corner to scroll through the images saved to Nina's camera roll. Surely there would be something incriminating, something Daphne could send to herself, to take this girl down for good. She flicked breathlessly through photo after photo, yet all she saw were screenshots of homework assignments, pictures of books—*books!*—and the occasional selfie with a dark-haired girl Daphne didn't recognize.

This was a waste of time. Nina was apparently smart enough not to take any photos with Jefferson, or any sexy lingerie photos, either.

The curtain rustled. Daphne quickly dropped the phone into Nina's purse and retreated a step. "This is utterly *perfect,*" she gushed. "I think we're done here."

"You think so?" Nina twisted back and forth to examine herself in profile. "Even with heels, it might be a little long. . . ."

Daphne nodded. She tried not to look too pleased with herself as she said, "Don't worry about that; Halo will hem it for you. I'll get one of the fitters now."

Poor Cinderella, Daphne thought smugly, *be careful which fairy godmother you trust. You might not have a gown for the ball after all.*

31

NINA

Later that week, Nina headed through the glass doors of Halo and turned toward the marble checkout desk. She was startled by how different the store looked from when she'd been here before: utterly empty and picked over, as if it had been ravaged by a pack of desperate socialites.

Thank god Nina had bought her own gown before the last-minute feeding frenzy.

The girl behind the counter, who'd been halfheartedly typing into her phone, glanced up at Nina's arrival. "Can I help you?"

"My name is Nina Gonzalez. I'm here to pick up a dress that was being altered," Nina explained. The salesgirl emitted a ponderous sigh and vanished into the back room.

When Nina had ventured here last weekend, she'd immediately felt overwhelmed: there were too many gowns to choose from, in far too many styles. She'd wished more than anything that she could ask for Samantha's help, except she and the princess still weren't speaking.

Nina's hackles had risen when Daphne showed up. She'd assumed they would exchange a few pleasantries and go back to ignoring each other, but to her utter shock, Daphne had suggested they shop *together*.

Nina couldn't think of an excuse fast enough. She felt the eyes of the whole boutique on them, and knew that if she refused, the story would make its way online—about how sweet Daphne had offered to help, but Nina had rudely refused. So she'd resigned herself to the inevitable and headed to the back of the store. Where she had ended up finding a gorgeous blue-and-black dress.

It was more than Nina had spent on an article of clothing in her entire life, but she told herself that it was worth it. Beatrice's engagement party was a big night for her and Jeff—because it was the first Washington family engagement that they would attend as a couple. In front of the entire world, and all the gathered press.

Nina shifted her weight impatiently. At least she was dressed more appropriately than the last time she'd been here.

It didn't come naturally to her, because this country-club look was pretty much the opposite of Nina's style, but she'd taken to thinking of it more like a costume than an outfit—as if she'd been cast in a movie. Today, for instance, she was playing the role of the Prince's Girlfriend, Picking Up Her Dress for the Ball. That character wore a long-sleeved dress, tights, and nude lip gloss.

"Sorry, I don't have your gown," the salesgirl said, emerging from behind a curtain that presumably led to the storeroom.

Nina glanced at the girl's name tag and tried a smile. "Lindsay. Do you know when it will be ready? I need to wear it tomorrow night."

Lindsay shook her head. "We don't have anything under your name."

"It's navy with a black overlay. I was getting it hemmed," Nina said, and realized she was babbling. She swallowed, trying to think of how Samantha would handle this. "I was here on Sunday with Daphne Deighton. Damien was helping us."

"Damien's off today."

"Can you please look again?" Nina ignored the stirrings of panic deep in her stomach.

The salesgirl moved to a computer. Her fingers clicked over the keyboard for a few moments, and she frowned. "Nina Gonzalez?"

"Yes." Nina almost said, *Don't you know me?* but caught herself just in time. This insta-celebrity thing was really messing with her head.

Lindsay's frown deepened. "But you canceled your gown order."

"What? No, I didn't."

"Yes," Lindsay insisted. She spoke the words crisply, with a sort of relish, as if she felt vindicated by this proof. "It's logged right here—you called later that afternoon to cancel. You said you'd found something else that you liked more."

"That wasn't me," Nina burst out. "I don't know who that was, but you must have mixed up the names, confused me with another customer. I didn't cancel this order."

Lindsay gave a sigh that clearly indicated this wasn't her problem. "We refunded your credit card, since we hadn't begun the alterations," she offered, as if Nina should be thrilled to have her money back.

Nina's heart thudded frantically in her chest. "The engagement party is *tomorrow.* I'm supposed to *be* there, at the ball, with Jeff!"

"I wasn't aware that you were attending with His Highness," Lindsay replied. Presumably this was to remind Nina that, as a commoner, she should have referred to Jeff by his proper rank.

"Where is the gown? I'll take it somewhere else for the alterations. . . ." Nina swallowed. She sounded borderline hysterical.

"I'm afraid someone purchased that gown a few days ago,"

Lindsay said, and Nina noticed that she was no longer pretending not to know which gown Nina meant. "Of course, you're welcome to browse the racks to see what's still available. Though I'm afraid most things left won't be your size. It's been a busy few days."

"What's going on out here?" A man with gray hair and wire-framed glasses stepped out from the back room. His eyes traveled over Nina with evident distaste. "Is there a problem?"

That was when Nina realized what was going on.

These people were trying to get rid of her. They knew precisely who she was, and didn't approve of her—her background or her style or the way she'd supposedly "stolen" Jeff. These were the people leaving all those ugly comments online.

A few stray shoppers glanced over, curious about the drama that was unfolding before them.

Nina had never in her life cried over *clothes,* yet now she felt wildly close to tears. She forced herself to swallow them back. Making a scene would only result in more unflattering coverage, alongside pictures of her looking flushed and angry.

How was she supposed to get a black-tie gown by tomorrow evening? For every other function like this, Nina had just borrowed something from Samantha, but she couldn't very well ask Samantha now. . . .

Her shoulders slumped. She remembered what Sam had said when she came over to Nina's dorm room and they got into that awful fight. *You're like a sister to me.*

She'd been so focused on all those memories of Samantha being thoughtless or selfish—but now another memory rose to Nina's mind. Of the time she'd gotten that awful bowl cut, the one Jeff had mentioned at Wawa. The girls at her school had teased her mercilessly for it.

When Nina told Sam what had happened—and that she was stuck with the haircut for months, until it grew out—Sam had found a pair of scissors and given herself a bowl cut, too, in solidarity. And of course, because she was the princess, she somehow managed to make it *fashionable*—turning Nina into a trendsetter, and saving her from fifth-grade social ostracism.

Nina had accused Sam of taking her for granted, but it struck Nina that maybe she'd taken Sam for granted, too. They had been friends for so long that she'd come to view their friendship as a permanent thing, as immutable and reliable as the stone of the Georgian Monument.

Nina cringed as she recalled some of the things she'd told her friend. Well, she was going to see Samantha at the ball tomorrow anyway; she might as well get a day's head start. Nina needed to ask for Sam's help.

And her forgiveness.

32

SAMANTHA

Samantha was sitting cross-legged on her couch, idly reading an article on her laptop, when she heard a familiar one-two-three knock.

She shoved the computer aside, certain she'd misheard, or that one of the footmen had heard her use this knock and was trying to mess with her. But when she opened the door, Nina was standing there.

Sam wished she could throw her arms around her friend and pour out everything that had happened since their fight. Nina and Jeff might have reconciled—Jeff had told Sam about it, right after it happened, and Sam had seen the photos of them together this past week—but she and Nina still hadn't spoken since that awful day in Nina's dorm room. The silence echoed with all the things they'd shouted at each other.

Nina cleared her throat. She was dressed totally out of character in a conservative dress and tights, her normally wavy hair pulled back.

"Sorry I didn't warn you I was coming over. I just—I was in the area, and I thought . . ." Nina trailed off in confusion.

Sam frowned. "Nina, what happened?"

"I can't believe I'm even saying this, but I've had a wardrobe emergency."

"Wardrobe emergency?" A smile tugged at the corner of

Sam's mouth. She was fairly certain Nina had never used those two words together.

Nina gave a quick nod, causing a few pieces of hair to slip from her bun. It made her look more like herself. "There was a misunderstanding with my dress alterations, and now I don't have a gown for tomorrow. And every store in town is entirely picked over. I was wondering if you knew where I could get one at the last minute?" she asked in a small voice.

Sam was no longer trying to hide her smile. Given the other, monumental problems in her life right now, it was a relief to be confronted with one she could actually solve.

"Sounds like we need to go shopping." She grabbed Nina's wrist and pulled her into the hallway.

"There are practically no dresses left in the whole city; I've been looking," Nina started to protest, but Sam just kept leading her down one corridor after another.

"We're shopping here." She stopped when they reached a metal touch screen on one wall. Sam scanned her fingerprints, and the door silently slid open.

Nina's eyes widened. "I didn't know you had biosecurity anywhere except the Crown Jewels vault."

"This isn't the Crown Jewels vault, but it's almost as good." Samantha stepped eagerly inside, and the motion-sensor lights clicked on.

They were standing in an industrial-sized closet, at least five times bigger than Sam's bedroom. On three of the walls were hanging rods, brimming with every kind of dress imaginable: formal gowns and short sequined dresses and wispy garden-party frocks. The final wall consisted of shelves lined in luxurious black suede, covered in accessories. There were hats and gloves and purses of every size, from functional leather handbags to embellished clutches so small that they could barely hold a lip gloss. Countless pairs of shoes were lined up like an array of brightly colored candies.

In the far corner, a seamstress's platform stood before an enormous three-fold mirror. A dimmer on the wall had settings for DAY, BALLROOM, THEATER, DINNER, and NIGHT. Sam had never really understood how *theater* and *dinner* differed from the *night* setting, but who cared? If nothing else, it was all fun to play with.

"Welcome," Sam intoned, in the voice of a game-show announcer, "to the Dress Closet."

"What are all these . . . I mean . . ."

"It's the collective closet of me, Beatrice, and my mom. Just the formal and event dresses. A lot of them have never even been worn."

Nina turned a slow circle. "How have I never been in here?"

"We've never had a Code Red wardrobe emergency before." When Nina didn't laugh at the joke, Sam cleared her throat. "Each time we had an event coming up, I would just pull a couple of options for you. I assumed you didn't *want* to come in here."

Nina winced at her words, and Sam realized she'd said the wrong thing—reminding Nina of all those online commenters who mocked her fashion sense. Nina tugged absently at the hem of her long-sleeved dress. "You're right. I don't know anything about this stuff."

Sam was glad the queen wasn't present to hear Nina call this room—filled with thousands of dollars of couture gowns, of intricate beading and gossamer fabrics and delicate hand-stitched sequins—*this stuff.*

"Don't worry, you're in good hands. Because I know a lot." A grin stole over Sam's face. "And I've been waiting for this moment for years. You, Nina Gonzalez, have no choice but to be my human mannequin."

Already she was prowling down the first rack, chattering as she went. "You have such a long torso, you'll fit better into Beatrice's gowns than mine. Which is too bad, since my style is *way* more fun," she teased, pulling out one exquisite gown after another. The peach high-necked one from last year's museum gala, covered in tiny crystals that caught the light. A gorgeous red one with black arabesques that trailed down the heavy full skirt. A dress of fuchsia silk that Beatrice once wore on a state visit to Greece. Sam draped them atop her arm, one after another in a vibrant multicolored stack.

Nina shook her head. "Sam, I can't let you do all this. I was saving up for my own dress."

"Great. Treat yourself to a mani-pedi tomorrow," Sam deadpanned.

"Seriously. I'm not supposed to borrow anything from your family."

Sam rolled her eyes. "Says who, the fashion police?"

"*Robert* said it, when he came to my house with a nondisclosure agreement!"

Sam fell still at that. Her grip closed over one of the felt-lined hangers, so tight that she almost snapped it. No wonder Nina thought that the Washingtons made her feel small.

"Forget Robert. He has no business telling you what to do. And if he says anything, I'll fire him."

"I'm not sure you have the authority to do that," Nina replied, though she was almost smiling.

"Please." Sam drew the word out so that it was two syllables. "Just try on a few things? You're my oldest friend in the world, and you have *never* let me dress you up, not like this."

"You're taking advantage of my desperation," Nina complained, but she obediently unzipped her dress and pulled on the first gown that Samantha held toward her, a slinky cobalt one covered in sequins.

"So what if I am?" Sam grinned, sliding various dresses along the titanium rods of the closet. "Are you really going to deprive me of something that brings me such joy?"

"You just like doing this because it gives you a semblance of control in a chaotic world." Nina twisted so that Sam could pull up the zipper for her.

Sam was caught off guard by the insight. But before she could answer, Nina turned back around to face her. Her cheeks were bright with color, her eyes sparkling.

"I really missed you, Sam."

It was enough to halt Samantha's hurricane of motion. She froze, dresses sliding out of her arms to tumble in a heap to the floor.

She stepped over the couture as if it were a pile of Kleenex and enfolded her friend in a hug. "I hated fighting with you."

"It was the worst!" Nina exclaimed. "I'm sorry I lashed out at you like that. It wasn't fair of me. I just felt so rattled, by the paparazzi and all those commenters."

Sam took a step back. "I've been thinking about what you said, about the way I've treated you. I'm really sorry," she said fervently. "I hate that I made you feel that way."

"A lot of it wasn't your fault."

"Still. Will you tell me how I can do better, moving forward?"

Nina smiled. "Right now you can watch me work through this enormous stack of gowns, and provide running commentary."

"That, I can definitely do," Sam assured her, and began to collect the scattered gowns from the carpet.

What a relief to know that with everything else going wrong in the world, this was one thing that had managed to right itself, after all.

As Nina tried on one dress after another, she and Samantha caught up on everything they had missed over the past several weeks: Nina's reconciliation with Jeff, and the fact that Nina had gone shopping with *Daphne*.

"That's really weird," Sam said bluntly. "Ex-girlfriends don't just go shopping with current girlfriends, not of their own free will."

"That's what I thought, too. Who knows, maybe she hoped someone would report the whole thing to the tabloids, and it would make her look good."

That was certainly plausible, but Sam couldn't help thinking there was more to the story. It felt a little too convenient to be a complete coincidence.

"Besides," Nina added, lifting an eyebrow, "you have no room to talk. I seem to remember you taking shots with Daphne on New Year's Eve."

Sam laughed; she'd almost forgotten about that. "Only because I couldn't find you!" she protested.

Though it had been kind of fun, trying to peel back the layers of impeccable behavior that encased Daphne like armor.

"What about you, Sam?" Nina asked. "Are you okay, with all the news about Beatrice and Teddy?"

Sam nodded slowly. "Beatrice and I talked. It turns out we've both misunderstood each other for a while. As for Teddy . . ." Her voice caught a little; then she forged on. "I'd be lying if I said I was thrilled about it, but Beatrice has her reasons for marrying him. And it's not like I can stop her. So I'm trying to get over it, as best as I can. Finding things to distract myself with. Speaking of which . . ." She looked at Nina's gown, which was covered in fluffy pom-poms along the bottom, and choked out a laugh. "You look like cotton candy that went through a shredder. Next."

"You and *Beatrice* are friends now?" Nina shook her head as she stepped out of the offending dress. "Just how long have we not been talking?"

"Too long."

"What caused you guys to make up? Did you find a common enemy or something?"

Yep. My dad's cancer.

Sam bit her lip against the words. She wanted to tell Nina about her dad's prognosis. She'd wanted to call and spill everything to her best friend from the very first moment she heard the news.

While unloading that secret might make her feel better, it also felt unbelievably selfish. It wasn't really Sam's secret to share. And honestly, she didn't want to put the weight of her dad's illness on another person's shoulders. Especially Nina's—not after everything she had recently been through.

Right now, what Sam and Nina needed was to keep playing this very elaborate game of couture dress-up.

"I guess Beatrice and I just had some catching up to do," she offered by way of explanation. "You know what they say, sisters before misters."

Nina snorted. "I don't think that's a real saying, but I'll let you have it."

Sam took the reject gown, smoothing its straps over the velvet hanger, then passed Nina a soft blue one. It spilled out into the room around them, a waterfall of pale silk.

"And on the bright side, hasn't Beatrice's engagement diverted the media attention from you and Jeff?" Sam watched as Nina stepped into the dress.

"Some, yeah. It's just disheartening, how many people hate me who've never even *met* me."

Sam felt a fierce wave of protectiveness toward her friend. "Want me to send security to rough them up, teach them a lesson?"

Nina turned back and forth on the platform, diplomatically ignoring Sam's offer. She looked, to be honest, like a blue-frosted wedding cake. "I can*not* wear this."

"Try one of these," Sam suggested, pulling over a few column dresses. "And promise that you won't read the online comments anymore. Those people are just jealous of how smart and poised and self-assured you are. And, you know, the fact that you're dating a prince."

"Sam . . ." Nina twisted her hands, seeming nervous. "Are you really okay with me and Jeff? I wouldn't want to make you feel weird, or uncomfortable. . . ."

"My two favorite people in the world, realizing how awesome each other are? Why would I not be okay with that?" Sam asked, a wicked gleam in her eye. "Of course, I expect you to name your firstborn after me, since I'm the one who brought you together."

Her friend's face turned beet red, making Sam roar with laughter. "Fine," she conceded. "Come to think of it, this family couldn't handle another Samantha."

Nina grinned, her face still flushed. "There could only ever be one of you, Sam."

33

DAPHNE

There was no thrill quite like that of walking into a party and knowing that of all the young women present, you were unquestionably the most beautiful.

Daphne sailed into the ballroom like a swan at sunset, her eyes glowing with reflected stares of admiration—and several of envy. Her gown swished pleasantly with her movements. It was a soft color caught somewhere between champagne and blush, with delicate straps that skimmed over her shoulders, and layers of featherweight tulle cascading over one another like petals. Her hair fell in lustrous curls down her back.

She saw Princess Juliana of Holland speaking with Lady Carl, who looked dour in a long black gown—didn't she know *anything* about etiquette? It was poor form to wear black to an engagement party. And here was the unfortunately named Herbert Fitzherbert, clumsily flirting with one of the king's handsomer equerries. Snatches of conversation floated all around her.

"—I would fire my assistant, except that at this point he knows way too much about me—"

"—No, the best avocado toast is definitely at Toulouse; I'll take you for brunch tomorrow—"

"—she's not rude; she's just French. If you wanted to be coddled, you should have worked at the Swedish embassy—"

"—I hear that Sedley intends to kill that bill the moment it hits the floor—"

They all paused to greet her as she passed, their breath catching a bit at her beauty. Daphne gave each of them a serene smile, revealing none of her anxiety, the way her muscles felt coiled and tense beneath her gown. She was like an Olympic runner poised before the gunshot that began a race. Waiting for Jefferson.

But then she saw Ethan Beckett heading toward her with long, loping strides, and Daphne's smile widened into something real.

"Dance with me?" he asked with his typical abruptness.

Daphne knew better than to say yes. She had a prince to find, a relationship to break up, and always, always, an endless supply of people to charm.

Instead she placed a hand on his, letting Ethan lead her through the crush and glitter of the ballroom.

He looped one arm around Daphne to settle it lightly above the base of her spine. With the other he reached to interlace their fingers. "You look far too pleased with yourself."

"Do I?" she asked lightly.

"You look as though someone just granted you an earldom." He gave his usual sardonic grin, and Daphne felt her own lips curling up at the edges.

"So, are you going to tell me your plan?" Ethan went on.

Daphne didn't deny it. He had a disconcerting habit of seeing through her no matter what she did.

"If I did have a plan, I would hardly share the details with you."

"I'd expect nothing less."

Ethan's movements weren't showy, yet they had an unexpected grace. He was self-assured, easy on his feet for someone so tall. Other, less glamorous couples flitted and chatted around them, making Daphne feel more striking by comparison.

"You're a good dancer," she observed.

There was a twist to Ethan's bow-shaped mouth. "Try not to sound so shocked, the next time you give someone a compliment."

"I don't make a habit of it."

Something sparked in the onyx of his eyes. "You're an easy partner," he conceded; then added, more softly, "We're well matched."

There was nothing Daphne could say to that. She knew just as well as Ethan why they danced so well together. Because Ethan knew her movements and she knew his—because, beneath the heated verbal sparring, they were ultimately the *same*.

The song ended. There was a burst of applause, and the band struck up another one. Daphne and Ethan, through some unspoken agreement, continued to dance.

"I'm going to miss you, you know," he said in an undertone.

"What do you mean?" Her heart had curiously picked up speed.

"Once you and His Highness get back together, I'm going to miss you." It was strange of him to refer to Jefferson by his formal title, but Daphne pretended not to hear it. Just as she pretended not to hear the subtext of what he was saying.

"I don't exactly plan on leaving."

Neither of them was smiling, as if they had reached some point that was beyond smiles. Although they were surrounded by hundreds of people, it seemed to Daphne that they were completely alone: a bubble of uncertain silence in a sea of noise.

"Daphne," Ethan said at last. "What do you want? Really."

Some strange part of her whispered an answer she refused to acknowledge. Daphne brutally silenced that voice.

"I want everything," she told him.

There was no need to elaborate. Daphne wanted a crown, which might very well be the only thing in the world Ethan couldn't give her, no matter how wealthy or powerful he became, no matter how much he schemed or struggled or succeeded.

"Everything," Ethan repeated drily. "Well, if that's all."

His words inexplicably made her laugh—and then they were both laughing, their laughter twining around them as they moved in the familiar steps of the waltz.

Ethan's eyes were still fixed on hers.

"What happens when an unstoppable force meets an immovable object?" he asked, so softly that he might have been talking to himself. At Daphne's curious look, he explained. "It's a paradox from ancient philosophy. What happens when an unstoppable force, like a weapon that never fails, meets an immovable object, like a shield that can't be broken?"

"Well?" She gave an impatient toss of her paprika curls. "What's the answer?"

"There is no answer. That's why it's a paradox. A riddle."

But Daphne knew. What happened was *sparks*. She caught her body inclining toward Ethan's and forced herself to step back.

She really should know better—especially after what had happened between them last May.

Daphne refused to let her mood ruin Himari's birthday party, though her smile felt increasingly precarious as the night wore on.

She was worried about her relationship. Things with Jefferson had been rocky for some time now; he was blowing her off, ignoring her for days on end, going out with his guy friends and letting himself be photographed with some random girl's arm snaking around his waist. Daphne had a panicked fear that when he graduated high school next week, he would break up with her.

It didn't help that he was currently in Santa Barbara, at the royal family's first wedding in decades. His aunt Margaret was finally marrying her actor boyfriend—and Jefferson hadn't invited Daphne as his date.

The tabloids were eating it up. DAPHNE DITCHED FOR THE WEDDING! read the headlines. Several blogs had reviewed the guest list in obsessive detail, wondering who might tempt Jefferson to cheat on her. Meanwhile the bookies had dropped her odds on marrying the prince from one in seven to one in eighteen, somewhere between his third cousin Lady Helen Veiss and the six-year-old princess of Mexico.

Daphne drifted aimlessly around Himari's house, a margarita glass in hand—that was her signature move at parties, to carry sparkling water in a margarita glass, because it looked so festive that no one ever questioned it—except that tonight its contents weren't sparkling water, but straight tequila. She kept hoping that if she drank enough, she might temporarily forget that her hard-won, high-profile relationship was unraveling at the seams. So far it hadn't worked.

When the party devolved into a sloppy free-for-all, everyone jumping and making out on the makeshift dance floor, Daphne hit her limit. She slipped outside, across the cool flagstones of the terrace, to open the sliding door of the pool house.

The pull-out couch had been made up with sheets and blankets: probably Himari's parents' idea, in case someone got too drunk at the party to make it home. It was so blessedly quiet in here. Daphne let out a breath and sank onto the edge of the bed.

And then the floodgates opened, and she began to cry.

"You okay?"

Ethan stood in the doorway. The light spilled out from

behind him, making him resemble one of those medieval paintings where the figures were limned in gold leaf.

"I'm fine," Daphne snapped, her pride kicking in. She brusquely wiped away her tears. Hadn't she sworn never to let anyone see her cry?

Ethan came to sit on the edge of the bed next to her. "What's going on?"

Daphne couldn't look away from the liquid dark irises of his eyes. They had spent so many hours together—of course they had, as the prince's girlfriend and his best friend—and Ethan had never acted anything but friendly toward her. But for some reason, Daphne had a feeling that he *knew* her. That unlike everyone else in their world, he wasn't fooled by the way she behaved. That he saw the thoughts swirling beneath her calm veneer.

Yet she couldn't read *him*.

She had long ago figured out Jefferson; he wasn't all that complicated. It had become a sort of game with her, to introduce topics seemingly at random—reggae music, the Spanish Inquisition, last year's congressional scandal—and try to guess what Jefferson would say. So far she hadn't been wrong once.

Not at all so with Ethan, who was maddening and elusive and impossible to understand.

"Can I do anything to help?" he insisted.

Daphne let out a breath, shrugging off his concern. "How long have you known Jefferson?"

If Ethan was surprised by her question, he didn't show it. "We've been best friends since kindergarten," he said. Which she already knew.

"And you stayed that close ever since age five?" Daphne hadn't meant to sound condescending. But if *she* couldn't hold the prince's interest for a mere three years, how had Ethan managed to do it for most of their lives?

He shrugged. "You know, the king was actually the one who

originally invited me over. I guess he thought it would be good for Jeff to spend time with someone from a different background. Someone middle-class." Ethan said it bluntly, without hesitation, almost as if he was proud to be a commoner. Then his gaze focused again on Daphne. "Why do you ask?"

She clenched her hands on the quilted bedspread and closed them into fists. "I need to figure out what I did to make Jefferson lose interest," she heard herself say, in a dull, hollow tone. "Otherwise he's going to break up with me."

She hadn't meant to confess that fear, especially not to Ethan, but the tequila seemed to have numbed the edges of everything and she no longer cared.

"That's ridiculous," Ethan said quietly. "Only a fool would throw away the chance to be with you."

Something in his tone made Daphne look up, but his face was as inscrutable and still as ever. She swallowed and explained. "Things between me and Jefferson have felt weird lately. And with his graduation coming up . . . I don't know what's going to happen."

Ethan must have been drunk too, the alcohol blunting the edges of his usual cynical courtesy, because his next words shocked her.

"Why do you care anyway, when you don't even like Jeff?"

Daphne blinked. "Of course I *care*. I lo—"

"You *love* him? Really?" Ethan's voice made a mockery of the word.

"I've come too far to stop now!"

The words were like champagne fizzing out of a bottle, impossible to suppress, as if Daphne's final emergency pressure valve had snapped at last. "I have been struggling for years to be perfect enough for the royal family," she said heatedly. "Do you have any *idea* how hard it's been?"

"No, but—"

"It's exhausting, and I can never let up, not even for a

second! I have to be constantly charming, not just to Jefferson and his parents and the media, but to every *single* person who crosses my path, even if it's only for a moment, because they will judge me by that moment for the rest of their lives. I can't ever stop smiling, or the entire thing will come crashing down around me!"

The sounds of the party felt very far away, like something in a dream.

Ethan swore. "If this is really what it's like, then maybe you and Jefferson *should* break up. Maybe he isn't the right person for you. Maybe," he went on, "you should be with me instead."

Daphne didn't know how to answer.

Her stomach was a turmoil of confused emotions—attraction and irritation, liking and hate—all clawing inside her for dominance, as if every last neuron in her brain had turned on in a wild electric light show.

Ethan shifted closer, a smooth quarter turn along the mattress. His eyes gleamed, dark and fervent and questioning.

This was their last chance to draw back, to pretend that none of this had ever happened and walk away. But they were both very still, a pair of quiet shadows.

Even in the silence, Daphne felt something crackle and spark between them.

Suddenly they were tumbling onto the bed together, a tangle of hands and lips and heat. She yanked her dress impatiently over her head. It fell in a whisper to the floor.

"Are you sure?" Ethan's breath sent little explosions all the way down her skin, like fireworks. It was the closest either of them came to acknowledging how wrong this was.

"I'm sure," Daphne told him. She knew precisely what she was doing, knew the promises she was breaking, to herself and to Jefferson. She no longer cared. She felt fluid, electrified, gloriously irresponsible.

She felt, for the first time in years, like herself. Not the public, painted-on Daphne Deighton that she showed the world, but the real seventeen-year-old girl she kept carefully hidden beneath.

♛

"Daphne? I need to talk to you." Her mother cut across the dance floor toward them, not even bothering to acknowledge Ethan.

"Oh—all right." Daphne wondered what the expression on her face had looked like, to send Rebecca rushing over here.

Her eyes briefly met Ethan's, and she saw his flash of understanding, and of disappointment. He nodded, stepping aside.

Rebecca's nails dug into the flesh of Daphne's inner arm as she dragged her away. "You don't have time for distractions, tonight of all nights."

"Ethan is Jefferson's best friend," Daphne said wearily. "I was just dancing with him for a few songs."

And remembering the night I lost my virginity to him.

"You could have been dancing with an emperor himself, and I'd still expect you to be present for the royal family's entrance," Rebecca hissed.

"Mother . . ." Daphne's steps slowed. "Do you ever wonder . . . I mean, is it all really worth it?"

Rebecca's grip tightened so fiercely that Daphne barely swallowed back a cry of pain.

"*Daphne.*" As always, her mother managed to convey a world of emotions in those two syllables. "I'm going to pretend you didn't ask that. Don't ever say anything like it again, not to me, and certainly not to your father. Not after everything we've done for *your* sake."

She stepped away, and Daphne pressed her hands together to hide their sudden trembling. Her mother was right, of course. She had been on this road for far too long to second-guess herself now.

There was a ring of red half-moons on the skin of Daphne's inner arm, where Rebecca's nails had been.

A commotion sounded at the Door of Sighs, and the herald emerged to bang his staff against the floor. "Their Majesties, King George IV and Queen Adelaide!"

Daphne watched along with everyone in the room as the king and queen strode in, followed by Beatrice and her fiancé. Moments later Samantha emerged, and then, finally, Jefferson.

He entered the ballroom alone, as was dictated by protocol: only someone engaged to a member of the royal family was permitted to walk alongside them. But he'd only progressed a few yards into the room when Nina Gonzalez detached herself from the gathered masses and came to stand at his side.

Daphne's stomach lurched as she watched Jefferson hold out an arm toward Nina.

She saw at once that her ploy at Halo had been useless. If anything, Nina looked even better in this: a scoop-necked column dress in a deep gray, its bodice and skirts heavy with charcoal beads.

"You have a job to do," Rebecca said quietly. As if Daphne were in danger of forgetting.

She forced herself to take a deep breath, fighting back the wave of frustration and resentment and envy that threatened to drown her. She could not afford to lose her cool over some *nobody*.

Nina might as well enjoy this hour with Jefferson, because it was the last one she would ever have. The moment Daphne could get her alone, she would move in swiftly for the kill.

34

NINA

Nina had been to a great many parties in the Washington Palace ballroom, but even she had never seen it so enchanted.

The space overflowed with flowers, green hydrangeas and calla lilies and vibrant orange dahlias spilling over every surface. Crystal chandeliers flung ribbons of light throughout the room. The light fell on revolving tulle skirts, on freshly pressed tuxedos, on the jewels that had been removed from vaults and safety-deposit boxes for the occasion as all these courtiers vied desperately to outglitter one another.

And everywhere she looked, Nina saw the *B&T* wedding monogram. It was printed in gold foil on the cocktail napkins, embroidered on the fabric of the skirted high-top tables, even painted on the band's drum set.

A dark-haired man, dancing only a few yards away with a woman in a crushed-velvet gown, met Nina's eyes. He stared at her with a mixture of disdain and boredom.

"Jeff," Nina whispered into the prince's ear. "Who is that?"

He turned to follow her gaze, then gave a huff of laughter. "That's Juan Carlos, the King of Spain's youngest son. We used to vacation with their family, at their summer palace in Mallorca." Jeff deftly led Nina farther from the Spanish prince. "He once asked Beatrice on a date—well, practically all the foreign princes did, at some point—but she said no."

"Beatrice turned down a prince?"

"I don't know why you're acting surprised. As I seem to recall, you've done it yourself. Multiple times," Jeff teased, an eyebrow lifted in challenge.

Nina flushed at the memory. "As I seem to recall, you deserved it," she said lightly. "And unlike Beatrice, I'm not a princess. I don't have to worry about issues of royal protocol or international relations if I say no to a *date*."

Jeff laughed at that. "Well, he and Beatrice would never have worked out anyway. His family calls him Juan-for-the-Road Carlos." Jeff lowered his voice conspiratorially. "Because he always brings a flask in his jacket pocket whenever he has to carry out official royal duties."

Nina stole another glance at the Spanish prince, still dancing with the woman in velvet. Her arms instinctively tightened over Jeff's shoulders. If Jeff and Sam weren't careful—if they didn't find something that mattered to them, some kind of *purpose*—they might end up like Juan Carlos: idle, world-weary, floating aimlessly from one royal function to the next.

It was just the constitutional danger of being the spare.

"You look amazing, you know," Jeff murmured. The desire in his voice, low and rough, abruptly cut off Nina's thoughts.

She bit her lip against a smile. "Sam helped. I wouldn't have a dress without her."

Nina's smoke-colored gown was sewn all over with beads. They swished and settled around her body, giving her the curious sensation that she was dancing through water. Her dark hair was piled atop her head like an evening cloud, a few tendrils escaping to frame her face.

"You don't look so shabby yourself," she added, with a nod toward Jeff's blazer: the one she'd borrowed on the terrace all those months ago. He'd even put on the aiguillettes and shining crossbelt, though the belt was empty of a sword.

"I *knew* you had a thing for men in fringe." Jeff gave a mischievous grin. "Though if I'd realized Prince Hans was coming, I would have worn my medallion for the Order of the Knights of Malta. It's the only decoration I have that he doesn't."

"Prince Hans?" Nina followed Jeff's gaze, to a spindly boy wearing square-framed glasses. "Is he . . . Danish?"

"Norwegian."

Nina tried not to roll her eyes. "I'm sorry, how many foreign royalty *are* there at this party?"

"As many as could get here in time." Jeff shrugged. "Hans's dad is one of Beatrice's godfathers."

Of course he was. Nina remembered a book she'd shelved in the library one day, *Minor Royal Families of Europe*, filled with pages and pages of family trees. She'd stared at them goggle-eyed—all those lines and branches, knotting and weaving over each other—before closing the book in exasperation.

Her eyes drifted to where Beatrice stood next to Teddy, surrounded by a crowd of eager guests.

"I still can't believe Beatrice is engaged. It all happened so quickly." Nina was thinking of Samantha—of how hard it must be for her, seeing Teddy with Beatrice. It made her feel almost guilty for being so happy when her friend clearly wasn't.

"I like Teddy," Jeff said roundly. "He's a great guy, and seems like a good fit for Beatrice, even if . . ."

"What?"

Jeff gave an uncomfortable shrug. "Clearly I'm wrong, but for a while there in Telluride, I kind of thought there was a vibe between him and Samantha."

Nina pursed her lips and said nothing.

"Beatrice has never been indecisive. I'm not surprised that she made up her mind about Teddy so quickly." Jeff's voice was soft over the delicate strands of the jazz music. "I guess when you find the right person, nothing else matters."

Nina nodded, understanding.

She wasn't sure she would ever get used to it all: the exposure, the unending public scrutiny. It was so much more intense now than it had been when she was just Samantha's friend. She'd been on the sidelines, sure, had watched plenty of photo calls and walked past plenty of lines of photographers, but they'd never spared her a second glance.

Being Jeff's girlfriend was entirely different. Nina still did a double take whenever she saw her own face on a tabloid, or heard her own name shouted in a crowd.

Though lately, Nina had noticed some of the coverage shifting its tone. She wasn't sure why: whether people had grown tired of the social-climbing angle, or the tabloids had simply found another victim to make fun of. Maybe other ordinary, non-aristocratic girls wanted to believe in the fairy tale—that they, too, could find a Prince Charming.

Whatever the reason, there was less venom here tonight than Nina had expected. She'd come to Beatrice's engagement ball thinking that it would be a nest of vipers: that her only real allies were Sam and Jeff, and everyone else would have firmly declared for Team Daphne. But she'd been pleasantly surprised by the number of familiar faces in the ballroom. Some were friends of her mom, some high school classmates of Sam and Jeff; others were people she'd never met, but who gave her smiling nods of approval.

Jeff's hands drifted lower on her back. Nina stepped a bit closer, hooking her arm around him, to tuck her head over his shoulder. Her body felt tingling and alert, her blood humming with the words she hadn't yet dared speak aloud.

Nina had been so afraid that she would lose sight of herself amid all the glamour and protocol, the inherently public nature of their relationship. But instead she'd found something much greater.

She loved Jeff.

And even though she had always known it—even though her love for Jeff went so far back that she could hardly remember a time before she loved him—Nina let herself learn it all over again.

35

BEATRICE

Beatrice felt like a mechanical wind-up doll, reciting the same few sentences over and over: *We are so glad you could make it*; *Thank you for the warm wishes*; *We are both thrilled.*

She couldn't afford to think too closely about the import of her words, or she might actually faint. Already she felt sweat sliding down her back beneath the stiff fabric of her dress.

Somehow it managed to evoke *bridal* without actually looking like a wedding gown—its silk panels a shade of cream so dark that it verged on light gold, adorned with taffeta detail. Her hair was styled in an intricate updo, the Winslow tiara perched on her head. Diamonds blazed like teardrops in her ears.

Countless nobles stood before her in order of precedence, all of them waiting to congratulate her and Teddy on the engagement. They wound around the side of the ballroom in a near-interminable queue. Beatrice kept imagining them breaking into dance, like some kind of aristocratic conga line.

She glanced over at her sister, who'd planted herself resolutely to Beatrice's left, as if Beatrice might suddenly need to lean on her for support. Ever since their conversation in the kitchens, Beatrice had noticed a new maturity to Samantha. She wasn't the same princess who'd laughed her way blithely through high school. There was a new edge to her, a new weight to her words.

Sometime in the last year, while Beatrice hadn't been paying attention, her little sister had grown up.

Beatrice had held it together through the dukes and marquesses, but they were still only halfway through the earls, and she felt herself beginning to fray. The line of courtiers seemed to stretch on and on forever.

Teddy—she still couldn't think of him as her *fiancé*—rested a hand on her back in a silent gesture of support. Maybe he'd noticed her drooping a bit.

"Robert." Beatrice turned to the chamberlain. "Could we take five?"

Robert's eyebrows drew together in a frown. "Your Royal Highness, it is customary for newly engaged members of the royal family to receive congratulation from all the gathered peers at the start of the celebratory ball." One of Robert's greatest skills was telling royalty *no* without actually saying the word.

To Beatrice's relief, Teddy cut in, his voice firm. "It's all right, Robert; we can pause. Or if you don't think it's inappropriate, I'm happy to accept congratulations on the princess's behalf."

"Thank you." Beatrice shot Teddy a grateful look. Gathering her plentiful skirts with both hands, she slipped out of the ballroom.

The moment she turned in to the hallway, Beatrice began to run. She didn't care where she was going as long as she kept *moving*, away from that room where everything was printed with an interlaced B and T. Beatrice didn't even remember giving her approval for that wedding monogram, but she supposed she must have. Everything related to the wedding had become a blur.

She stumbled past one of the downstairs sitting rooms,

where the guests had deposited their gifts at the start of the night, only to halt in her tracks.

"Connor?"

He stood near a wooden table that groaned beneath the weight of presents, most of them wrapped in ivory or silver paper. Although Beatrice and Teddy had insisted that all they wanted were charitable donations, everyone seemed determined to shower them with gifts.

"I know I wasn't invited," Connor hurried to say. He was out of uniform, wearing jeans and a sweater that brought out the blue-gray of his eyes. In his hand was a box tied with satin ribbon. "I just wanted to give you this, before . . ."

"Thank you," Beatrice said, because she had to say something, and her mind was currently incapable of forming any other words.

The right thing to do was to walk onward, away from Connor. To return to the ballroom, where her fiancé—and all the rest of her predictable royal future—awaited her.

Instead Beatrice stepped inside, pulling the door soundlessly shut.

"There's no need, Your Royal Highness," Connor said, a sharpness to those last three words. "I know you have to get back to your party."

"Please don't *Your Royal Highness* me."

He crossed his arms defensively. "What do you want from me, Beatrice? You made it perfectly clear how things stand between us. We've already said goodbye," he reminded her. "I just hope you're happy with the choices you've made."

"Maybe I'm not."

It came out barely a whisper.

Connor didn't move. "What does that mean?"

Beatrice felt her controlled court persona slipping away as easily as if she were unzipping a dress.

"I mean that we aren't over. Or at least, *I'm* not over *you*."

She took a heavy breath. "No matter what happens, I'll never be over you."

Slowly, she stepped forward and lifted a hand to his face: to trace over every freckle, every curve and shadow that had become so utterly familiar to her. More familiar even than her own reflection.

"Bee—" he said gruffly.

She grabbed his sweater with both hands and pulled him in to kiss him.

His mouth on hers was searing hot. Beatrice closed her eyes and clung tight to Connor. It felt like she'd been living in an oxygen-starved world and now could finally breathe—as if raw fire raced through her veins, and if she and Connor weren't careful, they might burn down the world with it.

When they finally stepped apart, Connor kept his hands wrapped tight around hers, as if he couldn't bear not to have some part of him that touched her. They both hurried to speak.

"I'm so sorry—"

"I never wanted to—"

"Beatrice," Connor cut in, and she fell silent. "I'll come back, if you'll have me. Be your Guard again."

The embroidery at the top of her gown stirred with her breath. "Really?"

He nodded solemnly. "These last couple of weeks have been torture. I realized that I can't bear the thought of a life without you. I'm not saying that I'll enjoy watching you marry him," Connor added, stumbling a little over the words. "But I get it, Bee. You're the heir to the throne and can't make your own choices."

He would come back to her. They would be together again. Beatrice tried to be pleased by this . . . but suddenly all she could see was Connor, kneeling before her in the garden, his heart in his eyes.

"I know better than to try to pick and choose which parts of you to love," he was saying. "I love you, Beatrice. *All* of you, even the part of you that is sworn to the Crown. Even if it means we can't really be together."

"I love you, too."

"All right, then. I'll ask to be reassigned to you." Connor smiled down at her. "At least this way we'll have each other."

Beatrice knew she couldn't take him up on his offer.

This thing between her and Connor was *real*. She was his and he was hers—that was simply the truth, perhaps the most powerful truth in this entire court. And something that true was something worth fighting for.

"No." Beatrice stepped back, shaking her head. "I can't ask that of you. You deserve so much more than a half life."

"What are you saying?"

Beatrice slid the diamond engagement ring off her finger, revealing the line of Sharpie inscribed beneath. For the first time in weeks, her smile wasn't forced.

"It's still there?" he asked, incredulous.

She hadn't been able to stand the sight of her finger without it. "I touched it up myself," she confessed, and took a breath. "Connor, I'm calling off the wedding."

Seeing Connor again was a sharp reminder of everything that Teddy wasn't. Beatrice liked Teddy, and understood him, and knew without a doubt that he would have been a great first king consort. If she'd never met Connor, maybe that would have been enough.

Except that she *had* met Connor. They'd managed to find each other in this messy, confusing, deeply flawed world. And now that she knew what it was like to truly love someone, Beatrice couldn't accept anything less.

"Really?" The naked hope in Connor's expression nearly undid her.

"Yes. I'll talk to my dad tonight, tell him I can't marry

Teddy." Her stomach knotted in dread at the thought of that conversation.

"What do you think he'll say?"

Beatrice wished she could tell Connor that it would all be fine. But after everything they'd been through, he deserved the truth from her. "Honestly, I don't know."

"He won't approve of me," Connor said quietly. "Neither will America. Look how much they freaked out about Jeff and Nina, and he's not even the heir. They'll never accept their future queen dating her *bodyguard*."

"If they really feel that way, then maybe I don't want to be their queen."

Connor gave an exasperated huff. "Don't be flippant."

Beatrice stepped forward, folding her body into his. After a moment, Connor let his arms loop over her and pulled her closer. She pressed her face against his chest, inhaling the familiar warm scent of him. The whole world felt suddenly lighter.

"I already lost you once. I can't bear to lose you again," she murmured. "I don't know what's going to happen, or how people will react, but we'll figure something out. Whatever it is, we'll do it together."

A clock chimed in the hallway. Beatrice wondered, suddenly, how late it was. All those viscounts and barons were probably still lined up to congratulate her for an engagement she had every intention of breaking before the night was over.

"I'm sure they're looking for you," Connor said, as if reading her mind. He grinned. "The sooner you go, the sooner you can take that ring off your finger."

Beatrice took a step toward the door and hesitated, torn. She hated the thought of walking away from Connor so soon, when she'd only just gotten him back. "Would you come with me? You could get in uniform, tell everyone you're assigned to me again."

"No offense, but I'm not going anywhere near that party," Connor said wryly.

"None taken."

"I'll be here for you when it's over," he assured her. "And, Bee—good luck with your dad."

"Thank you." She rose on tiptoe to brush her lips against Connor's one more time.

As she started back down the hallway, the princess straightened her rumpled dress, tucked back a piece of hair that had come loose from her bun. Her eyes were very bright, her lips a vivid pink. And she was smiling to herself, a secret flickering smile that made her seem to glow from within.

She looked, to everyone who saw her, like a young woman in love.

36

NINA

Nina was in the first-floor ladies' room when she heard the group of girls walk in. Their heels clicked in unison over the floor, their voices lilting and conspiratorial.

"Did you *see* what she's wearing? She sure upgraded fast, once she got hold of the prince's money."

"You really think he bought her that gown?"

"Her mom sure didn't, on a government salary."

Nina froze.

"I heard that she's so desperate for cash, she's been selling photos of *herself* to the tabloids."

A snort of disapproval. "You'd think she would have more style, having grown up around the palace."

"Come on, Josephine, you know you can't buy class if you weren't born with it." There was a chorus of snide giggles at that.

I dare them to say those things to my face, Nina thought, and swept furiously out of the bathroom stall. Her gown rattled with crystal beads like hail on pavement.

The trio of girls had clustered before the sink, which was made of an enormous slab of backlit pink quartz, its faucets shaped like swans' necks. Nina washed her hands, coolly ignoring the others. They exchanged a glance among themselves before fleeing the bathroom in a voluminous rustle of skirts.

She refused to let their small-mindedness ruin her night,

and yet . . . Nina swallowed. When it was just her and Jeff, everything felt so simple. But at times like this, the rest of the world came rushing back, in all its sordid ugliness.

Daphne Deighton chose that moment to walk into the bathroom. She looked resplendent in a delicate champagne-colored gown.

"Nina." Her gaze prickled on Nina's in the mirror. "You look amazing. It's too bad about the whole miscommunication at Halo, of course, but that gown is divine."

She was smiling as always, yet Nina had the sense of something hard and unyielding beneath the superficial warmth of her voice.

"Thanks," she said cautiously. Then the full import of Daphne's words hit her, and she paused. "How did you know about the mix-up at Halo?"

Daphne's self-control flickered, so quickly that Nina wouldn't have even noticed if she hadn't been watching for it. "Damien told me, of course. He felt terrible about the whole thing. I'm so glad it worked out!"

Nina could have nodded and left it there, but a suspicion had ignited in her mind, and she needed to know.

"Daphne," she said carefully, "are you the one who canceled my gown order?"

She expected Daphne to flat-out deny it. But to her surprise, the other girl spun on one heel and marched up and down the row of stalls, pushing on each door to make sure that they were empty.

Nina watched, speechless, as Daphne walked back to the entrance of the ladies' room and bolted the main door. When she turned, all trace of a smile had been wiped from her perfect features—as if a mask had dropped, and now Nina was finally seeing her for real.

"It was me," Daphne said simply. "It was *all* me, everything that's happened to you since you first got involved with

Jefferson. I gave the paparazzi your dorm address and helped them find incriminating photos of you. I planted the story in the tabloids. I called the boutique, pretending to be you, and canceled your gown order."

Nina blinked. She felt oddly caught off guard by the bluntness of Daphne's confession. "You did all that, just to try to get Jeff back?"

"'All that'?" Daphne smiled, a sharp glittering smile that matched the light in her bottle-green eyes. "Nina, I'm just getting started."

Nina stumbled backward. "You're insane," she said hotly. What had she been thinking, letting Daphne lock them in a bathroom together?

"I really do think you're a nice girl, so I'm going to give you some free advice. You need to end things now, before you end up hurt. You will never make it in the Washington family, not with your kind of background."

"My kind of *background?*" Nina spluttered. "For your information, the king and queen have always liked me."

"As Samantha's best friend, as the daughter of one of their *employees*, sure. As the girlfriend of their only son? I don't think so."

"My mom is a Cabinet minister, not a chambermaid," Nina said quietly. "And I'm sorry, what about your background makes you better qualified, the fact that your dad is a lord?"

"A baronet," Daphne corrected crisply, "and yes. Unlike you, I have been training for this job my entire life. Because it is a job."

"I don't—"

"Do you know who to call Your Serene Highness and Your Imperial Highness as opposed to Your Royal Highness? Can you identify the heir to the throne in every country—the

Prince of Wales and the Princess of Asturias and the French dauphin? Do you know the lineage of each of the thirteen sovereign duchies? How do you properly address a federal judge or a member of Congress?" Daphne paused from her monologue to take a breath. "You have no *idea* what it takes to be the prince's girlfriend."

Nina couldn't believe the bizarre list of job requirements Daphne had just rattled off. "Whatever your relationship with Jeff was like, ours is different. He doesn't care about those things."

"Your relationship with Jefferson is never just you. It's a public position. You are living in a goldfish bowl—constantly on display, and on trial."

Nina shook her head, though Daphne's words were eerily similar to what she said to Jeff not that long ago. Daphne saw that sliver of hesitation and pounced on it.

"The king and queen will never give Jefferson permission to marry you," she went on. "Never."

"Who said anything about marriage? We're *eighteen!*"

"Ah. I see." Daphne had the feline, self-satisfied look of someone who was very protective of her territory. "You're just messing around with him until he finds someone serious. Good. In that case, you won't be disappointed when it ends. Because there is no way you and the prince can ever have a future together, Nina. You're skating on melting ice. He might be into you now, but it's only a matter of time."

"A matter of time before *what?*"

Daphne lifted one shoulder in a sinuous shrug. "Before he realizes that you aren't long-term material."

Nina hadn't even thought of marriage—but now she couldn't help wondering if Daphne might be right. If she couldn't see herself ever getting serious with Jeff, what was the point of letting herself fall for him, and eventually being hurt?

Stop it, she admonished herself. This was exactly what Daphne wanted: to make her doubt their relationship—doubt Jeff.

Daphne took a step forward, probably expecting her to retreat, but Nina held her ground. Despite their ball gowns, their jewels, their elaborate hairstyles, they seemed to Nina like a pair of warriors tensely circling each other on the field of battle.

"You know what?" Nina declared. "I feel sorry for you. If what you say is true, if you really devoted your entire life to being some perfect princess figure—that's pathetic."

There was a dangerous gleam to Daphne's eyes. "Oh, no. *You* do not get to feel sorry for *me.*"

"I do," Nina repeated. "Because unlike you, I care about Jeff, the *person.* Not the fact that he's a prince."

Daphne laughed, but there was no mirth in it. "They're one and the same thing, Nina. You can't want Jeff like an ordinary man and ignore his positions and titles. If you don't know that, then you're a fool."

"Better to love him for real than to love him *because* of his positions and titles!"

"Oh my, you *love* him." The other girl smirked. "That really is too bad for you. Because Jefferson is going to come to his senses and get rid of you soon enough. Until then, I'll be right here, making your life a living hell."

Nina knew, with a chilling certainty, that Daphne meant every word.

"I'm going to tell everyone the truth about you. That you're a lying, manipulative—"

"I'd love to see you try." Daphne cast her a withering glance. "Who do you think they'll believe? I'm America's Sweetheart, and you're the gold-digging fame whore he rebounded to, before he eventually comes back to me."

Nina opened her mouth to retaliate, but no words came

out, because she knew deep down that it was true. America would take Daphne's side over hers.

"Someday you'll thank me for this," Daphne said quietly. "You don't have the stomach for this kind of life. I'm doing you a favor in the long run."

With that, she turned the bolt on the door and stepped out into the hallway.

Nina blinked, dazed. There was a love seat in the corner; she collapsed onto it in a sloppy heap of beads.

She sat there for a while, her chin tucked into her hands, staring blankly at the opposite wall. Light fell from the crystal chandelier overhead, which suddenly looked to Nina like a torrent of tears, frozen mid-fall by an evil snow queen.

How stupidly naïve she'd been, thinking she could just stroll into this party in a beautiful dress and everything would be okay. She didn't know how to navigate this court, with its layered promises and barbed favors. This court rewarded people like Daphne—cold, brutal people who did whatever the hell they wanted and never looked back. Nina couldn't compete with those people. She didn't *want* to.

This wasn't her world, and it never would be.

♛

Nina ran her hands up and down her bare arms against the cold. The wings of the palace sprawled to either side of her, flooded with moonlight. She was out on the balcony, the one with the birds' nest, where she and Jeff had watched the fireworks all those weeks ago.

This time, Nina wasn't surprised when his footsteps sounded behind her.

"There you are." Jeff's voice was warm, but then he seemed to take in her pallor, the bleak look on her face, and he hurried to close the distance between them.

"We need to talk," Nina said heavily.

Jeff slid out of his jacket as if to tuck it over her shoulders, but she drew back. He let his arms fall to his sides, chastened.

"Nina, are you okay? What happened?"

Your ex-girlfriend happened. She tightened her grip on the wrought-iron railings.

"I was so excited about tonight," she began. "Getting to be here with you, at an event that's important to your family. I thought we were ready for this."

"We *are* ready for this, Nina. I hope you know how much it means to me that you're here."

She shook her head. "You might be ready for this, but I'm not. All the lies and pretending, that ballroom full of two-faced people—I can't do it."

"I told you, forget the internet commenters," Jeff insisted. "My family loves you; everyone who matters loves you."

"Are you sure your family approves of me?" Nina forged ahead before he could interrupt. "I'm not talking about Sam; I'm talking about your parents. Do you honestly think they would give us permission to get married?"

She half expected Jeff to defend her, but instead he flinched. "Isn't it a little soon to be talking about marriage?"

"It would be, if we were a normal couple and I didn't have to worry about whether or not I'm *suitable!*" Nina hated herself for parroting Daphne. But like all good insults, Daphne's words had contained a kernel of truth. That was why they cut so deep.

"I'm not trying to freak you out, or be unreasonable," she added helplessly. "But I also have no desire to enter a relationship that's doomed from the start. I don't want to date someone whose parents are ashamed of me."

Jeff reached for her hand, and this time Nina let him take it. "Where is this coming from?"

She let out a breath. "Daphne cornered me in the ladies'

room and told me to break up with you. She's been out to get me from the beginning. She sabotaged my gown—"

"What happened with your gown?" Jeff cut in, confused.

"—and she's the one who planted those photos of us in the tabloids, the ones taken outside my dorm! She *sent* the paparazzi there that night!"

"Daphne had no idea about us. No one did, remember?"

"Are you sure you didn't tell her at New Year's?" Nina couldn't keep the jealousy from her voice. "I saw you two talking out on the patio at Smuggler's. You looked pretty close."

"What do you want me to say? Yes, Daphne hit on me at New Year's, but I turned her down, told her that I was with someone else now." He shook his head in disappointment. "Come on, Nina. I thought you would at least be gracious in victory."

"Being gracious," Nina said darkly. "Sounds like yet another of the many things that Daphne can do, and I can't."

The darkness felt tense and heavy, and somehow more ominous than before. Nina struggled to breathe. Then something Jeff had said clicked into place.

"You *did* tell Daphne. Even if you didn't tell her my name," she insisted. "After you told her you were seeing someone, she clearly figured out that it was me. Then she sent the press to my dorm!"

"Do you realize how paranoid you sound?" Jeff asked, incredulous. "Daphne hates the press. She would never do that. I know she can come on strong, especially to someone like you, but she wouldn't hurt me like that."

It wasn't lost on Nina that he'd said *hurt me.* Not *us.*

"To 'someone like me'?" she repeated, stunned. "You mean, a *commoner*?"

"Of course not. I just meant, someone who hasn't known Daphne for years."

"You met me when we were six," she reminded him. She

didn't have to add that it was much longer than he'd known Daphne.

Jeff glanced down at the tip of Nina's shoe, peeking out from beneath her gown. "Daphne and I ended on good terms. We're still friends. Whatever she said to you, I'm sure it was well intentioned."

Was he seriously taking her side? "I can't believe you ever dated her. She's awful."

"Why are you being like this? I'm with *you* now. What does it matter what happened in the past?"

"Because I don't think it's actually *in* the past!" Nina burst out. "Daphne clearly isn't done with you—and from the way you're defending her, maybe you aren't done with her, either!"

She tore her hand away from Jeff's grip. "She's a manipulator, Jeff. She's been lying to you from the beginning."

"Nina—"

"It's absurd that I'm supposedly the gold-digger, when it's really Daphne. I like you *in spite of* your position, and Daphne likes you *because* of it!"

The prince's jaw tightened. "Daphne and I dated for almost three years," he said. Nina recoiled a little at the reminder. "I think I would have known if she was lying to me that whole time."

"No. You're just too blinded by her looks to see it," Nina insisted. "She's been playing you, Jeff. Using you. She should win an Oscar for this, because it's the performance of a lifetime—making you think she cared about you, when all she cares about is being a princess!"

"So now you're accusing her of being a sociopath," he said quietly.

"Exactly! She faked your entire relationship, and if you can't see it, you're even more foolish and shallow than I used to think you were!"

Nina stared determinedly out at the city, furious with herself for crying, but it was too late.

If only she had proof of what had happened in the bathroom. But it was her word against Daphne's. And if Jeff was going to choose Daphne's side over hers . . . well, she had her answer right there.

Jeff let out a breath. "I don't want to make you any promises that I can't keep, about marriage or where this is going. I'm not trying to mislead you in any way. All I know is that I want to give us a fair shot."

"We *did* give us a fair shot, and it didn't work," Nina said quietly. "I can't handle all of this. The reporters, the constant scrutiny, the fact that your ex-girlfriend is determined to get rid of me—even the fact that your lawyer emailed me a *relationship contract*—it's too much."

Jeff didn't answer right away. He seemed stunned by her words.

"Nina . . . ," he said at last. "If it was just us, if I was a normal guy, would things be different?"

Of course they would, Nina wanted to say, except that the very notion was nonsense. The thought of him as a so-called *normal guy*, as one of the disheveled college kids who worked for his beer and pizza money, was ridiculous. Jeff could only ever be the Prince of America.

Just as Nina could only ever be a commoner.

"It won't ever be *just us*, Jeff."

He nodded. "I really am sorry."

She turned a tear-streaked face to him. "Me too."

They stood there, both of them leaning toward each other, but not touching.

"I guess this is it, then," Jeff said at last. "See you around."

He dropped a final kiss on her brow, more like a friend saying goodbye than a boyfriend. Then he walked back into the palace, the doors shutting behind him with a definitive click.

Nina leaned her elbows onto the railing. Her stomach had seized in an undeniable cramp, as if all the pain and sadness in her body were wringing her like a towel, twisting tears from her eyes.

She needed to get out of the palace, and this time, she wasn't coming back.

37

SAMANTHA

I am not jealous, Samantha reminded herself, as she drifted around her sister's party like a stray snowflake. It felt petty to be jealous at a time like this. Beatrice's engagement was a matter of state, a *dynastic* decision, and their father was dying— and compared to that, it felt selfish for Samantha to be yearning for Teddy. There was so much more at stake here than her own teenage heartbreak.

Her rational brain knew and accepted all of this, but that didn't make it any less painful.

At least Nina and Jeff seemed happy. They'd been attached to each other all evening, smiling goofy lovesick grins. Sam didn't see them on the dance floor anymore, though. Probably they had slipped off to be alone.

The person she did keep seeing, no matter how consciously she tried *not* to, was Teddy.

Ever since their conversation in the Crown Jewels vault, she and Teddy had done an admirable job of avoiding each other. It seemed like he was traveling back and forth to Boston anyway. When she did see him, Sam murmured a polite greeting and quickly moved on.

But tonight Teddy seemed to be everywhere. Sam realized that some stupid part of her was tracking his movements, with a low hum of alertness that seemed to operate under the surface of her consciousness.

He looked gorgeous in his tuxedo, his blond hair slightly longer than it used to be—gorgeous, and utterly off-limits to her. Sam gripped the stem of her glass so tight that it left an indentation mark on her fingers. She had almost, *almost* come to terms with the fact that she was giving him up. That decision had been much easier when he wasn't right in front of her.

There were plenty of other young men at this party, if she wanted to distract herself. Sam forced herself to whirl across the dance floor with them, one after the other: Alastair von Epstein, Darius Boyle, and the infamous Lord Michael Alden, who'd defied his family's wishes and became a professional swimmer. He was even cuter in person, with that perfect white smile that was all over cereal boxes and toothpaste commercials.

Samantha was certainly dressed for flirtation. Her dramatic red trumpet gown matched her vivid lipstick, and her hair tumbled in curls down one shoulder, ruby studs glinting in her ears. It all had a glamorous, old-Hollywood feel.

She made a concerted effort for a while—looking up at Michael through lowered lashes, laughing at his jokes even when they weren't funny—but her heart wasn't in it.

"Sam, can I talk to you for a minute?"

Beatrice had come to stand behind her, uncharacteristically alone.

"Of course," Sam replied, curious. She followed Beatrice to a corner of the colonnaded terrace, behind a towering spray of white peonies in a cut-glass vase. A young man in the uniform of the Revere Guard shadowed their movements, eventually settling along the edge of the ballroom.

"What happened to your other Guard? The tall, dreamy one?" Sam didn't recognize Beatrice's new security detail.

"Connor?" Her sister let out a strange breath that was almost a laugh, her voice higher-pitched than normal. "He'll be back. He was just on temporary leave."

Something was different about Beatrice tonight. The moonlight struck living sparks from the prongs of her tiara, cast a pale glow over her face. She looked softer and more beautiful than Sam had ever seen her.

Beatrice glanced around their surroundings, making sure no one could overhear. Then she leaned in close. "I'm calling off the engagement," she said abruptly.

"What? But—*why?*"

"You were right; Teddy and I aren't in love. We shouldn't make this kind of commitment, not when there are other people out there for us. People we *could* fall in love with," she added, with a significant glance toward Sam.

"What about everything you said, about how you need to get married before—" Sam stopped herself from saying *before Dad dies,* but Beatrice understood.

"I'm going to talk to Dad tonight, as soon as I can get a minute alone with him. I know he won't be thrilled," she admitted. "But hopefully he'll come to understand."

Sam glanced back toward the ballroom. At all those hundreds of people, who'd come to celebrate the love story of Beatrice and Teddy.

"You're sure?" she whispered. The wind howled in her ears, drowning out the laughter and gossip of the party. "You're really going to tell the world that you've changed your mind?"

Beatrice shook her head with an irrepressible smile. "Who cares what the world thinks? The only people whose opinions should count right now are our family's and Teddy's."

It was such an un-Beatrice answer that Sam could only blink, speechless.

The wind tugged more insistently at the skirts of their gowns, pulling the pins in their hair. Still neither of them moved.

"I can't believe you would do this for me," Sam managed at last.

"I'm doing this for *us*. There's so much that you and I can't control about our lives, being who we are, but there's no reason we should have to make this kind of sacrifice."

That was when Samantha knew.

"You're seeing someone else," she guessed.

The expression on Beatrice's face—surprise and nervousness at being caught out, but most of all a bright, beaming excitement—was confirmation enough.

"Promise me you won't say anything until I've talked to Dad."

Sam wanted to take her sister's hands and squeal in excitement. To think that careful, duty-bound Beatrice had been carrying on a clandestine love affair. "Who is it? Anyone I know?"

Beatrice's smile faltered. "You've met him, yes," she said slowly.

"Is he *here* tonight?"

When Beatrice nodded, Sam glanced breathlessly back toward the party, wondering which of the young men inside was her sister's secret boyfriend.

"It's not going to be easy," Beatrice said hesitantly. "This guy . . . he isn't as eminently suitable as Teddy."

"Few people are." Sam tried to make a joke of it.

"He's a commoner."

Sam blinked in shock. Now she understood why Beatrice had asked all those weird questions about Aunt Margaret. She wanted to know what would happen if she couldn't stomach marriage to any of the young men on their parents' list. If she followed her heart instead.

"I know," Beatrice went on, reading Sam's expression. "It's less than ideal. What can I do?"

"You'll figure it out. Just . . . one step at a time. Focus on getting out of your engagement with Teddy first, before you try to get into another one." Sam tried to sound encouraging.

She had no idea how her sister was going to manage something as utterly unprecedented as marrying a commoner.

Beatrice sighed. "I'm not really looking forward to sharing the news with Dad. Or with the media. I wonder what the protocol is, for breaking off a royal engagement. Has that even *happened* before?"

"Oh, sure!" Sam exclaimed. "In the nineteenth century more weddings were called off than actually took place. It happened all the time when political alliances shifted."

"Great. I'll tell Dad we can look back at Edward I's broken engagement as a precedent." Beatrice gave a strangled laugh, then fell silent. "The people are going to hate me for a while."

"Maybe," Sam conceded. "Or maybe they'll be proud of you for knowing your own mind, and being brave enough to put a stop to all of this."

Beatrice nodded, though she didn't seem convinced.

Sam's eyes drifted back toward the ballroom. "Does Teddy know yet?"

She remembered Teddy's remark when he told her that Beatrice had proposed: *You can't say no to the future queen.* He would never have been able to break their engagement himself—not with the fate of his family, his entire community, on his shoulders.

But if Beatrice called it off, there was nothing the Eatons could say in protest.

Sam's sister shook her head. The golden light from the party played over her profile, gleaming on one of her earrings, casting the other half of her face in shadow. "You're the first person I've told."

She might be overstepping, but Sam had to ask. "Could I be the one to tell him?"

"I thought he deserved to hear it from me . . . ," Beatrice began, then seemed to change her mind at the expression on Sam's face. She smiled with unmistakable relief. "Come to think of it, maybe you *should* be the one to tell him. Isn't it the maid of honor's job to handle wedding complications?" She said it lightly, as if calling off the wedding of the century was nothing more than a garden-variety *complication*.

Sam threw her arms around her sister. "Thank you."

And despite her efforts to avoid Teddy all night, despite the fact that she'd just spent the last ten minutes out here on the terrace, Sam realized that she knew exactly where he was.

He stood near the edge of the dance floor, surrounded by a semicircle of well-wishers. Sam beelined toward him. She felt suddenly like she was floating, like an infectious fizzy joy had lifted her off this planet altogether and she would never come back down.

Teddy glanced up in surprise. He clearly hadn't expected Sam to seek him out tonight. Neither had she, until now.

"Beatrice wants to see you. I think to take more photos," she announced loudly. Then she angled her head away from the crowd, so that only he could read her lips. *Coatroom, five minutes,* she mouthed, and sashayed away before he could question her.

He was there in four.

She'd been pacing back and forth in her anxiety—well, *pacing* wasn't the right word given the confines of the space; she could only take one step in each direction. She kept thinking of the last time she'd been in here with Teddy: at the Queen's Ball, back when she'd still been the heedless girl who chugged a beer in a coat closet. Back when all she'd known about him was his name and the warmth of his smile.

"I shouldn't have come." Teddy stood uncertainly in the doorway.

"What are you, a vampire that needs to be invited over the

threshold?" Sam tugged him inside, shutting the door behind him. "It's okay, I promise."

"Sam, no." He retreated a step, his hand already on the doorknob. His code of honor struck Samantha as something rare and fine, a remnant from a previous century.

"Beatrice is going to break off the engagement."

Sam was alert to his response, so even in the darkness she saw Teddy's stunned, wide-eyed expression. He let his hand fall slowly from the door. "What?"

"She's calling off the wedding," Sam said again.

"Did she tell you why?"

"Because she loves someone else."

"Ah," Teddy breathed. "I thought she might."

"You . . . what?"

He shifted his weight, causing the lush furs behind him to rustle and sway with the movement. Sam forced herself to stay still, though every atom of her body buzzed with his nearness.

"There were times when Beatrice got a distracted look on her face. And I knew she must be thinking of something else—or some*one* else," Teddy said slowly, and shrugged. "She never smiled like that about me."

"Teddy . . ." If only there were a light in here—she needed to *see* him better, try to figure out what he was thinking.

"Not that I blame her," Teddy went on, his voice rough and unreadable. "Since I was doing exactly the same thing."

He was talking about her—wasn't he?

It took every ounce of Sam's self-control not to venture closer. "So you aren't disappointed?"

"Honestly? I feel relieved. And happy for your sister, that she's found someone she loves. She deserves that."

The cloakroom was very quiet, as still as the sumptuous furs that hung around them. Sam felt hyperaware of every inch of darkness that separated her from Teddy.

371

His voice cut through the silence. "What happens next?"

"Beatrice is going to talk to our dad tonight, tell him her decision. Then I'm sure they'll get Robert involved, figure out the best way to break the news—he'll probably make you do another interview, or maybe a press conference. And you'll have to give back all the presents stacked in that room. *And* cancel next weekend's cake tasting," Sam added, in that nervous rambling way of hers. "I was really looking forward to that."

"Samantha. I meant what happens next for *us*."

Sam swallowed. She felt suddenly like she'd melted, like she was nothing but lightning encased in skin.

"Last time we were here, you said that you refused to take orders from me."

"That depends on the order."

"Well, I was *hoping* that you would kiss me, but since I can't command you, I guess I'll have to—"

Her next words were silenced as Teddy lowered his mouth to hers.

It no longer seemed to matter that Sam couldn't see him—that he was darkness, and she was darkness, and darkness swirled all around them. Because everything in the world had narrowed to that single point of contact. To the searing feeling of Teddy's mouth on hers.

She hooked her arms around his shoulders and yanked him closer. Teddy reached under her curls to cradle the base of her neck, his other hand slipping around her waist. Sam's breath caught in her throat. They stumbled back onto the furs, and Teddy knocked his head against a shelf, but not even that broke apart their kiss.

"We should get back," Teddy whispered at last, his breath warm in her ear.

Sam nipped one last time at his lower lip, just because she could. She felt rather than saw him smile against her skin.

"If we *must*," she said dramatically, and forced herself to step back. She was dangerously close to dragging Teddy up to her bedroom, no matter the consequences.

"Sam." Teddy ran a hand through his hair, a shadow against the dark. "I'm sorry for the way this all happened. It hasn't been especially fair to you."

"It hasn't been fair to any of us." Sam thought of Beatrice, cornered by their dad into proposing when she didn't really mean it.

"I *like* you," Teddy said baldly. "In Telluride, I kept wishing that I could hit pause—keep spending time with you, learning more about you. What I'm trying to say is, you deserve better than this. Than hiding with me in a coatroom."

His words warmed her. "I do wish it was a bit more spacious," she teased, but he didn't take the bait.

"I just . . . I would hate to cause problems for you, with your family."

Whatever happened, Sam knew that she and Beatrice would be in it together. "What about you and *your* family?" she asked, deflecting.

Teddy heaved a quiet breath. "I don't know," he admitted. "I hope we can figure something out. If we don't, I guess I'll learn what it's like to lose everything."

"Not everything. You'll still have me."

Sam felt for his hand, and Teddy gripped it hard.

"We're going to have to give people time, you know," he said. "Neither of us comes out looking very good here. I'll be the guy dating his ex-fiancée's sister, and you're the maid of honor dating the former groom."

"They'll get over it eventually. Stranger things have happened when it comes to royal weddings," Sam declared, with more confidence than she felt.

"Such as?"

"Louis XIV had an affair with his brother's wife. Henry VIII married *his* brother's wife." Sam laughed. "You've also got the medieval king Hardecanute—that means 'Tough Knot'—who died of drunkenness at a wedding feast. I'm serious," she insisted, at Teddy's skeptical look. "He literally drank himself to death!"

"I believe you." Teddy was clearly fighting back his amusement.

"Are you laughing at me?"

"Never," he said quickly. "I'm just thinking about how difficult it's going to be, being with you. Difficult and unpredictable and never, *ever* boring."

She flushed in pleased self-consciousness.

"Okay—why don't I go out first, and then you wait a couple of minutes, just in case. Meet me near the bar?" Teddy suggested.

Sam nodded as he slipped out the door. Only a few seconds had passed before she darted out into the hallway, the hem of her dress dragging on the floor as she caught up.

"Oh—Teddy!" she cried out, with studied nonchalance. "I'm so glad I ran into you!"

"I thought we agreed that you were waiting a couple of minutes," he whispered, though he was grinning.

"Let me have my way, just this once."

"I have a feeling it's never going to be *just this once* with you," Teddy answered. "Though I have to say, I'm okay with it."

38

DAPHNE

Daphne was chatting with the Countess of Cincinnati when Nina ducked past the doors to the ballroom. She looked pale and slightly shaken, though she wasn't crying. Daphne felt grudgingly impressed by that.

She watched Nina cast one last lingering glance over the party, as if committing it all to memory, then leave in a swish of gray glass beads.

Daphne looked over at her mother, flush with victory. Rebecca had been right after all: the way to break them up had always been through Nina, rather than Jefferson. Rebecca met Daphne's gaze and cut her eyes meaningfully toward the prince.

But Daphne wasn't about to rush. The last thing she wanted was for Jefferson to feel *pursued*.

It wasn't until the night was winding toward a close—the crowds at the bar thinning, the dance floor slowing down— that she went to find him.

Jefferson was, predictably, in the Reynolds Room: a small chamber down the hall from the ballroom. Its windows were lined with persimmon drapes, a massive couch curled up before them like some great sleeping animal. In the corner stood a built-in bar. It was rarely staffed, though on one occasion Daphne had seen the king himself back there, mixing martinis.

The prince sat on a gleaming barstool, his body slumped forward, his elbows propped on the bar. An expensive bottle of scotch sat before him. There were shelves of crystal tumblers along one wall, but tonight it seemed like the prince had dispensed with the niceties and was drinking straight from the bottle.

Daphne pulled the door shut behind her, and the sounds of the party were rapidly cut off.

Jefferson barely glanced up at her arrival. "Oh, hey."

"Rough night?" she asked sympathetically, undeterred by his tone. She'd always been able to charm Jefferson out of a maudlin drunk mood. "Looks like you could use a friend."

"What I could really use is a drinking buddy."

Daphne pulled herself onto the barstool next to him. "Where's Samantha? She was a fantastic drinking buddy in Telluride."

She saw Jefferson's flicker of recognition. "That's right. Weren't you two taking shots?"

It was nice to know that he still couldn't look away from her, even if he wanted to. "Who, me?" Daphne asked, with false innocence. She kicked off her rhinestone-studded heels and hooked her feet over the lower rung of the barstool. "What are we drinking?"

He slid the scotch toward her, something challenging in his attitude, as if he didn't really expect her to join in.

"Cheers," Daphne said lightly. The bottle felt heavy in her hand. She took a long sip, then set it on the bar, slowly and with some style.

Now she had the prince's attention.

"Everything okay?" Her gauzy champagne-colored dress cascaded around her as she leaned forward. In that moment, Daphne knew, everything about her seemed soft and angelic, from the pale curve of her neck to her rose-colored lips to her fingernails, painted a translucent pink.

Jefferson heaved a sigh. "You've probably heard, but Nina broke up with me tonight."

"No," Daphne breathed. "I hadn't heard."

He shot her a curious glance. "She said some pretty weird things about you, actually. She accused you of sending the paparazzi to her dorm, to break the story about us."

Daphne let her mouth fall open in a perfect O of shock. "I had no idea that you guys were dating. Let alone what dorm she lives in," she said, with a confused laugh. "Besides, I would never do something like that. You know how much I hate the press."

"That's what I told her. But . . . where would Nina get an idea like that?"

Daphne sensed his uncertainty. And she had known this was coming—that Nina would fling accusations about her to the prince. Which was why she'd come prepared.

Nina was no longer here, and as King George I once said, history is written by the victors.

"I'm sorry. This is all my fault. All this confusion, I mean," Daphne explained, in answer to Jefferson's puzzled look. "I told Nina earlier tonight that I blamed myself. I guess she misunderstood."

"Blamed yourself? For what?"

"She clearly felt out of her depth." Daphne said it gently, so that it somehow didn't come out like an insult at all, but more like a quiet observation. "She wasn't equipped to handle all the attention she was getting. I tried to give her some advice when we went shopping—"

"You went shopping with Nina?"

"We ran into each other at Halo, and I helped her pick out a dress." Daphne sighed. "I probably shouldn't have made an effort. She clearly thought I was interfering. I just wanted her to learn from my mistakes."

Jefferson nodded, silent. He glanced at the fireplace, above which hung a famously unfinished portrait of his grandparents King Edward III and Queen Wilhelmina. The top half was complete, but the bottom dissolved into charcoal sketch lines, the Queen Mother's dress transitioning from flame-colored paint to wisps of pencil. After her husband died, she refused to let the artist finish the painting; and so it would remain like this, forever incomplete.

"Nina doesn't like you," Jefferson said abruptly. He still wasn't convinced by Daphne's explanation.

Of course she doesn't. Daphne gave a serene nod. "I don't blame her. She knew what I was thinking tonight."

"What were you thinking?"

Daphne lifted her eyes to meet his, then swept her thick black lashes down over her cheeks.

"How I still feel about you. I won't say that I'm sorry you and Nina broke up. Because I'm not."

She let the words fall between them like dice, tossed in some cosmic game of chance, except that Daphne left nothing to chance. Jefferson wasn't going to kiss her; she knew that much. It was too soon. She just needed to say the words and let them percolate in his mind.

He shifted awkwardly, as if he wasn't quite certain how to behave around her after what she'd said. Still, Daphne waited a moment. Too many people were unnerved by silence, but not her. She knew what could be accomplished in a beat of silence, if you were willing to let it unfold.

"Thanks for sharing this," she said at last, and reached across him for the bottle of scotch, to take another long sip before passing it back to Jefferson.

He cleared his throat. "Remember when we came in here and played Apples to Apples?"

"You and Ethan kept trying to make it a drinking game!" Daphne recalled. "It was so long ago, I can't remember who won. . . ."

Jefferson gave a sardonic smile. "Not me, if my hangover the next morning was any indication."

"Wasn't that a school day?"

"Oh, yeah. I'm pretty sure I begged you to bring a breakfast sandwich to the alley for me." The students of St. Ursula's and Forsythe weren't supposed to visit each other's campuses, but there was a narrow strip of grass between the two—uninventively called "the alley"—where you could meet between periods for a quick kiss. Or, in Daphne's case, to deliver Gatorade and a breakfast sandwich to your boyfriend.

"I miss those days." Daphne's smile was tinged with nostalgia. "Everything else aside, I miss being friends with you. So many times I've caught myself reaching for my phone, because there was something I wanted to tell you, and then . . ."

Jefferson's hand was right there on the bar between them. Daphne knew how easy it would be to lace her fingers in his, but she didn't want to spook him.

Instead she sighed and looked down, the diamonds in her ears swinging and catching the light. "I wish we could be friends again."

The prince nodded, slowly. "I don't see why we can't be."

Later that night, Daphne started toward the main double doors of the palace. She had just said goodbye to Jefferson—well, *goodbye* might be overstating it; she had poured him into the helpful arms of one of his security officers. She had briefly considered going upstairs with him, but decided against it. She didn't want him to think of her as the rebound from Nina, when Nina had always been the rebound from *her.*

And anyway, they'd gotten too drunk, sliding that fifth of scotch back and forth as they reminisced and laughed over old memories. Daphne decided that it was better to end now, on a high note. She had rekindled the spark, and that was enough for tonight.

Daphne didn't bother heading back into the party; there was no one else she needed to see, and her parents were long since home. She paused at the front hallway to collect her coat from a footman. Even though she'd taken much smaller sips than Jefferson, she felt the scotch pulsing languidly through her veins. She was quite drunk.

And exhausted. That was the thing about success; it could be even more draining than failure. It had felt like a marathon: all these days and nights of scheming and plotting, breaking apart a relationship and holding herself ready in the wings. She'd been running on fumes and raw determination, and now there was nothing left to hold her upright.

The palace's circle drive was always chaotic after a big party. A long queue of people twisted around the front porch, each of them waiting for one of the courtesy cars, which the palace provided free of charge after a night like this. Daphne allowed herself a sigh and started toward the back.

"Daphne? Can I give you a ride?"

She was somehow unsurprised to see Ethan at the front of the line, holding open the door of a town car.

Daphne paused in the moonlight, her coat dropping from her shoulders. There was something new and sharp in the air, something she should ignore. But she didn't.

"That would be great. Thank you," she murmured, and slid after him into the backseat. Ethan leaned forward to give the driver her address.

"We can drop you first. This *was* your car."

"It's okay," Ethan said quickly, and smiled. "Chivalry, and all that."

Daphne realized that she didn't actually know where Ethan lived, had never been to his house, had never even met his mom. She wondered, fleetingly, why he'd never invited any of their friends over—if his mom didn't approve of them, or if Ethan had reasons of his own.

"So? How did it go?" Ethan demanded. Through the tinted windows, the city was a gold-flecked blur. The skyscrapers of the financial district huddled against the horizon, honeycombed by scattered office windows that were still illuminated.

"Nina broke up with Jefferson."

"Congratulations." He gave a slow, quiet clap. "Though I have to say . . . I'm surprised you're not still with Jeff, after a victory like that."

She could have told Ethan that Jefferson was too drunk, that she'd done more than enough for one night. Instead all Daphne said was, "Well, I'm not."

He lifted an eyebrow. "I'm curious. How did you manage it?"

It suddenly felt like such a relief, sitting here with Ethan, not hiding anything. Throughout the conversation with Jefferson, Daphne had been on high alert, monitoring her every word and gesture. But with Ethan she could just be herself.

She told him everything she'd done to Nina, from the beginning.

The car took a sharp turn, and since neither of them was wearing a seat belt, the weight of Ethan's body lurched against hers.

He quickly moved away, though with less distance between them than there had been.

"I'm impressed," he declared, when Daphne had finished her story. "Sabotage *and* intimidation—you've outdone yourself. You really decimated that girl."

Something about his phrasing needled her. "Did you ever doubt me?" she asked testily.

"Never." Ethan paused, as if uncertain whether to say his next words, then went ahead and said them anyway. "It's too bad that Jeff doesn't appreciate the half of what you're capable of."

"That's not true—"

He barked out a laugh. "Jeff doesn't know you like I do.

381

All he sees is what you look like, which is a damn shame, because your mind is the best thing about you. Your brilliant, stubborn, unscrupulous mind, and the sheer force of your willpower."

Daphne wanted to protest, but Ethan was looking at her with an expression she had never seen before.

It was the look of someone who knows you, knows the best and worst parts of you, knows what you have done and what you are capable of doing, and who chooses you in spite of it all. It was a look Daphne had never seen from Jefferson in all the years they had been dating.

"Stop it," she hissed, and then again, with greater volume: "Just *stop*, okay? I don't know how to win with you!"

"Daphne. It isn't always about *winning*."

"Of course it is!"

She reached up to smooth her hair, feeling powerful and unsettled. Before she could lower her hand again, Ethan caught it in his own. His thumb traced small circles over the back of her wrist—intent, slow, lazy circles that made Daphne's breath catch. She didn't pull away, though Ethan's face was suddenly close to her own. For once there was no sardonic tilt to his full, sensuous mouth.

"Ethan . . ." Daphne meant to sound reproving, but her voice came out dangerously uncertain.

When he finally lowered his mouth to hers, it seemed inevitable.

The kiss snapped down her body like a drug, coursing wildly along her nerve endings. Daphne pulled him closer. She knew this was a foolish mistake—that she was throwing away all her years of hard work. She didn't care.

The choice should have been so simple: on the one hand was Jefferson, the *prince*. Everyone wanted them to be together: Daphne's parents and Jefferson's parents and *all of America* and, ostensibly, Daphne.

Yet here she was. It was as if the touch of Ethan's lips on hers had short-circuited her brain, and nothing else mattered anymore.

Somehow she'd moved to sit atop him, straddling his lap. They both fumbled in the dark, shoving aside the frothy mountain of her skirts. His lips traveled down her neck, and she tipped her head back, letting her hands curl possessively over his shoulders. She felt as if she and Ethan had become a pair of blades striking to make fire, like sparking against like.

Ethan was right about one thing: Jefferson didn't know the real her, and he never would.

39

BEATRICE

Beatrice couldn't grab a moment alone with Teddy until the party was nearly over.

There were simply too many guests, all of them eager for their own personal moment with the groom- and bride-to-be. She caught Teddy's eye a few times, and an invisible flicker of communication would pass between them—but then another well-wisher would pull him aside, or the photographer would request Beatrice for a photo, and they would again spin off in different directions.

A few partygoers still lingered on the scuffed dance floor. Footmen approached them with glasses of water, gently trying to herd them toward the entrance, where a long line of town cars stretched around the circle drive. Even the flowers in their towering arrangements seemed to have lost their bloom, stray petals already falling to the floor.

Beatrice finally turned to Teddy and asked for a moment alone. He nodded in understanding, and she led him toward the side of the dance floor, behind a column of rose-colored granite.

"Teddy, I'm so sorry about everything," she hurried to say. "I hope you know that I . . . I mean, I never should have . . ."

"It's all right," he assured her, his blue eyes subdued. "As long as you're okay." The sentence upticked at the end, making it into a question.

"Not yet," Beatrice admitted. "But I think—I hope—I will be."

Teddy gave her a soft smile, one that she certainly didn't deserve. "What can I do to help?"

It twisted her guilt like a knife, that Teddy was being so honorable and thoughtful at a time like this. That even when she was breaking off their engagement, he still focused on making things easier for *her*.

"Please don't tell anyone yet." She was eerily reminded of making the same request when she proposed, though for drastically different reasons. "I need to break the news to my dad first. Then we can figure out the next steps."

Teddy nodded. "I'll keep behaving like your fiancé until I hear otherwise from you."

"Thank you," Beatrice murmured. "And thank you for being so understanding about all of this. For not hating me, even after what I've put you through."

"I could never hate you." He reached for her hand, nothing romantic in the gesture, but as if he wanted to forcibly transfer her some of his strength. "Whatever happens, know that you can always count on me. As a friend."

Beatrice nodded, unable to speak.

When they reemerged into the remains of the party, the Eatons had lined up to say their goodbyes.

They were all here: Teddy's parents, the Duke and Duchess of Boston; Teddy's younger brothers Lewis and Livingston; and the youngest sibling, their sister, Charlotte. Even if she hadn't met them already, Beatrice would have known at once that they were related. They all had that look about them. A golden-haired, patrician, photogenic look that made you think of playing football outside, fresh-baked apple pie, and windswept Nantucket summers. They seemed utterly at ease in their ball gowns and tuxedos, as if they woke up and got dressed in black-tie attire every morning of their lives.

"Thank you for coming," Beatrice told each of them, with a clasp of their hands; this family wasn't the hugging type.

"I'm so thrilled. So thrilled!" Teddy's father boomed, throwing a jocular arm around Teddy's shoulders.

Beatrice caught the awkward half hug of goodbye that Teddy gave Samantha, and stifled a smile. Maybe if they were lucky, both Washington sisters might end up with a happy ending.

It wasn't until the Eatons had left that Beatrice cleared her throat. "Dad? Could I talk to you? Alone."

"Sure. Let's go to my office for a nightcap," he suggested, still beaming.

Beatrice followed, to settle opposite her father in an armchair. A footman must have kept the fire going all night, because it blazed contentedly in the massive stone fireplace.

She wished she could relax into the chair like the young woman she was: pull her feet up onto the cushions and tuck them to one side, lean her head back. But she wasn't permitted that kind of informality, because right now she wasn't a daughter talking to her dad.

She was a future queen, talking to the current king. That was the context in which she and her dad had begun this discussion—*a matter between monarchs*, he'd said, when he told her that he was sick—and that was how she would continue it.

The king reached for the decanter on a side table and poured bourbon into a pair of cut-glass tumblers. He handed one to Beatrice, who immediately took a sip. Liquid courage, right?

"What a night," he mused, still buoyed by his good mood. "You looked so beautiful, Beatrice. So regal. I'm proud of you."

The only way to spill the news was all at once, she thought, and steeled herself.

"Dad, I want to call off the engagement."

The jubilant smile slid off his face. "What are you talking about?"

"I can't marry Teddy. I don't love him."

There was a sudden urgency to her words, as if she'd broken open a tap and now they were pouring out like water, faster than she could catch them. "I *tried* to fall in love with him, really. I knew how much it meant to you. But I can't do it, Dad. Not even for you."

The king nodded. "I understand," he said, and the knot in Beatrice's stomach began to loosen. This had been so much less arduous than she'd expected. She should have known her dad wouldn't pressure her—

"We'll push back the wedding. That gives you and Teddy more time to get to know each other," her dad went on, oblivious to Beatrice's dismay. "We haven't announced a date anyway. We'll tell the planning committee that you need another six months, slow down the pace. Maybe you and Teddy could take a trip—spend quality time together, away from all the public appearances. I know my illness has put everything on a compressed schedule," he added, his eyes downcast. "I'm sorry that I made you feel rushed."

Beatrice's hands clenched frantically in her lap. "The timing isn't the problem, Dad. A year from now, I won't want to marry Teddy any more than I do tonight."

Anger flashed in the king's eyes. "Did he do something to hurt you?"

"Of course not," she said impatiently. "Teddy is great, but—"

"Then what is it?"

"I've fallen in love with someone else!"

"Oh," her father breathed, as if all he could manage right now was the single syllable. Beatrice didn't dare reply.

"Who is it?" he asked at last, in a wooden kind of shock.

"Connor Markham."

"Your *Revere Guard?*"

"I know he's not from your preapproved list of options," Beatrice hurried to say. "That he isn't a nobleman. But, Dad—I love him."

The wind whistled and howled at the windowpanes. The fire hissed, sparks flying up as logs resettled. Beatrice reached for her glass, to take another nervous sip of the bourbon. It glowed a deep amber in the light of the fire.

"I'm sorry, Beatrice. But no," the king said at last.

"No?" she repeated. Was that really his response—to flat-out deny her request, as if she were a child asking to stay up past her bedtime?

"Surely you see that it's out of the question." Her father paused, giving Beatrice time to nod in agreement. When she didn't, he forged ahead. "Beatrice, you can't break off your wedding with Teddy Eaton—who comes from one of the very best families in the country, who is smart and honorable and kind—because you're in love with your Guard."

She tried not to wince at the way he said *one of the very best families in the country,* as if that were something the centuries-old titles actually measured and ranked. "Connor is all of that, too, Dad. Smart and honorable and kind."

"Teddy graduated with honors from Yale. Your Guard never went to college, barely even managed to complete high school!"

"You're the one who always says that there's more than one kind of smart!" Beatrice gritted her teeth. "I know there isn't historical precedent for this, but that doesn't mean it's *wrong.*"

Her father didn't answer right away. He clinked the ice in his glass, his eyes still fixed on the fire.

"Remember what your grandfather always used to say, about how the Crown divides you into two people: one public, the other private? That you are Beatrice the future queen and Beatrice the young woman, all at once?"

Beatrice twisted her engagement ring back and forth, sliding it off her finger and on again. She had a sudden urge to throw it across the room.

"I remember," she answered.

"It will stay that way your whole life. It gets even worse when you're a parent, and have a child who becomes heir to the throne." At last the king looked up, directly into Beatrice's eyes. The sheer grief in his expression knocked the air from her chest. "The parent in me is overjoyed that you've found love. Of course it doesn't matter to me, as your father, who you are with—as long as that person treats you well and makes you happy."

"But . . . ," she supplied, when her dad fell silent. She was shocked to see his eyes gleaming with tears.

"That other part of me, the part that answers to the Crown, knows how impossible it is. If you were anyone else in the country . . ." The king winced and put a hand over his chest, as if he were in pain. "But you have never been just *anyone*. Beatrice, you cannot be with that young man and be queen. You would have to give up everything for him."

She felt herself bristle. "You used to tell me that nothing was impossible, that we could find a solution to anything if we thought carefully and creatively enough."

"That was about political problems!"

"From what you're telling me, this *is* a political problem! That law is two centuries old. Maybe it's time we had a commoner on the throne!" She cast him a pleading gaze. "You're the king, Dad. Surely there's something you can do. Sign an executive order, or submit a new law to Congress. There has to be a way out."

Her dad's face was very grave as he spoke his next words: "Even if there was something I could do, I wouldn't do it."

"What?" Beatrice cleared her throat, fighting not to scream. "You seriously won't help me marry for love?"

"Beatrice, I always *wanted* you to marry for love," her father insisted. "I just hoped that you would fall in love . . . within certain guidelines. That's why I invited those young men to the Queen's Ball. They are much more suited for this type of life than Connor is."

Within certain guidelines. Beatrice was ashamed to realize that it might have worked: that she might have talked herself into loving Teddy, eventually, if not for Connor. She shifted onto the edge of her seat, her voice scathing.

"You honestly think that I shouldn't be with Connor because he's a *commoner?*"

Her father shook his head wearily. "Beatrice, you've studied the Constitution backward and forward. Don't you know by now that the Founding Fathers never did anything without good reason?" He poured himself another splash of bourbon. His mouth was set into a grim line, his eyes shadowed. "That law is there to protect you, and the Crown, from situations like this. From . . . misalliances."

Tears pricked at Beatrice's eyes. She needed space, needed a minute to *think* a way through this. "Why won't you at least give him a chance?"

"It isn't about me, Beatrice. If I was the only person you had to convince, you would already have my blessing," her father said quietly. "But I know how flawed the world is— how fiercely people are going to judge you, as America's first queen. I know the near-impossible task that lies ahead of you. Trust me when I say that if you marry Teddy, he will help lessen that burden for you in a thousand small ways. Teddy will lift you up, will support you. He will be an *asset* to you, while Connor would prove nothing but a hindrance. And you can't afford a hindrance. It's going to be difficult enough for you as it is."

"Because I'm a woman," Beatrice said flatly.

Her father didn't argue. "Yes, exactly, because you're a woman, and the world will make everything exponentially more difficult for you. It isn't right, or fair, but it is the truth. You are going to be the *very first* Queen of America. You have a steeper road to climb than all the eleven kings who came before you. You will have to do so much more to prove yourself, to earn the respect of foreign dignitaries and politicians and even your own subjects. I have been trying for years to help prepare you, to make things as easy for you as I can, but it's still a challenge that you will face every single day."

"Connor *knows* all of this, Dad. He's seen my life up close, and he hasn't been scared away. I can lean on him as a source of support." *I already do.*

"He will drag you down," her father said brutally. "Beatrice, I'm sure he means well, but that young man has no idea what he's signing on for. How is he going to feel after years, *decades*, of being constantly told he's not good enough? Of sitting quietly by your side at thousands of state functions? He will be forced to sublimate his entire *life* to the demands of the Crown." The king took a bracing breath. "Connor may love you now, but is his love for you strong enough to withstand all of that?"

Of course it is, Beatrice wanted to say. The words failed to reach her lips.

"The law might seem outdated and ridiculous to you, but there's wisdom in it," her father maintained. "Why do you think so many of our forefathers married foreign princesses? It wasn't just to seal political treaties. It was because no one else was capable of taking on this job. No one else, aside from the children of other monarchs, had been raised since *infancy* to lead millions of people."

"You're underestimating Connor," Beatrice tried to say, but her voice broke.

The king wiped at his eyes. "Beatrice, I'm trying to protect you both. Even if it *was* possible for you to marry Connor, it would be a mistake. Someday, when he realized just how much he'd given up for you, he would regret this choice. He would come to hate you for it—and worse, he would come to hate himself."

Beatrice couldn't move. She felt utterly transfixed by her father's words.

"But . . . I love him," she said again.

"I know." Her father's hand tightened around his glass. "If it's any consolation, you aren't the first monarch to face this kind of sacrifice. Plenty of kings who came before you gave up someone they loved, to satisfy the demands of the Crown. Myself included."

His words didn't sink in right away. When they did, Beatrice's gaze snapped up. "*What?*"

"I loved someone too, before your mother."

Her blood hummed with shock. The only sound was the quiet popping of the fire.

"Who . . ." Beatrice's lips felt dry and cracked.

"She was a commoner."

"What happened to her?"

"I haven't seen her in a very long time," he said gravely. Beatrice was too distracted to realize that it wasn't a complete answer.

Her father had been in love when he was young, and had given up that love to marry Adelaide. Beatrice tried to imagine letting go of Connor like that: never seeing him again, never knowing if he'd eventually moved on, married someone else. Her heart twisted in anguish at the thought.

"Beatrice, I know you love your Guard now, but the kind of love you're talking about—it doesn't last." The king paused to cough before continuing. "Your mother and I weren't in love when we first married. We *fell* in love, day by day. Real love comes from creating a family together, from facing life together—with all its messes and surprises and joys." He sighed. "I know you don't love Teddy now, but I also know that if you marry him, you'll come to love him. In a real way. *That's* the kind of love you can build a future on—not whatever you feel right now for Connor."

Beatrice sat there in silence for a while, staring blindly at the fire. Her mind spun with everything her father had told her.

"No," she said at last.

The word fell like a stone into the silence.

The king's head angled toward her. "What do you mean, no?"

"I mean that I don't accept this. You might believe in this law, might think that it somehow protects the Crown, but I refuse to be bound by it. I'm not like you or Aunt Margaret." A new stubbornness glinted in her eyes, and she stood up.

Her father grimaced. "Beatrice, please don't say things like that."

"Why not?" Her words gained momentum, avalanching faster and faster in the white-hot heat of her anger. "I have spent my whole *life* chasing this idea of perfection—trying to be the perfect princess, perfect daughter, perfect future queen. And for what?"

The king's eyes were glassy, the blood drained from his face. "For America," he said, and coughed again.

"Is *America* going to love me the way Connor does? Listen to my secrets and kiss me good morning and tell me my dreams are worth chasing? All I've ever done for America is give and give and *give*, and still America wants more! When will it ever be enough?"

Beatrice had never in her life spoken like this. The words unlocked some astonishing new part of her—as if she'd opened the door to her suite and found that it contained more rooms than she'd ever imagined, all shimmering with possibilities, just waiting to be explored.

"Maybe things would be easier if I did walk away!" she said hotly. "Let the law strip me of my titles and remove me from the succession—I don't care. Let Samantha be the first queen instead!"

Beatrice knew she was lashing out like a cornered animal, that she didn't mean what she said. Or . . . did she?

She thought of Samantha, blazing through the ballroom as confident as an empress.

What if Beatrice *wasn't* queen?

Her father stared at her, his features twisted into a grotesque mask of horror. "Please, Beatrice . . ."

That was all he got out before he lifted a hand to his chest, seized in a fit of coughing.

And kept coughing.

The flash of Beatrice's anger rapidly dissipated as she watched her father double over, his hands braced on his knees. His face was reddening, his eyes squeezed shut, his coughs louder and more ragged. A chill of foreboding chased its way down her spine.

"Dad!" She grabbed a bottle of water from the side table, trying to pour some into his mouth, but it didn't work; the water just dribbled uselessly over his chin.

The king slumped down, to fall on his hands and knees.

"*Help! Someone, help! It's the king!*" Beatrice sank onto the carpet next to him. She realized dimly that her gown was splattered with bright red blood—her father's blood, which he was coughing up, and she could do nothing at all to help him.

It was only a matter of seconds before his security stormed through the doorway, but those few seconds were the longest of Beatrice's life. Everything seemed to dissolve into a panicked, multicolored haze. All Beatrice could hear was the ragged, uneven sound of her father's breath. The prongs of her tiara dug mercilessly into her skull.

"Dad—it's going to be okay, I promise. I'm right here,"

she said brokenly, her hands on his shoulders, until one of the security team gently pushed them away. She kept talking as the EMTs arrived to load him onto a stretcher.

This was all happening too fast. Beatrice felt a scream building inside her but forced herself to bite it back; or maybe she was biting her tongue, because she felt blood in her mouth, edged with the metallic taste of fear.

"I'm so sorry," she kept saying over and over, as if it were a prayer. "Stay with me, Dad. *Please.*"

40

DAPHNE

Daphne blinked, slowly waking. Through her windows the sky was a leaden gray, streaked with the first dim lights of dawn.

Next to her, his breaths soft and even, lay Ethan Beckett.

She sat up abruptly, hugging her creamy satin sheets to her chest as her room—her *mistake*—snapped into dizzying focus. Her dress lay in a disheveled mound of tulle on the floor, alongside the shoes she'd kicked off, and scattered pieces of Ethan's tux: a reproachful trail of evidence, reminding her what they had done. Again.

Ethan stirred next to her, but stayed asleep. For a moment Daphne let her eyes drag over his form: his long torso, his muscled shoulders, the shadow of his lashes on his cheekbones. His hair curled at the nape of his neck. She remembered how, just hours ago, her hands had been tangled in that hair, her head tipped back as she swallowed a moan. Daphne winced at the memory.

If only she could rewind it all like an old-fashioned cassette tape, or better yet, yank the tape out altogether and punch a series of holes through it.

She didn't understand the current of desire that pulsed between her and Ethan, in spite of what happened last time, or maybe because of it. Maybe what she and Ethan did together had forged some dark bond between them, as if they were heroes—or rather, antiheroes—who'd ventured together to the underworld, and now their fates were forever intertwined.

No. Whatever this was, Daphne had to break it off, now.

Ethan must have felt her eyes on him, because he blinked slowly awake. "Hey," he murmured, with a yawning smile, and reached to pull Daphne back down toward him. She ducked from under his arm and scooted back.

She hated him for looking so sexy right now, warm and rumpled and creased with sleep.

"Ethan, you need to leave."

He let out a breath and sat up. "Let's at least talk about this."

"There's nothing to talk about."

He shook his head defiantly, almost defensively. "Daphne, that's twice now that you and I have thrown ourselves at each other. I'm not saying I know what it means, but don't you think we owe it to ourselves to figure it out?"

"As far as I'm concerned, nothing happened. We're going to put this behind us, just like we did before."

Except that last time was much, much worse.

Ethan held her gaze steadily. "I can't keep pretending that nothing has happened between us."

"Nothing *should* have happened between us. We can't do this to Jeff!" Daphne hissed, startled into calling him by his nickname for once.

"We're not doing *anything* to Jeff," Ethan argued. "Look, last time we had plenty reason to feel guilty. But this is completely different—you're not dating him anymore. I refuse to act like this was some drunken mistake."

The gray light had crept farther into the room, touching an old music box atop the high-topped vanity where Daphne's jewelry gleamed. Thrown over the back of her desk chair was a delicate black scarf that Jefferson had given her, after she once mentioned that she wished she had one, for all the cocktail parties they attended in cold weather. That was the kind of boyfriend Jefferson had been. The type who remembered stray comments and acted on them. Or at least, who sent one of his family's assistants to act on them.

"Jefferson is your best friend, and I dated him for almost three *years*. This . . ." Daphne gestured angrily around the room, indicating the rumpled sheets, the pieces of clothing scattered like debris in the aftermath of an explosion. "This has to stop."

"You're seriously telling me that last night meant nothing to you?"

He had her trapped. She couldn't admit that it meant nothing. Not after she'd slept with him twice, when she'd never slept with Jefferson in all their years of dating. But she refused to be bullied into saying anything she might regret. She refused to verbalize feelings that she should never have had in the first place.

The silence stretched to a breaking point. Ethan lifted an arm as if he was going to reach for her, then seemed to think better of it.

"You're lying to yourself," he told her. "Pretending that this is only physical, that it means nothing, when we both know that's not true."

For a split second, Daphne let herself imagine what it would feel like to say yes. To tell Ethan that she chose him. To fall back into the warm circle of his embrace, let him keep looking at her in that charged and magical way.

Their reflections glared at her from the mirror on her wall: Ethan staring at her with those glittering dark eyes, Daphne's gaze darting back and forth with indecision. Both their figures were cast in a ghostly blue glow. It was coming from her phone, Daphne realized, which was blowing up with messages. She reached over to grab it off her side table.

Her home screen was covered in dozens of tiny bubbles.

They were all alerts labeled BREAKING NEWS, their level of panic steadily increasing as the night had progressed.

His Majesty the King has been admitted to the ICU at St. Stephen's Hospital. . . .

His Majesty is on life support, having suffered a coronary thrombosis. There is no current update on his condition. His family is with him at this time. . . .

The king, in the *hospital?*

Daphne's heart rate spiked as her fear and uncertainty kicked into overdrive. But so, too, did her decades of training.

This was drastic, earth-shattering, *devastating* news, and Daphne had missed it because she was in bed with the wrong boy. She sent up a silent prayer of thanks that her parents hadn't already stormed into her room to tell her.

"The king has been hospitalized," she told him, in a crisp, no-nonsense tone. "You really need to leave. Take the back staircase; otherwise my parents might see you."

She stepped out of bed and stalked over to her closet, where she picked out an outfit: a demure cardigan and dark-wash jeans, a cross necklace on a silver chain, suede booties. Did she have time to wash her hair, or should she just pull it into a low ponytail?

"What are you doing?" Ethan asked, watching her movements.

A detached sort of calm had settled over Daphne's shoulders. The things she'd been thinking just two minutes ago, about her and Ethan, now seemed like the wildest and most outlandish impossibility. "I'm going to the hospital."

"To be with Jeff."

"He needs to be surrounded by the people who love him right now." Daphne lifted her eyes to Ethan, as unruffled as if they were old friends saying hello across a garden party. "I assume I'll see you there, later."

Ethan stepped out of bed and began to get dressed, his

movements angular and vengeful. A muscle worked in his jaw. Daphne watched his expression shift rapidly from disbelief to hurt to anger. *Good*, she thought. Anger was the safest. Anger she knew how to handle.

"Fine, Daphne." Ethan's shirt was half buttoned, his jacket thrown over his arm, his shoes knotted at the laces and held in one hand. "If that's how you want things to be. I'll leave you to enjoy your victory the way you want to. Alone."

His voice was eerily quiet. "Because that's what you'll be if you choose him, you know. *Alone*. Even if you get what you want someday, and have a ring on your finger and a crown on your head and a big elaborate title before your name. There will still come a moment when everyone else leaves the room and it's just the two of you. You, and a prince who hardly knows you at all. I hope it's worth it."

The plaintive echoes of that word—*alone, alone, alone*—seemed to chase after her, long after Ethan had shut the door.

41

NINA

"My turn," Daphne purred, an eyebrow lifted in unmistakable challenge.

Nina fanned out her cards and held them close. Their ornate black and red faces, printed with clubs and diamonds and spades, stared impassively back at her. Her hand was no good.

Daphne set down the jack of hearts with a flourish. "The knave," she declared, using the old-fashioned term—from back when face cards represented the royal family, when the knave was meant to signify the prince, the one who broke hearts.

There was nothing for Nina to play, and Daphne knew it. She gave a narrow smile. "I win," she declared. Nina watched as she swept everything on the table toward her, her eyes glinting with avarice.

Daphne piled the jewels into her lap, then glanced up at Nina in cold surprise. "What are you still doing here? You know you don't belong."

Nina sat bolt upright, her heart thudding dully in her chest. It had only been a dream.

Then the events of last night rushed over her in painful detail—her confrontation with Daphne, her breakup with Jeff. After that, Nina hadn't been able to go back to campus, where she would be surrounded by all those eager, curious eyes. She'd asked the courtesy car to bring her home instead.

At least here she wouldn't be bombarded by constant

reminders of Jeff. Everything else, even her dorm room, felt too tangled up in memories of him. She couldn't even get herself a post-breakup Wawa milkshake, because now that, too, seemed to belong to her and Jeff.

This was exactly why Nina hadn't wanted to get close to him in the first place: because she'd known, deep down, that it wouldn't work out. That no matter how much they wanted to be together, circumstances would always conspire to force them apart.

The early-morning light touched on all the familiar comforts of her childhood bedroom: the old wicker screen in the corner, her brass light fixtures, the deep purple of her throw pillows. It was warm up here, a dry dusty warmth that Nina wanted to wrap around her like a blanket. She realized that she'd fallen asleep with her arm tucked around her old stuffed cat, Lenna, which she hadn't done in years.

Nina started to turn her face stubbornly back toward her pillow, only to hear noises coming from downstairs. It sounded as though someone was crying. She pulled a terry-cloth robe over her old pajamas and trotted down the stairs barefoot.

Her parents were on the couch together, Isabella tipping her head onto Julie's shoulder. The light of the television flickered over their faces, underscoring the shadows beneath their eyes. Isabella had a box of tissues in her lap, which she kept nervously picking at. Both women were sniffling.

"What's going on? Is everything okay?"

Her mamá lifted a tear-streaked face. "The king is in the hospital, in critical condition."

"What?"

Nina's mom shifted wordlessly, letting Nina wedge herself on the cushion between them. This was how they always used to watch movies when she was younger—Nina in the middle, surrounded by her parents' warmth, the competing scents of their perfumes.

Her mamá reached for the remote and turned up the volume. "All the cable networks have suspended their regular shows. It's been round-the-clock coverage."

A reporter stood before St. Stephen's Hospital, one hand stuffed into the pocket of her black peacoat and the other clutching a microphone. "To all the viewers just now joining us, we have been covering this unfolding story since two a.m. Eastern time, when the king was rushed to the hospital after his daughter Beatrice's engagement party. The palace has not yet issued an official statement about his condition. All we know is that His Majesty is being treated in the intensive care unit of St. Stephen's."

Nina shook her head. "I *saw* him last night at the party, and he seemed fine. He even danced with the queen for a while! How could this happen?"

The king was always so vibrant, with that booming, larger-than-life laugh. It seemed impossible that illness could strike someone so utterly alive.

"It just *happened*," Julie said softly. "There's no how or why for this kind of tragedy. No explanation. Not everything gets to make sense."

Nina fumbled in her pocket for her phone and dialed Sam's number, but it went straight to voice mail. She wondered how her friend was holding up, how *Jeff* was holding up.

This was the worst kind of tragedy, wasn't it—the kind you didn't see coming. Some things, like breakups or fights with your best friend, you could at least prepare for. But there was no bracing yourself for something like this: for the heart attack that struck at random, mere hours after your daughter's engagement party.

"Do you remember the day he was crowned?" Isabella's voice cut through her thoughts.

"Vaguely." They had staked out a spot on the edge of the parade route, eager to catch a glimpse of the new king and queen. Nina recalled clutching a small American flag on a wooden stick and waving it furiously, remembered buying a cherry snow cone from a street vendor and licking its syrupy sweetness from her fingers.

"Strangers were talking to strangers, everyone acting as though the entire capital had become one giant street festival." Isabella still held a tissue in her hands. She began folding it over and over into an ever-shrinking triangle. "I never thought I would get the chance to actually work for him, and then . . ." She sighed. "He's been such a good king."

A chill ran down Nina's spine at the finality of her mamá's words. It sounded as though she was already *mourning* him. "We don't know what's going on. He might make a full recovery."

"The palace hasn't made any statement. That's not a good sign," her mamá countered. Well, she of all people knew the inner workings of the palace infrastructure.

Nina thought again of the twins. Of the entire royal family, huddled together in one of those bleak waiting rooms, waiting for good news that might never come.

"You should go to St. Stephen's," Julie chimed in, as if reading her daughter's mind. "I know Jeff and Samantha could use a friendly face right now."

Nina hated the thought of letting her best friend go through this alone. But there was no way she could face the prince right now. "Mom, no. I can't."

"I know it'll be weird, seeing Jeff after last night," her mom said gently. "But you should be there for Sam's sake."

Nina knew her mom was right. But then she thought of last night, of how Jeff had automatically taken Daphne's side. How easily it had apparently been for him, to walk away from their relationship.

"You don't understand. It wasn't exactly a normal breakup."

"That makes sense, given that your relationship was hardly normal."

Nina could only nod in agreement, pulling a pillow onto her lap to hug it.

"Do you want to talk about it?" her mom went on. When Nina didn't answer right away, she tried again. "It just seemed like you and Jeff were so happy together. I can't understand what came between you."

It wasn't what *came between us,* Nina thought, *but* who. The glamorous, insidious Daphne Deighton, getting what she wanted, just like always.

Nina took a breath and told her parents everything that had happened.

When she finished, her mamá's face was mottled with anger. "How *dare* she. I always knew there was something off about that girl—what a little—"

"I feel sorry for her," her mom cut in. "She's clearly lost sight of reality."

Nina nodded. "That's what makes her so dangerous. There's nothing she won't do in order to get what she wants."

"Let me get this straight," Isabella went on, pulling one leg up to cross it over the other. "You're giving up, just because Jeff's terrible ex-girlfriend cornered you in a bathroom and said some nasty things?"

"I'm not *giving up.* I'm just sick of it all: the paparazzi attention, the way the palace kept butting into our relationship. The fact that I had to dress differently if I wanted to be with him. Everything Daphne said was simply the icing on the cake."

Her parents' eyes met over her head. Nina could practically feel their indecision, the silent messages crossing and colliding between them.

"Nina, I would be lying if I said we were thrilled when you

first told us that you and the prince were dating," her mamá began—which was a generous way to phrase it, given that they'd found out from the tabloids. "But it was also clear to us that you and Jeff really cared about each other. That kind of feeling doesn't come along very often. It's worth fighting for, worth defending. Especially from people like Daphne."

Nina shifted. "Fight Daphne? You don't understand what she's like."

"Oh, Nina. I've gone up against the Daphne Deightons of the world a thousand times over." Isabella let out a mournful sigh. "You think your mom and I don't know how it feels, being told that we aren't good enough, that we don't belong? I am a gay Latina woman in a position of enormous power in the king's administration. That has won me far more enemies than it has friends. Every day I face people like Daphne— people who fight dirty, who think that they are entitled to anything in the world that they want, simply because they can reach their greedy hands out and *take* it."

"Exactly!" Nina exclaimed. "How on earth can I win against someone like that? Fight fire with fire?" The thought of trying to out-manipulate Daphne was daunting. No way could Nina wage that kind of social warfare.

"Of course not."

Julie combed her fingers through Nina's hair: a soft, distracted gesture. "Your mamá and I look to each other to stay grounded. People like Daphne—who walk around the world hurting others, hiding their real selves—*those* people are the unlucky ones. You can't worry about them. All you can do is be yourself, wholly and unapologetically. You don't have to change for anyone, not even for a prince. And if Jefferson doesn't love you just as you are, then he isn't the young man I thought he was," she added softly.

Nina shook her head. "I don't know. . . . Jeff and I said

some pretty harsh things to each other." Hadn't she called him shallow and selfish?

"Oh, sweetheart. Someday you'll understand that words are just that—words. They can hurt, but they can also heal."

They all looked up at the TV, which had panned to the crowds gathering outside the hospital. The capital must be totally shut down this morning. What looked like thousands of people had flocked to the streets, talking in low, somber tones. Strangers hugged one another; police monitored the intersections, to protect people who walked into the road, blinded by tears.

The reporter was saying something else, about how the stock exchange would suspend trading until further notice, but Nina wasn't listening. All she could think about was this enormous outpouring of love and support for the royal family. She had to be part of it.

"Moments like this have a way of smoothing out the rough edges of things, to help us see what really matters," her mamá chimed in.

Nina thought of what Jeff had said that night on campus, when he'd surprised her with the Wawa milkshake. *You're already part of our family,* he'd told her. *You belong with us—with me.*

She stood up, running a hand distractedly through her hair, which was still matted with hairspray from last night's dramatic updo. She needed to go, now. No matter what had happened between her and Jeff, she needed to be there for Samantha.

"Do you think—" She broke off, glancing uncertainly at her parents. "Do you think he'll want to see me?"

"I don't know," her mom said honestly. "But there's only one way to find out."

♛

Barely twenty minutes later they pulled up outside St. Stephen's. Julie was driving, still in her pajamas, with Isabella perched in the passenger seat, casting worried glances back at Nina. They had insisted on giving her a ride so that Nina wouldn't have to deal with parking.

Nina had watched in terrified awe as her mom cut across lanes of traffic, blazing through yellow lights with abandon. For once it didn't seem to matter. There was barely anyone on the road. Coffee shops and laundromats were shuttered and dark, TEMPORARILY CLOSED signs fastened over their doors. A hush had fallen over the capital, as if everyone were anxiously holding their breath, putting their own lives on hold while their king's life lay in the balance.

They pulled up outside the emergency-room doors, avoiding the cameras and microphones clustered near the side entrance. Nina saw the corner of the Royal Standard fluttering over the hospital roof, alongside the American flag—as if anyone didn't already know that the king was in residence.

"Good luck, sweetie," Isabella murmured, when Nina threw open the car's rear door. "I love you."

"Love you too, mamá." Nina's eyes darted to Julie, and her smile wavered. "Thanks for driving, Mom. Wish me luck."

Nina provided her name at the front desk, and was relieved to learn that she'd already been added to the list of preapproved visitors. "I know they'll be glad to see you," the administrator offered. She glanced at Nina's empty hands, a question in her eyes.

Nina tried not to reveal her consternation. Was she supposed to bring flowers? She'd come in such a frantic hurry that she hadn't even thought of it.

Daphne probably would have come with a gift, but then, Daphne wasn't the one here. Nina was.

When she reached the private wing where the king was being treated, Nina halted. A pair of palace security guards stood at the double doors. Recognizing Nina, they stepped aside to let her through.

Her steps quickened. The waiting area was just ahead. What would she say to Samantha, to *Jeff*? She couldn't worry about it, Nina decided. She would have to just trust that the right words would come to her in the moment.

And suddenly, there he was—stepping around a corner, his face heavy with sadness. Nina ached for him. She opened her mouth to call out a greeting—

Daphne turned the corner next to him.

Nina stumbled back, retreating behind the heavy bulk of a soda machine. She watched in mounting horror as Daphne slipped her arm through Jeff's: an intimate, confident gesture. Her face tipped up to his in concern and she nodded, listened to something he said. She had on a demure charcoal-colored sweater and simple cross necklace, a light dusting of makeup on her face.

She looked perfect, as always—perfect and expensive, where Nina was rumpled and stale, her eyes red-rimmed from a night of crying.

Had Jeff seriously called Daphne to ask her to come with him to the hospital?

Nina fought off a wave of dizziness. Just twelve hours ago, she and Jeff had been together, holding tight to each other on the dance floor, and now he was back with *her*. It confirmed everything Daphne had said. His relationship with Nina had been nothing more than a single off-key note, a blip interrupting his *actual* relationship.

In the end, Daphne really was the one who had all the cards.

Nina knew that the strong thing to do would be to walk out there anyway. To sit next to Samantha and put an arm around her, tell her best friend that she was here for her, no matter what happened.

But Nina wasn't brave enough for that. She retreated before Jeff or Daphne could see her.

As she shuffled blindly down the hallway, it seemed to Nina that the only noise in the entire hospital came from her. It was the sound of her heart, shattering all over again.

42

SAMANTHA

Samantha had memorized the artwork on the opposite wall. She knew every subtle gradation of its color, every twist in its pattern. She would have stared out the window just to change things up, except that the waiting room had no window.

Maybe the room had been designed this way on purpose, to keep people from watching the sun move through the sky: so they wouldn't note the passage of time and get even more anxious than they already were. As good an explanation as any, since there was no clock in here either.

She glanced at her phone to check the time. It was still in airplane mode; she'd switched it hours ago, when she couldn't handle any more breaking-news alerts. Almost noon. Had it really been ten hours since they'd arrived here? It all felt surreal, in the sticky dark way of a bad dream.

Sam decided to flick her phone off airplane mode. Her screen immediately filled with notification bubbles, messages of support flooding in from everyone she knew. One of the texts was from Nina: *I am so, so sorry about your dad. I wish I could be there at the hospital with you. Know that I am thinking about you nonstop. Love you.*

Sam sent a single red heart emoji in reply. It was all she was capable of, right now.

She'd been in her bedroom when she heard Beatrice's shouts from the opposite side of the palace: raw, panicked shouts that didn't at all sound like they had come from her sister's throat. Sam had stumbled down the stairs, still wearing her red trumpet gown, its skirts spilling around her bare feet like a pool of blood. She'd watched, powerless, as the EMTs loaded her father into the back of a medical van. The ribbons of his uniform fluttered each time the gurney rattled.

The queen stood alongside Samantha. The lights of the ambulance danced luridly over her features, only a slight tightening of her jaw betraying her emotions. Beatrice swayed a bit next to her, as if alcohol—or, more likely, shock—had made her unsteady on her feet.

They had watched, utterly mute, as the van left for the hospital. Its siren echoed around them, an angry streak of sound tearing through the streets.

Moments later they had rushed into a waiting car and followed, to gather here in this anonymous waiting room, where they'd spent the night doing exactly that. Waiting, and hoping.

The doctors had appeared every half hour with a non-update, letting them know that, once again, the king's condition hadn't changed. He was still on life support.

They weren't letting anyone in to see him, not that he was awake anyway. But Sam couldn't help thinking that it didn't bode well. She was morbidly reminded of the French court, where members of the royal family were not allowed to visit relatives who were ill, because it was believed that if a king or queen witnessed death, the entire country would be cursed.

Sam shifted, causing her chair cushions to squeak in protest. No one even looked up. Jeff was in the seat next to her, his head hanging in his hands, Daphne on his other side. Sam felt too stunned to even question Daphne's presence right now. She just kept hold of her mom's hand, her mind whirling uselessly from one thought to another.

Queen Adelaide had barely spoken since they reached

the hospital. Her hand was clasped around her daughter's, so tight that the nails dug into Sam's palm. Sam barely felt it.

In the corner knelt the Queen Mother, the white beads of her rosary clicking in her hands as she mouthed her litany of prayers. She hadn't stirred in hours. If anyone could *pray* the king back to health, Sam knew, her grandmother could.

Beatrice sat slightly apart from everyone else, perched on the edge of her seat, looking as terrified and fragile as a porcelain doll. Teddy's hand rested tentatively on her shoulder, though Beatrice seemed oblivious to the contact.

He kept glancing toward Sam, and their eyes would meet in a silent bolt of communication. She knew they were tempting fate, staring at each other across the room, but everyone else was too wrapped up in their own anguish to really notice. Sam wished more than anything that Teddy could sit next to *her* instead—that she could feel the reassuring warmth of him while everything else was falling apart.

But it had all happened so fast, he and Beatrice hadn't announced they were calling off their engagement. Which meant that Teddy would have to keep playing the part of Beatrice's fiancé a little while longer.

Sam tugged absently at the sleeves of her high-necked sweater, wondering which of the staff had picked this out. She and her siblings had been at the hospital only a few minutes, still wearing their ball gowns, when Robert had rushed over with a packed bag of "comfortable clothes." Sam had been hoping for yoga pants and a sweatshirt, but then, appearances must always be maintained.

She'd pretended not to see the other outfits tucked at the bottom of the bag—a black dress and heels, in case they needed to leave the hospital in mourning.

"I need a minute," she declared, and gently detangled her hand from her mom's grip. She had to go somewhere, anywhere, if only to get out of that waiting room and its oppressive silence.

There was a break room down the hall. Someone had brought a delivery of food up here: muffins, bananas, a large bowl of berries. As if the royal family possibly wanted *catering* right now.

Sam wasn't hungry, but she needed to do something with her hands. As long as she kept moving, she could scare away the dark thoughts—which were like shadows, multiplying and stretching in her mind. She busied herself making tea, heating hot water in a machine and choosing a tea bag without noticing the flavor.

When she heard footsteps, Sam turned around, half hoping Teddy had followed her. But it was her twin brother.

"You'd better not let Grandma see you with that," Jeff joked, nodding at her mug. His heart clearly wasn't in it, but Sam appreciated the effort all the same.

"I know, I know. A princess drinking tea—it's the end of the monarchy." Though America hadn't been at war with Britain for two hundred years, everyone still acted as though drinking tea were a deeply unpatriotic act. The palace refused to even serve tea at any of its events, only coffee. Which wasn't even *grown* in America.

"You okay?" Jeff asked softly.

"Not really."

At the choking sound of her sob, he came forward and threw his arms around her. They stayed like that, hugging, for what felt like a long time.

Sam didn't bother with words. There were some feelings that words couldn't express; and anyway, this was Jeff, who understood her on an elemental level. Who had once shared the rhythm of her heartbeat.

Finally they broke apart. Blinking back tears, Sam grabbed a miniature jar of honey and spooned some into her tea. "I know this is ridiculous, given everything else that's going on, but I have to ask." Because she was curious, and because she needed to distract herself, if only for a second. "Why is Daphne here instead of Nina?"

Jeff gave a strange laugh, acknowledging the banality of her question. "I assumed that you knew. Nina broke up with me last night."

"Seriously?" Sam sank into one of the plastic chairs. Jeff pulled out the one next to her and slumped forward, elbows on the table.

"She told me she wanted no part of this," he said helplessly. "The media, the scrutiny. It was too much for her."

"But . . ."

But you both looked so happy last night, Sam wanted to protest. And the day before, in the Dress Closet, Nina had been beaming and blushing at the mention of Jeff. What could have possibly happened to change her friend's mind?

She looked again at Jeff's face, and the questions died on her lips. Her brother was suffering enough without having to relive every detail of their breakup.

"Jeff . . . I'm so sorry."

He nodded morosely. "When Daphne came to the hospital this morning, I couldn't turn her away."

Now Sam understood Nina's text. When she first read it, she'd been too numb with grief to question why Nina wasn't coming. It was because Nina didn't want to face her ex-boyfriend the very day after they broke up. Sam didn't especially blame her.

"I'm sorry I made things awkward with your best friend," Jeff added, as if reading her mind.

"It won't be awkward," Sam assured him, though she worried he was right. Her friendship with Nina might not be the same after this, because there would always be the ghost of Jeff between them. A space where he should have been.

Jeff picked up a muffin, then set it down again. "This all happened too fast," he said quietly. "Everything is changing, and I don't know how to stop it. I just want it all to go back to the way it was."

"I know," Sam agreed.

And yet . . . after the events of the past few months, things would never go back to normal. Jeff was right. Everything had changed. Or perhaps *she* was the one who had changed. Because Sam was no longer content to let the days skip idly by.

For so much of her life, she and Jeff had been aligned on nearly everything. They posed for a joint press portrait each year on their birthday, attended the same soccer camps, were raised by the same nanny. They communicated in truncated twin-speak—*this; sure now?; okay time.* Even as they grew older, they attended the same parties, hung out with the same group of friends. They kept no secrets from each other.

They had always felt like two sides of a coin: the pair of court jesters, the frothy fun twins. The emotional cannon that their family sent out whenever they needed to distract America.

Sam wasn't sure when that had shifted. Perhaps it was her father's illness, or Teddy's words, which had percolated in her mind ever since Telluride.

All she knew was that Jeff no longer felt like her second self. That for the first time in her life, she felt closer to her older sister than to her twin brother.

Maybe this was what it felt like to finally grow up.

43

DAPHNE

Daphne should never have doubted her abilities.

When she'd arrived this morning with a bouquet of lilies and asked the hospital staff to admit her, Daphne hadn't been certain they would let her through to the royal wing.

She'd been startled when Jefferson came down the hallway himself and threw his arms around her with surprising emotion. "Thank you for coming. It means a lot to me," he'd said roughly. "Will you stay?"

"Of course."

He'd led her to the waiting room, where they sat in a pulsing, anxious silence. Jefferson kept reaching for Daphne's hand, as if seeking the simple reassurance of human contact.

She hadn't realized that it would be so easy. That after months of careful plotting and maneuvering, months of calculation, all it had taken was a single act of tragedy for Daphne to work her way back in.

But then, events like this had a way of changing people; or rather, of *revealing* their true selves. It whittled parts of them away, until they emerged honed and clean like a sharply fletched arrow.

Daphne, certainly, had been forever changed by what she did to Himari.

She kept stealing glances at the prince, wondering what he was thinking. Did this mean that they were back together? At the end of their conversation last night, they had agreed simply to be friends again—but surely friends didn't sit here all day, holding hands in a hospital waiting room?

A small, shrill voice in Daphne's head reminded her that she had woken up this morning with Ethan. She had gone straight from Jefferson to his best friend, *again*; and the fact that she'd slept with Ethan sent her mind tumbling down a dark tunnel of memories, of all the terrible things that had happened after the first time she hooked up with him.

She didn't like thinking about it. Daphne had a readily adaptable moral code, but even she couldn't come to terms with what she'd done. Her best option was to compartmentalize it: tuck it into a dark box and leave it alone. Most of the time that worked.

But after what Ethan had said—after waiting here all morning for good news that never came, just as she'd waited the day Himari fell—the box was open, and now all the memories came rushing back.

Daphne felt an overwhelming need to talk to someone, to unburden herself. Even to someone who couldn't hear.

"Do you mind if I step out for a second?" she asked, giving Jefferson's hand a squeeze.

"Of course not," he assured her.

Daphne stood with a nod, smoothing her hair carefully over her shoulders. When she reached the elevators, instead of heading down, she went up, toward the long-term care ward. She'd walked these steps to Himari's room so many times, she could have navigated them blindfolded.

"Hey. It's me," she said, just like always, as she took the chair by Himari's bed. Her gaze traveled instinctively to the medical monitors, where Himari's life was reduced to a series of numbers and squiggly green lines.

"I was thinking about the time we met. Do you remember when we were partners for that ninth-grade project?" They'd

been assigned to research an era of history. Himari had immediately insisted that they focus on the Roaring Twenties. *We can
wear boas for our presentation,* she'd pointed out, in a *duh* sort of
tone, as if the very mention of boas negated any other argument.

Daphne had laughed. *You had me at boas.*

That afternoon, Daphne went over to Himari's house to
try on the costumes in her family's attic. As they stood there
facing the mirror—both of them giggling and preening, their
eyes sparkling above the mound of feathers—their friendship
had been sealed.

Daphne slumped her elbows onto her knees in a distinctly
unladylike position, and sighed. "I wish you could answer.
Every time I come, I wonder what you would say to me if you
could reply. I wonder if you even *like* my coming."

Daphne wasn't sure why she visited Himari so often. *Keep
your enemies close,* as the saying went—except that Daphne
still had trouble thinking of Himari as an enemy. Even after
everything.

"Maybe you hate me," she went on. "You have every
right to."

She didn't usually talk this much on her visits, not anymore. These days she mostly sat in silence, brushing her
friend's hair, watching the beat of her pulse on those glowing
monitors. But today Daphne felt a strange impulse to voice
her secrets. Today she could practically see them—they were
here in the room with her, lurking in the corners, flapping
about on great leathery wings.

"You probably don't care, but I'm about to get Jefferson
back. He was seeing this new girl, Nina, but she ended it.
Well, I *made* her end it." Daphne reached to take her friend's
hand, closing her other palm over Himari's fingers. "Also, not
that you would approve, but I slept with Ethan again."

♛

Daphne hadn't dared acknowledge what had happened between her and Ethan at Himari's birthday party.

She'd woken in the middle of the night and slipped away before anyone could see her, while Ethan was still snoring in that fold-out bed. If she never spoke it aloud, she told herself, it would be as if the whole thing had never happened.

Until the following week at Himari's house, when Himari confronted her about it.

"So," Himari said, turning to Daphne in cool disapproval. "When are you going to tell the prince about you and Ethan?"

"Excuse me?" Daphne spluttered.

They were in Himari's bedroom, trying on their dresses for the next day's graduation party. A party at the palace, which they had planned to attend together, as best friends.

Himari rolled her eyes at the denial. "Don't play dumb, Daphne. I saw you and Ethan at my birthday party, in my pool house. How long has *that* been going on?"

She'd seen them, but said nothing about it until now? Daphne's eyes flicked guiltily to Himari's window, to look out at the scene of the crime. The floodlights made the pool house look brighter than ever, as if Himari had highlighted it for just this purpose.

"I kept thinking you would tell Jefferson yourself." Himari stared levelly at her friend. "Though I guess I wouldn't say anything either, if I was dating the prince—and supposedly waiting till marriage—and I'd been sleeping with his best friend. Classy move, Daphne."

"I haven't *been sleeping* with Ethan! It was just that one time, and it was a mistake! I want to erase the whole thing and pretend it never happened."

"You can't erase something like that." Himari's face was spiteful, her dark eyes glittering with condemnation.

"My relationship with Jefferson isn't any of your business, okay?"

"It's my business because I saw it! You might be okay with *lying*, but I'm not."

"Let me explain," Daphne attempted, but Himari cut her off.

"Explain? To me?" She gave a hollow, merciless laugh. "The one you owe an explanation to is *Jeff*. He's the one whose trust you betrayed. But I'm going to give you one last chance. You tell Jeff by the end of the party tomorrow night, or I will."

Daphne swallowed. Her throat felt sandpaper dry. "You're blackmailing me?"

Himari gave a narrow smile. "I prefer to think of it as strongly incentivizing you to do the right thing."

"Why do you want to hurt me?"

"From where I stand, *you're* the one hurting *Jefferson*. Don't you think it's time you took a step back? Let him date someone else for a change?"

Daphne stared at her friend in numb disbelief. She should have known. Himari wanted the prince for herself.

Of course, other girls always wanted Jefferson. Daphne had been fending them off throughout their relationship, at parties and at school and even on the streets. Jefferson literally couldn't walk in a parade without girls screaming at him, holding signs that said MARRY ME, JEFF! Daphne had long ago resigned herself to watching girls preen and flirt before him, throw themselves at him as if she weren't standing right there.

But never had she suspected that her best friend was angling for him, too.

She wondered if she and Himari had ever really been friends, or if Himari had been posturing the entire time. Waiting for the moment when Daphne might slip up, and she could swoop in to take her place.

"If you think he's going to jump from me to you, you're wrong."

Himari gave a harsh laugh. "Maybe he will; maybe he won't. I guess we'll find out."

There was a hardness to Himari that Daphne had never seen before. It created an answering hardness within her. She felt like she no longer knew her friend at all.

She told Ethan to meet her outside school the next day, in the alley between their two campuses. He was at least half responsible for the events of that night—and he couldn't afford for the truth to get out either. Not if he wanted to keep his best friend.

When she told him about Himari's ultimatum, Ethan frowned. "Maybe we should tell Jeff ourselves. Preempt her. If it comes from us, we can spin it the right way."

Daphne struggled to keep her voice down. The alley was mercifully empty right now, but you never knew who might turn the corner. "You can't be serious. There's no right way to *spin* this, Ethan! Jefferson can't find out. It was just a one-off mistake, something we never should have done, and that we both regret."

"Was it?" he pressed, with a curious, half-watchful look. "Of course."

The strangest thing was, Daphne didn't actually feel guilty. She knew she should, they *both* should: this was a terrible double betrayal, the girlfriend and the best friend. Yet the only guilt Daphne had managed to muster up was a vague sense of guilt for not feeling any guilt at all.

She realized with a start that she didn't actually regret what she'd done.

All she regretted was that she'd been caught.

"I don't see how we can stop Himari from telling him, if her heart is set on it," Ethan said slowly.

Daphne rolled her eyes in frustration. Why didn't he seem more determined to fix this?

"Maybe we can undermine her," she mused, thinking aloud. Her shoes crunched on the pebbles underfoot as she paced back and forth.

Daphne felt her mind spinning and clicking like the gears of a watch, racing down a thousand possibilities every second. What they needed was a way to sideline Himari—make her seem ridiculous, even farcical, so that if she did tell Jefferson what she knew, he wouldn't believe a word she said.

"If only she would get drunk at the party. Then her accusations will come across like incoherent ramblings."

"Even if she does get drunk, she won't forget what she knows," Ethan reminded her. "How does this prevent her from going to Jeff another time and telling him everything?"

He was right. They needed leverage.

"If we get her drunk enough, then she might do something ridiculous. Something we could take photos of, to hold against her—threaten her that if she ever told Jefferson about us, we would show the photos to her parents."

Ethan nodded. "They're so strict with her, it just might work," he agreed. "Fight blackmail with blackmail. Except . . ."

"Except it's Himari, and we both know she won't get drunk and do something incriminating," Daphne finished for him. No matter how often people urged her to let loose, Himari never had more than a single glass of wine. She was too scared of her parents' punishments. The one time they'd caught her and Daphne sipping wine coolers outside, they'd threatened to send Himari to a military school if she ever did it again.

Panic swept through Daphne, a harsh, cold panic that wiped all thoughts from her head.

It was only then, when her mind was brutally empty, that she knew her plan. It didn't even feel like she'd come up with it, more like someone else had written it for her, in stark block letters, and now she was finally able to see.

"What is it?" Ethan prompted, reading her expression.

"We could make her *seem* drunk."

"What are you suggesting, that we roofie her?" Ethan said it jokingly, but when Daphne didn't laugh, his eyes widened in trepidation.

"Hear me out," Daphne said quickly. "We could slip a little something in Himari's drink—not a lot, just a minimum dosage. If she does say anything, it will seem like drunken incoherent ramblings. Or she might just pass out on the couch before she gets the chance. Everyone will think she drank too much, too quickly. And she obviously won't be in any condition to rat on us. We take some photos of her, just to be safe—to hold over her head in the future."

"Daphne. Please tell me you're joking."

So Ethan wasn't going to help her. Fine, then. Daphne would do this on her own. The same way she did everything else.

"Never mind. You're right," she agreed, too quickly to be fully convincing. "I'll find another way."

But of course, there was only ever one way for Daphne. Onward and upward, just like always.

That night at the palace, she slipped a few ground-up sleeping pills into Himari's drink.

It was easy, really; no one knew that Himari and Daphne were feuding. All Daphne had to do was ask another girl to please hand this glass of wine to her friend.

Himari grew instantly, visibly drunker, her words louder and more pointed, and then a few minutes later she retreated to a sitting room. Daphne stood near the doorway with Jefferson, watching as Himari tilted her head back onto the expensive pillows of the couch, her eyes fluttering shut.

The party ebbed and flowed around Himari for several

hours. Daphne saw Jefferson's protection officer frowning at Himari's sleeping form, but he never made a move to do anything, which Daphne found reassuring. He was medically trained—if Himari was in danger, wouldn't he say something?

As the night wore on and people grew drunker, the passed-out girl became something of a meme. People posed for selfies with her, making a thumbs-up in front of Himari, whose mouth was open, a stream of drool falling onto the couch. Daphne wasn't surprised. Himari had always been snobbish and inscrutable, and humiliation of the proud was one of mankind's favorite sources of entertainment.

She knew from Ethan's angry looks that he'd figured out what she'd done. But she did her best to keep him at a distance. She had enough to worry about right now without his self-righteous accusations.

Finally, later in the night, he found her alone.

"I can't believe you," Ethan whispered, jerking his head toward Himari.

Daphne shrugged. She knew this was an absurd plan, but what other choice did she have? Her reputation, her *relationship*, was on the line.

"She's going to be fine. Her pride will be a little bruised, but she'll survive that. I really am watching her," Daphne added, in a plaintive voice. No matter what Himari had said, no matter that she'd thrown away their years of friendship like a pile of trash, Daphne would never truly hurt her.

Ethan cast Daphne a curious, inscrutable look.

"What are you going to do, tell on me?" she demanded, her chin tipped up in challenge.

"You know I wouldn't." He paused. "You're terrifying, though." The way he said it, it sounded oddly like a compliment.

"Terrifyingly brilliant," Daphne amended.

A laugh rumbled deep in Ethan's chest. For an instant,

Daphne felt herself wondering what it would be like to feel that laughter—*really* feel it, her body tucked up against Ethan's, skin to skin. "Remind me never to get on your bad side," he told her.

"I think you know better than to ever try."

They had drifted wordlessly into the other room, toward the table of drinks, only to stall partway there. Daphne forced herself to ignore the flickering sensation that Ethan's gaze kindled in her chest.

Neither of them saw Himari rise drowsily from the couch and head toward the back stairs, the ones off the downstairs hallway. Even in her drugged-out state, she was determined to go up to Jefferson's bedroom, to tell him the truth about Daphne. And probably for other reasons.

It wasn't until she heard the unearthly sound of Himari's screams that Daphne realized the other girl had made it halfway up the stairs—and tumbled right back down.

♛

Daphne shifted on the hospital chair, her grip still closed over her friend's hand. She wished more than anything that things had gone differently. That she'd listened when Ethan had tried to talk her out of this ridiculous plan, that she'd forced Himari to negotiate—hell, that she had done what Ethan wanted in the first place, and told Jefferson the truth herself.

Losing her virginity to Ethan was bad enough, but drugging Himari was far, far worse. It didn't matter that Daphne had only meant for her to pass out and sleep it off. It was *her* fault that Himari had fallen and hit her head—*her* fault that her friend had been in a coma for the last eight months.

No one could ever find out the truth of that night. Especially not Jefferson.

"I'm sorry," Daphne whispered again, and let out a sigh.

What was done was done, and now that it had happened,

Daphne felt more permanently fixed on her path than ever before. She had lost too much—hurt her friend, traded away the last tattered scraps of her conscience—to give up now. She needed to see this through. Too many sacrifices had been made along the way for her to go anywhere but ruthlessly forward.

Daphne glanced up sharply. There was a slight pressure on her hand.

A shiver trailed down her spine. Her eyes cut sharply to Himari's face, but it was as blank and drawn as ever. Still, her fingers tightened around Daphne's in a barely perceptible squeeze. Almost as if she wanted to reassure her friend that she was still in there.

Or to let her know that she'd been listening to every word that Daphne said.

44

BEATRICE

It's all my fault. It's all my fault.

The words echoed over and over in Beatrice's head, an awful, hideous mantra, and there was nothing she could do to dispel them, because she knew that they were true.

She had told her father that she didn't want to be queen, that she wanted to renounce her rights and titles so that she could marry her *Guard*, and the shock of it had given him a heart attack. Literally.

Our Father, who art in heaven . . . All the prayers that Beatrice had memorized as a child came rushing back, their words filling her throat. She kept reciting them, because it gave her something to occupy her brain, a weapon to wield against her overwhelming guilt. *Love believes all things, hopes all things, endures all things. Love never fails.*

But what kind of love was that verse talking about? The kind of love she felt for Connor, or for her father, or the protective love she felt for her sister? What about the love Beatrice felt toward her country?

If her father died—

She couldn't bear to finish that sentence. She wanted to scream, to beat her fists against the walls and howl her anguish, but there was a blade of strength within her that refused to let her break down.

Connor was here, in uniform. He stood unobtrusively to

one side of the waiting room, trying to catch Beatrice's eye, which she steadfastly refused to do. She couldn't bring herself to send him away—but she didn't dare talk to him alone, either.

"Your Royal Highness, Your Majesty." One of the doctors hovered in the doorway, addressing Beatrice and her mom. "Could I have a moment with you both?"

Beatrice felt her heartbeat skip and skid all over the place. She nodded, not trusting herself to speak, and followed her mom into the hallway.

The doctor shut the door behind them. "The king's condition is not very promising."

"What do you mean?" The queen's voice was as level and calm as always, though her hands visibly trembled.

"As you know, the king's cancer is spreading from his lungs. What he suffered last night was a coronary thrombosis, meaning that one of the blockages caused by his cancer made its way into an artery, cutting off blood flow to his heart. That caused the heart attack."

Thrombosis. Even the word itself seemed evil, those sibilant Ss coiled together like a nest of snakes, about to sink their fangs into you.

Beatrice's mom leaned against the wall to steady herself. She hadn't even been aware that her husband *had* cancer until they reached the hospital last night and the king's chief surgeon informed her. "Shouldn't he have recovered from the heart attack by now?"

"It did some damage," the doctor said delicately. "The greater problem is that the cancer is still there. And now we're having trouble stabilizing His Majesty's breathing."

Tears shone in the queen's eyes. Her earrings from the party last night were still twisted in her ears: a pair of enormous canary diamonds, so big they almost looked like miniature lemons. "Thank you," she managed, and returned to the waiting room. But Beatrice didn't follow.

She glanced up at the doctor, swallowing her fear. Even though she already suspected the answer, she had to ask. "Could the coronary thrombosis have been caused by a shock?"

The doctor blinked, politely puzzled. "A shock? What do you mean?"

"If something happened last night that really surprised my father—something he hadn't expected," she said clumsily. "Could that have caused the blood clot?"

"A shock cannot create a clot in itself. It can only accelerate the process by which the clot enters the bloodstream. Whatever . . . *startled* your father last night," he said tactfully, "may have contributed to the timing. But the king was already sick."

Beatrice nodded. She tried to stave off the fear that crept through the cracks in her armor, to keep the placid Washington mask on her features. It was getting harder by the minute. "Could I . . . could I see my dad?"

Maybe it was what she had just confessed, or maybe he simply felt sorry for her, but the doctor stepped aside. "Five minutes," he warned her. "There can't be any more stressors to His Majesty's system."

It's okay. I already told him that I'm in love with my Guard and that I want to renounce my claim to the throne. There's nothing left I can say that will shock him any more than I already have.

"Thank you," she murmured, as graciously as she could.

The hospital room was thick with silence, broken only by the methodical beeping of clustered machines. Beatrice hated them. She hated all those illuminated lines and ridges, plotting her father's pulse as it struggled to right itself.

When she saw him, panic seized her with ice-cold fingers. Her legs suddenly felt unsteady.

Her dad was in a hospital gown, tucked beneath the blankets on the narrow bed. His face had a blue-gray tinge. Something about the angle of his arms and legs seemed awkward, as if they were superfluous limbs that he no longer knew how to employ.

He'll be fine, Beatrice told herself, but she could taste her own lies. This didn't look like fine.

"Dad, please," she begged. "Please hang on. We need you. *I* need you."

Some deep emotion in her voice must have reached through the fog of his pain, because the king stirred. His eyes forced themselves open.

"Beatrice," he rasped.

"Dad!" She gave a cry of joy that was part grateful laugh, and turned to shout for her mom. After all these hours, he was conscious again. Surely that was a good sign. "Mom! Dad's up, you need to—"

"Wait a second. There are some things I want to tell you."

Her father's voice was quiet, but there was an urgent gravity to it that silenced her. He reached one hand, feebly, to take Beatrice's. She clasped both her hands around his, so fiercely that the signet ring of America pressed uncomfortably into her palm, but she refused to let go.

She couldn't help thinking of the last time she'd been at a hospital bedside, when her grandfather had used his dying breath to remind her that the Crown must always come first.

No, she thought fiercely. Her dad couldn't die. It seemed so impossible, so cosmically unfair, that he could die when they all needed him so desperately. He was only fifty years old.

"I need you to know how much I love you," he told her, before a fresh wave of coughing racked his chest.

Beatrice forced back the tears that threatened to spill over. "Stop it, Dad. You can't talk like this. I won't let you."

There was the faintest hint of a smile on his lips. "Of course not. I have every intention of getting better. Just . . . wanted to say these things, since they're on my mind."

She knew that an apology might upset him. It would only

remind him of what she'd said in his office, which had *caused* his heart attack in the first place. Beatrice forged ahead anyway. "Dad, about last night—"

"I'm so proud of you, Beatrice. You are incredibly smart, and wise beyond your years." He didn't seem to have heard her. "Trust your judgment: it's sound. If someone tries to push you into something you have a bad feeling about, take another look at it. Don't be afraid to ask for help, from your advisors or from your family. There is so much glamour, so much pomp and circumstance. Don't forget . . ." His voice began to trail off, but he forced the last few words out as a whisper. "Don't forget that it's your *position* being honored, and not yourself."

Beatrice held tighter to him, as if she could keep him here through sheer force of will. "Dad, I'm sorry. About Teddy—"

"Don't be afraid to push back against your opposition. It won't be easy for you, a young woman, stepping into a job that most men will think they can do better. Harness some of that energy of yours, that stubbornness, and stick to your beliefs." He spoke carefully and slowly, each word underscored by a wheeze or a bit of a cough, but the words were certain. Beatrice had a sense that he'd memorized them. That he had been lying here in his hospital bed, composing them in bits and snatches, in the moments he hovered near consciousness.

"Dad . . . ," she said, in a faint voice.

"It's been the greatest honor of my life, helping prepare you to take on this role. You are going to be a magnificent queen."

Beatrice bit her lip to keep from crying. "I love you, Dad."

"I love you, too, Beatrice," he said heavily. "About Connor . . . and Teddy . . ."

His head tipped back against the sheets, his eyes fluttering shut, as if the effort to stay awake had been too much.

Beatrice let out a single anguished sob. He didn't need to

finish that sentence for her to know what he meant. He was telling her that she needed to let go of Connor—to marry Teddy, and start the rest of her life.

She felt the grinding and turning of some axis deep within herself as the human part of her fell silent and the part of her that answered to the Crown took over.

"Your Royal Highness." The doctor creaked open the door. "I think it's time you let the king rest."

"I don't . . ." Beatrice didn't want to leave when her father was like this, when he'd just expended so much energy on that speech. It felt somehow that she was tempting fate.

"It's all right, Beatrice. I'm going to sit with him awhile." The queen appeared in the doorway. She'd washed her face and redone her makeup, clearly trying to hide the evidence of her tears. "Why don't you step outside? You could take Sam and Jeff. I'm sure the crowds would love to see you. Many of them have traveled a long way to be here right now."

The last thing Beatrice wanted to do right now was a walk-about, but she lacked the emotional strength to say no. "Okay. We'll be back soon."

She gave her father's hand one last squeeze, then headed out to give her siblings, and Connor, the heads-up.

Sam and Jeff immediately agreed with her plan. "That's a nice idea," Sam said softly, running a hand through her ponytail.

"Teddy. You'll come with me, right?" Beatrice's voice nearly broke, but she held out a hand toward him. "It would be good for the country, to see us together right now."

There was a moment of strained silence. Beatrice felt Teddy's questioning gaze, felt Samantha's radiating resentment as they both realized the import of her words.

She couldn't end her engagement with Teddy, not right now. Not after the threat of leaving him had literally sent her father to his *deathbed*.

None of them spoke as they headed down the elevator and out to greet the waiting crowds.

It was a sunny afternoon, the sky overhead a Byzantine blue that felt distinctly at odds with what was happening in the hospital room upstairs. The golden light streamed down on them, making Beatrice wish she could shade her eyes, or wear sunglasses. She forced herself to blink until her vision adjusted.

The air felt cold and sharp. She drew in a great lungful of it, as if by breathing double she might somehow breathe on her father's behalf. Then she turned toward the expectant crowds.

Beatrice couldn't remember the last time she'd been part of a walkabout this subdued. Usually they were festive, because usually they were part of parades or parties: children cheering and waving flags, asking her to pose for selfies or sign her autograph.

Today she simply shook hands, accepted a few hugs. Many people handed her flowers, with notes or cards for her dad. She murmured her thanks and passed them all to Connor. As she handed things to him, she occasionally let her fingers brush his, in a silent, selfish touch. Even after she stepped away, she felt the weight of his grave gray eyes resting on her.

She had no idea how she would find the strength to give him up. Not after everything they had already been through.

Beatrice forced herself not to think about that. She focused on nodding and shaking hands, on making her lips recite a string of sentences over and over: *Thank you for being here. We appreciate your prayers. Your presence means so much to my father.* For once she was relieved to do this—to fall back on her training and become the marionette version of herself, let ritual take over.

She was vaguely aware of Teddy doing the same thing a few paces away from her. Sam, on the other hand, had retreated as far from Beatrice as possible. Beatrice could still feel her sister's gaze, boring like daggers into her back. She knew Sam was angry with her for appearing with Teddy in public, when she'd said that she was calling off the engagement.

A few times Beatrice reached for a water bottle and took a sip, hoping it would settle her stomach, which suddenly felt so empty. Or maybe she was empty. Maybe she was as cold as her sister had always thought, driven only by duty. She felt as hollow and heartless as this plastic bottle, utterly empty of everything.

It wasn't until her father's surgeon came running down onto the main steps of St. Stephen's that she knew.

The doctor stumbled forward like a white-robed ghost, Queen Adelaide behind him. Lord Robert Standish froze, his arms full of dozens of bouquets. He let them all fall to the ground in his shock, roses and tulips and soft white freesias blanketing the steps like a carpet of tears.

Connor turned to Beatrice, sorrow—and his love for her— etched on his features, right there for all the world to see.

"I'm so sorry, Bee," he whispered, shocked into forgetting protocol. "I'm so, so sorry."

The entire world seemed to be spinning, and gravity was shifting, and Beatrice felt like she'd collided with something impossibly hard. Maybe this was all just a nightmare. That would explain why everything felt tinged with a slight glow of unreality—why the world had gone fuzzy and shimmering at the edges.

She dug her nails into her palm so sharply that tears sprang to her eyes, but she didn't wake up.

"No," someone kept whispering. "No, no, no." It took a moment for Beatrice to realize that it was her. She felt fragmented by anguish, as if she'd reached some edge within herself she didn't know was there, some boundary of grief and fatigue and pain that no one should ever venture to.

Connor was the first to come to his senses and bow—a

deep, ceremonial military bow, lacking only a flourish with a sword to make it complete. Teddy quickly followed. Jeff gulped, then did the same.

Beatrice's face was stinging. She wondered if it was tears, freezing on her very skin.

For a single drawn-out moment, she let herself be a young woman who cried.

She was crying for her father—her king, but also her dad. She missed him with a fierceness that clawed at her from within.

She cried for Teddy and Connor, for Samantha, and for herself, for this last moment of girlhood that she was about to leave behind. For all the kings who had come before her, who had faced this same precipitous moment when their entire world ground to a halt.

Samantha crossed one ankle behind the other and swept into a curtsy. Her face was tear-streaked, her eyes hollow with shock.

Queen Adelaide followed suit. She curtsied slowly, her back as unbendingly severe, as unflinchingly straight as a poker. "Your Majesty," she whispered.

And then they were all bowing. Row by row, everyone gathered here—the silent crowds that had come out in support of her father—sank into bows or curtsies before Beatrice, causing a ripple of obeisance to domino silently back toward the street.

There was a creaking sound overhead. Everyone glanced up sharply as the American flag sank to half-mast, its fabric whipping and fluttering in the wind. The Royal Standard stayed where it was. It was the only flag that was never lowered, not even after the death of a sovereign—because the moment that one monarch died, another was automatically invested. The king is dead; long live the queen.

The Royal Standard represented Beatrice now.

Hundreds of eyes rested on her, camera lenses ready and filming.

Beatrice knew what was expected of her in this moment—what an heir to the throne was supposed to do in their first appearance as king or queen. She and her etiquette master had discussed it once, many years ago, but it had felt so distant and abstract back then. She felt suddenly grateful for that conversation, that this moment was planned out *for* her. That she had a script to fall back on, since her mind felt so utterly numb.

Facing the people, Beatrice plunged into a deep court curtsy, low and reverential. And she stayed there.

Her head was lowered, tears silently tracing down her cheeks. There was dignity and elegance in every curve of her body. Beatrice held the motion perfectly, like a dancer—honoring the people her father had served, promising that she, too, would give her life in their service. This curtsy was a symbol of the covenant she was making, to be the next monarch.

She stayed that way until she heard the peal of the church bells across the street, announcing the death of the king.

The bells began to echo throughout the city, clanging a deep and somber note through the capital. Beatrice imagined that everyone was frozen before their TVs or radios, or watching the live coverage on their phones—as if, for this single moment, the rush and clamor of the entire modern world had fallen still.

When she finally lifted herself up, she was Princess Beatrice no longer.

She had become Her Majesty Beatrice Regina, Queen of America, and long may she reign.

ACKNOWLEDGMENTS

When I first started working on the concept for *American Royals* back in 2012, I hardly dared to hope that it might become a published book. It all still feels like a dream come true! I am so grateful for the support and guidance of everyone who's made this book possible.

To my editor, Caroline Abbey: thank you for taking a chance on me. I don't know what I would do without your wisdom, your fierce sense of humor, and your willingness to spend hours discussing all things royal.

I couldn't ask for a better publishing team than the one at Random House. Michelle Nagler, Mallory Loehr, Noreen Herits, Emily Bamford, Kelly McGauley, Jenna Lisanti, Kate Keating, Elizabeth Ward, Adrienne Waintraub, and Emily DuVal: thank you for everything you have done to bring *American Royals* to life. Your enthusiasm and collective brilliance never cease to amaze me. I also owe special thanks to Alison Impey, the creative genius behind this utterly striking cover.

Joelle Hobeika: thank you for your sharp editorial insights, your understanding, and most of all your belief in this project all these years. And thank you to everyone at Alloy Entertainment: Josh Bank, Sara Shandler, Les Morgenstein, Gina Girolamo, Romy Golan, Matt Bloomgarden, Josephine McKenna, and Laura Barbiea.

I am constantly in awe of my foreign-sales team, Rights People. Alexandra Devlin, Allison Hellegers, Harim Yim, Claudia Galluzzi, and Charles Nettleton: thank you for bringing *American Royals* to so many languages around the world.

I am grateful for the unwavering support of my friends, who have talked me through plot points and alternate-history timelines with far more patience than I deserve. Sarah Mlynowski, I appreciate all your creative help. Margaret Walker, you deserve a special shout-out for being my on-call scholar and American-history enthusiast.

None of this would be possible without my parents, who taught me to believe that I can accomplish anything I set my mind to. I love you higher than the sky. Lizzy and John Ed, you have always been my greatest champions and also my best friends. And finally, Alex—as you well know, sometimes even authors are at a loss for words. All I can say is thank you for being with me on every step of this journey.

IS AMERICA READY
FOR ITS FIRST QUEEN?

MAJESTY

AMERICAN ROYALS II

NEW YORK TIMES BESTSELLING AUTHOR

KATHARINE McGEE

Turn the page for a sneak peek at
AMERICAN ROYALS II: *MAJESTY*!

SAMANTHA

The reception hall of the G&A museum was a crush of people.

The guests smiled and laughed, posing for the photographer, raising their voices over the sound of the string quartet in the corner. They exclaimed their excitement over the exhibit, speculated about the details of the royal wedding— what color the bridesmaids would wear, who would design Beatrice's gown.

Right now, Sam hated all of them.

She hated them for being so gullible and stupid, for buying into the absurd charade of Beatrice and Teddy's relationship. Couldn't they see that it was all for show, orchestrated by the palace's PR team?

Ever since Beatrice and Teddy had set a date, the entire nation had erupted in wedding fever. Sam had seen it everywhere. Restaurants were naming new dishes and cocktails after the couple. Dozens of fitness studios already claimed to offer Beatrice's pre-wedding workout routine. Even tonight Beatrice and Teddy were the guests of honor at the museum's opening of a new exhibit titled *Royal Weddings Through the Ages*.

If only Nina had agreed to come. Sam scanned the crowd, searching frantically for Jeff. Instead, she caught sight of her sister across the reception hall.

Of course, Beatrice was surrounded by a cluster of people. In her hyacinth-blue dress embroidered with rosettes, a smile pasted on her face, she looked like a beautiful porcelain doll. That was Beatrice—always charming, always *on*—unlike Sam, whose batteries seemed to constantly gutter and die out.

The queen's eyes darted up to meet Sam's, and her picture-perfect mask slipped, revealing the real Beatrice: a woman who looked uncertain and achingly alone.

Sam ventured a step forward.

Then something caught Beatrice's attention, and she glanced away. Sam followed her sister's gaze—to Teddy.

Sam watched, utterly oblivious to the rest of the room, as Teddy made his way to Beatrice. His tie was the same shade of blue as her dress, making them seem like a matched set. He said something charming—at least Sam assumed it was charming, from the way everyone laughed—and placed his hand lightly over her sister's.

Drawing in a sharp breath, Sam stumbled back. Her eyes burned, but she wasn't crying. She needed to get *out* of this reception hall, far from Beatrice and Teddy and all the rest of them.

She wove blindly through the crowd and pushed open a door marked STAFF ONLY. A server looked up, startled. "Excuse me—I mean, Your Highness—" He was pushing a catering cart, and Sam heard the unmistakable clink of jostling wine bottles.

"Don't mind me," she muttered. The startled waiter had barely registered her words before Sam had leaned down and lifted a bottle of sauvignon blanc from the cart. Then she was sailing past him, through a heavy unmarked door, and emerging into the spring night.

A narrow balcony wound around the side of the museum. Still clutching the wine bottle in one hand, Sam draped her elbows onto the railing. The iron felt blessedly cool against her feverish skin.

Below her stretched the capital, a jagged quilt of light and dark. It had rained that morning, and headlights flickered through the misty radiance, making the cars seem to float above the shimmering pavement. The scene blurred disorientingly in her vision.

She hadn't realized how much it would sting, seeing Teddy with Beatrice. *I don't care,* she thought furiously. *I hate them both. Beatrice and—*

There was a brief struggle in her chest, pride warring with affection; but at her core Sam was a Washington, and pride won out. It didn't matter that once upon a time she'd thought she was in love with Teddy.

He wasn't her Teddy anymore. The warm, blue-eyed boy she'd loved to distraction was gone, and in his place stood a stranger: someone distant and honor-bound and terrifyingly like Beatrice.

She'd thought he was different. But in choosing Beatrice, or duty, or whatever he wanted to call it, Teddy had proven that he was just like the rest of them. He was part and parcel of this whole stuffy institution, which had never understood or valued her.

Sam already felt like she'd lost her sister, and now she'd lost Teddy, too.

Her hand closed around the railing so tight that her palm hurt. Sam glanced down and saw that the iron was carved with a pattern of tiny faces: woodland sprites laughing in a sea of leaves and flowers. They seemed to be mocking her.

Letting out a ragged cry, she lifted her pink satin heel and kicked the medallion in the center of the railing. When it didn't budge, she gave it a few more kicks for good measure.

"I don't know what that railing ever did to you," remarked

a voice to her left. "But if you need to attack it, at least set down the wine first."

Slowly, Sam turned to look at the tall, broad-shouldered young man who stood a few yards away.

She had a feeling she'd met him before. He wore an expensive gray suit that set off his ebony skin, though his tie was askew and his sleeves rolled up, giving him a decidedly rakish air. When his eyes caught hers, he grinned: a cool, reckless grin that made Sam's breath catch. He looked a few years older than she was, around Beatrice's age. Sam felt something in her rise to the challenge of his liquid dark eyes.

"Just how long have you been lurking out here?"

"Lurking?" He crossed his arms, lounging carelessly against the railing. "I was out here first. Which makes *you* the intruder."

"You should have said something when I came outside!"

"And miss that epic royal tantrum? I wouldn't have dreamed of it," he drawled.

Sam's grip on the railing tightened. "Do I know you?"

"Lord Marshall Davis, at your service." He bent forward at the waist, executing a perfect ceremonial bow. The words and the gesture were elegant, the type of thing any nobleman might have done when meeting a princess, yet Sam sensed that he didn't mean a word of it. There was an irreverence to the gesture, as if Marshall was exaggerating his courtesy in contrast to her own undignified behavior.

He rose from his bow, his mouth twitching with suppressed laughter, just as his name clicked in Sam's memory. Marshall Davis, heir to the dukedom of Orange.

Orange, which spanned most of the western seaboard, hadn't joined the United States until the nineteenth century. Marshall's family wasn't part of the "Old Guard," the thirteen ducal families knighted by King George I after the Revolutionary War. But given how spectacularly wealthy they were—Orange had always been one of the most prosperous duchies in America—the Davises probably didn't care.

Sam tried to remember all the snatches of gossip she'd heard about Marshall over the years. He was a stereotypical West Coast playboy, who surfed and went to parties in Vegas and was always dating some Hollywood starlet or vapid aristocrat.

Come to think of it, hadn't Marshall been one of the young men invited to the Queen's Ball last year as a potential husband for Beatrice? If only she'd picked *him* instead of Teddy.

He nodded at the wine bottle. "Would you mind sharing, Your Royal Highness?" Somehow he made even her title sound like a source of amusement.

Sam barked out a laugh. "I hate to disappoint you, but I forgot a corkscrew."

Marshall held out his hand. Bemused, she passed him the bottle. Moisture beaded along its sides.

"Watch and learn." He reached into his pocket for a set of keys before jamming one into the cork. Sam watched as he twisted the key in quick circles, gently teasing the cork from the neck of the bottle until it emerged with an eager *pop*.

Sam was impressed in spite of herself. "Nice party trick."

"Boarding school," Marshall said drily, and handed her the sauvignon blanc. Sam hadn't brought any wineglasses, so she went ahead and drank straight from the bottle. The wine had a crisp tartness that settled on the back of her tongue, almost like candy.

"I've always wondered if the stories about you are true." Marshall caught her eye and grinned. "I'm starting to think they are."

"No more or less true than the stories about you, I imagine."

"Touché." He reached for the bottle and lifted it in a salute.

They passed the wine back and forth for a while. Silence thickened around them, light leaching from the sky as night settled its folds around the capital. Sam felt her thoughts turning brutally, relentlessly, back to Teddy and Beatrice.

She would show them. She didn't know how she'd show them, but she would do it—would prove just how little either of them mattered to her.

Next to her, Marshall rocked back on his heels. He was always moving, she realized: shifting his weight, leaning against the railing and then away. Perhaps, like Sam, he felt constantly restless.

"Why are you hiding out here instead of enjoying the party?" she demanded, curious. "Are you avoiding a clingy ex-girlfriend or something?"

"Well, yeah. Kelsey's in there." When Sam didn't react to the name, Marshall let out a breath. "Kelsey Brooke."

"You're dating *her?*"

Sam wrinkled her nose in disgust. Kelsey was, in her opinion, the worst type of starlet—the kind who chased publicity, constantly posting photos of her private jet or designer shoe collection. Last year Kelsey had halfheartedly launched a luxury bedding company, only to abandon the project midway through.

"I *was* dating her. She broke up with me last month," Marshall replied with an indifference that didn't fool Sam.

He shifted again, and the fading light gleamed on a pin affixed to his lapel. It reminded Sam of the American flag pin her dad always used to wear.

Following her gaze, Marshall explained, "It's the official Orange logo." The pin depicted a bear, its teeth pulled back in a menacing growl.

"You have grizzly bears in Orange?"

He shrugged. "I think it's meant to be a sign of strength."

An old, familiar instinct stirred within Sam. Knowing that

she was being difficult, and deliberately provocative, and just a bit flirtatious, she reached out to unfasten the pin from his jacket. "I'm borrowing this. It looks better on me anyway."

Marshall watched as she pinned the bear to her dress, right at the center of the bodice, near her cleavage. He seemed torn between indignation and amusement. "You should know, only the Dukes of Orange can wear that pin."

"And *you* should know that I'm entitled to wear anything you can wear. I outrank you," Sam shot back, then blinked at her own words. She'd said nearly the same thing to Teddy last year—*I outrank you, and I command that you kiss me.* And he had.

"I can't argue with that logic," Marshall replied, chuckling.

Sam's pulse quickened. Her blood seemed to have turned to jet fuel, her entire body buzzing with recklessness. The pain of seeing Teddy with Beatrice felt muffled beneath this new and sharp emotion. "Let's go back inside."

Marshall set the bottle down with deliberate slowness; Sam noticed that it was nearly empty. "Right now?" he asked. "Why?"

Because it was fun, because she wanted to stir up trouble, because she needed to do *something* or she felt like her chest would implode.

"Think of how furious it'll make Kelsey, seeing us together," she offered, but something in her tone must have given her away.

Marshall's eyes lit on hers in a long, searching look. "Which of your exes are *you* trying to make jealous?"

"He's not my ex," Sam replied, then immediately longed to bite back the words. "I mean, not technically."

"I see." Marshall nodded with maddening calm, which somehow made Sam even more defensive.

"Look, it's none of your business, okay?"

"Of course not."

Silence fell between them, more charged than before. Sam wondered if she'd revealed too much.

But Marshall just held out an arm. "Well then, Your Royal Highness, allow me the pleasure of being your distraction."

As they headed back into the party, he let his hand slide with casual possessiveness to the small of her back. Sam tossed her head, her smile blazing. She forced herself to keep looking at Marshall so she wouldn't search the crowd for Teddy. She didn't want him thinking she'd spared him a moment's consideration.

If she spent the rest of tonight with another future duke, Teddy would see just how little his rejection had hurt her—that he'd never actually mattered to her at all.

Chris Bailey Photography

KATHARINE McGEE

is the *New York Times* bestselling author of the Thousandth Floor series. She studied English and French literature at Princeton and has an MBA from Stanford. She's been speculating about American royalty since her undergraduate days, when she wrote a thesis on "castle envy"—the idea that the American psyche is missing out on something because Americans don't have a royal family of their own. After several years in New York and then in California, Katharine now lives with her husband in her hometown of Houston, Texas.

katharinemcgee.com